WATCH FOR THE CURE

Kahvahl moaned, twisting about on the floor. "A promise. Victory. We trusted an infidel and were betrayed."

"Us? Who is us . . . Iran?"

"All governments spawn corruption." Kahvahl closed his eyes, murmuring. "True believers . . ."

"Why were you betrayed?"

"The man used us. He has hidden power. . . . First the United States will fall, then Europe."

"What? How?" Hendrix's voice shook with urgency.

"The microbe is merely a device. . . . Watch for the cure. . . . Watch for the cure. . . ."

Books published by The Ballantine Publishing Group
are available at quantity discounts on bulk purchases
for premium, educational, fund-raising, and special
sales use. For details, please call 1-800-733-3000.

REPLICATOR RUN

Rainer Rey

FAWCETT GOLD MEDAL • NEW YORK

A Fawcett Gold Medal Book
Published by Ballantine Books
Copyright © 1997 by Rainer Rey

All rights reserved under International and Pan-American Copyright Conventions. Published in the United States by Ballantine Books, a division of Random House, Inc., New York, and simultaneously in Canada by Random House of Canada Limited, Toronto.

http://www.randomhouse.com

Library of Congress Catalog Number: 96-90999

ISBN: 0-449-18337-8

Manufactured in the United States of America

First Edition: May 1997

10   9   8   7   6   5   4   3   2   1

To my father, Dr. William H. Rey,
who named me after a writer

And to my wife, Cathy,
who helped me become one

ACKNOWLEDGMENTS

As with many books, the author draws information and support from many relatives, friends, and professionals.

My personal thanks to my brother, Oskar Rey, for his legal guidance; to my father-in-law, Dr. Richard Kirk, and to Dr. Mark Dedomenico for their medical advice; to Victoria Parker, librarian, for her patience with research help; to Colonel Ron Myers (USAF, ret.) for assistance.

To my family, Ashley and Bobi Rey, Joan Rey, Rita and Steve Bauman, Sharon Collins, Dick Otis, Nick and Rene Otis, Sascha and Kevin Ward for the pats on the back. To Dale Bailey for being a fan; to Kim, Lucas, Tom, Tim and Kathy, Mary Beth, and the whole Kirk clan.

To friends Larry and Sharon Boileau for their early help, to Dale and Donna Holpainen for encouragement, to Nancy Boyden for a keen eye, to Shannon Weiss and Pat Starr for a push now and then, and to Doug Boyden, Mike Subert, and Cliff and Cleo Forbes for their friendship.

Thanks to a nurturing editor, Elizabeth Lyon, and to Leslie Kellas Payne for additional discipline, and to Charles Snelling, a fellow author, for his gusto.

And finally, gratitude to Diane Gedymin for her initial insight, to my agents, Anna Cottle and Mary Alice Kier, who continue to inspire and motivate, and to Leona Nevler for her editorial guidance.

Over a period of twenty-four hours, several dozen children, throughout America, contracted an unexplainable rash.

Accustomed to the amazing workings of the human body, the parents of these young ones anticipated a predictable outcome: their children's skin would be whole again.

Gordi Skerit was one of these children.

He was due home from school.

And he was late.

PROLOGUE
MAY 1, THE FIRST DAY

Ann Skerit brushed the crumbs from the kitchen counter with a washrag and turned, looking toward the back fence at the rose-colored sky. She wiped a wet hand over her forehead and stepped over to the sink to gaze out the window.

No sign of Gordi.

The curtains billowed. Cattails waved by the pond. The wind had kicked up from the east and brought the peculiar odor of rusted mink cages.

At one time the corroded prisons had held hundreds of furry little creatures. But a decade ago virus enteritis swept through the entire miniature mink community at the Skerit Ranch and obliterated the population.

Morton, Ann's husband, refused to part with the cages because mink ranching had always been a way of life for the Skerit family. His father had been born on this ranch and had died from a heart attack, devastated by the crisis.

Ann shook her head, remembering the heartbreak, small animals twisted in agony prior to death. The episode left Morton bitter and unwilling to rebuild the business.

Mink cages. Sometimes she felt as if she were imprisoned in one of them.

Ann leaned farther out the kitchen window. "Gordi!" she called.

No answer. Only the rustle of the breeze through the long grasses near the barn. The hissing of the tall green-and-yellow shoots reminded her of the snake pit at the reptile exhibit outside Red Lodge, Montana. Little Ann had stared at the faces of the vipers, their eyes as dead as those of their victims. If snakes could talk they would whisper and be gone. Like ghosts. Snakeskin. Scaling. Gordi's rash had that odd flaky look to it.

Where was he? Perhaps somewhere out beyond the hill at the far end of the pond with its willow trees, frogs, and dragonflies.

She pulled back inside and listened to the eerie quiet within the house. The only sound, the ticking of the grandfather clock in the hallway.

Morton wasn't due home from the packing plant for another hour.

Ann walked over to the refrigerator to get some iced tea. The heat of a late-spring day lingered in the kitchen. She poured the cold brown liquid into a glass, put the pitcher back, and took the ham off the second shelf of the refrigerator. She felt the cool air on her legs.

Closing the door, she glanced out the window again.

A small round orb had appeared at the crest of the hill in the distance. It bounced slightly, revealed a tiny pair of shoulders, and finally, against the deepening sunset, Ann saw the figure of her nine-year-old son, dressed in over-alls, moving slowly toward the house. His gait seemed awkward. Was he all right? Maybe just tired from base-ball practice. Her worried thoughts were interrupted by ringing. She put the ham down, bustled to the phone on a tiny oak stand in the hallway.

"Hi," Morton said, on the other end of the line. "Listen, I'm sorry, honey, Dexter wants me to stay another hour. Gotta load a freezer truck. I won't be too much later."

"Gordi's just about home. I took some ham out."

"How's his rash?"

"I don't know. He's still outside." She heard the kitchen door open and shut again. "Just a minute, he just came in." She covered the mouthpiece with her hand. "Gordi," she shouted, "I'll be right there."

A strange sound from the kitchen.

"Come when you can, Morton. I'll have dinner ready," she said quickly.

"Be there shortly," Morton assured her. "Maybe we can play some gin on the porch after dinner."

"Okay, darling. I love you."

Ann hung up, straightened her apron, and headed for the kitchen. "Gordi," she said. "Gordi, that was Daddy. He says he—"

She bit off the last word as she rounded the doorway, the scene unfolding like slow-motion film: wind through the open screen door, the spilled lunch box with a half-eaten sandwich, the baseball cap and mitt lying on the porch. And her blond baby boy, Gordi, curled up on the kitchen floor, as if he had fallen from the rafters.

"My . . . my God! Gordi—"

"Mama, my throat," he whimpered. "It's sore. And my—"

"Honey, don't move. Just . . . just . . . let me help you." Scooting the chair from under the small desk by the mirror, she dragged it across the floor and placed it behind him.

She helped him up. "Sit down, angel."

"Mama, I'm scared. I was down at the pond when I started to feel sick."

"It's all right, baby." She settled him into the seat.

"Look at my arms." He whimpered again. The baseball jersey was pulled up to his elbows.

"I see it, sweetheart." She felt a touch of nausea. What

had been a rash yesterday was now a series of open sores. "Does it hurt a lot?"

"It's startin' to, Mama. It stings." He tried to hold back the sobs.

She noticed eruptions on his forehead, partially hidden by his curly hair. Realizing he should not see his face, she blocked the space between the child and the mirror on the wall. "You must have done something to aggravate your skin. It looks like you messed with a beehive."

"No."

"I don't understand. When you left this morning you were just a little red. Now it's like—" She stopped, imagining the look on her face. She didn't want to alarm him. Too late. His fear turned to tears. She wanted to touch him but was afraid. Scaly reptilian spots had appeared on the boy's head and arms. The skin looked as if it were curling away from itself, revealing flesh underneath.

"We've got to call the doctor, honey. Can you walk?"

"I'm scared to move, Mama."

"All right." She tried to keep the panic out of her voice. "Just sit there a minute." About to head for the phone, she patted the unmarred portion of his hand for the first time. Inadvertently, she pulled away. Gordi's skin was incredibly hot, like no fever she had ever felt.

Ann rushed to the phone, dialed 911. In the kitchen, Gordi cried louder, agony trembling in his voice.

The stubborn phone rang repeatedly. Finally, an operator came on the line. "Nine-one-one."

"I need an ambulance." Ann tried to keep her voice steady. "This is the Skerit home, eleven-thirty-four Sutton Way."

Gordi began to scream.

"What is it?" asked the woman's voice on the other end.

"That's just it. I don't know," Ann stuttered. She thought about calling Morton, but Gordi's cries had reached a panicked crescendo. "Please. I don't have time. Call my husband, Morton Skerit, at the Jackson Chicken Plant. Tell him to meet me at the hospital. There's been an accident." Ann heard the thud as Gordi's body hit the floor. She dropped the phone, knocking over the tiny oak phone stand. Rushing to the kitchen, she saw her child writhing on the linoleum. He was hyperventilating. Blood trickled from the corners of his mouth where sores in the mucous membrane had ruptured.

"My God! Gordi!" She knelt down beside him. "God help you." She held his shoulders, wanting to alleviate the pain, not knowing how. Tears streamed down her face. Filled with anguish, she surveyed his arms and forehead.

Gordi seemed oblivious, mercifully unconscious, his body barely moving. He wasn't screaming anymore, but his rapid breathing continued.

To her horror, Ann noticed that in several areas the skin had separated even farther. At various points on his arms, the sores had taken on a bluish cast at their outer edges, as if the skin were dead.

THE SECOND DAY
1:18 A.M.
Cable News Broadcasting Offices
San Francisco

A breaking story on a sick kid named Skerit? Devin studied the note he had received from Amy. It was like her to alert him to "hot" items that broke at the network, even though he had been relegated to producing low-key regional feature stories like the one he was editing now with Tony Cavello, his engineer.

Disease. Dan Canon would likely handle it. The science editor specialized in sensationalism. Devin disliked the Princeton graduate's penchant for overstatement, melodrama.

Devin looked up at the monitor, watched himself walk across the screen. He addressed the camera as he crossed in front of a line of fruit trucks. Satisfied with the smoothness of his delivery, Devin leaned forward and tapped Tony's sweatshirt on the shoulder. "Marry this scene with Take 61, and you'll be done."

Deep in thought, Tony froze his hands on the keyboard. "Where's that located again?"

"About six minutes in, where I'm commenting on labor strife in the Napa Valley."

"Oh, yeah."

Devin stretched. "Then leave a VHS on my desk for review."

Tony looked up from under his bushy black eyebrows. "This airs tomorrow?"

6

"It could . . . as filler."

"You got it, Commander."

Devin pulled his camel-hair blazer off the back of the leather chair and headed for the door of the editing bay. "Later."

Tony grunted affirmation.

Devin checked his reflection in the window of the editing booth, ran a hand through his salt-and-pepper hair, and threw Amy's note in the wastebasket.

Devin wanted to go home, hoping for a sound night's sleep. He had been burdened with a seventeen-hour editing shift due to a shorthanded staff.

As he stepped into the brightly lit hallway a stabbing pain landed behind his left eye. He squinted his way to his office.

The room was mercifully dark. He fumbled around in the closet for the duffel bag that held his workout clothes, looking for a roll of breath mints. He found them and went to the desk to retrieve car keys from the top drawer. The polished picture frame on the credenza caught his eye. The color photograph of his ex-wife, Susan, automatically cued a replay of their many years together, ending with a flashback of that final day when she walked out forever.

He stuffed the keys into his jeans, shook off the ghosts, and left the room. This time of night the hallways at CNB were quiet, except there, near the news department. A cackling laugh, a hoarse cough, someone yelling, running in with late copy. He avoided the scene and found the elevator.

The door opened, revealing a button-nosed young woman. Her face broke into a dimpled smile.

Devin greeted his protégée. "Hey, lemon drop."

Blond and frequently smelling of her lemon-scented soap, Amy Klein had quickly picked up the nickname.

She had joined Cable News Broadcasting three years earlier. She had attended UC Berkeley, where she graduated with honors, became an assistant producer at another network for a while, had some on-camera experience, and now functioned as a field producer. On the occasions when she could manage it, she wound up on camera herself. Versatility at Cable News Broadcasting was an asset, but due to its positioning, CNB sometimes served as a kind of purgatory for those either rising or descending within the ranks of the television industry.

"Did you get my note?"

"Yeah, thanks." Devin smiled back, crunching the last of the mints. He stepped into the elevator. She made room, reminding him of Peter Pan with her short hair and tights. Amy was like the kid next door with enough drive to run the neighborhood.

"Are you going to see Freeman?" she asked hesitantly.

He shook his head and reached for the elevator panel. He was certain Frank Freeman wouldn't even consider him for the story. "No, I'm going home."

Amy covered the button with a small hand. "Devin. This story should be yours."

"Sounds more like a Dan Canon disaster." He gestured to the panel of buttons. "Push lobby."

"Come to Freeman's office. Let's do the story together."

"I'm going on eighteen hours, Amy. I'm wasted."

"You couldn't be that burned out."

He remembered when *burned out* was a tenement building, a smoking bunker in Iraq, the hull of a crashed jet. But not him. Never lost it. Just lost Susan.

"Devin, you're not listening. Show Freeman you really want this. He'll send you. I know he will."

Maybe she was right. It would be his first lead-story

opportunity since the divorce. He smiled at her. "Always pushing."

She shrugged. "You pushed *me*, taught me more than I could ever thank you for." Amy noticed as Devin reacted to a sharp pain, pressing a hand against his side. "What's wrong?"

Yesterday's martial-arts class had aggravated an old football injury. "Barbecued ribs," he said.

"That you ate?"

"No. How they feel."

Before he could stop her, Amy pushed the button for the twenty-second floor.

"You schemer," he said, shaking his head.

She affectionately tapped his arm. "Freeman put me on the Skerit assignment."

He looked up as the floor numbers began to climb. "Fine. You shoot it, and Canon can hype it."

"He's such a bore. I don't want to go with him." She pouted. "Come along. I need your advice. I'm nervous about waiting."

"Waiting?"

"New York, Devin. ABC."

"Your tryout?"

"I'm beyond that," she said. "I sent a sample tape of myself. I'm one of ten finalists for a morning news position. Live screen tests next week in Manhattan. I have a real shot at this." Her eyes flashed with delight. "Thanks to you."

Devin had encouraged Amy to do more on-camera work, but questioned her odds. Wasn't she too young to get this position?

"Good. I know you'll do fine," he said pragmatically.

She wanted more, pumping him for reactions. "Come on, get excited." Amy was like an enthusiastic big-footed puppy, and invited the same kind of affection. "Go with me."

He inhaled deeply. "To New York?"

"No. Bellingham. Let's do this story together." She beamed like a pixie. "I can do the field footage, you do commentary. Come on. *Ask* Freeman."

The elevator lights flashed. Eighteen, nineteen, twenty. The silence seemed unnatural. He had to admit, though exhausted, he was interested. "Okay, what's the deal?"

Her mood changed. "Strange skin problem that's killing kids. A little girl died in Macon, Georgia."

"Macon? I thought—"

"That's another case. These aren't pretty pictures." The elevator doors opened, and they walked down the plum-colored carpet to the administrative offices.

"Then you've seen video," Devin said. She would have scoped out the story before anyone else.

"Yes. Freeman has it cued up in his office." As CNB's national news director, Freeman worked all hours. Though CNB ranked a distant second to CNN and broadcast worldwide via satellite, it was still a relatively small operation.

The secretaries had gone home long ago. Devin and Amy passed their vacant desks and reached the large brass double doors that opened to the executive suites.

Fifty feet from Frank Freeman's door, Devin saw the large black man, sitting straight-backed on the edge of the conference table near the TV monitor, a remote control in his hand. He tended to revert to military bearing, a throwback to his days in the service. Devin noted the wet patches under his arms.

At the sight of Devin and Amy, he launched into a diatribe, welcoming them all the way down the hall. "Amy, where have you been? There's fresh news breaking on this thing." He took a huge breath. "Parks? I thought you were doing regional features, a Napa Valley dispute or something."

Devin gave Amy a sidelong glance and began his retreat. "Just a detour."

Amy grabbed him by the arm. "Devin wants to see the footage."

Hearing her say it, he realized she was right. "Do you mind, Frank?" he asked.

Freeman paced the floor like a nervous hippo in suspenders. "I had Canon slated for this job." Devin liked Freeman, but his boss was manic about work and often transferred tension to his people. Freeman glanced nervously into Devin's eyes, as if to measure him. "Why do you want to see the tape?"

Devin noticed the expectation on Amy's face. "I'm interested in the story."

"You?" Freeman had concerns about Devin's state of mind since the divorce; his lack of motivation had kept the star anchorman on the sidelines. "You think you'd want to tackle this? You look tired."

Devin smiled to take the edge off. "What good newsman doesn't?"

Freeman appeared reluctant to deny him; asking Devin to leave would be an insult. "Well, I suppose it couldn't do any harm. Take a look while I brief Amy." He gestured forcefully to the chairs across the table. "Sit down, both of you. I don't have much time." He hoisted his ponderous weight onto the edge of the conference table.

Devin fantasized its collapse.

Amy sat down and Devin dropped into one of the high-backed plum-colored chairs next to her. His shoulders felt snug between the padding.

Freeman pointed to the TV screen. "This footage came over satellite. A little girl died in Macon, Georgia, just before midnight. Local station WMAZ picked up coverage of her entering the hospital. Apparently took a couple of hours before anyone back there thought it important enough to send to us. CNN must also have it by now. Check it out."

Devin watched as the television monitor flickered. The tracking settled down and the picture flipped forward, locked into play. The video revealed a stretcher being wheeled from an ambulance by two attendants. Two more followed, one holding an IV bag, the other supporting a grieving mother.

The small girl on the stretcher lay motionless. Her face and arms, exposed, were blotched and bloody. Incredibly, the skin around multiple open wounds was trimmed in black, as if each wound had been opened by a flame.

"Holy shit," Devin said, under his breath. The blackened skin reminded him of the burned and broken bodies of Iraqi children he had seen during the Gulf War, but never anything he had witnessed in civilian life.

On-screen, a reporter in a trench coat stepped in front of the camera as the stretcher passed behind him and was carried up some steps to an emergency-room entrance.

The reporter raised a microphone. "The cause of little Debbie Collins's injuries are unknown. The nurse at the Millcrest School reports that Debbie collapsed this morning, and has, from all indications, been seriously burned. However, no one remembers fire in the area." The reporter assumed a sophisticated pose, turned to the camera. "Debbie Collins's friends and their parents are obviously shocked by her sudden collapse. Hopefully, the doctors here at Hardiway General Hospital will be able to explain exactly what happened to Debbie. More on this story as it develops. I'm Archie Campbell for WMAZ *News Watch*." The picture rolled on as the reporter froze in his pose. Then, relaxing, he gestured to the cameraman. "Was that pretty cool?" the reporter asked. The picture went to black.

Devin shook his head. "Sympathetic, wasn't he?" He turned to Freeman. "The sores on that kid. Burns?"

"They look it," Freeman said, clicking the picture off with his remote.

"I don't think so. Burns don't come in bits and pieces. They cover the body. They don't polka-dot like that. Poor kid looked like she was abused by some maniac with a hot poker."

"The scary part"—Amy reached over and touched Devin's hand—"is that the Bellingham kid, Gordi Skerit, has them, too."

"Same scattered burns?" Devin remembered an Iraqi boy's body blown onto a heap of rubble by an incendiary bomb. In the sunlight, white bone had shown through the seared flesh on the back of both thighs.

Amy nodded.

"There's more." Freeman got up. "Dispatch just called and told me they have satellite footage on two similar cases in Tucson and New Jersey. The Tucson kid died thirty minutes ago. They're running tape downstairs right now. Brutal. And newsworthy. Disease Control Center teams are scrambling. Early medical reports suggest this thing develops faster than any infection on record, deadlier than the Ebola virus."

The statement shook Devin only briefly. "A catastrophe bit. You're sending Canon, of course?" he asked. Besides thriving on terror, Dan Canon had set his sights on a future anchor position at the station.

"I was. He's preparing his disaster special, this fits right in," Freeman answered.

"Oh, his sociopathological special, that's right. Waco. Oklahoma City. I understand he's even pulled library footage on Rwanda," Devin said, turning to Amy. "News

at eleven. The bloodier the better." Her face fell. He had
forgotten. She had been a production assistant in Rwanda
during the bloodbath of '92. "Sorry, I meant—"

"I know what you meant. It's okay." She got up and
set out for the door, suddenly morose. "I'm going to
gather my gear. I think the two of you ought to talk about
this."

"Amy . . ." Devin rose from the chair. She started
down the hallway. He wanted to follow, hesitantly
looked back at Freeman.

"Let her go," Freeman said. "Shut the door and give
me a minute."

Devin grabbed the brass handle and yanked. The latch
clicked. "I thought you were in a hurry." He stood at the
end of the table, his hands resting on the chair back.

The big man walked down the table's length, came
close enough to stand on Devin's toes. "Devin, I respect
your past. You were the best anchorman I've ever seen.
Time magazine agreed with me. Of course that was
before . . ." Freeman stared off into space.

Devin knew exactly where Freeman was heading. The
same old discussion about how his divorce made him
dysfunctional, perhaps cost him his previous job. He
didn't need reminding. "Frank, I came up here because I
thought I might have a shot at this story. But if you're
going to replay the Susan scenario all over again . . ." He
brushed his hair from his forehead and turned toward
the door.

Freeman grabbed his arm. "Just a minute. Don't get so
testy. I agreed we'd let you ease back in. But it's been
nearly a year. I'm worried about putting you back in the
saddle. I need razor-sharp, focused work on this."

Devin gently pushed his hand aside. He liked Freeman
but hated strong-arming. "I just worked seventeen hours.
You consider that focused?"

"It's different on the front line."

"I know that."

Freeman's meaty hand grabbed the back of the chair. "I'd like to see you put the same energy into your work that you put into your karate classes."

"My stories are on time," Devin said, sounding more defensive than he wanted.

"But they're flat." Freeman's face reddened. "Maybe you've lost your edge."

Freeman had finally spit it out. Devin's eyes narrowed. He'd been treading water, stuck in feature work, soothed by the pace. The edge. Frank hinted he might never get it back.

He tried not to be offended. "I haven't lost anything."

"That's not the way I see it. You're over forty. It's time to *kick* butt or butt out." Freeman was laying it on, like a judgmental father. "I hired you because you used to be great."

"You're saying I'm not?"

"I don't know. Something changed. Maybe it *was* Susan."

Betrayed by the suggestion that divorce could conquer him, Devin squared his chin. "Why keep bringing that up?"

"Something's gotta get you in line."

"In line? This isn't West Point." Devin tried not to lose it, aware of the frustration in his voice. He moved toward the door. "And I'm not one of your plebes." He interpreted Freeman's badgering as a dare. He felt suddenly empowered. "I don't blame you for pushing me, Frank. Questioning my focus. Maybe I haven't shown you a lot lately. Maybe it's time I did." He grabbed the handle, swung the door open. "I'm focused. Ready to work." He turned, left Freeman staring as he walked down the hallway past the glass cases where Emmy Awards glistened under the spotlights. Five of them were his.

"Where the hell do you think you're going?" Freeman called.

Devin stabbed himself in the chest with his thumb. "Me? I thought Bellingham might be nice."

Huffing, Freeman set his large body in motion. As Devin walked, Freeman caught up, stride for stride. "You can't do that. You take this assignment *only* if I give it to you. What the hell am I supposed to tell Canon?"

"Tell him there's a chemical spill in L.A. I'm covering the Skerit kid."

They had reached the elevator doors. "What about the Napa story?" Freeman asked.

"It's done. Besides, second-rate time fillers are something I'm no longer interested in. I'm covering *this* story. If you don't want it, someone else will."

Freeman grabbed Devin by the arm. A couple of drops of Freeman's sweat spotted Devin's blazer. "You're threatening me to get this assignment?"

"No. I'm just *taking* this assignment."

"And what if you blow it?"

Seeing the look in Freeman's eyes, Devin realized if he wasn't careful, he might lose his second job in three years. He wanted the spotlight, but his confrontation with Freeman had put him on his guard. The countdown had begun. The camera was rolling.

Freeman stared at him, perspiration running down his temples.

Devin searched for a line. "I'll give you all you want. When I do, we'll talk about that anchor position," he said, surprised at himself.

"Anchor?" Freeman grumbled as the elevator doors opened. "God, you're ahead of yourself. I haven't even agreed to Bellingham, and you're discussing promotions."

Devin put a finger on Freeman's chest. "No problem."

Freeman bristled. "I think it's in serious doubt."

"In your mind maybe. Not in mine."

Devin looked into the elevator. Amy stood at the door. She must have heard their exchange. She seemed energized.

"I'm sorry I walked out before," she said. "Immature on my part." She studied their tense faces. "Immaturity can mess up even the best relationships. Devin, are you coming?"

Devin glanced at Freeman expectantly.

Freeman waved a thick hand and began lumbering back to his office.

Devin couldn't read his status. He gazed after his boss. "Well, Frank?"

Freeman stopped, looked back over his shoulder, ignored Devin. "I've called ahead for crew support from a local station KVOS. Amy, you're producing this story, how you handle it is up to you. There's a chartered Learjet leaving for Bellingham in forty-five minutes," he said. "Take whatever help you need and be on it."

THE SECOND DAY
5:05 A.M.
Atlanta

Dr. Samuel Gordon lay on his back in the four-poster bed, sheets mounded on his chest. He was a big man, thick all over. Since his wife's death, he rarely slept well. Responsibility clouded his mind, even during the night. His hulking frame would shift restlessly and covers would eventually land on the floor. They were there now.

Feeling the chill on his thighs, he woke as the doorbell rang. He answered the door in his massive maroon bathrobe.

"Sorry to disturb you, sir." It was John Richards, his assistant. Not a good sign. "I thought, being so near morning . . ."

"That's fine." Gordon impatiently ran a fleshy hand through his black hair. "Out with it."

"It's a flash fire." There were few other reasons for an off-hours visit. Due to his girth, Gordon never drove. Richards had the limo running at the curb and had dressed hurriedly. His curly red hair was a mess.

"Come in." Gordon gestured toward the staircase. "Who's reporting?"

Richards seemed reluctant to answer. "State health people and hospitals. Several sites."

"Several?" The word frightened him. Viral flash fires were typically restricted to one area. "I'll get dressed. Come upstairs. Where are they?"

Richards grasped the bleached oak banister and followed him. "Macon, Georgia. Bellingham, Washington. Tucson, Arizona, and Trenton, New Jersey. Documented cases."

Gordon paused at the landing. "God. There must be a mistake."

"There may be more," Richards said hesitantly. "We've got several direct calls from MDs."

Gordon found a tentlike pair of gray slacks, set his weight down on the bed, and fought with the legs. "Nearby?"

"No. Columbus, Laramie, and L.A."

"That's impossible. Unrelated. Christ, I wish these guys wouldn't ring us every time there's a measles outbreak." Gordon found it reprehensible that some incompetent doctors would overreact to puzzling patients. "Reliable pathology on the documented cases?" He managed to fasten the button of his slacks.

"None yet. Speculative diagnoses. We're sending teams now."

Gordon conquered the stubborn zipper. "Quarantines?"

"Only a few of the sites."

"Any contagion?" He reached for the white shirt.

"None documented. But, Sam, the symptoms. Fever. Severe external hemorrhagic extrusions." Richard's foreboding tone fit into an expected nightmare scenario.

"I don't like it. Sounds like filovirus. Epithelial characteristics?"

"Severe mucous-membrane damage."

Gordon didn't want to hear it. As director of the Disease Control Center, he lived each day awaiting the arrival of the ultimate microscopic killer. Was this the day? He prayed not.

"Patient characteristics?" Gordon reached for the tie slung on the bedpost.

"Both male and female."

Gordon nodded, fussing with the ends.

"And under twelve."

Gordon stopped. "What?"

"All documented cases are kids."

Gordon fingered the knot of the tie pensively. He found himself grateful he had no children of his own. "You're certain?"

"That's what we're told. 'Course we're only into the infection cycle thirty-six hours."

"How advanced is it?"

"Well, the patients went from a rash to being comatose in two days. The Macon patient died three hours ago. Others are critical. ER admittances. ICU treatment."

"Too damned fast. My coat." Gordon grabbed his shoes and socks, tucking them under his arm, heading for the door. Gordon grunted as he started down the stairs. Richards followed with a gray herringbone blazer, size fifty-eight.

Gordon walked out the front door barefoot, lumbering toward the Lincoln limo where a uniformed driver with a mustache waited, holding the back door open.

"Hello, Carter." Gordon slid into the backseat. Richards joined him. Gordon struggled with his size but managed to lean down and put his socks on. Carter walked around the car and got into the driver's seat.

"You remember the Classic Containment Module, Richards?" Gordon asked as he slid his right foot into a black shoe. He had helped design the disease control plan. His left foot cramped, but he managed to get it in. "It assumes we can outflank an outbreak. How do we fight on multiple fronts at once?" He laced his shoes and looked up, finding Carter waiting for instructions. Gordon waved a hand. "My office. Step on it."

A sliver of sunlight appeared over the parkway as the long black vehicle left the elite neighborhood and raced toward the Disease Control Center.

THE SECOND DAY
2:15 A.M.
Bellingham, Washington

Ann Skerit felt like a dead tree, a hollow, dried-out shell. Her sapped energy would return only if she were allowed to see her son.

She pressed her face against the cold glass of the hospital window. Below, the flashing red light moved along the bright white stream of the I-5 freeway through Bellingham. It ran up the ramp, exited to the west, and slowly passed through streets until it disappeared into some trees. Reappearing, it found its way up to the entrance of County General Hospital, revealed itself to be an ambulance. As it moved up the driveway leading to the emergency room, the pulsing light rotated on its roof.

Ann leaned off to one side. Two orderlies ran out, helped the driver. They opened the back doors and lowered two stretchers onto the cement. Ann wanted to see the injured people. Tonight she felt a kinship with anyone who might be hurting.

She turned away from the window.

Her husband, Morton, sat on the couch in overalls, clutching his knees.

All night she had watched him hide his pain. She knew he was wrestling with the urge to shout at the doctors, and understood his anger and frustration.

The soundless electric clock on the wall pulsed on. The silence in the room weighed heavily on her.

Gordi lay in a coma, somewhere down the hall.

Earlier tonight, he had been wheeled from the ambulance into the emergency room below. Ann thanked God that Morton had arrived at that moment.

She almost lost it when the nurses reacted to Gordi's incredible deterioration. They asked abrupt, aggressive questions about whether Gordi had been burned, speculating loudly about the blackened peeling of his skin. Over the din, Ann told the doctor that Gordi had had no contact with fire or toxic chemicals.

Dr. Orteig, on duty in the ER that evening, gave Gordi a quick examination and rushed him up to intensive care. Dr. Orteig. Cold. Apparently hardened by endless years of trauma.

Morton and Ann were ordered to wait. They waited for one hour, two, then three. There was little to do with idle hands and shuffling feet.

Ann gazed out to the lights of Bellingham, glistening like a cluster of stars. Stars. Gordi's favorite song when he was a toddler: "Twinkle, Twinkle, Little Star." He sang it many nights before bed. She managed a thin smile, remembering Gordi's excitement about baseball practice. He had returned home the first day with his red-and-white baseball uniform. Fragile, yet proud. He had his father's pride.

The leather couch creaked. Ann looked up.

Morton had shifted his weight. He fussed with the brim of his Cincinnati Reds cap, sighed heavily, and got to his feet. He walked over, stood next to her. She watched him in the dark reflection of the window.

"Can't think of nothin' else?" he asked softly. "Ann, could he have fallen into a bunch of lye? There wasn't any acid around the yard or nothin'?"

"Morton." She shrugged. "You saw the way his arms looked yesterday. They were a little red. The calamine lotion should have helped. Today, in the kitchen, he was hot as hell with that bloody skin, then it got worse."

She spoke gently. Morton suddenly looked much older. More like his father had looked the year before he died. She tried to erase that vision.

Morton wiped his palms on the thighs of his jeans.

She saw her own reflection in the blackened window. Globe lights hung from the ceiling like a series of moons in the waiting room behind her. In the illumination they cast, she saw the glistening tracks of tears marking her cheeks.

"It was like a plague, ripping into our little boy," Ann whispered. "I couldn't do anything."

She turned to her husband, leaned toward him, a willow branch about to break. Morton raised his arms like two oak beams on an aging drawbridge. Ann lost her resolve and fell into his embrace. Her tears soaked into the arm of his blue windbreaker.

He led her to the leather couch. They slumped down and sat together frozen in silence. Bulbs in the yellow globe lights buzzed. The second hand on the clock dragged across the white face. Ann watched it move from one black mark to the next. A siren, approaching in the night, was the only sound in the room besides their breathing.

Then, down the hallway behind the swinging doors, she heard the squeak of a pair of pacing shoes approaching rapidly.

A frizzy-haired nurse burst through the entrance and gestured toward them. "The doctor needs you," she said. Ann gathered her light sweater around her shoulders and stood up.

"What is it?" Ann's voice quavered.

"Follow me, please," said the nurse. Morton rose

without a word. "This way." The nurse urged them to hurry.

"Gordi?" Ann asked. She could feel panic rising in her throat. She tried to contain it.

"The doctor wants to talk. Please." She took Ann by the elbow. Morton supported her other arm. They passed through the doorway and moved down the hall.

Morton removed the cap from his head. He stuffed it into the pocket of his windbreaker. They passed several dimly lit rooms. Ann heard a moan from one of them. Some relatives of the suffering occupant huddled near the bed. A woman cried in another room. Her bent shadow on a drawn curtain reminded Ann of her mother's osteoporosis.

"God. Where is he?" Ann asked. The hallway seemed endless.

"The detoxification area," the nurse said, looking sideways at Ann through her glasses.

"What for?" Morton asked.

"To isolate him. Dr. Orteig felt it would be best."

They passed under the bars of fluorescent lights, spaced evenly down the length of the hallway. Finally, a doorway. The sign read NO ADMITTANCE.

The nurse stopped outside. "In here." She pushed the heavy door. They followed her. She led them to a small room immediately to their left. "Please sit down. The doctor will be with you in a moment."

They found their places: Morton in a wooden chair and Ann on a wide windowsill.

Ann felt sick. She couldn't bear to look at Morton. Her nausea might get worse if she had to deal with his expression. Instead, she looked out into a darkened alley. No trees. Nothing. Just a brick wall on the opposite building. She ran her eyes up a tarnished green drainpipe that hung against the ragged red brick. A brassy taste crossed the back of her tongue. The pipe's links and angles reminded her of the wooden snakes she had bought in Seattle's Chinatown the year she and Morton were married. A footstep. The door.

Dr. Orteig entered. "I apologize for the long delay," he said matter-of-factly. His tunic looked crisp and dry. He had changed it. Ann stood up, clutching her hands.

Cap in hand, Morton launched himself to his feet. "What's the delay? Why couldn't we see him?"

The doctor looked at Morton, then Ann, apparently searching for words. "Mr. and Mrs. Skerit," he said, running a hand through his gray hair. "Gordi's condition has worsened, I'm afraid." He had a pale, narrow, pointed face like a rodent. "I . . . to be honest, I've never seen anything quite like this. I've considered a chemical burn, shingles, chicken pox, a strep infection. None of the diagnoses make sense."

Morton crushed the baseball cap with both hands. "You sound like you don't have a good goddamn idea what's wrong with him."

Ann touched Morton on his arm.

Orteig retreated a step. "We're doing our best to deal with it. He's lost plenty of blood due to epidermal extrusions on his body. Abnormally high pulse. He's running a fever of a hundred and five. The congestion in the bronchial passages is critical. It's caused by a breakdown of the mucous membranes. He's bleeding internally."

Ann's stomach turned. She felt blood rush to her head.

Orteig picked at the dry skin on his earlobe. "I fear it may be viral. God knows we've had enough speculation about new viruses."

"What are you saying, Doctor?" Morton's tone had turned helpless. Ann noticed the sweat on his cheeks.

"Mr. Skerit," Orteig said calmly, "outbreaks of new

viruses have been recorded occasionally. Ebola, for example. Now, I'm not suggesting—"

"What about Ebola?" Morton's eyes were rimmed with red.

"A very powerful strain. But I'm not—"

"How do we find out?" Ann asked. "Does it look like Ebola?"

Orteig put two hands up, apparently asking for calm.

"If it *is* a virus, Gordi's rate of deterioration suggests something more potent than we've ever encountered. But it's strange that the toxicity is also quite pronounced. Dermatology shows similarities to an Ebola inflammation, but the good news may be that Gordi's ailment has developed incredibly fast, more like the reaction to a chemical burn." Orteig seemed scattered. "I've suggested the state health department send people out to your home as soon as they can."

Ann could no longer tolerate the doctor's meandering. "Is he going to make it?" she cried.

Her outburst made Morton advance two steps toward Orteig as if he were going to hit him. The doctor sidestepped Morton, moved to Ann, placed a thin hand on her shoulder.

"I promise we'll do all we can. I've asked attendants to bring up bulk ice. We've put Gordi in a pH-balanced solution and kept it very cold, to curtail the bleeding." He looked from Ann to Morton and back at Ann. "All right. It's time you saw him. Follow me."

Ann and Morton accompanied him to a neighboring room, bathed in an eerie blue glow. Orteig led them to a curtain. Ann and Morton stood at the doctor's side like apprehensive children.

"I told you ... this is the only way I know how to handle this," Orteig said. "Gordi's feeling no pain. He's simply asleep." He pulled the cord. The curtain parted. A deep aqua light spilled into the room.

Ann looked through the reinforced glass into the detox chamber. Two nurses stood by a glass tank filled with a blue liquid in which Gordi was immersed. An oxygen mask covered his face. His blistered wrists were strapped down. IV tubes hung from his arms. Ann had never seen anything so ugly. She collapsed back into her husband's arms, buried her head in his chest, and wept.

"That's what you're doing for him?" Morton asked hoarsely.

Ann forced a look at the doctor.

"All we can do, at this point." Orteig moved a step away, avoiding her eyes.

Ann brushed tears from her cheeks, grabbed Morton by his jacket sleeve, pushed him closer to the detox window. They stared at their son. Ann noticed the frizzy-headed nurse enter the room.

"Doctor, the phone," the nurse said, pointing to the wall receptacle.

"I'll take it in my office."

"I think you better take it here. Dr. Keefer is very anxious to talk with you."

Orteig nodded toward the Skerits and shushed her. "Since when do you tell me where I accept my calls?"

The nurse shook her head humbly and tiptoed over to his side, talking so low that Ann could barely hear. "Doctor, I don't think you can go back to that part of the building," the nurse said.

"What?"

"Dr. Keefer insists on a quarantine immediately."

Orteig threw a look in Ann's direction. "Keep your voice down. Quarantine? For this wing?"

"Right, with no further admissions to this part of the building."

Ann could no longer contain herself. "What is it?" She turned from the glass, confronting the doctor.

"Just one moment, please, Mrs. Skerit." Orteig took the phone off the receiver.

Ann approached the nurse cautiously. "Nurse, may I talk to you?" The nurse put a forefinger to her lips. Orteig had his back turned.

"Dr. Keefer is on the line," the nurse said to Ann. "He's in charge."

"Dr. Keefer?" Orteig said, pushing the button for one line. Apparently, there was no one there. He pushed another. "Dr. Keefer. Yes. What's this about a quarantine?" Morton was still standing by the blue glass, his face pressed against it.

"What does he mean?" Ann asked the nurse.

"Dr. Keefer's been in contact with the Disease Control Center," she whispered. "There have been other cases like Gordi's. That's good, Mrs. Skerit; we may get answers from other cases."

"What's the prognosis on the Macon girl?" Orteig pressed his body into the wall, shielding the phone from the others. Ann could still hear him. "I see. All right. And the boy in Tucson?"

"How many others?" Morton asked, turning from the window. The nurse shrugged. "How many others?" he repeated.

Orteig suddenly appeared agitated. "But if Atlanta runs things, we'll be wrapped in plastic for days. What? Oh, all right." He hung up and stared at the floor.

Ann moved over to him. "The other children. What happened?"

Orteig lifted his gaze to hers, then glanced at Morton.

Ann saw the scene in her mind again: Gordi slumped on the floor, the open screen door, the spilled lunch box and the baseball mitt, the rush of the wind.

Dr. Orteig had a strange, nervous look in his eye. "It's too early to draw any firm conclusions, Mrs. Skerit. With several other cases like Gordi's reported, we come under national jurisdiction. Viral paranoia. Who knows. We'll just have to do our best." He was at the door leading to the detox room.

"But, the other cases . . . how are they?" Ann asked.

"Nurse. Bring some cots in for the Skerits."

"Doctor, please answer me." Her resolute tone caused Orteig to stop, look over his shoulder.

The calculating rodent suddenly looked afraid. "No further news on cases elsewhere," Orteig said. "But official word from Macon and Tucson . . ." He hesitated.

Ann's eyes brimmed with tears again. "Tell me."

Orteig spoke quietly, forming each word with clinical precision. "Both patients died several hours ago."

THE SECOND DAY
9:23 A.M.
Bellingham, Washington

"Is Dr. Orteig the one who dealt directly with Gordi?" Devin asked, pulling on his shirt cuff. "Can we talk to him?"

"I have instructions," Dr. William Keefer, the hospital director, said coldly. Keefer reminded Devin of his English teacher in high school, round and bald. What remaining hair he had appeared glued onto his head with tonic, giving it a moist sheen. Medical degrees hung like badges of honor in the white-walled office.

Devin yawned. A half-hour nap on the flight up hadn't been enough. Amy's energetic conversation had kept him awake. Crisp starched sheets in the hospital rooms on the way to Keefer's office coaxed him toward sleep. He fought through it.

"You appear to have made an exhausting effort to join us, Mr. Parks. But I've told the Seattle press, and I reiterate to you, I won't allow anyone to see Orteig. As you've probably gathered, he has his hands full. And frankly, there's no further information."

Devin looked down at the spools of Amy's small tape recorder turning quietly on her lap. Gottlieb, the local part-time cameraman from station KVOS, had been forced to wait out in the grip truck. "How about a telephone hookup with either Mr. or Mrs. Skerit?" Devin asked. An innovative idea for someone half-asleep.

"I have no strong objection," Keefer said, obviously patronizing him. "However, we're testing Gordi's parents. They're hardly in a position to chat with reporters." He said "reporters" as if it were an insult.

Devin ignored it. "Tests? Have they come down with it?"

Apparently irritated, Keefer rubbed his mustache. "Don't try and make this an epidemic. It's a preventive measure."

"So we can talk with Mrs. Skerit later?" Amy asked. It was worth a try.

"I'm sorry. There's no guarantee. Now, if you don't mind. That's all." Keefer spoke with finality. So much for the Q&A.

Devin looked over at Amy and shrugged. "We'll come back later."

Later . . . this afternoon. Devin might be able to get a quick nap in between. Feeling the weight of his weariness like heat from a stove, he visualized a nearby motel they had passed on the way in. He could catch two or three hours. There'd be a puffy pillow, bedcovers turned down, and two little mints the maid would leave with a scented card. He'd read the three-line poem about peace and enjoy some. He prepared to rise.

"Just a minute," Amy interjected. She placed a manicured hand on the desk and leaned forward. "Withholding information won't protect the public. They know. We've had hundreds of calls about these kids since early this morning."

Devin gave her a sidelong glance. Keefer appeared to be a man with definite boundaries. If she pushed him too far, he might close up completely. The thought of her potential job in New York made her more aggressive about getting a story from this iceman.

"I think you'll find," Dr. Keefer said in a calculating

tone, "that the Disease Control Center in Atlanta will be your only source of information, Miss Klein."

"Call me Amy."

"Whatever. The DCC will make any official statements."

Devin didn't appreciate his rudeness. "Then we'll call Atlanta."

"Good luck. The DCC has stringent policies." Dr. Keefer nudged his gold-rimmed glasses up the bridge of his nose. Then he buttoned his white tunic and rose, signaling the end of the interview.

"Thanks for your . . . indulgence," Devin said in a tone that meant just the opposite. Keefer squinted at him, apparently getting the message. Then, as if deciding how to respond, he pointed toward the door. "Mr. Parks, Miss Klein. Let me show you something."

Amy gathered her recorder and notebook and stood.

Devin got to his feet.

Dr. Keefer had exited his office, headed down the hall. Amy and Devin caught up.

Keefer stopped at the corner. "Look down there." He gestured down the corridor. A wall of hard plastic stretched tightly over a double doorway. Two state policemen sat in chairs outside the entrance to the wing. Devin wondered if they were there to keep people out or victims in.

"That wing is as airtight as it can be," Keefer said. "Exterior windows, the service elevator, everything. You'll find policemen outside guarding the perimeter. Dr. Orteig, some nurses, the Skerits, and their son are virtually in a vacuum. Orders from Atlanta, not from me. I spoke with Orteig face-to-face for several hours through that plastic. He's in direct communication with the Disease Control Center. All new information will be issued from that office, not from this hospital. This is serious business."

Dr. Keefer began to backpedal toward his office. "Sorry, that's the way it is."

"Is every single person involved with Gordi's case inside there?" Devin pointed to the plastic.

"Every . . . one," Keefer said, turning away. "Good . . . luck to you both." He was off down the other hallway in a brisk walk.

Devin reacted to the strange hesitation in his answer. "Doctor?" he called.

Amy gazed after him, and sighed. "There goes nothing."

Devin watched intently as Keefer disappeared around the corner. "I think the doctor's lying. Somebody else had contact with Gordi. Keefer isn't sure."

"Don't you think they would have rounded everybody up?" she asked.

"In the confusion, maybe not."

Amy gave him a sly smile. "I'll talk to some staff members." She started for the nurses' station.

Devin leaned against the wall. "Sure, if you want. But before you fly off, tell me why there are no other reporters lingering around these hallways. Have you figured that out?"

She stopped. Turned back to him. "They don't have a nose for news."

"No. They've gone home. We missed it. The story's coming out of Atlanta. The news will originate from back east by satellite. If there *are* new leads they aren't happening in this hospital. We'll have to look somewhere else."

"Good, let's go," she said, tugging his sleeve, chomping at the bit.

He chuckled. "Okay. But I've gotta get a couple of hours of sleep or I'll drop."

"What do you expect me to do while you log zees?"

He took her by the arm. "Catch some lunch."

"I'm surprised at you," she said, pulling her arm away. "After what Freeman said?" One of the nurses at a computer looked up. Devin noticed and gave her a disarming smile, then shushed Amy with a finger to his lips. Amy responded with a doubting look. As much as she liked Devin and respected his past, she suddenly questioned his resolve. "This story could mean everything to you," she whispered.

Everything? he thought. Memories of hot success turning a marriage cold. His bewilderment over women and careers. His career cost him a wife. A political career stole his mother away. Now he found himself at odds with a career woman over his desire for a few hours of sleep.

He relented. "The motel can wait. I'll catch a nap in the grip truck."

Her face softened. She stared at the tops of her shoes. "All right. If you have to, Devin." He didn't like her sympathetic tone, made him feel like a doddering senior.

"I've got an idea," he said. He pulled Amy over to a nearby window. The rolling hills of Bellingham stretched out under slate-blue overcast skies. "The Skerit farm is out there," he said. "Out in Lynden. That's where we're going."

"Great!" She actually bounced.

Devin found himself envious of the anticipation in Amy's eyes. She flushed with excitement. God. To feel that fever, again. Passion for a lead.

"But only after we get clearance. While I rest, you and Gottlieb take the rental car, hit the sheriff's office, and make sure we can get into the home." Devin pointed at her face. "Will that hold you? I'll nap in the truck, and by the time you get back, I'll be fresh."

She cocked her head. "What if I'm only gone for half an hour?"

"Whatever. I'll be ready. We'll go. Okay?"

She nodded, placated for the moment.

Devin led her down the hall toward the nurses' station, then gestured, noticing the men's room. "Just give me a minute." Devin looked over his shoulder as he pushed on the white door. "Don't go anywhere." He couldn't help but smile.

She stood, slightly pigeon-toed, the recorder dangling in her hands.

As he entered the rest room he marveled at her energy. It reminded him of his own youth. Thoughts of past glories, images of sitting at the anchor desk on a three-camera set at WLS with his own makeup woman.

He looked at the white tiles as he stepped to the urinal. No matter how many times he'd been in hospitals, they gave him the willies. Something crawling on the walls.

Finishing, he stepped to a sink.

A sound behind him. Someone in the handicapped stall. With the latch on the door broken, Devin could see a gnarled blue-veined hand grasping the chrome rail. An elderly man grunted as he defecated.

Devin turned the faucet on hard to mask the sound.

He found himself repulsed by old age, dreading it. Soaping his hands, he looked up. In the mirror, beneath the slightly graying black hair, the steel-blue eyes were framed by recent wrinkles, a contrast to the fresh face that had beamed on billboards and buses in Chicago. Bright red letters. Tune in at 6:00 P.M. for Devin Parks with world news.

It was way past six, but Devin vowed it wasn't too late.

The old man in the stall wheezed. Devin heard him whistle through tired tubes.

Hospitals. Like prisons. Get out of here. Away from this indignity.

He turned off the water.

The old man in the stall grunted again, and Devin cringed, hearing splashes in the bowl. Life's squalor. It was out there. He'd seen it before. He was suddenly struck by a foreboding chill. Keefer's attitude. Cold, clinical, a common reaction when there was something to hide. Could the disease be as devastating as Freeman intimated? An Ebola? Something even worse? He dried his hands quickly and escaped from the rest room, rushed out the white door only to find that Amy was nowhere to be seen.

When he reached the grip truck, their driver, Alan Gottlieb, wasn't inside. Had Amy grabbed him? The rental car was missing. They were probably both on their way downtown to the sheriff's office.

The clouds above had darkened.

Devin looked around the parking lot of the hospital beyond the main walkway. A slow but steady stream of patients, medical people, cars passed by the shrubbery.

He decided to check the doors of the truck. Open. Good. He climbed up into the passenger side of the cab and noticed the note on the dash. It read: *Back in five minutes.*

That made no sense. Why would Gottlieb leave a note if he were with Amy? Maybe, because Gottlieb was the only crew member available at the early hour of their arrival, he and Amy had gone back to KVOS to pick up a grip.

Devin sat in the seat, his eyes heavy. He nodded once and leaned over, rested his head against the truck window. Closing his eyes, he slumped against the door.

Dreams came frequently during restless sleep. Often—

for instance, now—he became master of a panoramic horizon without end and marveled at the black-and-white fantasy.

Levitation took him high into the sky, where he directed the dream. He flew over pastureland, mountains, and finally a town.

A large crowd of people looked up. He swooped down over their smiling faces with arms spread wide, and then shot back up into the clouds. In full command of his powers, he soared through a colorless atmosphere like an eagle without feathers. But as it had done before, the dream suddenly took an ominous turn.

His flight dropped him back down to a tall church spire, where, weakened, he clutched the top with both arms and legs, barely able to hang on.

The crowd below became angry, shouting derisive comments. They threw rocks. One nearly hit his head. Another one went by. Then, a jagged piece of stone struck him in the shoulder. He was about to fall.

His next conscious feeling, someone tugging his arm.

"Amy," Devin said, floating somewhere between dimensions.

"Mr. Parks, wake up."

Devin fought the dusty irritation under both eyelids. He squinted, focusing on the person sitting next to him in the driver's seat, the dark, curly-headed freelance kid. Gottlieb, wearing a wet orange KVOS windbreaker, tapped him on the shoulder.

"Where's Amy?" Devin asked.

"I thought you knew."

Devin shook the sleep out of his head. "What? You mean you haven't seen her?"

"No. I went looking for you guys."

"But the rental car . . ."

"It was here when I left, now it's gone. What are we

going to do?" Gottlieb asked. He said *we*. Ever since they met that morning, the kid had made it apparent he was excited being around professionals from California.

Gottlieb's rookie grin motivated him. Devin sat up, rubbed his neck, gratified to feel better. Sleep had refreshed him. "We'll wait for Amy. If she's not here in five minutes, I guess we'll head for the Skerit farm without her."

"Let's use those five minutes."

"What do you have in mind?"

"I think I'm onto something." Gottlieb's smile widened. He had the sinewy look of an Israeli freedom fighter. "How much would CNB pay to find someone who saw the Skerit kid up close?"

Devin blinked. "What are you talking about?"

"I was down the street." Gottlieb pointed. "There's an old guy tellin' stories about seeing the sick boy."

Devin gestured to the hospital through the light drizzle that fell on the windshield. "Hospital staff members are locked up in that wing."

"That's right. Hospital personnel. This guy's the groundskeeper. Late last night he turned off the sprinklers when the ambulance pulled in. He's good buddies with the drivers. Had beer with them after."

Devin perked up. "Ambulance drivers?"

"Yeah, but forget them. They're upstairs like you said." Gottlieb waved a forefinger. "But he's not."

"The groundskeeper. He wouldn't be under observation because he's not part of the medical staff." Devin sat up straight. Something stirred in his gut. This time it wasn't pain. "Where did you say he was?" He wiped his eyes.

"The general store." Gottlieb gestured to an Old West replica of a feed store two blocks away.

Devin saw it through trees that dotted the hospital grounds.

"All right." He stretched his shoulders, pointed to the vacant lot across the street from the store. "Pull up over there, far enough away so it doesn't intimidate anybody. If he's legit, we owe you a bonus."

"I'd appreciate that." Gottlieb grinned from ear to ear, both of which stood out from his bony head. A good guy, Devin thought. Straight arrow. Devin felt a twinge of excitement. Fire in his belly. Gottlieb maneuvered the white grip truck across the asphalt onto the wet grass under some large maple trees, away from other cars.

They jumped out.

Devin put a hand up over his eyebrows to see through the mist. He and Gottlieb scurried across the damp grass out to the open pavement of the street.

Rain fell harder. They broke into a sprint.

Devin cut around a puddle on a weakened left knee, just to see if it still held the weight. It felt good to move. He hadn't enjoyed a full run in months. He used to do forty yards in 4.8 seconds in full football pads.

They crossed the remaining fifty feet and hustled up the wooden stairs of the building, approached the front door, under the sign that read BARTON'S FEED AND GRAIN.

Devin turned to Gottlieb. "Don't show yourself. Lag behind and point him out. Let's not scare him."

Gottlieb nodded, still smiling.

Devin opened the squeaking door and entered. A small cowbell sounded over his head. Several men and two women prowled the shoddy-looking aisles for merchandise, making the ancient wood floor creak. Devin noticed dust on the cans. Del Monte beans. S&W asparagus. Carnation evaporated milk to his left, and a large display of Tim's Cascade Potato Chips.

A large woman in an apron stood behind the counter. "Can I help ya?" Her hair looked like a beehive, wrapped in a bun.

"Um, no . . . just looking for now, thanks." Devin gave her a friendly smile. Which man was the groundskeeper? He looked back for Gottlieb, who crept along in the next aisle by the brooms.

Peering over the molasses jars, Devin gestured toward a man in a plaid hunting cap.

Gottlieb shook his head.

Devin moved on past turpentine, paints, and jars full of brushes.

Gottlieb coughed from behind a tool display. He stood on tiptoe, pointing at another grizzly-looking man in a beard, wearing a raincoat and a wool hat.

Devin nodded appreciatively and made his way around the end of the aisle toward the man, who fingered a hose nozzle, studying the price.

"Excuse me," he said. "You work at the hospital?"

"What's that?" The man laid the nozzle back into the bin.

"You're the groundskeeper at the hospital."

"Got different jobs . . . hospital's one of them."

"Good," Devin said. "I'd like to talk to you for a minute. That's my friend over there . . ." He pointed to Gottlieb, who gave a little wave.

"KVOS," the man said. "You're TV people."

"That's right." Devin noticed the fat woman behind the counter stare at him intently. He spoke guardedly. "Could we talk outside?"

"In the rain?" the man asked, with a quizzical look.

"We've got a nice dry truck." Seeing the man's hesitation, Devin quietly reached for his wallet. Television networks normally didn't pay for interviews, but to avoid a delay, he slipped a hundred-dollar bill into the man's hand.

The man gazed down at his palm, then up at Devin. A faint spark glinted across his blue eyes. A mischievous smile played at the corners of his bearded mouth as he looked down at the bill again. "You want to talk to me? Outside?"

"That's right. Now, why don't you come along." Devin's low, reassuring voice seemed to work.

The groundskeeper followed like a child, clutching the hundred-dollar bill.

Devin threw Gottlieb a nod, and the young man ran out the door ahead of them, presumably to fire up the generator.

Across the wet grass under the maple trees, Devin and the groundskeeper fought back the rain. Devin squinted at him as they approached the truck. "What's your name, sir?"

"Name's Twilly."

Gottlieb had placed two HMI lights in the back of the truck. He switched them on and held the back doors open. The man stopped in his tracks.

"What are them lights for? What are we doin'?"

"We're going to ask you a couple of questions, Mr. Twilly. Now please get in." Devin put a hand on his back as Gottlieb grabbed him by the elbow, hoisted him up over the bumper and into the truck.

Twilly removed his hat, staring into the lights. "What questions?" He turned his attention to Gottlieb, who had moved toward the cab of the truck and placed a video-chip camera on his shoulder. "What's that for?" He stuffed the wool hat into his raincoat.

"We're taking your picture while we talk." Devin gave his arm a reassuring pat, pulled another hundred-dollar bill out of his pocket for bait, led Twilly farther into the truck. "We appreciate your doing this." He unfolded a director's chair, gestured for Twilly to sit. Then he grabbed a pencil microphone off a stand and handed the end of the cord to Gottlieb.

Twilly's eyes widened in the gleaming light as he sat down. "I've never been on TV." He shook slightly, seemed tempted to run, was about to rise, but Devin came forward with the microphone, placed a hand on his shoulder.

"Rolling?" Devin said to Gottlieb, keeping his eyes on Twilly's face. The cameraman's grunt was affirmation enough, and Devin began, trying not to intimidate Twilly with the formalities of an interview. "Mr. Twilly, why aren't you at the hospital right now?"

"My day is done." Twilly spoke quietly. "I'm headin' home to the missus, that's all." He stared at the camera.

"But weren't you asked to stay by one of the doctors?"

"Nope. Never been," Twilly said. "Probably never will."

"Don't you realize that there's a quarantine at the hospital because of the Skerit boy?"

Twilly looked at Devin for the first time.

"I understand the ambulance drivers who brought him in are friends of yours," Devin continued. "You had beer with them after work yesterday."

"Just one," Twilly said.

"They're being held for observation. Because they had contact with the Skerit boy. But you're out here walking around."

"I wasn't that close to him. Maybe like from me to the camera fella there, that's all. I seen the kid for a minute out back by the emergency doors."

"What time was that?"

"It was about eight forty-five, I guess."

"A bit late for groundskeeping, isn't it?"

"Like I told you, I got different jobs. Yesterday I was supposed to work at the hospital in the late afternoon, after I mowed the Elks Club ball field. Plenty of light left this time of year."

"Fine. But you saw the Skerit boy?" Devin tried to steer the conversation back to the main topic.

"Yup."

"Can you describe what you saw?"

Twilly's brow furrowed. He stared at his lap, apparently gathering words, brought a withered hand up to his forehead, rubbed it back and forth for a moment.

"Mr. Twilly?" Devin prompted.

"Well . . . the poor little kid was unconscious, that was plain to see. They had a needle stuck in his arm. And, his skin . . . was all black and patchy here and there, like he'd stuck parts of himself into a blast furnace. You know, kinda like a hot dog gets after bein' barbecued too long." Twilly apparently searched for a simile. "I don't know. I don't think I ever seen that kind of a burn. Looked like the devil had seared the kid with the breath of hell itself . . ."

THE SECOND DAY
8:10 A.M.
Kanaapali Beach, Maui

The lives of Jaktar and Dr. Victor Glant had become entwined through time and circumstance. The man called Jaktar was the time keeper. And Glant was the victim of circumstance; his past was about to crash violently into his future, which was to be short-lived.

Alone in the lobby rest room, large and muscular, Jaktar looked in the mirror and adjusted the tight black wig so it fit more comfortably. Jaktar surveyed his angular face. The black hairpiece looked natural. He enjoyed it. He had Moroccan blood, dark skin, and felt comfortable in Hawaii. Dark complexions were normal, after all. The shock of curly blond hair his Swedish mother had left him was now hidden under the toupee. An only child, he hated his mother and her lily-white skin. He hadn't seen her since he was fifteen. His father was dead, his mother incarcerated for killing him.

He pressed his upper lip with the fingertips of both hands. Spirit gum held a black mustache firmly in place. Its ebony lines made his face even more beautifully dark.

Girding himself for the task ahead, he flexed his shoulders and walked out of the rest room into the crowded lobby of the Horizon Hotel.

For seventy-two hours a severe wind had whipped the shores of Maui, keeping the beaches closed.

During this last day Jaktar watched visitors at the hotel

curtail their activities to card playing on their private lanais, walking through the rain-soaked gardens, and sightseeing on the round-the-island bus tours. Jaktar followed two of these tourists closely, checking their movements, waiting for an opening. He had been careful not to stay too close. It was unnecessary, since he wore a directional audio enhancer in the pocket of his cream-colored blazer. Aimed properly, he picked up conversation seventy-five feet away.

Jaktar enjoyed wearing loud clothes.

Audacity gave him strength, like a peacock spreading his tail to impress its mate. In this case, the mate was murder, and he loved it dearly.

Murder had become a worldwide occupation. Jet travel allowed assassins to operate efficiently anywhere.

Today it was Hawaii. And Dr. and Mrs. Victor Glant were targets.

Jaktar had disposed of Dr. Leo Metzger in Evansville, Indiana, the day before yesterday. A risky kill. He had followed Metzger to his club, disguised as an air-conditioning repairman, and found an opportunity.

Metzger sunbathed frequently, likely trying to change that unwanted white skin.

Jaktar had quietly slipped the lock of the private booth, held the tanning-bed lid down, and put a handkerchief doused with chloroform over Metzger's face. Then he had inserted a long hypodermic needle under Metzger's sternum.

Jaktar smiled, remembering how his victim's legs had thrashed under the plastic lid until, inevitably, everything went quiet. Calmly leaving the body, he had walked out of the club undetected.

An overnight flight out of Chicago had brought him here, to seek his present quarry. The peacock was again in full regalia, flamboyant and focused on the hunt.

Seated in a large white wicker chair, he awaited the Glants' arrival. If they were going anywhere, they had to pass by this strategic vantage point in the lobby. Having made a bogus wrong-number phone call, he knew they were still in their room.

Jaktar looked at his watch. There was now some urgency.

He had received word, only an hour ago. His people had botched an assignment, and Dr. Thomas Hendrix had escaped capture. Normally, his assistant, a North Korean named Sing Chu, was highly reliable. Jaktar had trained him personally. The assignment should have been routine. Jaktar reasoned that Sing Chu and his tactics team could handle the abduction, though kills were easy compared with captures. According to information Jaktar received during the short call from the mainland, Hendrix had been cornered in the hallway of his apartment. Then a medical emergency, a heart attack in the next unit, brought a flurry of firemen and paramedics into the building. Hendrix disappeared in the confusion.

Jaktar wasn't upset. Not in his character. Emotions were like loyalties, commodities to be managed to his advantage. He prided himself that others might be flustered or hurried by these circumstances. Even though the kill was a rush, he would not rush the kill. He was an accomplished craftsman and a businessman, ready to finish this job then move on to supervise the next one in Virginia, where Hendrix was last seen.

Another look at his watch. Raising his eyes, he discovered a woman in a canary-yellow top with apparently little to do but block his view.

"Oh, hello," she warbled. "What a handsome watch you're wearing. Do you have the time?"

"Always," Jaktar replied.

She cocked her head, expecting more. He stared at

her with his dark eyes, imagining a bullet hole in her forehead.

"Well, pardon me." She moved off toward the registration desk, revealing Victor Glant and his wife, Melba, waddling down the hallway toward the lobby. The two heavyset people turned into the small gift shop near the arcade.

Jaktar pushed the earpiece farther into his right ear, but the couple's conversation became garbled with background noise.

The Glants appeared to be engaged in lively discussion. They disappeared into the recesses of the shop, emerged a few minutes later, headed in his direction.

He picked up a newspaper, disguised his surveillance. Glancing past the *USA Today* issue, he listened to their conversation.

Dr. Glant wore a T-shirt he had evidently just purchased.

"You saw the yellow flags, you idiot," Melba Glant scolded.

"A man occasionally makes up his mind, and I made up mine," Victor Glant said. "I'm ready for a swim!"

"You're crazy." Melba wore a multicolored muumuu.

Glant stabbed the air above his head with a chubby forefinger. "Experienced swimmers can go." He pointed to the words *surfer dude* emblazoned across the T-shirt.

She softened her tone. "Victor, come to the pool with me. We'll read . . . maybe play some backgammon."

"Backgammon?" Glant asked. "I paid twelve dollars for this shirt. I intend to try it out."

She grabbed his arm. "You're not going alone."

"Good. Then you're joining me?"

Melba shook a finger in his face. "I'm going to make the lifeguard stop you."

"Nonsense. I'll show him my T-shirt, and he'll want to come."

"The waves are too high."

"Oh, nonsense," Victor bellowed across the lobby.

Jaktar heard the pronouncement even without the earpiece.

Glant slapped the T-shirt over his rounded belly with both hands. "I'm off," he said proudly.

Melba looked around. She seemed embarrassed that other hotel guests might witness the spectacle.

Jaktar took the opportunity to move to the elevator. From the corner of his eye he saw Glant spin around and head for the stairs to the beach.

"Victor, please don't go."

"I'll meet you at the pool, later," Glant yelled to his wife as he disappeared down the stairs.

In the elevator, Jaktar pushed "11" and the "close door" button. Outside the converging doors in the lobby, a man in a straw hat voiced his disapproval, just missing the trip. Jaktar began his ascent.

Glant's penchant for surf-swimming had been listed in his dossier, and Jaktar had hoped for this moment. It might have come sooner, if the off-season storm hadn't closed the beaches.

Jaktar exited the elevator at a brisk walk.

Opening the door to room 1124, Jaktar grabbed the Ruger rifle from the closet and moved to the window overlooking the beach.

Jaktar had been trained to use his eyes like a hunting hawk, no peripheral vision, just intense focus on limited square feet, a small patch of beach below, where Victor Glant kicked off his sandals.

Jaktar followed Glant as he stumbled toward the white water with its six-foot breakers. The scientist screamed with delight, threw himself into the water, and was immediately covered by a wave. He came up on the other side and looked back toward the beach. Few people there.

Momentarily, Jaktar broke focus, surveyed the rest of the scene.

A mother and two small children dumped wet sand onto a small sand castle off to the north.

Lifeguards in red trunks folded towels near the guard shack up near the grassy hotel grounds. One peered toward Dr. Glant but was immediately distracted by a female partner.

Eleven floors above, Jaktar heard her laugh.

A couple of distant joggers approached this way from a few hundred feet to the south. No other distractions. Bad weather kept most people indoors and many of them were eating a late breakfast.

Jaktar seized the moment. He pulled two rubber gloves from his jacket and put them on, snapped a silencer onto the weapon. Then he dropped down on one knee on the seat of the chair placed near the window. Resting an arm on the back of the chair, he propped the high-powered scope rifle against his shoulder. He drew a bead on Dr. Glant through the vertical metal railing of the lanai. In the scope, it appeared as if he were only a few feet away.

Jaktar watched Dr. Glant bob in the surf. Between waves, he moved less erratically. Crosshairs of the sight came to rest on the gray hair on the back of the doctor's head.

Jaktar used the bald spot as a bull's-eye, and squeezing the trigger slowly, he let go a round.

The silencer hissed, the bullet left the barrel, exploded the back of Glant's head 270 feet away.

The impact snapped his head forward, rolled the body onto its stomach. A red blotch formed on the ocean forty feet from shore.

A wave rolled over his rounded back, covering the words *surfer dude* on the green, yellow, and blue T-shirt, as Dr. Glant sank beneath the surface. Then he was gone. Red water dissipated, churned by the waves.

Jaktar felt a wave of excitement shudder through his body. He closed his eyes, relishing it. When it had passed, he wiped the weapon clean and laid it on the bed.

He stood in front of the dresser, rearranged himself, discarding the wig and mustache.

He would leave the room just as it was. He had disposed of his luggage after arriving, and left no traces except the unmarked weapon, contraband provided by the organization in Hawaii.

He brushed a hand through his blond hair and looked down on the dresser at the pot of hot licorice herb tea he had ordered from room service.

As was his habit, he took a small glass cup he carried in a belt pouch and poured himself some refreshment. Each murder required a new crystal. At the beginning of his career, he had purchased a set of twenty-four. There were five left that would likely be used in this current campaign. The licorice caressed the back of his throat. Another full sip. The tea tasted minty sweet. Just like the kill.

THE SECOND DAY
5:26 P.M.
Williamsburg, Virginia

Dr. Thomas Hendrix had been in hiding, convinced that someone was trying to capture or kill him.

He stared at the flashing red sign outside the motel. The light seemed to pulse inside his brain as thoughts flipped into consciousness like information on a computer screen, contained and orderly.

He reviewed his options. The government was unapproachable; they might even be behind his failed abduction. His daughter Ginelle was likely the only person who could help him. If he could talk to her.

He moved the cheese snack farther down the bedspread, placed the pizza box closer to his knees.

Ginelle. God grant she was safe. A marvelous daughter. Object of his affection and pride, though in recent years she had become judgmental, sometimes refusing to speak with him.

He chewed on a cracker, musing how she had chosen to follow in his footsteps as a biochemist, yet disagreed with his career choices. Their estrangement was all the more painful since they were the two surviving members of the family.

He hoped that time would heal the rift.

Presumably, his would-be abductors didn't know where Ginelle was. She wasn't at home. He had checked. After several phone calls he discovered she'd gone to

Washington to visit the Smithsonian. He was pretty sure she'd stay with her friend Julie in Reston, Virginia.

He smiled. Ginelle loved the Smithsonian.

As a small girl, she had tried to reach through a glass case to touch a monarch butterfly. Her little face had clouded with disappointment as her fingers stubbed on the pane. She had looked up at her father with those huge green eyes. A beautiful child.

She was beautiful now, often burdened by the some-times unwelcome attention of men. And, perhaps because of her mother and sister's deaths, she seemed somewhat self-protective. Of course, within the cloister of academia she had had her share of male friends—professors, colleagues. He smiled. They were too much like her father to hold her interest. Fortunately, she had kept her address and phone number confidential. Thank goodness, under these dangerous circumstances.

Hendrix had left an urgent message for Ginelle in Reston, to call the motel when she returned.

He brushed the crumbs off the colorful bedspread and opened the pizza box. Still warm. As he examined the pepperoni and cheese his mind continued to click. As always, his restless thoughts organized themselves into highly complex patterns, something he cursed when he longed for peace. Of course, it was that very ability to deal with multiple concepts simultaneously that allowed him to work molecular machine problems, and had been the reason for his success.

Reaching for pizza, he funneled his mental energies to his current dilemma: where to hide. He could go back to Yale. But his association with his alma mater was well known. Better to find somewhere safe out of the country. Switzerland, he thought. He reached for a piece of pizza, then dropped it.

For the first time he realized how disturbed he was.

His hands were shaking so badly that he could barely hold the food.

He pushed the pizza box away, reached for the remote control on the bed stand, and clicked on the small set. The news would take his mind off his current plight.

He searched and found channel 32. CNB's evening report. He had switched over from CNN some time ago because he liked CNB's frequent science and industrial features.

On-screen, a reporter held a microphone in front of a frightened-looking man in a camera truck. Hendrix noted the reporter's name, written in gold letters at the bottom of the screen: DEVIN PARKS. As Devin's voice became audible in mid-sentence, he heard: ". . . and Mr. Twilly is one of the few people who has actually seen the patient up close. The hospital is sealed. It's virtually impossible for reporters to contact the staff or doctors working on this bizarre case. But whether the Skerit boy is alive or dead is unknown. No diagnosis, yet. All we know is that Gordi Skerit's symptoms resemble others in various geographic locations. So far, the Skerit boy is the only patient with this condition here in Washington State. I'm Devin Parks reporting to you from Bellingham for CNB News."

The screen cut to the news set at CNB headquarters in San Francisco, where anchorman Frank Worthy resumed his story. "Both Devin Parks and Amy Klein will remain in the Northwest to cover this developing story."

Worthy turned a page on the desk and looked back at the camera. "Unconfirmed reports indicate there may be as many as twenty-seven cases of this mysterious ailment throughout the nation." A map of the United States came up on the screen next to Frank Worthy's face and lit dots appeared as he spoke. "Besides documented similarities in the cases in Bellingham, Washington; Macon, Georgia; Tucson, Arizona; and Trenton, New Jersey;

there are now reports coming in from California, Minnesota, Kansas, Nebraska, Ohio, and Maine. These suggest the ailment is either causing a 'me-too' hysteria, or actually occurring in multiple locations nationwide. Call this an ailment? A disease? Its true causes are vague and difficult to determine. For further comment, we go to our science editor, Dan Canon."

"A disease?" Hendrix said absentmindedly, groping for a slice of pizza, his eyes riveted on the television.

The screen showed a younger, collegiate type with dark hair and glasses, wearing a tweed jacket.

"Thank you, Frank. The degree of alarm about this mysterious ailment is unique. Rather than the clustered pattern of Legionnaire's disease, which occurred in various locations in the East, or the geographic constraints of the respiratory virus which struck primarily in the Southwest, we have a phenomenon here so dynamic and so spread out, it defies logic. Dare we say the word *Ebola*? No. The characteristics of this contagion resemble, and yet are also unlike, the plague in Zaire. Remember, Ebola has a three-week incubation period and is transferred by physical contact. These cases developed in the last twenty-four to thirty-six hours in multiple locations far from one another. There is no known relationship between the current victims, although it is worth noting that they are all children. Some similarity exists in the kind and severity of symptoms, according to eyewitness reports of relatives and bystanders. The body's reaction is what you might expect to see from Hollywood special effects. Epidermal deterioration, internal bleeding, and finally a phenomenon which looks like third-degree burns about the head and body. No wonder panic surrounds the unfortunates who contract this frightening ailment. I believe that's the reason we've had so much media attention on something so short-lived."

"Do we have any official reaction on this, Dan?" Frank Worthy asked. "Any word from state governments or health officials?"

"Not yet. We've attempted to contact Washington, but there has been no official response. Dr. Samuel Gordon of the Disease Control Center in Atlanta was unavailable for comment. There should have been an official statement by now, if some kind of chemical accident or laboratory biological hazard had occurred . . . the kind we've seen in fiction and film. But nothing of the kind. We simply know a quarantine's been dropped around medical facilities housing victims. And no recommended action. I would anticipate school closures and similar measures if this thing is indeed communicable. The only advice we can offer people at this time is—"

"Dan. Let me interrupt you, if I may," Frank Worthy said, "for a live report from our Los Angeles office via satellite. We now join Brook Hanford, our reporter in Los Angeles. . . . Brook?"

Dr. Hendrix barely noticed that the cheese, crackers, and pizza box had fallen off the bed. He adjusted his glasses. His mind raced. The young fair-skinned reporter in Los Angeles appeared on the screen.

"Frank. The whirlwind nature of this 'disease,' if we can call it that, is evident here in Los Angeles, where we now have *five* cases reported. All are young children. I'm standing on the front steps of Providence Hospital, where I'm about to be joined by Dr. Arthur Dempsey, chief pathologist for the California Department of Health. Dr. Dempsey has seen patients admitted here and in two other medical facilities across town, and has chosen to make a public statement. He is due any moment."

"Brook, you're saying Dr. Dempsey *requested* to appear?" Frank Worthy asked, now on split screen with the other reporter.

"That is correct. We've been asked to air video taken at the hospital of one of the young patients, Sandy Cochran. Dr. Dempsey feels it's important the viewers see the—oh—just a minute, here he is. . . ."

The screen showed a well-dressed man in his fifties descending the steps of the hospital in a dark suit, joining the young reporter in the glow of the lights. Brook continued, "Dr. Dempsey, we're live to our headquarters in San Francisco. As you requested, the video is cued up and ready."

"Thank you, Mr. Hanford." Dr. Dempsey spoke in a deep, gravelly voice. He squinted into the lights shining brightly under the California night, pulled a piece of paper from his breast pocket, and referred to it. "I have instructions from Dr. Samuel Gordon at the Disease Control Center in Atlanta to make the following announcement. Other media throughout the country will be similarly notified at the earliest opportunity. In the video you are about to see, you will witness symptoms of a victim with an affliction which has no clinical name, yet is rapidly becoming a national concern." He turned to the young reporter. "How will I know what we're seeing, Mr. Hanford?"

"The monitor, over there, Doctor."

"Oh, yes. All right. What you're seeing now is a close-up of young Sandy Cochran's left arm. Notice what appear to be severe burns on the skin. These hemorrhagic skin eruptions are a consistent symptom developing several hours after fever. In some cases, the fever is accompanied by vomiting, dizziness, and fainting."

"Holy God," Hendrix said, completely absorbed by the coverage. He got to his feet, stood petrified, stared at the television screen.

Dr. Dempsey continued. The screen showed shots of the young girl's face. "Sandy's parents allowed us to take these pictures at my request, so others might become immediately aware of the situation. If your child has signs of what you think is flu, sore throat, fever, or exhibits anything more than symptoms usually associated with a common cold, we advise you to call your physician. I've talked with doctors around the nation by phone this evening, and it's apparent we're dealing with something destructive and deadly. I have confirmed reports of deaths from this new illness in Macon, Tucson, Bellingham, Trenton, and Los Angeles. Other reported cases are critical . . . comatose and dying. In each patient, high fever and external skin damage simultaneously accompanied internal injury to mucous membranes and eventually lack of consciousness. This has, in some very specific locations of the country, become"—the stress on Dr. Dempsey's face was obvious as he tucked his notes back into his jacket—"a medical emergency."

He looked straight into the lens. "Be assured, the department of health and other government agencies are investigating the problem. We'll find an answer. In the meantime we recommend schools, clubs, and camps in nearby vicinities to these cases be closed tomorrow. People should check with their local authorities. Now we have, as yet, no clue as to how the disease spreads, or what implications secondary infection might have. We have word that some parents of afflicted children now show similar signs of illness. Namely, Mrs. Skerit in Bellingham and Mrs. Collins in Macon, Georgia. Both came down with the symptoms."

Dr. Dempsey turned to Brook Hanford, who appeared tense. "Believe me," Dempsey said, half to Hanford and half to the camera, "I wouldn't be making this announcement if it weren't absolutely necessary."

Dr. Hendrix flicked the remote control and faded the

volume on the television to silence. Dr. Dempsey was still on-screen mouthing the words.

"Jesus," Hendrix said quietly, "someone let it out." He paced the floor of the motel room. "The maniacs finally did it! Maniacs!"

He pictured the isolated desert outpost. Laboratory animals. The experimental chamber.

The phone rang on the bed stand. He stepped on the pizza box, whirling back toward the bed. His daughter Ginelle was on the line.

"Why did you call, Dad? Your message sounded very strange."

"Ginelle," Hendrix said. "Thank God. Where are you?"

"I'm in Reston. Julie and I just returned. What are you doing at a motel?" He could hear her disgruntled tone. He had imposed on her.

"Don't say anything to Julie about this."

"About what? What's the problem?"

He breathed hard, yet tried not to reveal his panic. "Three Asian men tried to abduct me." Better to mention the news broadcast later.

"My God."

"I would have been forced to go with them if poor Mrs. Brodnick in 3B hadn't had a seizure. As I was led down the stairs the building filled with firemen. Aid cars everywhere. I took the opportunity to yell, 'I'm a doctor.' Paramedics grabbed me and dragged me upstairs to help. In the confusion my assailants disappeared."

"Who were they?"

"I have no idea. Their leader had a horseshoe-shaped scar on his forehead." Hendrix recalled the intensity of the man.

"I don't understand." She sounded concerned. "Why would someone—"

"Ginelle, please listen. Have you seen the news? They've announced a dreadful disease."

"I hadn't heard."

"You will. Just turn on the news. Something terrible is happening. Do you still have the keys for the lab in Richmond?"

"At the university?"

"No. The lab where you worked on the gene pool."

"The biochemistry lab at the Commonwealth Institute?" It was the only nearby facility with molecular equipment.

"Correct. Do you still have access there?"

"I have security clearance through the campus."

"Good. Meet me there tonight."

A pause.

Ginelle must have been digesting his request. "I . . . think you better explain," she said. The judgmental tone again. "Don't tell me this has anything to do—"

"I'm afraid it does." He couldn't hide the guilt in his voice. "The ailment they've described sounds like the replicator."

"Oh God. What do you mean, sounds like?"

"The symptoms are identical. The television broadcast showed young children who have it. I've seen all that before. Not on people . . . on monkeys. Something no one else was ever supposed to see. Back in the desert, several years ago, when I was working with Leo Metzger, Victor Glant, and Ahmar Kahvahl . . . the Black Diamond Project."

A long silence. Then a chilled response. "I hate this. All of it. I wish you had listened to me."

He admired her forcefulness, even when he took the brunt of it.

"Please," he pleaded. "Let's not get into all that again. I need you now."

Almost to herself: "Somehow I knew you would pay for that horrendous government contract. I . . . I don't think I should get involved."

"You must. If you don't, it'll be on your doorstep in a few weeks. Yours and everyone else's. It's spreading. Please, Ginelle. Whoever did this obviously has no conscience. They may even be looking for you." He regretted using fear as a tool, but without her help, he could not even begin to do what he had to do.

"If they are, it's obviously your fault."

"I'll see that you're safe. We can straighten things out if you help me work. There's no time to waste. Do they have plenty of plasma available?" A pause. He could see her face. Pride. Determination. And beneath, the strength of spirit.

"I think we can get it from the genetics department." Thank goodness. She had shifted in his direction.

"Good. I'll need several carbon extracts, access to the computer, and some negatively ionized plutonium mesh. And when you arrive, make up some RBC-16. We'll check the enzymatic grid to ensure we use the right formula."

"What are we trying to do, Dad?" she asked with resignation.

"If my memory serves, and with God's help, we'll find a formula for a vaccine."

"What about the government? What about Metzger, Glant, and Kahvahl? Shouldn't you try to reach them?"

"No. Ginelle, if this is the replicator, it's been deliberately planted. God help us if it makes a run."

"A run?"

"An unobstructed string of infection. If I succeed in formulating an antidote, we'll contact the necessary officials. Until then, I don't trust anyone. I never trusted Metzger or Kahvahl. And Glant . . . he's undoubtedly somewhere in Hawaii. He goes there every year."

THE SECOND DAY
9:45 P.M.
Widmark Hotel
Bellingham, Washington

Amy had returned late and they agreed to meet for dinner.

Now, in the hotel's plush dining room, they sat opposite one another in a booth. Amy's mood was hard to read. She had taken it upon herself to visit the Skerit farm and Gordi's school without clearance and without Devin. Devin was glad that she had taken the initiative, but he was also proud that he was the one who had landed the Twilly story and garnered national exposure. He had found the lead; she had gathered some valuable still shots. Now he had to praise her efforts and make sure she wasn't disappointed.

"How could you possibly get away with it?" he asked admiringly.

"When the health-department people got to the Skerit farm," she said, "I had already been inside. I got back in my car, so they thought I had just arrived."

Still chewing, Devin pushed his plate away. "Smart." He took a sip of Cabernet to wash away the last of the New York steak, realizing how much he wanted her to have her day in the sun. "I'll bet you'll have a feature story on the Skerit family as soon as we get back." Not fully recovered from his long sleeplessness, he had been waylaid by the deep red wine and two predinner martinis. He realized he was beginning to slur his words.

"You think Freeman would let me? It makes sense." Her shiny blond hair reflected the candle glow. Tonight, she looked quite mature, like the daughter he might never have. She had blossomed both personally and professionally.

"Of course he will. Who else has coverage on victims' homes? Quarantines kept them out, whatever." Seizing the moment, he raised the wineglass briefly. "You're the one with an inside story."

"Let me show you the Polaroids," she said, bouncing on the leather seat of the booth.

"Sure. You could do a live read with inserts over the pictures."

"Here." She grabbed the leather clutch purse she had placed at her side, undid the clasp, and pulled them out.

As Amy sorted them Devin scooted around so he could see them better, and was suddenly affected by the sight.

"This is the kitchen," Amy said, toning down. "Pretty graphic. That's blood smeared on the linoleum."

Devin frowned. "God, poor kid. I forgot about the bleeding."

"Here's two of the back porch."

Devin pointed. "What's that?"

"I assume it's Gordi's lunch box. His baseball glove was still lying by the door, just as he must have left it."

The shots brought home to Devin the reality of the trauma. "We sometimes forget, don't we?"

"Forget?"

"Just like that reporter in Macon, remember? He was fired up by the story, didn't think about the victim."

"Am I like that?"

"I'm not talking about you. I'm talking about all of us . . . newspeople. It's such a fine line, staying removed enough to tolerate the trauma, yet involved enough to stay human."

"You've done it."

"You think so?" he asked. "I don't know. After Iraq, I buried myself in my career. Didn't look to either side. Straight at the camera, nowhere else."

"After Rwanda, I did the same."

"I understand. But at least we're here talking about it. That's very important."

Amy gathered the pictures quickly as the busboy arrived. They both remained silent as he cleared the dishes. Then, as the young man left, Devin looked up and found Amy staring at him.

"You're a cool guy, Devin. Some woman ought to appreciate you."

Catching a hint of something beyond youthful adoration in her expression, Devin glanced away. "One did once."

"You've never told me, what happened?"

He couldn't face a rehash of those painful events. "Not tonight," he said. "Show me the rest of the pictures."

"There's not much more."

He reached. "Come on."

She put the photographs back on the table and singled out the last few. "I took wide shots of the house. Full shots of the hallway."

With memories of Susan stabbing at him, Devin took another sip of wine, trying to concentrate. He picked up the last photo. "What's this?"

"Weird. The way they still had all those animal cages out back. Maybe they ran a mink farm at one time."

He shuffled back to the first shot. "In the kitchen, weren't you worried about infection?"

"No. Not with no one else there. I washed my hands carefully." She stacked the pictures and put them aside.

Devin sought to keep the conversation going, forestall

any further mention of his past. "What about Gordi's school? Anything?"

"Not really. I tried talking to the baseball coach, but he was at practice. A young guy who was his assistant, a janitor of sorts, had apparently left a couple of days ago. So, aside from a few teachers' comments about how nice Gordi was . . . nothing concrete."

Now her enthusiasm had him wanting to lend importance to her afternoon. He leaned back from the candle glow and smiled broadly. "It's been a great day."

"It has," she said dreamily, as if suddenly distracted.

He wondered what she was thinking. "Something on your mind?"

"I'm glad you did the Twilly story," she said, toying with the dessert spoon on the white tablecloth. "It's just what you needed. How did Freeman sound on the phone?"

"You know him. He acted as if it were expected. Asked us to get our butts back on the plane, but I told him I needed a rest, and that we were staying." Devin had arranged for Carl Clemmer, a chartered Learjet pilot, to meet them at the airport in the morning.

"Overall, Freeman must have been happy with you."

"Just luck. If Gottlieb hadn't dropped by that store—"

"Yes, but you knew how to handle it."

He couldn't help feeling a touch of pride. "I admit I was stimulated."

"Of course." She dropped the spoon and fussed with the tablecloth. "Devin. Ever since I was a reporter on my high-school newspaper, my dad encouraged me to be in the news business. I was so pleased to get the CNB job. I yearned to be the first one there with the most to say."

Her strange wistfulness gave him pause. "What's going on in that head of yours?" He put a hand on her arm. "Why so pensive, all of a sudden?"

"Devin. After I went out to the Skerit home, I called my dad in Iowa. I kind of felt like it. I don't know why. I guess the tragedy at that farmhouse and the deaths in other families around the country just kind of hit me."

"That's what we were talking about. I understand."

"Dad had been trying to reach me, too."

"Oh?"

"Yes. I had given ABC my home number, not wanting to have them call the office."

"What do you mean? They called your dad?"

"Yes."

"And?"

Her face suddenly lit up. Moisture formed in her eyes, glistening in the candlelight. "I got it," she said simply. She choked up.

He couldn't believe what she had just said. "What do you mean?"

"They gave me the job. I don't have to go back for a live test. They liked my tape so much they hired me based on the sample I sent them." She laughed through her tears.

He stared at her. He had never really considered she might succeed. "Gee. That's wonderful."

"I start in two weeks." She wiped a little tear from her cheek. "Just think, I'm a cohost on a morning news show in New York!"

Was she actually leaving? Devin fought his ambivalence. His protégée, a good friend, had actually landed her own show, while his career barely treaded water. He looked around the room. Only one other couple sitting in a back booth. The waiter glided by, and Devin caught his attention, waving a hand. "You have Dom Pérignon?"

The man in the high-cut tuxedo jacket paused at their table. "Of course."

"Great. A bottle, please."

The waiter nodded and headed for the kitchen.

"Devin, I don't want any," Amy said softly, as if embarrassed.

"Oh, come on. Let's celebrate your new job." What irony that he had tried to pump her up about her work while she had quietly one-upped him.

Amy smiled shyly. "Well, I guess it is kind of special."

"Special? It's spectacular."

The waiter was back with two glasses and a bottle of extra-dry champagne. "Monsieur." He presented Devin the label.

Devin nodded. "Fine. Amy, you must have some."

"Well." She stared at her glass. "Maybe I will."

The waiter poured a sample for Devin to taste, and after Devin's approval, finished pouring both glasses.

Devin raised his glass in the candlelight. "To you and to New York." While Amy smiled and took a sip Devin downed his champagne and grinned.

"Why did you do that?" Amy asked.

"What?"

"That." She pointed at his empty glass.

"Just celebrating." He mustered a smile and poured himself some more, then topped hers. Setting the bottle down, he took another large gulp and stared into the candle on the table, watching the flame wriggle.

"Devin." She took a sip and looked at him curiously. "You're okay with my going to New York, aren't you?" She stopped talking and searched his eyes with a sudden wistfulness. "If I even thought you might . . ."

Might what? What was she saying? "What do *I* have to do with it?"

"More than you know. Your caring, and . . ." She seemed to shake herself. "Anyway . . . I wanted to follow my dream."

"Sure. That's what dreams are for," he said, taking another swig. "They flit around so you can follow them."

"You sound like you're bitter about that."

"I've seen dreams come true." He finished the last of the champagne.

She gave him a reproachful look. "I don't understand."

"Understand? We're celebrating." He sounded edgy. He told himself to calm down.

"My leaving has upset you."

"God," he laughed halfheartedly, "more power to you. It's a great excuse to have a good time." Devin captured the waiter's attention again. "Ah . . ." he said. "There you are. Bring us another bubbly for the future Barbara Walters." The waiter nodded, straightened his bow tie, and retreated to the kitchen. "And you're so much cuter," Devin mumbled, looking back at Amy.

Her eyes moistened. She refused to look him in the face, stared at the tablecloth.

He had offended her with his flippancy. Uncalled for. Devin's guilt gained a new dimension. "I'm sorry," he said, trying to take her hand. She pulled away.

"I'm a serious newswoman, Devin. I always have been."

He was amazed at the anger in her voice.

"I didn't mean—"

"I've appreciated your advice and your support, but I think I deserve more than your condescension."

The word hit him like a shot. He nodded pensively. "I apologize for the lack of respect. Somehow I seem to do that."

"Do what?"

"Hurt people I care for."

She picked up her purse and started to knead it, frustrated. "You haven't hurt me." Her tone softened. "I'll miss you."

Devin felt an alcoholic mist hovering around his he The world looked fuzzy. "I'll miss *you*," he said, suddenly immersed in his own melancholia.

"Devin, I think we should call it a night."

But Devin didn't want to go back to his room alone, and he felt more secure sitting in one place. She began to slide out of the booth. He tried to prevent her from rising.

"Don't," she said. "I'm getting the check. It's time to sleep."

"I'm sorry, please sit down. I'll just drink water." He held up an ice-filled glass, hanging on to her with his other hand. "Look. *Agua*. H_2O." He drank a gulp. But as she pulled away he spilled some on his tie. He smiled as disarmingly as he could. "Water under the bridge."

She slouched back into the booth, gave him an understanding look, and shook her head. "Devin, I want you to know we'll always be friends."

"You. You're a special person," he said. She reacted with full dimples, and he felt momentarily reprieved.

He managed to focus on her. "We will stay in touch, you and I, won't we?" His words had become quite slurred. He was now fully convinced that he had consumed far more than he should have. He wondered if his prattle sounded like the ramblings of a street bum.

She moved away. "Of course we will. But now, let's pay the check and go."

Dizzily, Devin swung around and stared into the candle. "You know what Barbara Walters says . . . we're in touch so you be in touch." He pulled the candle forward, moving the light closer to his face. "Hate to lose contact with those we cherish." The candle flickered. "It's tough enough just to tune in to each other. Just when we think we've got a steady signal, somebody changes the channel." He lifted a finger and brushed the flame with it, back and forth several times, leaving the flesh in the fire long enough to feel a tickle of pain. "Sometimes my brain feels like one big satellite dish. The whole world is on satellite, I can't seem to tune in to myself." He came out of his daydream, trying to recall his whereabouts. The booze had really hit him.

Devin looked up, surprised to see Amy holding the check. He groped for his wallet, searching for his credit card.

"Here. I have mine." Amy pulled a green company charge card from her clutch purse.

Devin nodded, grabbed the bottle, and poured the remaining champagne into his glass. The waiter hadn't delivered the second one. Amy must have refused it. Devin stared at the candle's wavering dance. The room grew darker. He barely noticed the waiter appearing at her elbow to take the credit card. Everything had gone black around the small orb of light.

"Devin." It was Amy. She spoke through a dull fog.

He suddenly realized that they were walking to the elevator together. Where had the candle gone?

"Devin. I don't feel well."

"What's that?" They were in his room. No. Hers. Then he was in his bed alone. He had his pants off. Still wearing his shirt. It seemed as if just a few minutes had passed when there was a knock at the adjoining bedroom door.

Amy's face peeked through the opening. "I think I'm going to get sick." Her voice was strained.

"What? Oh. That's just the champagne," he said, rolling over into the feather pillow. He was unable to open his eyes.

"I only had one glass."

He drifted away. Someone in the next room. Flushing toilets. Breathing . . . panting. More dreams, until the light woke him, shining in his eyes. Devin strained to see the clock radio. It was 6:33.

The room slanted. Taste of acid at the base of his throat. He buried his head beneath the pillow. Another stretch to see the time. 9:17. Light through the room drapes. The phone. Ringing. He dragged his face across the dry sheets. Reached. Answered.

"Hello?"

"Parks, is that you?" It was Freeman.

"Wrong room. Sorry." He dropped the phone onto the nightstand.

The small voice railed at him from the phone. "Devin. Don't hang up! Are you there?"

"Boy, am I." He talked at the phone from a distance, his face draped off the edge of the mattress.

"Parks! Pick up the phone."

Devin obeyed.

"Let me call you back. I'm in the shower." His arm, like a hairy crane, maneuvered the phone across the crevasse between the bed and the nightstand.

"What? Well, dry off. There was an interesting call for you from some doctor back east."

"I don't know any doctor back east."

"Let me give you the number."

"I'll call you later." Devin put the handset back onto the receiver, then, thinking better of it, rested it on the nightstand, eliminating the possibility of further calls. Devin lay staring at the ceiling, which moved in a slow arc. The door to the adjoining room was still open. Amy. He got up on one elbow.

"Amy?" No response. A moan. "Are you feeling any better?" he called.

He managed to sit up. Feet on the floor. He shuffled to the open door and knocked. "Are you dressed?"

No answer. He leaned into the room.

There. A lump of blankets on the bed. Amy's curly blond hair, partially covered.

He tiptoed into the room. The black pantsuit she had worn lay on the floor next to the bed.

Devin touched Amy's shoulder. "Amy."

He pulled the sheet back, revealed her forehead. Freckles. Her face. More freckles than he remembered. He bent down to take a closer look. Devin's thoughts were fragmentary, shapeless, pointless. Then, suddenly, an electric shock fired up his tailbone and filled his chest. He was only a foot from her face.

"Oh, Jesus!" Devin said, seeing the red spots on her skin. "Amy, wake up."

She blinked several times, and struggled to keep her eyes open. Devin put the back of his hand on her neck. She was burning up.

"Amy. Have you looked in the mirror?"

"No. I can't move."

Devin pulled the blanket down. "Don't, Devin. I'm cold."

"Just a minute, sweetheart." He struggled with her, able to get the edge of the blanket down over her shoulder. She used her other arm to try to recover the blanket. He saw the redness on her hands, and her left forearm.

"Cover me, please."

"Amy, you don't understand." He had to tell her. "God. I . . . I think . . . you have it."

THE THIRD DAY
6:14 A.M.
Atlanta

Dr. Samuel Gordon stared at the monitor. A steady column of statistics rolled slowly up the screen, indicating the number of cases now confirmed as Unknown Disease #7.

"Flash fires," or health incidents that had an impact on the general public in the United States, were placed into various groups, depending on their severity and their origin. Chemical events were categorized as "S" incidents due to their Synthetic nature. Radioactive events were classified as "R" incidents, Bacterial as "B," Virus as "V," and so on. Last year there had been six Unknown Disease cases reported in the United States. They appeared and disappeared without diagnosis, killing a number of people and receding into the environment.

UD#7 was sweeping the country.

"I think we've seen enough of the numbers, Stella." Gordon looked over to the dark-haired microbiologist on his left. The swivel chair creaked under his massive weight. "Bring up the frequency grid."

Dr. Stella Chang's fingers danced on the computer keyboard. The attractive Chinese-American scientist punched up the enlarged screen, revealing a steel-blue map of the United States.

A dot pattern in red appeared in groups across the map, with heavy concentrations in certain areas.

"Look at that," Gordon said. "Spread out like a nuclear strike."

"Over thirty-three thousand cases projected by tomorrow night," Chang said, crossing her legs.

Gordon heard the sound of nylons rubbing as one leg touched the other. "I never anticipated this type of pattern," he said. "We've sent sixteen flash-fire teams, covering as many as fifty different concentrations of this damn thing. It looks like artificial implantation. Senator Kemper may be right. He's convinced it's a conspiracy."

"Why is he involved?"

"He shouldn't be, not as chairman of the Armed Services Committee. But he's motivated by his links with pharmaceutical special-interest groups he gained on the Hill. I can't remember when he hasn't had a bug up his ass about our operation."

"Not this bug."

"No, much to my regret." Gordon sighed. "It might keep him busy enough to leave us alone. But then, Georgia is his state and we're in Georgia. That makes us one of his amusements."

Dr. Chang peered over her pearl-rimmed glasses. "I was curious. No infection outside the country?"

"None yet."

"Several isolated cases in Canada near the border." Chang pointed to the monitor. Red dots reflected in the lenses of her glasses.

"Leakage," Gordon said. "Contamination from travelers. I actually wish there *were* cases elsewhere. Anywhere. Anywhere overseas, so there's evidence of unilateral infection. Otherwise, who knows what the political consequences might be." A red light flashed on the panel over the computer screen. A woman's voice came over the intercom.

"Dr. Gordon. Urgent call from Washington."

"Senator Kemper's office?" Gordon asked.

"No, sir. It's the White House."

"I'll take it in my office, thanks."

"What are you going to say to him?" Chang asked.

Gordon gestured to the computer monitor. "What would you tell him?" A new red dot appeared every few seconds as new cases of UD#7 were reported.

Gordon walked behind Stella Chang's chair and patted her on the shoulder. He lumbered his 270 pounds across the iron grating and climbed the metal stairs. He reached the top of the stairway, took a left, walked along the ramp that ringed the control center. Several personnel sat at monitors, which formed a U shape in the sunken operating platform. The platform was known to staff members as the Flashpoint.

The Crisis Building of the Disease Control Center resembled a military installation. Guards from every service branch protected the facility, which was built to become the command post in a chemical-warfare crisis. Heavily fortified with cement, the structure resembled a bunker. The interior Flashpoint deck was built largely of metal and glass so staff members had visual contact at all times.

Above, executive suites held a dominating view of activities below. Dr. Gordon's office commanded the center of this row.

He nodded to a marine standing guard at the door and entered his office. At his desk, he was about to touch the red button on the phone when John Richards, his assistant, rushed in, carrying printouts and photographs.

"Do you need these?" He handed the materials to Gordon, statistical summaries of the last hour's reported cases, plus glossy eight-by-tens from microscopic negatives.

"Thanks . . . thank you, John."

Richards looked around as if to find a chair. Gordon pointed at the door. "John. I said thank you."

"Oh . . . sorry," Richards said. He had been party to Gordon's conversations with the president before and apparently hadn't expected to be dismissed.

Gordon watched him as he moved awkwardly to the door and down the glass hallway. Richards was the most efficient assistant he had ever had, and he respected his work ethic.

Gordon touched the red button reserved for official calls from the federal government. The president was on the speaker phone.

"Sorry to keep you waiting, Mr. President." Gordon sat down in the large brown leather desk chair.

"Dr. Gordon. I hope you have something useful to tell me," the president said through the speaker. "I don't want to shut the country down. We'll be at a complete standstill. Show me some good reasons *not* to do that."

"I've got thirty-three thousand reasons you *should* do it. That's the case count by tomorrow night. Growing every second."

"Thirty thousand! God, the last I heard it was six or eight."

Gordon referred to the computer stats, making sure of his data. "It's a geometrical progression, sir. Compounding itself by the minute."

"The National Guard is closing airports, harbors. A curfew would stop it, wouldn't it? I mean that's the idea, isn't it?" Gordon heard the strain in the president's voice.

"Too early to tell. We're learning more by the hour."

"What do your research teams report?"

"Identical symptoms in every patient they've seen. The disease is singular in origin, although incidents are spread out across the country in a random fashion. Symptoms are universal. The necrosis is so distinctive—"

"Nec . . . cells dying?"

Gordon didn't expect the president to be fluent in medicalese.

"Yes, sir. Decay of tissue in the victims is unique. It spreads like an infection, yet the disease characteristics indicate unusual toxemia."

"Can you define it?"

Gordon paged through the lab photographs until he came to an extreme close-up.

"One of the victims was close by in Macon. Allowed us to take blood serum. Early analysis indicates it enters the victim through respiratory and digestive tracts. Behaves more like a virus than a bacteria." Gordon looked at the print of Debbie Collins's blood cells in stark black-and-white. "It penetrates membranes easily. Travels through the blood. Attaches itself to hemoglobin. Once it takes a ride, it works into the nervous system. Neurologists at the U.S. Army Research and Development Command have shown that the disease spreads into the nervous system after interior organ damage. Subsequently, it appears in peripheral nerves in the skin . . . external symptoms similar to herpes zoster, commonly known as shingles."

"Shingles? That's a glorified skin rash, isn't it?"

"Yes. Part of the greater herpes family of viruses. But this beauty has a mean streak. Moves incredibly fast and finishes the job with efficiency. Autopsies show the skin and mucous membranes suffer in the process, but the final cause of death arises from a damaged central nervous system, namely the brain, which explains the comatose condition of patients just prior to death."

"Have you checked with USAMRIID?" He referred to the United States Army Medical Research Institute of Infectious Diseases. "Are they missing anything?"

"One of the first things I did."

"Well?"

"I spoke with Blake Pendergast over there. He's the head virologist and a hell of a good man. No biohazard accidents. No contamination. Pendergast looked at tissue samples. He categorizes this as a Level Four hazard . . . the worst. Seeing the reports on victims, he first thought it might be a mutation of Ebola Zaire. We've discussed that one with you."

"I remember it well."

"Symptoms are similar. Yet Ebola mushes up internal organs quite visibly. This baby does irreparable damage, of course, but the deoxygenation creates more of a drying effect, not the jellylike tissue breakdowns of Ebola."

"So you're sure it's not Ebola."

"Pendergast is absolutely sure. Ebola's a filovirus . . . long and ropy, like RNA strands." Gordon put a finger on the photographic print. Off the tip of his fingernail, Debbie Collins's dead cell was filled with oblong football-like compartmentalized objects. "This thing is uniquely smooth and ovular."

"Ovular is unique?"

"Very. Most viruses are globelike and rough-edged. Exceptions are Ebola and Marburg, another ropelike African strain." Gordon's eyes followed the smooth outer edges of the oval structures. "This has a synthetic look to it."

"Synthetic. The joint chiefs are convinced we've been struck by a chemical attack from a foreign power."

"That's impossible. Unless there's something you're not telling me."

"Like?"

"I've heard there were cold-war experiments in our recent history, Mr. President. So secretive, you may not even know about them. There have been rumors of government nanotechnology projects with chemical, or worse . . . genetic weapons."

"As a junior senator in the seventies, Dr. Gordon," the president said, "I was haunted by the dark side of research in this country. It's an unspoken issue. Internal security measures within the government are frighteningly convoluted at times. I fear someone, somewhere, developed something like this on their own, right under our noses, cloaked as a biogenetic project."

"I'm afraid I'm not privileged in those areas, Mr. President."

"Of course. They're classified."

"Classified from whom? Me?" Gordon tossed the photograph on his desk in disgust. "The man who inherits the problem?"

"The military complex in this country controls that sensitive arena. There's a lot of work done in the private sector, as you know."

"No government control over those firms?"

"I wish I could tell you the government is capable of that kind of control," the president said. "Frankly, private nanotechnology research is so specialized that few outsiders can make judgments as to whether it's ethical, moral, or legal, for that matter."

"A frightening idea," Gordon said. "Ironically, that's where we have the greatest hope for cure."

"The private sector?"

"Yes. Pharmaceutical labs. For vaccine. We're making our information available to them."

"I don't care who does it. I'm counting on you to give me an answer soon. You know that. Jonathan Swain, my national security adviser, believes he should come down to help you expedite things. I agree. Gordon, I don't have to tell you the importance of this standstill. If we keep people home and stop international commerce, we'll be on the verge of economic collapse in a matter of days."

THE THIRD DAY
10:24 A.M.
Bellingham, Washington

"It's okay, Officer, I'm with the press." Devin nervously showed his credentials and pushed past the police guard into the foyer of County General Hospital.

For the moment he was exclusively in charge of saving Amy's life. He dealt with the responsibility by remaining mentally one step removed, as if he were watching an imaginary playback of himself on the news. He reasoned if that's what it took to keep from cracking up, he would work with it.

After an anxious wait at the elevator, he decided to take the backstairs. He was in superior shape, but this morning, exercise upset his system. Breathing grew harder with each step; he struggled for lucidity in the face of his hangover.

Befuddled, he had called Freeman back from the hotel, explaining that he was taking Amy to the hospital. On the drive over, he decided to leave her in the rental car in the parking lot, until he felt assured he had reason to bring her in. He felt sure that once inside, she might never leave.

As Devin reached the second-floor landing an orderly passed him on the stairs, looked him over curiously. Devin turned his head as he went by. He was reluctant to be recognized, and panting as he was, he didn't want to breathe on the man . . . just in case.

Although he showed no signs, Devin suspected he might well have the disease himself. If he *was* a carrier, there was nothing he could do, except save Amy and then deal with his own condition.

His ribs ached from exertion. He climbed, rationalizing, imagining the renown he might gain by describing his own symptoms on television. After a full flight of stairs he dismissed the fantasy, realizing it was rummy bravado, an evasion, a mental game to avoid facing fear.

He reached the third floor, passed a service hallway.

A foul organic odor hit him in the face. Silver trays filled with someone's physical remains lay on a cart, covered with a plastic sheet. He grimaced. An attendant had mopped the area with pine-scented ammonia. The combination of the two revolting smells brought a visual to mind, a Christmas tree hung with dead rodents. He regretted his flair for imagery.

Shaken, Devin walked down the hall to the familiar nurses' station, sweating profusely. He showed his press pass and demanded a surgical mask, making an urgent appeal to see Dr. Keefer.

The women treated his request casually. Their white dresses, along with their professional aloofness, disturbed him. He wanted to yell at them, but he chose caution. Two cops at the entrance of the quarantined wing were just out of earshot. Inadvisable to draw their attention. Yet somehow he had to get his way.

He leaned over the nurses'-station counter, spoke quietly yet intensely, perspiring heavily and claiming he had pressing news about the disease. He had to see Keefer.

It worked.

The needle-nosed head nurse, wearing a black leather watchband, handed him an olive-green surgical mask at arm's length, which he strapped on. Then a broad-backed woman in white was assigned to the task of leading him down the hall.

The rotund woman showed him to a creamy-white inner office, some thirty yards from the restricted quarantine space.

Devin took a seat on a wooden chair next to an empty desk, apparently used for patient consultation, judging from its clinical nudity. The only item of color in the room was a magazine in a battered wooden rack on the wall. Devin wondered what patient might consider reading the trade rag. The title: *Anesthesiology Quarterly*.

After several apprehensive minutes Devin gratefully acknowledged Dr. Keefer as he entered, dressed in a tunic, carrying a clipboard. He was still round, balding, and now enraged.

"Why are you so sweaty? And what the hell do you mean barging in like this?" he asked. Devin didn't attempt an answer. Keefer wasn't waiting for replies. He seemed totally exasperated. "There's no need for that mask in this part of the building." As if wearing protection were a personal insult.

Devin wiped his brow. "Let me be the judge of that."

"Mr. Parks, your paranoia is understandable but unnecessary. If you can shed some light on the disease, let's hear it. This better be important."

"I think you'll find it interesting," Devin said, as calmly as he could. "It happens that I've witnessed a patient's infection firsthand."

"What do you mean?" Keefer sounded skeptical.

"I've just come from someone who I believe is infected."

Keefer reared back, slamming the clipboard on the desk. "My God, man, do you realize what you're saying? You may have it, too. Did you have intimate contact with this person?"

He had touched Amy's hand. Carried her to the car. "No." Devin somehow didn't feel guilty lying. He'd have to find a way to set things right.

"Well, who is it? They're a walking time bomb." Keefer's balding head appeared shinier in the fluorescent ceiling light. "They could infect scores of others."

"Well, she won't. She's in a secure location."

"She?" Keefer pursed his lips, making his mustache stand out from his face.

"Yes. Amy Klein, my assistant, whom you met."

"That's impossible. She had no contact with patients here."

"That's right, she didn't."

As if influenced by Devin's perspiration, Keefer became moist around the eyes. "That means another local source. Tell me what's going on."

"I will. If you tell *me* what's going on." Devin felt more in control.

"I don't think you're taking this thing very seriously." Keefer's eyes darted around the room.

Devin noticed him place a finger on the intercom button. "I wouldn't do that. If you don't cooperate, I'll leave her where she is, and she'll infect dozens of people trying to find me."

"Parks, are you blackmailing me? I don't take kindly to intimidation."

"And I don't imagine you'd take kindly to more deaths either. Educate me fast, or you'll endanger your local population."

Keefer stepped back, genuinely surprised, his face as white as his tunic. "What are you demanding?"

"I want into the inner circle. I need to know what's really happening."

"You won't find it pretty," Keefer said.

"I came prepared. Start shocking me."

Perturbed, Keefer fingered the stethoscope that hung around his neck. "God, you're arrogant."

"Like many doctors."

"And disrespectful. Hell, I'll have you arrested." Keefer reached for the intercom button.

"Go ahead. Detain me and the time bomb keeps ticking."

Keefer's mustache twitched. His skin went to a raspberry shade. He walked over to an inner door and opened it.

"All right. Keep the mask on and go in there."

"You first, Doctor. And keep your hands off intercom buttons."

Keefer ushered him through a large conference room that led to another hallway, a route to the quarantine section. As they came to a large window, through the glass, Devin saw several masked nurses in surgical garb attending three unrecognizable patients, each immersed in an ice bath. He noted the see-through arrangement.

"This is a maternity ward," Devin said, awed.

"Used to be. We moved maternity to a new wing a month ago."

Devin pointed. "Is one of them the Skerit boy?"

"No. He died. That's his mother, Ann, and his father, Morton." Devin pointed to the third bath. "Dr. Orteig," Keefer said solemnly.

"Gordi's doctor?" The disease had crossed to the caretakers. "Are they the only ones?"

"The ambulance drivers will soon be beyond help. Three nurses in back have early signs of infection, as does the groundskeeper." A chill rattled up Devin's back.

"Twilly? Is he there?"

"Yes. None of the others are comatose yet, like the Skerits. But Orteig is right behind them on the timetable."

"Timetable?"

"Ann Skerit is nearly gone. She was exposed well over thirty-six hours ago. That's the terminal threshold, according to the stats we're getting from the Disease Control Center. Morton, having more body weight, is deteriorating more slowly. Orteig follows, several hours behind Ann in exposure."

Devin envisioned himself following Twilly. "How do you know all this?"

"We get hourly updates." Keefer reached over to the glass window for an intercom button.

Devin restrained his arm. "Doctor . . ."

Keefer shook him off. "Relax, I'm going to speak with Orteig." He paused, gritting his teeth. "Do you understand what we have here, Parks? A frightening killer. I've never read, never heard of anything like this motherfucker." The expletive surprised Devin, though it was understandable. The crisis had stripped Keefer of his bedside manner. "Now, I'm going to give Orteig an update. I promised. This intercom feeds to the one next to his head. Do you see it?"

Devin noticed the small box with speaker mesh sitting on a stand next to Orteig's bath.

"Whether he's dying or not, he's still a doctor," Keefer said bitterly. "He wanted to hear the lab information. You wanted to learn. Here's your chance."

He angrily pushed Devin aside. "Orteig. Can you hear me?"

The frizzy head in the ice tank moved. From this distance it looked as if it belonged to a trampled doll, thrown disrespectfully into a bin.

Devin heard a voice and looked up. He was listening to Orteig through the large speaker above the window formerly used by maternity-ward parents to hear new babies cry. What an irony for a doctor to be dying in that same room.

"They're working day and night, Orteig," Keefer said over the intercom, trying to sound encouraging. "Early lab results from the Macon autopsy confirm the disease is unclassified. Can you hear me?" he asked. "Orteig, are you awake?"

"Awake," Orteig mumbled. His voice sounded thin, distant, like an old gramophone recording.

Keefer looked at Devin. "He made me promise to explain. I'm going to whether he can hear me or not."

Devin nodded.

"Cellular deterioration occurs following a molecular exchange of oxygen. The oxygen tie means the disease particles are easily airborne. That's why you and your staff were infected. Do you understand?"

"Easily . . . yes," Orteig said. Keefer gave Devin a helpless look.

Devin interrupted. "You mean someone has to breathe infected air to get sick? What about handling objects?"

"We believe the disease is contracted by touch or breathing recently infected air."

"How recent?"

"Probably no longer than a few minutes." Keefer referred to notes in his hand.

Devin wondered about the Skerit farm and Amy. A few minutes. No recently infected air out there.

Keefer pushed the intercom to continue. "The autopsy lab results show the disease uses oxygen as a host vehicle."

"I'm sorry," Devin whispered. Keefer glared at him. "Do you mind if I ask questions?"

Keefer reminded Devin of a pastor interrupted during a funeral eulogy. "What is it?" he asked.

"What about the oxygen?"

"Oxygen easily combines with fluids and other gases. The disease is transmitted outside the body with no problem."

Devin nodded politely.

Keefer turned back toward the delirious Orteig. "The Collins girl had primary inflammation on the extremities. Damage to the mucous membranes in the respiratory system followed, as it did in Gordi Skerit. But secondary victim reports show primary infection in the lungs, like your own, Doctor."

Keefer's explanation to his dying colleague made Devin uncomfortable. It seemed ludicrous . . . a medical ritual, diagnosis to the dying.

Devin glanced over at Orteig, awaiting some kind of affirmation. Orteig remained motionless.

Keefer would not relent. "Body weight determines the rate of infection. Women and children are most susceptible. Atlanta has been able to isolate and identify the disease as a new unknown strain." He stared through the glass. "But they're working on an antidote, Orteig. There's progress. There's always hope."

Devin looked through the glass expectantly. No sound.

The attending nurse took a step toward Orteig, looked over at Keefer, and shook her head. She bent down to the intercom. "He's slipped into a coma, Doctor."

Keefer appeared shell-shocked. He blinked, shook his head and turned to Devin.

"Is that it?" Devin asked.

"Yes." Keefer sighed. "I didn't describe the final stage. The disease is similar to herpes in another respect. It eventually affects the brain, causing the coma Orteig just experienced."

"But you said there was hope."

Keefer's shoulders relaxed. "To be totally honest, Mr. Parks, we haven't found the answer to AIDS after twenty years." His manner became more accommodating. He seemed suddenly to view Devin as a comrade in crisis. "We don't even know what this horror is, yet. How the hell would we cure it? There are thousands of cases by now. With its short incubation period, we can't tell who's sick and who's not until they drop."

Keefer was quite correct. Devin hadn't recognized it in poor Amy. Poor Amy. Out in the car, alone. He would have to surrender her to this place of hopelessness. It was time to tell Keefer.

"Doctor, I suppose I better—"

"Excuse me, gentlemen." A nurse interrupted, entering the hallway.

"A call from a Dr. Hendrix," she said.

Keefer's eyes showed his confusion. "Hendrix? I don't know a Dr. Hendrix."

"The call is for Mr. Parks."

Keefer turned and looked at him suspiciously. "My. You're apparently already in your own inner circle."

The nurse wasn't finished. "And, Doctor, you have a call on line three from the Disease Control Center."

"Fine. Parks, use the phone in the anteroom. When you're done, come to my office. Let's talk."

Devin nodded and followed the nurse into the next room. She gestured to the small black phone on the table.

Devin removed the surgical mask and picked it up. "This is Devin Parks." Someone coughed on the other end of the line. "Hello," Devin said. "Doctor . . . Hendrix, is it? Can I help you?" Silence on the line. "Doctor?" Devin asked, anxious for a reply. "Dr. Hendrix, are you there?"

"I'm here, Mr. Parks."

"What can I do for you?"

"I saw you on television. Your report on the diseased children."

Devin felt mildly flattered. "Yes. How did you find me?"

"I spoke to a Mr. Freeman at your home office in San Francisco. He informed me you might be at the hospital by now."

Devin marveled that Freeman told a stranger. "What else did he tell you?"

"Very little. But I fully understand how disease can make a hospital suddenly important." An inane comment, or was he searching?

"That's fine. Doctor, I have things to do."

"You do indeed. We have things to discuss."

"About what?"

"The disease, Mr. Parks. It appears to be unstoppable."

"That's what I'm afraid of. I've seen it."

"The Skerit child?" Hendrix asked.

"Others as well."

"Yes. I'm not surprised."

Devin disliked his lofty tone. "Doctor, come to the point."

"You're speaking with a man who has a cure."

Shocked, Devin looked around the small room, as if someone might be listening.

Hendrix continued. "My formula can immunize potential victims."

Not wishing to appear naive, Devin used skepticism as a defense. "Are you some sort of publicity hound?"

"Don't underestimate me, please."

"If this isn't a crank call, why don't you give your formula to the health department and get on with the treatment."

"I can't do that," Hendrix said. "I want *you* to do that."

"Me?" Devin felt as if a giant hand had grasped him by the shoulder.

"Yes. I have my reasons."

Devin's voice rose with intensity. "This sounds a little strange, you know what I mean?"

"You probably suspect me to be an eccentric, Mr. Parks. But believe me. I'm deadly earnest. I saw your newscast. I'm fully familiar with the symptoms of the disease and how to cure it."

"How? This thing is brand-new."

A moment of silence on the other end of the line.

"Old diseases are familiar because they've been diagnosed. Like deadly children they were born into the world and named. But others, yet unrecognized, exist among us without our knowledge. Have you read Shakespeare, Mr. Parks?"

"What the hell does Shakespeare have to do with it?"

"*Hamlet.* 'There are more things in heaven and earth than are dreamt of in your philosophy.' When the Creator made the earth he kept a ledger . . . an accounting of all natural things. We meddle with the books, and the numbers may never add up again. I'm guilty of that arrogance. I'm one of the meddling bookkeepers. God help me for my presumption. I researched this disease. Tell me, are you infected, Mr. Parks?"

The question struck Devin in the gut. "I may well be."

"I suspected as much."

The giant hand of destiny gripped more tightly, just as sentiment clamped his gut. "A friend of mine is infected."

"Who? The female associate traveling with you?"

"Yes," Devin said, dumbfounded. "How did you know?"

"Mr. Freeman told me you were taking someone named Amy to the hospital. My memory of the newscast is quite vivid. It's a good guess, since women are more easily infected. Children most of all."

"Lesser body weight. That's what Dr. Keefer said."

"Is this doctor with you now?"

"No. He's in his office. I think he wants to clap me in irons."

"Don't permit that. Your mission is to reach me. Fast action will save thousands of lives."

Devin felt the giant hand lift him to a pinnacle of anticipation. He teetered between reluctance and potential notoriety. "What do you expect me to do?"

"I understand you have a chartered jet. Leave immediately. Don't bring anyone along."

Notoriety aside, he felt the weight of responsibility return. "But Amy, she'll die."

"Ah, of course, yes, bring her."

"Carl Clemmer, our pilot?"

"No others, please. I'll see to it that your other friends become vaccinated soon. After we've successfully made contact."

"Doctor, one question." The view from the pinnacle became expansive; opportunities dotted the landscape. "Why me?"

"I knew you might need my help. And I'll recognize your face. I don't know the faces of many infected television people, but I know yours. Your professional status is valuable to me. You'll soon see. Besides, I have little time to screen applicants." Hendrix spoke calmly. "Now, get your Amy to me immediately. I can vaccinate both of you and save your lives. I'm the only one who can help. If you don't do what I say, death is inevitable."

Devin felt the pinnacle tilt forward. He was strapped in the front seat of life's roller coaster. "All right. Where do you want me to go?"

"Richmond, Virginia. For reasons I am unable to explain now, I won't reveal my exact location. Just go to a private nightclub on State Street in downtown Richmond called the Chorus Line. You and Ms. Klein should meet me there at seven o'clock tonight. Come alone."

Devin put the phone down, strapped the mask on his face, and checked the hallway. Empty. He moved quickly to avoid meeting Keefer. He couldn't afford delays.

"I'm going out to get a camera," he said as he passed the nurses' station.

Once out of sight, he flew down the backstairs.

In the stone lobby, he slowed to a walk.

He approached the front door, removed the mask, and strolled by the cop. Halfway down the walkway, he broke into a run and reached the car.

Amy lay in a fetal position in back, her spotted face covered with perspiration.

He slid into the driver's seat, started the car, and gunned the engine.

"Devin," she said. "What are we going to do?"

"Fly, sweetheart. Fly to make you well."

THE THIRD DAY
9:36 P.M.
Richmond, Virginia

In a drizzle outside a once-popular private club, the Chorus Line, Devin and Amy huddled in the darkness. He held her close, having covered her with a fuzzy blue blanket he had taken from the Learjet. It was tucked under her arms and crumpled up around her head, so her face wasn't visible.

She spoke to him, her voice muffled by the cloth. "Devin."

"Shhh, Amy, save your strength."

"What time is it now?"

Through the mist, a digital clock flashed on a bank facade down the street.

"It's after nine." The adrenaline that fueled him on this adventure had left him some time ago. Enthusiasm for a Hendrix news story had waned. No Hendrix—no story. And without Hendrix, Amy would surely die. Dejected, he shuddered, fighting thoughts that he himself might soon show signs of disease.

"What if he doesn't come, Devin? He should have come by now."

He didn't have an answer.

She coughed. "You're sure there'll be enough vaccine? What about Carl?"

A lump formed in his throat. She was concerned about others despite her own critical condition. "We'll handle it." He swallowed hard, doubting he could handle *any-thing* without further intervention.

He needed help. Help for Amy, for himself, and for Carl Clemmer, the Learjet pilot, waiting at the airport, presumably infected by air he had breathed in the enclosed cabin during the flight from Washington State. Believing Amy had the flu, Clemmer had flown them to Richmond. Hendrix had to keep his word so that later Devin could get to Clemmer with the vaccine.

Devin stared down at the wet pavement. Streetlights reflected on the asphalt, each light a bright starburst on the petroleum blackness.

The street was quiet. Too quiet. Downtown Richmond was empty.

Looking up, Devin saw faces in apartment houses across the street. When he glanced in their direction, they ducked back behind curtains, reclusive cliff dwellers in the canyons of the city. Another face gawked from a second-story window of another dirty brick building. As Devin stared, trying to make out the features, curtains ruffled and the face vanished. He felt awkward, sitting on the step of the nightclub, a vagrant, while viewers peered fearfully at him from behind their drapes.

Had Hendrix been on time, Devin might have addressed these same people on a national broadcast. By now he would have taken possession of the vaccine and turned it over to the scientific community. His report would have been on all networks, not just CNB.

The world would have watched, not just inhabitants of these tenements.

Unlike Devin and Amy, these people observed a national curfew, which the president of the United States had announced in an address only hours before, sharing news that the Disease Control Center projected a signifi-cant number of potential victims in every state.

After listening to that address, Devin spoke with Freeman from the plane, explaining his opportunity for an exclusive. Freeman expressed concern about Amy, but Devin got the feeling his boss wouldn't have known what to do if the Lear had returned to San Francisco with a sick crew. Devin understood and resigned himself to temporary isolation.

For all his misgivings, Freeman vigorously encouraged Devin to meet with the phantom doctor, and pledged the network's support. And why not? CNB might have an exclusive on the most important breaking story in the country. Freeman reminded Devin that his press pass could be used for unlimited travel. Press and the military personnel were free to move despite the disease.

Devin made good use of his ID for a cab ride from the county airport, vowing to get vaccine to the unknowing cab driver who had been exposed as well.

Amy shivered, seemed frail. Was her life dissolving before his eyes? Her future in New York? All of that, his responsibility.

Little to do but keep her talking. Better than just sitting there.

He peeked around the blanket. "Amy. You with me? We have no choice. We have to wait here."

"I understand."

He leaned farther forward to see her. She drooped, tilted her head away. He made out ends of eyelashes, the rest of her damaged face hidden.

It occurred to him that he must speak with her now. The disease had drained her. She might be comatose soon. "I want to ask you something."

"Devin. I feel like I'm falling, and there's nothing below me." She sounded breathless.

Was she aware of the emptiness of death approaching?

He tried not to think about it. "Hold on," he said. "Just a couple of questions about the Skerit farm. All right?"

She nodded and nearly fell forward.

He supported her, felt guilty about disturbing her. "The things you touched in the house . . ." She nodded. "Anything appear contaminated?"

She mumbled something. She had washed her hands.

Her body felt fragile. He found himself clutching her harder to make sure there was still substance underneath the blanket. "You handled quite a few things?"

She shook her head. "No."

"Things that belonged to the boy."

She nodded.

"What were they?"

"Lunch box. Baseball glove."

"Was there food . . . in the lunch box?"

She pouted as she spoke. "A sandwich. Didn't touch it."

"And the mitt?"

"I put it on."

"On your hand? Why, for God's sake?"

"I used to play."

He choked up at the pitiful reply. "Amy." He hugged her. Only a day ago her young face had been radiant. It had glowed.

"What about you, Devin? Do you feel okay?" She sounded terribly weak.

"I'm all right," he lied. He felt strangely off balance. Something had happened in his body.

He was distracted by a rumble. A motorcycle.

A cop had passed the club earlier, apparently not noticing them as they hid in the alcove. Now, with his motorcycle growling, the cop made a second pass down the other side of the street. He seemed to spot them, made a U-turn, swung around, and rode up onto the sidewalk. Leaving the cycle idling, he dismounted and sauntered over. In his gas mask, he looked ominous, like a caricature from a science-fiction film.

He grasped a nightstick in his gloved right hand. "What's the problem here?" the officer asked in a muffled voice.

Devin clutched Amy more tightly. "We're waiting for a friend."

"Haven't you heard? There's a curfew. The epidemic. You should be home." The officer stooped closer, trying to see Amy under the blanket. "What's the matter with her?"

"I know about the curfew, Officer," Devin said. "I'm with the press." He had reached inside his coat to get his card. The officer made a sudden move with the nightstick, punching Devin with the end of it just over the breast pocket, pinning his hand to his chest. "I'm getting my press card," Devin said, startled by the move.

"Keep your hands where I can see them. What's wrong with the woman?" The officer bent over to look at Amy's face.

Devin moved his hand, placed it on the blanket that covered Amy's head.

"Let me see her face," the officer barked. "What have you done to her?"

Devin became aggravated. "Done to her? Nothing."

"Then let me see her." The officer reached out with his other gloved hand.

"Really, Officer, please leave us alone."

"You want me to take you both in?"

"No."

"Why isn't she saying anything? Let me see."

Devin realized he had no option left. "Goddammit," he shouted, pulling the blanket off Amy's head. "Look. She has it!"

The officer recoiled in horror, seeing Amy's face

dotted with open sores. "Holy shit." He nearly fell back over his motorcycle.

"If you don't want it, you better get your ass out of here," Devin said.

The cop appeared convinced. He mounted the bike. "All right," he said. "But I'm calling in. We'll get an aid car out here. Don't move. Wait till they come." He lifted the kickstand, maneuvered the bike back. "Don't move!" He hit the throttle, driving the bike down the sidewalk out of sight.

"Devin," Amy whispered. She sounded awful.

"It's okay, Amy. He's gone."

"I think I'm going to get sick again."

"Here, lean over this way." Devin adjusted himself to support her weight.

She rolled over sideways and vomited on the cement stoop of the club entrance. Yellow bile splattered the pavement. She had thrown up in the head when the Lear-jet refueled in Chicago. It was then he noticed the eruptions had become worse, put the blanket over her so Clemmer wouldn't see. But her deterioration progressed rapidly from a morning fever to a nearly delirious state by afternoon.

Her survival hinged on Hendrix's appearance.

Devin glanced at his watch. It read 9:43. From the darkened alcove, he glanced up at the two-story building across the way. More faces gaped.

Amy leaned heavily on his shoulder and went limp. She had slipped into unconsciousness.

That shook him. He wanted to go somewhere, find someone, do anything. He was about to get up when he heard a noise, a whirring sound up the street.

A gray-and-white Volkswagen van was rolling slowly toward them. Some twenty feet away it stopped.

The woman driver of the van seemed reluctant to approach.

Devin squinted, trying to see her features under the street lamps. The van moved slowly again, up to the curb.

A woman with long blond hair and large dark eyes leaned over and rolled down the passenger window. "Parks?" she yelled.

"Yes, right here." Devin waved.

"Where's my father?" The woman sounded worried.

"Your father? You mean Hendrix?" Devin asked, taken aback.

"Yes. I'm Ginelle Hendrix." She slid across the seat to the window. "Where is he?"

"That's what I'd like to know. He hasn't been here. I'm sorry. Can you help us? She's very bad."

Devin lifted the blanket so Amy's face was visible.

"Oh my God!" Ginelle jumped out of the van. She wore a denim skirt and a peach-colored blouse. Her gait resembled that of a dancer as she ran across the sidewalk and knelt next to Amy. She immediately pulled the blanket back farther, examining her. "She's in an advanced stage."

"I know." Devin wondered why Ginelle wasn't frightened.

"No sign of my dad? You're sure?"

"Sorry, no."

Ginelle looked up and down the street nervously. "Anyone else?" she asked, putting an arm around Amy.

"Just a motorcycle cop, a few minutes ago."

"We've got to get her out of here." She began to gather the blanket in order to lift Amy. "Help me."

Devin rose and lifted Amy's torso as Ginelle grabbed her feet. They made their way to the back of the van. Devin held Amy as Ginelle opened the door. She climbed in to help lift Amy's bulk into the cargo area.

She waved him on. "Get in. Make sure she's comfortable."

Ginelle moved to the driver's seat. No other seats in the van, so Devin squatted on the white enameled steel floor next to Amy's prone body, holding her head.

As Ginelle put the VW into gear she looked back at Devin. "Not even a message from Dad?"

"Nothing since we arrived."

She swung around from the steering wheel, tears in her eyes. "I don't know what to think."

"What is it?" Devin asked softly.

"He was to call me the minute he made contact with you. I left him working at the lab. We were exhausted. He told me to go home and get some sleep. When he didn't call, I waited until I couldn't stand it anymore." Devin watched her face in the rearview mirror as Ginelle guided the van down a back street. Her eyes showed her confusion as a tear rolled down her cheek. "He told me this could happen. My father went up against an incredible power to save everyone. Including you. He knew it was dangerous. It could be the end for him."

"What power? What do you mean?"

"Can't you imagine the organized effort it takes to successfully pull off an attack like this?"

"The disease. It's no accident?" Devin asked.

"No. On the contrary. It's a vicious strategy."

Amy moaned. Devin looked down. A string of saliva trickled out the corner of her mouth. He cradled her head in both hands.

"Since you apparently know what Amy has, you must realize that *I* have it, and that *you'll* have it, too," Devin said.

"What's your first name?"

"It's Devin. Did you hear what I said? We've both got

it. I already feel it inside of me." He was suddenly aware of the fear in his voice.

"When I get to my home, Devin, I can give you an injection. My father had the vaccine with him. But he gave me a single extra vial to keep, as a backup."

"What do you mean, one vial?"

"One dose. A single treatment. I've had mine. There's not enough left for two."

Devin's body shook with revulsion. Had the disease taken hold of him? He hadn't had a reaction like that since he'd been on an Iraqi battlefield. A corporal to whom he'd been talking shot a thirteen-year-old boy running at them with a hand grenade. The obscenity of the boy's death had overwhelmed him.

"But what about Amy?"

"From what I can see, she's too far gone."

"Are you sure?" Devin asked desperately. "Can't we try something else?"

"It's my father's formula, not mine." She shifted the VW, grating the gears. "I'm afraid to return to the lab. Besides, even if we could figure out what to do, it would take too much time. I'm terribly sorry."

"A hospital then, anything," Devin shouted.

"Devin, I'm giving you the facts. There is no other cure. Amy's beyond help, but we can save you with the one dose."

"What about the others? Our pilot. The people in Bellingham. They may all die." Devin felt moisture form in his eyes as he confronted Amy's fate. He felt trapped. "We flew all the way out here. God. We don't even know if it works," he said petulantly.

An icy silence followed. They moved past a statue of General Lee in the center of a downtown Richmond intersection.

"I may not approve of what my father did professionally, Mr. Parks," she said slowly, without turning around, "but his success with this vaccine is unquestionable."

"Approve of him?" As he himself began to feel delirious Devin's frustration turned to anger. "How could you approve of a man who says he invented this god-damn obscenity?"

Ginelle whirled in the driver's seat, eyes flaring. Then, struggling to calm down, she turned back to the steering wheel and spoke carefully. "This atrocity wasn't my father's doing. He shunned it, and our government. Don't question my father's intentions. He's already heard it all from me. But don't judge him before you know all the facts." She shifted gears, again looking back at Devin. "Dad put himself in danger for you. He was determined to give you the vaccine. If nothing else, I'll accomplish that."

She picked up speed on a wide street.

In silence, Devin held Amy. He pushed the blanket aside, uncovered her head. They passed under street-lights, and intermittent flashes of brightness crossed her ravaged face. The skin had separated around the cheek-bones. Small red gashes formed around the mouth.

Devin couldn't bear it anymore. Feeling sick, he looked toward the windshield.

His eyes rose to meet Ginelle's in the rearview mirror. For the first time he noticed how dark they were.

He wondered how dark his life was about to become.

THE THIRD DAY
Somewhere on the Road
10:15 P.M.

As Dr. Thomas Hendrix regained consciousness and opened his eyes, he saw nothing.

Am I blind? he thought, sitting up. "Is anyone there?" His words rang emptily in the darkness, and as they faded away he heard the pounding of his own heart and some kind of steady drone that hung in the air.

He rubbed his forehead and winced. There was swelling over his left eye. The pain made him nauseous, weak.

Someone had clubbed him outside the lab; he had put the car key into the door of his Mercedes, heard a rustling in the bushes behind him, turned, and blacked out.

He clutched the sides of his jacket. My God, the vials, he thought. Where are the vials?

Running a hand over his coat and down his pants, he found nothing. No wallet. No pocket change. The insulated satchel, the hypodermic needles, and the vaccine vials for the reporter . . . gone.

"What have you done with it?" Words drew no response. "Show yourselves."

His captors had apparently left him alone.

Since they chose not to answer questions, he decided to explore his surroundings.

In the darkness, he sat up and felt the underside of his seat. Rough cloth. Wooden legs. Canvas covering. A cot. Gaining confidence, he rolled onto his knees, worked his hands along the framework. Leather belts and buckles hung under the head of the bed. Scooting down to the foot of the cot, he reached down and found similar straps underneath.

What kind of a bed was this? Slender legs attached to grated metal, set into steel sockets, bolted to the floor.

His eyes began to adjust to the gloom. A sliver of light emanated from ten feet over his head, possibly shining through a small vent.

Leaning on the cot, now aware of a high-pitched whine all around him, he made out a huge shape that loomed at the other end of the room.

"God, it's my car," he said, rising to his feet, trying to fathom it. Suddenly dizzy, he lost his balance and stumbled, put one hand down onto the cot to steady himself.

He fought to stand upright, yet wobbled back and forth. The floor moved. That high-pitched whine. The whine, that drone, was the sound of truck tires beneath him on pavement.

I'm inside a large vehicle on a highway, he thought.

He took a step in the darkness, another, slowly making his way. His outstretched hands touched something hard. Cold. Metal. Smooth and solid. A wall.

Rocking with the movement of the vehicle, Hendrix searched the confines of his moving prison and found a corner. The rear of the truck, he thought. No. The front. Difficult to tell which direction the truck was going.

Reversing his direction, he found another corner near the Mercedes. Hendrix reached out, felt the door handle and the sideview mirror of the car. The vehicle felt comfortably familiar. They were captives together.

Leaving his old friend, he moved farther along the expanse of the wall, found a third corner. Then, working his hands along the steel wall at that end, he felt a groove in the surface, approximately an inch wide. He bent down. It ran to the floor. He squatted, tracing its course, fingers working down to a mesh grating, on which he stood. Rising again, his hand followed the groove to its upper limit, roughly a foot and a half over his head. There, it took a sharp right turn. He felt along for about three feet, found another sharp right angle as the groove headed back toward the floor.

A way out, Hendrix thought, gauging the perimeter of the door. No handles or hinges at the opening, only a small panel with buttons.

Must be hydraulic.

In the murky light, he worked back toward the opposite end of the chamber, toward the Mercedes. A few more steps and he had passed the cot and was next to the car. Suddenly he felt an uncomfortable shift of weight that lifted him off his feet.

His body slammed into the front wall. The world exploded, as his nose smashed into smooth, cold steel. He fell backward like a rag doll onto the grated floor. Dots of light filled his vision, flickering brightly in the darkness.

He moaned, felt wetness on his mouth. Saltiness on his tongue. Blood ran down over his lip. He used the sleeve of his tweed blazer to wipe it away.

Touching the bridge of his nose, he winced. The tips of his fingers encountered a ragged edge of skin.

His glasses. Had they cut him? No. They were missing. He would have felt them against his face.

With head pounding, he crawled back to the cot and painfully hoisted himself onto the edge.

Moments passed as he sat with his head in his hands, at a loss what to do, weary, disoriented. Finally, the pain in his face subsided.

He was about to get to his feet again when a hydraulic hiss at the end of the chamber startled him.

Red light formed along the grooves of the door near the Mercedes. A sliding panel opened, revealing the dark silhouette of a muscular man who was walking slowly toward him. Blond hair stood out on top of this phantom's head, backlit by the red glow. The stranger's features were indistinguishable. He stopped a few feet away.

Hendrix rose slowly.

"You *are* awake," the man said, speaking in a thick accent. Difficult to judge his age.

"Where am I?" Hendrix asked.

The man didn't answer. Instead, he turned his head to the door and yelled, "He's awake!"

Two sinewy Asian men in black tunics entered. Hendrix thought they resembled the men who had tried to abduct him at his apartment.

"I asked you where I am."

The tall man pointed. "Lie down on the cot, Doctor."

"And I demand to know who you are, and where you're taking me." Genuinely frightened, Hendrix attempted to convey authority.

The large blond man stepped forward. "We follow orders. Lie down."

One of the smaller men moved to the head of the cot, the other to the opposite end.

Hendrix attempted to step away, but the tall blond man grabbed him by the right elbow. With a viselike grip, his fingers dug deep into the soft frontal part of the joint, making Hendrix cry out, while the man's other hand clamped Hendrix's wrist. A twisting motion flipped Hendrix back onto the cot.

"If you had not been so important to the organization, you would be dead," the tall man said.

Hendrix groaned. "What organization?"

The man ignored the question, nodded to one of the other men, who took a long hypodermic needle from his tunic pocket.

"What are you doing?" Hendrix asked. "Who are you?"

"The name is Jaktar, Dr. Hendrix." He pulled one of the leather straps across Hendrix's chest, leaned down, and buckled it. "I should kill you . . . but they won't let me—yet."

At this range, Hendrix saw him more clearly. Jaktar was oddly handsome, with sharp and angular features. Dark skin contrasted with white-blond hair. The combination was strange, almost inhuman.

"Do you realize what you've done?" Hendrix asked, looking from Jaktar to the others. "You know what's in my satchel?"

"What do you take us for . . . fools, Doctor? You are not here by accident. It's destiny." The man spoke abruptly; the accent was difficult to place.

"Destiny? Did you cause the disease?"

As Jaktar smiled Hendrix was awed at the width of his mouth. It was as if someone had slashed it out of his face. "A naive question from the man who invented it."

"What are you talking about? Are Metzger and Glant involved?" Hendrix asked. "What about Kahvahl?"

The reflected red glow of the doorway flickered in Jaktar's black pupils. They were large, like a cat's. "Glant and Metzger are no longer involved, Dr. Hendrix. Kahvahl's greed condemned him. He no longer fascinates us. You, on the other hand . . ."

"What about me?"

"If you were not useful, you'd be dead."

"Mr. Jaktar. Is that your name? The vaccine in my satchel can save thousands of people. I can make it work. Let me explain."

The three men leaned over him. Jaktar spoke in a foreign tongue to the man at the head of the bed, who dangled a needle in plain sight.

"Very well, Doctor. Time for explanation has arrived. A shot of scopolamine will loosen your tongue, and then you will give us the information we want. Do you understand?"

"No. No drugs." Hendrix struggled. "I have so many questions." His mind filled with things he desperately needed to know. "My daughter. You haven't harmed her, have you?"

"Your daughter. Exactly," Jaktar said. "You are about to tell us where she is."

The man at the head of the bed leaned down, placed the tip of the syringe at the left side of Hendrix's neck a few inches above his clavicle. As he felt the sting Hendrix saw white, heard an ethereal whirring of jet engines. "Ginelle," he said softly.

In a fog, he heard Jaktar speak to him, whispering in his ear. "We couldn't find her, Doctor. Not in the Richmond phone directory. Unlisted. Commonwealth University registries show no address. But you can tell us where she lives."

Hendrix felt as if he were in a dentist's office with a rubber dam in his mouth, lips flapping limply, while Jaktar, the oral surgeon, pulled words out of his throat. Without wanting to, he spoke, forgot why he shouldn't, and lapsed in absurdity.

At ease and no longer worried, Hendrix swelled with a childlike euphoria. Now language flowed from him like a stream of water into the room.

He lost the sense of having a body. His head had separated from his chest at the neck. His abdomen, floating several feet below, relaxed as his stomach muscles went soft.

He suddenly wondered if he were urinating. Filled with a warm, pleasant sensation of being held on a tether, he hung somewhere off the edge of reality.

THE FOURTH DAY
1:35 A.M.
The Kingsgate Apartments
Richmond, Virginia

Beautifully detailed tapestries hung on the living-room walls of Ginelle's large apartment, surrounding Devin with picturesque pastoral scenes. One, woven in pastel green, showed an old manor house in a lush countryside, a reminder that order might prevail somewhere in the world.

The thought occurred that they were somewhat old-fashioned for a woman who looked like Ginelle. Yet their age comforted him. He desperately needed structure.

This disease scenario in which he played a role had been written by some maniac, and Devin was left in it, searching for his cues. Devin knew he had a part to play, but he was damned if he knew what it was.

He felt ridiculous lying on this leather couch with the thermometer in his mouth. Yet, he hummed a delirious tune, studying the various sculptures in the room, attempting to interpret them. These lovely old pieces, fashioned in a time of hope. What would the sculptor hew in this time of madness?

Odd how his mind flitted about, dwelling on art.

Was he trying to avoid thoughts of the inevitable?

A sound behind him. He rolled over, stared back at the refrigerator light shining on the kitchen floor.

Ginelle's moving shadow, the clicking of her leather slippers on the hardwood.

She walked into the hallway and rummaged in the storage area. He remembered some comment about storing lab materials under the stairs. That made some sense of the clinking glass tubes.

The sound wavered and he lost it. Sequential time disintegrated. No difference between recent impressions and memories of a distant past. Freeman. Dan Canon. Dr. Keefer.

He felt weaker. Emptiness crept into his chest. Suddenly a wave of depression, images of his own potential death. He was able to get a handle on their origin; destructive thoughts brought on by fever.

The bedroom door was ajar. He strained to see the nearly naked body in the master bedroom. The shape of her legs. Amy. Her boots sat at the foot of the bed. He remembered. Ginelle had removed all of Amy's clothing except her bra and panties. Skin eruptions made the garments a mess. Her tight pants were entirely impractical. Ginelle said the bloody sores stuck to her sweater.

Devin found his hallucinations filled with abrupt shifts. He could be immersed inside his mind, then suddenly across the room critically appraising his own condition.

Seemingly from nowhere, Ginelle appeared, moving slowly across the floor. She leaned over and took the thermometer out of his mouth. Long blond hair touched his face. It smelled clean and sweet, redolent of gardenias.

She sat on the edge of the sofa sternly looking at the thermometer, then put it back in his mouth. "Keep your mouth closed."

His mouth felt like mush. The thermometer, like a cigarette, hung on his lip. He reached up and grabbed it, poked it back in. For the first time he saw the pale orange liquid through the syringe in Ginelle's other hand.

He spoke with the glass tube clenched in his mouth. "Are you giving that to me?" He fought the urge to take the last available dose.

"With your consent." She had moved down to his knees, far away, just out of his reach.

"Consent?" He felt ashamed that a part of him yearned for life, yet with remorse. "I want you to give it to Amy," he said angrily.

"We apparently need to talk this through one last time." Moments passed as he studied her. Her eyes dark and cool. A deep green. She pulled the thermometer out once more and held it up to the brightness of the brass floor lamp. Translucent emerald flashes showed in her eyes just before she squinted. She twirled the thermometer with her slim manicured hands. "You have 103.8."

"What does Amy have?"

"Last time I checked, over a hundred and five. It's difficult to take her readings because she's unconscious. Her true temperature is academic."

"Academic?" Amy's well-being, as large as his own life.

"Yes." She hesitated. "It's important you understand. Amy is beyond help." She said it deliberately. "I'm doing what I can for you. But taking the shot is a life-and-death decision with an untried cure. I feel uncomfortable giving you the serum without your complete consent."

"You sound like a doc."

"I'm a Ph.D not an MD." She set the thermometer on the stone coffee table.

"Then how can you be sure about Amy?" he asked.

"I am," she said.

He struggled to focus, pushing the delirium back into his consciousness. His throat ached. Swollen tonsils. He reached up and tried to unbutton the collar of his shirt.

"You need my help?" she asked.

"Yes, goddammit."

"I mean the shirt." She scooted up near his waist, reached out to loosen the button.

"You know what I mean." He pushed her hand away. "I have to be sure she's gone before I—"

"You're angry. I understand that. But angry or not, you *must* consent."

Nowhere to run. Time to confront her death? Amy's future. The job in New York. If only he could save Amy by sacrificing himself. He mulled the words over. . . . "A greater gift hath no man than to lay down his life for his friend." Inscribed on his gravestone. He lingered with that fantasy momentarily and then caught himself, realizing his thoughts were flying out of control. He felt ridiculous.

Ginelle interrupted his meandering. She scooted up higher toward his chest, holding the needle in front of his face.

"What?" he asked. She hadn't spoken.

The room began to undulate, shifted like a TV screen with a faulty horizontal hold. So this was it . . . the end of the broadcast.

"Devin," she said, "I'm losing you."

What the hell did she mean?

"Devin!" She sounded frantic. "Tell me it's okay."

The shade of his eyelashes fell over his vision, obscuring her panicked face. He saw small veins in the thin skin of his lids, spread out against a deep purple infinity. But he grabbed for the last shred of sanity.

"Yes," he said. It was all he could manage to utter.

Someone held his left arm, pushing his shirt higher over the elbow.

He strained to look down.

"Make a fist," she said from the next room. No. She

was right there, tightening a rubber strap around his biceps.

The needle. Into his flesh. He saw the small rubber stopper inside the top of the tube begin to descend and then stop. A bit of his own blood entered the syringe and then exited back into his body with the rest of the vaccine. She pushed the plunger all the way. The world turned slate gray with streaks of black swirling against a shimmering sky.

He was high in the air, clinging to the top of that same spire, looking back over his shoulder. He recognized faces in the crowd. One, his dead mother. She carried a campaign poster in her right hand. On her lapel, she wore a pin emblazoned with the gubernatorial seal of the state of Iowa. Her breasts. One had partially fallen out of her gray tweed suit. The nipple was swollen.

Other faces in the crowd. His father stood in the back, dressed in dirty overalls, the smell of compost around him. Amy. Her face fresh and unblemished. She bounced next to Devin's father, tugging his sleeve violently. She yelled, "Wake up! Wake up!" in his dad's ear, over and over.

Suddenly the townspeople were far below. Strangers threw rocks up at him. The missiles whizzed past his head. His grasp on the church tower weakened. The crimson sun rose on a black-and-white horizon off to his left. A rock struck him in the ear. He was about to fall.

She touched his forehead.

"Amy?" he said.

"No, Devin. It's me. How do you feel?"

He flew out of a wind tunnel. His feet were about to touch down. "Where's Amy?"

Ginelle's face. She pointed to the other room. "Where we left her . . . in there." The door was closed.

"Oh God. How long was I out?"

The room was filled with daylight. The peach blouse was gone. She had dressed in a dark blue cotton T-shirt with a denim skirt. Her arms were toned and shapely. Spotless.

"I let you sleep. It's been about five hours," she said.

"You gave me the injection, didn't you?"

She nodded.

"Amy?" he asked, craning his neck.

She shook her head. "She's barely with us."

Tears wet his cheeks. His hair was drenched. Wading out of pity, he refocused on her eyes. She looked so concerned, like someone watching an animal suffer. God, he must look pathetic!

She responded to his misery. "You need to rest," she said.

Time to suck up his guts.

"What about you?" He recovered a remnant of dignity. "Don't *you* need some sleep?"

"No. I felt I should look after both of you. It appears you've improved. Do you feel the vaccine?"

Devin nodded. Strangeness oozed through his mouth. He smacked his lips. An odd flavor, mixed with saltiness of his tears.

She watched as he ran his tongue over his teeth. "You taste it, don't you?"

"Vinegar," he said. "It tastes like vinegar."

"It isn't, of course. But that's correct. I experienced the taste after I had my shot." She spoke softly, steadily.

"This whole thing is crazy." He felt impotent. A strong need for self-expression. Time to be more than a victim. He tried to get up. She put a hand on his chest.

"Give it a bit more time. Your body's been through a great deal."

Folding his hands across his chest, he stretched his

back. Every muscle ached. He felt bruised, as if he'd played several football games in one day. At last, his thoughts cleared. Lucidity had its liabilities. Once again, he confronted the dreaded realization.

"What's with Amy?"

"Her pulse was down to twenty-four beats a few minutes ago. It's almost over." Ginelle. Calm and sympathetic. Sudden softness in her eyes pushed him to despair.

"Oh, Jesus," he said. He wasn't cursing, rather addressing the God to whom he hadn't prayed since he was a child. He raised his left forearm over his face. Silent sobs shook his chest. He felt her grab his wrist, squeezing firmly. She didn't speak, letting him release his grief.

He took the opportunity and wept, visualizing his dinner with Amy in Bellingham. Youthful hope, her innocence.

Steeped in anguish, he became awkwardly aware of how he must appear to the woman with him. He struggled to regain his composure.

Somehow, she sensed his embarrassment and removed her hand.

He looked up, wiping his eyes.

The change in Ginelle's face. The worried daughter had become a caring healer. "Amy's feeling no pain. It will end without trauma."

"Are you certain? Her suffering. I can't stand the idea."

She sighed. "Imagine what it's like out there."

He visualized the chaos. "What have you heard?"

"Emergency news broadcasts. On the radio while I was changing." She sat up. "The president has called out the troops in response to the unrest."

"It was quiet downtown."

"That was last night. Today they're in the streets. The

government estimates there are over thirty thousand con-firmed cases nationwide. Certain segments of the popula-tion panicked. Especially right-wing groups who think we're being attacked by our own government. Vigilante groups are rioting. I heard about demonstrations outside hospitals. Some shootings. Gang marches in Detroit, Watts is aflame in L.A., and National Guard troops are guarding Washington, D.C. The president deployed them to try and maintain order."

He nodded, picturing crowd scenes, breaking glass, and burning buildings.

"Any news about your father?" he asked cautiously.

"No." She got to her feet, walked over to the window.

He watched her carefully, impressed with her grace, regretting the question.

"He's all that I have left," she said, taking the white fringe of the curtain, kneading it with both hands. "My mother and sister are gone." She froze, obviously lost in memories, staring through the drapes. Soft sunlight spotted her brow. Golden highlights danced in her hair. She pulled a handkerchief from her hip pocket and wiped her eyes.

"I'm sorry." He spoke softly. "When did you lose them?"

"It's been a while. Mother went four years ago. Cancer." She gestured around the room. "These tapes-tries and statuettes are all I have left of her. She came from Romania."

Now the strange decor made sense to Devin.

"And my older sister, Lisa, died in a climbing acci-dent." Long sigh. "She fell into a glacier in Switzerland. A search was useless."

He had no reply. Trying to fathom her feelings, he compared them with his own. To him, family was a farce. He recalled the degeneration of his relationship with his mother due to her political career. And his father? A living question mark. How could you lose someone you never found? Fatherhood. A joke. Never really there. Now completely gone. Myths. Just poetic tributes on a cold tombstone.

"You'll find your dad." He realized the comment sounded inane. But he meant it. She loved her father. Ironic. Having this conversation with Amy lying in the next room. Ginelle seemed distracted, glancing out the window.

"I was just thinking," he said, "about my family."

"Could I request . . . none of *your* personal history, if you don't mind." She turned, penetrating him with a look. "You and I are alive. That's all that's important. We're living examples of my father's cure."

"In the van you said . . . you had criticized him."

"He and I were estranged for several years."

"Why?"

"I think that's enough of *my* personal history."

"I disagree. It may have profound consequences . . . medically speaking. You know what I mean?"

"All right. In a professional context."

"I don't even *know* your profession. What do you do, anyway?"

"I'm an independent researcher, supported by grants. DNA and RNA work for the National Institute of Health. Most of my work is done at Commonwealth University."

"Viruses?"

"As they relate to cancer, yes."

"So you work on viruses. Your father did. So why the estrangement?"

"Viruses. Not man-made microbes. There's a distinction," she said angrily. "First of all, my work doesn't destroy. Our split was my choice. I was critical of Dad's chemical-warfare research." The tone softened. "But when I saw him again and worked with him at the lab two days ago, I understood his reasons, I forgave him. Now he's gone." Her attempt to keep her voice from shaking failed. "Look, I don't mean to cut you short. But I don't have time to get to know you. I'm focused on one thing, finding my father." She took a step forward. "I suppose that means discovering the origin of this epidemic."

"The two may be the same thing," Devin added.

"Yes. That's why knowing as much as possible about Amy's experience may become meaningful for lots of reasons. Tell me, when was Amy exposed?"

"Late, the day before yesterday."

"How did it happen, do you think?"

"At the Skerit farm."

"Are you sure?"

"It could have happened at the hospital. But I don't think so."

"Then she had direct contact."

"Yes, apparently." He tried to remember Amy's comments. "She . . . touched some of the boy's things."

Ginelle softened. "How unfortunate. Anything in particular?"

"A baseball glove."

"Anything else?"

"Nothing specific . . . a lunch box."

"Ah! She touched that?"

"No. Just the mitt. I can't be sure." He'd been drunk on champagne the first time, and somewhat delirious the second time Amy had told him.

"What about you? When were you infected?"

"Infected?" Somehow the word shocked him. "When I saw her four hours later, I guess," Devin said. "Assuming Amy was already contagious."

"You said you had drinks and dinner. Did you get any closer than that?"

"What are you asking?"

She rephrased her question. "The drinks. How much did you have?"

"A couple, I guess . . . I don't quite remember."

"Two?"

Was she judging him? "Yes and some champagne; quite a bit."

Ginelle seemed fascinated. "Do you normally drink that much?"

"What is this? AA?"

"Tell me."

"No. I hardly ever drink. But Amy was celebrating a new job. Why?" His voice had become edgy. He told himself to ease off.

"And Amy . . . any alcohol that evening?"

"Just one glass of champagne." Devin's mind flashed to the waiter's cold look. Amy's attempts at conversation. His spinning bed.

Ginelle looked at the closed door of the adjacent room, where Amy lay. "She lost her battle with the microbe more quickly because of her lighter body weight. And her small alcohol consumption." She stepped closer to him. His eyes were even with her knees. "The disease is slowed in victims who have elevated blood alcohol levels. Extends the incubation period."

"I had more time?"

"Several hours, it seems. Alcohol restricts oxygenation and the microorganism rides red blood cells when the RBCs are oxygenated, traveling through the bloodstream. By now your bloodstream should be clearing up." She sat down on the couch and reached for his face. He flinched. "Easy! Let me look." She raised one of his eyelids, looked into one eye, then the other. "The whites are still slightly discolored," she said. "That's one of the symptoms. The eyeball shows the effect faster than the skin. If you'd been aware, you would've noticed Amy's eyes turning blue prior to skin eruptions."

If he had been aware? "Her eyes were closed most of the time," he responded.

"I see." Ginelle studied his face. "Is she your lover?"

"God. What a question."

"Well, is she?"

"She's . . . no. An associate. A friend."

He caught the glimmer of a smile. She had one-upped him, even in this gloomy moment. He noted her high cheekbones, the straight, elegant nose.

He felt the need to change the subject. "How did your father concoct a vaccine so fast after he'd been away from it so many years?" he asked.

Sadness returned to her face. "In his words, deadly formulas are difficult to forget."

"Well, in any case, I'm grateful to him." Even though he sensed she was hiding something, he felt a tug, the need to help her. "You're very worried, aren't you?"

"Yes. I feel that he's still alive, but the people responsible are holding him for some dreadful reason."

"But who were they?" He stirred, trying to roll over.

"Lie still. Let the vaccine do its work."

"Any idea who it could be?" he repeated.

"I don't know. Dad's not sure. Only a few people shared his knowledge of the replicator. That's what Dad calls it . . . a replicator."

"Something that duplicates itself?"

"Yes." She stared, searching his eyes. "It enters cells, kills them, duplicates, and moves on." Ginelle's eyes seemed to change shades with her moods. They were changing now. She had become much more pensive.

"Can I trust you?" she asked softly. "I'm not sure I have anyone else I can talk to." For the first time she was allowing herself to show vulnerability.

"Of course you can." He reached out. Took her hand. The green eyes moistened. Her fingers felt warm in his. He smiled. Then she slowly dragged her hand away, placing it in her own lap. She sat on the edge of the couch with her knees together. Her long blond hair draped off one shoulder.

"Dad worked on a project called Black Diamond," she said. "A private research project under a government grant." She pointed to the crook of his arm. "Your blood contains Black Diamond research; one of several biochemical-warfare experiments conducted at the time. Dad left the project after one year."

"So you think the men who made the 'replicator' subsequently released it?"

"Dad thinks so, yes," Ginelle said.

"For what possible purpose?"

"Who knows?"

"Why destroy hordes of people? An accident?"

"Not the way it happened. Accidents don't happen in multiple locations. News reports say the outbreak occurred simultaneously in any number of states. You're a reporter. Does that sound reasonable to you? Something else. The replicator was highly virulent. Formulated in two parts, precisely so accidents would *not* happen."

"Replay that for me."

"Dad says they stored the disease in an unmixed state. The alpha portion of the formula consists of a toxic chemical base. The beta portion is a computer-generated mechanism; the replicator. A replicator commands reproduction and cell penetration." She spoke with her hands, showing the two parts in the air. "Alpha and beta are individually dormant. Mixed together they become lethal. It simply couldn't have been an accident."

"All right." He rolled over to face her. "Assume it was a willful act. A group of researchers flew around assembling formulas just in time to infect hundreds of people. Terribly cumbersome. Makes no sense either. These men your dad worked with, were they about your father's age?"

"Approximately."

"Tell me about these guys."

"Dr. Glant, Dr. Metzger, and Dr. Kahvahl. Dr. Kahvahl had the biobasis for a simulated virus. Glant and Metzger contributed to the component structure. My father brought his expertise in molecular fragmentation."

"You know the ingredients?"

"Just sketchy details of RNA coding grids. I have no knowledge of the replicator's triggering mechanism. I simply assisted Dad. The exact molecular fraxinations are beyond my understanding. I don't believe he wanted me to know."

"Why?"

"To protect me."

She looked sad again, but he had succeeded in engaging her in conversation. "I'm having trouble visualizing a molecular machine."

"Imagine a mini–tissue simulator smaller than a molecule, containing tiny operative mechanisms. These mechanisms have cloning keys, allowing the machine to replicate itself within a precisely balanced environment: human hosts. Although animals were used in prior experiments, *this* version of the microbe is specific to the human system." She sculpted the air with her slender hands as she spoke. "Unhampered, the replicator guides an infectious run within the body . . . a wildfire that consumes everything in its path. This 'run,' as Dad calls it, occurs on a larger scale within the population, a death sweep."

"Okay. So, your father's phone call?" He lifted a hip, adjusting his weight on the couch.

"Dad hoped you and the media would help. He wanted to heal Amy and have you present her as proof of the cure to the Disease Control Center. Convinced, the government would distribute his vaccine."

"I thought your father distrusted the government."

"Yes. But he felt fairly confident about the Disease Control Center. They seemed separate from the intelligence community. Dad intended to remain safely in the background while you and Amy flew to Atlanta." She sighed and stretched. "That's the essence of the story. You were lucky he gave me an extra dose. But . . ." Her green eyes changed shades, again, turning bluish. "Poor Amy." She rose and walked to the door of the master bedroom. She hesitated, looked back at him once more, then as if resigned to the unpleasantness, she entered.

Through the open door, he saw Ginelle lean over Amy's still form in the shadows of the other room. God, he thought, is this it? Ginelle placed a hand on Amy's neck. Dread wrenched his gut. What was taking so long? He closed his eyes and wished he could pass out again.

The delay became a rare torture.

He heard the door creak and opened his eyes to see Ginelle return, walking back slowly on tiptoes. She had a solemn look on her face.

"I'm sorry, Devin. She's gone."

Devin flashed on Amy's father, the excited phone call about the job at ABC. He felt emptiness suck down through his body, leaving him with nothing inside. He wanted to get away. From this place. From Amy. From himself. From everything. He shielded his eyes with his forearm, breathing hard.

"Devin, I'm going back to check the Internet for any breaking reports and then lie down for a while." Ginelle sounded very tired, unwilling to share her feelings further.

Amy had shared hers.

The world had turned a bit colder.

Ginelle's smooth voice had grown hollow. "When I wake up, I've got to get on with it," she said. She came closer and bent down. "Amy can't be the medical example my father intended. But you can. You're evidence of a successful recovery."

He felt dehumanized, refused to make eye contact.

"I want you to consider what that means," she continued as she walked toward the den. "Please think about it."

He dropped his arm, venturing a glance. "Think about what?"

"Help me complete my father's mission." She turned and disappeared down the hall before he could answer.

THE FOURTH DAY
4:44 P.M.
Baghigra, the Sudan

William Galbreath, an official in the British Foreign Office, sat under the whirling fan in his small office. He had insisted that the entire room be decorated in white. White reminded him of cleanliness and coolness, soothing him in the brutal climate of this country.

Galbreath's desk was neatly appointed with a beautifully embroidered leather pad, a golden clock with the face of a lion on either side, and a pearl-inlaid letter opener. The handle of his ivory cane, which rested against the corner, was shaped in the likeness of the same lion. It showed his respect for England, and the former empire of which it was the symbol, although he believed fiercely in modern postcolonial ideology. In his mind, he served England best by showing the rest of the world his country embraced rights of the people it once colonized, embraced those people as partners not subjects. Galbreath spoke the language of enlightened diplomacy while showing respect for the past.

A fond possession sat on the desk, a photo of his mother and himself shaking hands with Queen Elizabeth. It showed a young Galbreath, with silver-blond hair, in a blue blazer, and his mother, Lady Fiona Barrington, presenting the Queen with a Barrington saucer, a rare pattern she had designed.

He particularly liked the photo because it juxtaposed the

old nobility, represented by his mother, and the new social order, represented by himself. He had renounced his title, much to his mother's dismay. She still supplied him with elegant dishware, however, and now, buried in thought, he fingered the stem of the handle of a Barrington cup that sat on the desk, filled with rare Chinese tea.

A peasant boy named Ahdari sat across from Galbreath, obviously anxious about the Englishman's reaction to the distressing photograph he had brought.

"And where did you say you found this?" Galbreath asked skeptically, studying the picture.

"Outside the ruins on the east side of town, sir." Ahdari appeared nervous.

Galbreath heard his shuffling sandy feet. The boy was covered with dust. Each time Ahdari moved, Galbreath envisioned a small cloud forming around his clothing, and wondered what kind of damage the finely stitched fabric of the chair he sat on might endure from the filth.

"You know I would not have allowed you in here under normal circumstances," Galbreath said. "Your uncle's a successful merchant and an important man, or I wouldn't have given you the time of day."

"That is why I am so grateful," the twelve-year-old said, smiling. Three front teeth were missing. "I knew this was a rare and unusual picture of something very strange, indeed. My friend Oki told me you would be the one to show."

Galbreath noted the young boy's manipulative flattery. "Oki?" he asked, fingering the top of the cane.

"The son of the well digger."

"Oh yes. I've seen the two of you begging outside the market. Why do you beg, when your uncle is so wealthy?"

"He is wealthy because he does not give his money to my father or other members of the family," Ahdari said.

"Wealth in our country requires a great deal of care. Otherwise people will take what you have, and quickly."

At this, Galbreath couldn't help but smile. "So you think I will give you money if you give me this photograph?"

"And the others," Ahdari said.

"What others?"

"There are more. In a small metal box which was buried in the sand behind the ruins."

"And all of them like this one?" Galbreath asked. "Of some wretched person that has been burned to death?"

"Oh yes. There are at least a dozen different people like that, sir, in the pictures, I mean."

"All black, like you?"

"I could not tell, sir. The burning made them all seem to be of the black race. If you burn a white man enough, will he not also be black?" Ahdari's innocence forced Galbreath to smile again. "There are some children in the photos, too. If you come, I will show you. But, sir, you have not yet agreed to pay me."

"I will pay you, if the pictures are truly important."

"Look at the photograph, sir. Does it not look to be something very worrisome?"

"All right," Galbreath said. "Show me where you found this."

Ahdari leaped out of the chair.

Galbreath rose, fetched his Akubra hat, his khaki coat, and his cane. "Let's take the back way to my car, you little rascal."

The two of them exited through the heavy wooden door into the sun, the boy skipping, kicking dust, and Galbreath, using his brass-handled cane, limping behind.

Galbreath had been in Baghigra five weeks. He made it a point to meet as much of the local population as time would allow. A retired English secret agent, his current mission on behalf of Her Majesty's government was overtly diplomatic—to assess more efficient use of foreign aid to Sudanese farming communities. His secret activities entailed the investigation of an Islamic fundamentalist guerrilla movement. The British Foreign Office tracked potentially dangerous groups that might threaten foreign governments.

This particular resurgence of the jihad originated in southern Sudan in the 1950s. Getting into the backcountry was the only way to roust out leaders of the movement, who had become more troublesome through car bombings and subversive leaflets, distributed on the streets.

The ride to the edge of town in the ancient Bentley would not be long.

Baghigra was a meager village.

It sat near a tributary of the White Nile, which only ran wet during the winter months. In summer, the dry riverbed served as a reminder that the African sun ruled the land. Through maintenance of several vital wells, the village sustained its people, who numbered just over three thousand.

In a few minutes Galbreath and Ahdari arrived at the eastern ruins, located three and a half kilometers from the town. Galbreath had heard these buildings had been destroyed fifteen years before for unknown reasons.

As the car approached the mounds of sand and stone, Galbreath spotted the boy named Oki sitting on a large rock. His bicycle leaned against the boulder.

"Oki stayed to guard the ruins," Ahdari said enthusiastically. A cloud of dust swirled around the motorcar as it stopped.

Galbreath stepped out, with Ahdari close behind.

"I told you he would come!" Ahdari shouted.

"Hello, hello." Galbreath slammed the car door,

hobbled toward the boy, making holes in the sand with his cane. "Ahdari tells me you know where there are more of these." He lifted the photo in front of Oki's face.

"Yes. Over there, behind those bushes," Oki said.

Galbreath squinted in the late-afternoon light, gazing to where he pointed. He limped in that direction.

Oki jumped off the boulder and the two boys trailed him as he hobbled toward the bushes.

"You have the head of a lion on your walking stick," Oki said. "Are you a hunter of great animals?"

"I was." Galbreath pictured himself three long decades ago, walking the steppes with his friend Arthur. Memories of Arthur's smile and the bright gleam of the African sun on the tusks of the charging elephant intermingled. The cane Galbreath carried was fashioned from those same tusks.

The admission of being a hunter was obviously too tempting for scrawny Oki. "Is that how you became a three-legged man?"

Galbreath smiled at the unintended reference to the Oedipus myth. The Sphinx, in the guise of a mad bull, had robbed him of his long stride.

"Yes," he said wistfully. "But now I am a hunter of men." Before the boys could ask the meaning of the phrase, Galbreath held the photograph to their faces. "So you found this some distance from the ruins. What were you doing there?"

"Digging," Oki said. He looked a great deal like Ahdari, but was even filthier.

"I see that by your clothing."

"We were pretending to dig a well like Oki's father!" Ahdari said eagerly. He looked over at Oki as they walked. The boys smiled at each other. Ahdari seemed particularly proud that he had succeeded in bringing Galbreath along. They walked a hundred or so paces before reaching the dry, withered bushes.

"Here. Here it is!" Oki said, running ahead and jumping into a large hole.

Galbreath noticed the mound next to the hole. "You dug all this earth out of there?"

Oki looked up. "Father always digs deep when he makes a good well." He used both hands to scoop loosened earth from the bottom of the hole. "We hid the box in case you would not come." After a few moments he uncovered a rusted metal container, which, from all appearances, had been weather resistant.

Oki handed the box to Galbreath. The rusted hasp had no lock on it. He opened the lid. The black-and-white photographs inside were in remarkably good condition.

As the boys stared at him expectantly Galbreath looked through the photos one by one, examining them carefully.

He shook his head in disgust at a few of the pictures. Several showed young native children lying on white sheets, skin shriveled and torn in various parts of their bodies. Three pictures of one boy, either dead or near death when they were taken, included close-ups of his face, deformed by the lumps of the shattered skin. A bit of mucus hung from a blistered lip.

Galbreath uttered a grunt. "They are absolutely disgusting."

"These people have been badly burned," Oki said, nodding at Ahdari.

"So it would appear," Galbreath replied. "So it would seem to be." He put the pictures back in the box and looked down at the two boys. "You were right. These are worthy of payment." He reached into his khaki pants pocket. The boys came forward anxiously. "And I will pay you well for them." He counted out the money. "But only if . . ." He hesitated, giving them an intense scowl. "Only if you do not say anything to anyone about them."

Oki and Ahdari looked at each other, serious expressions on their innocent dirty faces.

"Not even our parents?" Ahdari asked.

"Not for now. And if you do not say anything, I will pay you just as much again in three days. Is it a bargain?"

The boys changed frowns to smiles and leaped up and down.

"Oh yes, sir," Oki said. "We will come to your office in three days."

"Good," Galbreath said. "That will give me time to try to find out who might have destroyed these buildings, and who could have buried these photographs."

The boys shouted with glee and bolted back in the direction of the car. They cavorted through the brush, their naked feet kicking up small puffs of ocher-colored dust in the late-afternoon light.

Galbreath watched them with affection. Then, before leaving, he carefully put the pictures of battered people in his breast pocket, looked up, and surveyed the land. He had chosen to work on this continent. He loved all things natural, including the inhabitants of Africa.

The long sunset rays turned the tall grasses into a sea of golden needles, stretching toward the purple mountains in the east.

The ruins to his left sat like great warts on the back of the open prairie.

He felt deep rage that some abhorrent force could defile this haven of natural innocence with acts of unspeakable cruelty.

THE FOURTH DAY
9:59 A.M.
Kingsgate Apartments, Richmond

Devin woke and stared at the ceiling. He followed the wainscoting around the four corners of the room.

He stretched his neck, brought his hands up in front of his face. Turning them over, front to back, he was gratified to find them steady. His recovery seemed to be progressing.

Suddenly restless, he needed to act. Time to move on.

The room felt different. Ginelle's apartment no longer soothed him. The formality of her home now made him uncomfortable. Perhaps the fact that she clung to the past, her dead mother's antique furnishings, staid tapestries and statues, made her seem odd.

He felt a yearning for the flavor of San Francisco. His apartment in Mill Valley. The Embarcadaro. His office. He belonged there, could follow the disease story from there. It was time to get back.

He would contact Amy's father so he could arrange for her burial.

Ginelle had expectations, but was his participation in her plan really necessary?

After all, she obviously didn't know all the facts. If Dr. Hendrix was unsure about the origins of the disease, maybe he was dead wrong about other things. The government might not be involved at all. Maybe Ginelle was not truly who she said she was. Maybe Devin had been used as a pawn to set up Hendrix's disappearance.

Devin visualized Dr. Hendrix, the conspirator, disguised in a white panama hat, sitting under a palm tree at some overseas resort.

He sat up, rubbed his face. A growth of beard. He hadn't had a shower in two days. No wonder he felt edgy, uncomfortable.

Ginelle was apparently still asleep in the den toward the rear of the apartment. He would have to find a way to leave without waking her.

Devin tossed the blanket off his lap and tried to stand. He smiled at his infirmity. Wobbly. Hungry. He reached up, touched his forehead. The fever was gone. But he'd perspired profusely. His slacks were moist, particularly around the waist. The shirt had somehow come off during the night. He may have torn it off. He remembered that the fabric had felt rough to his skin.

Bare-chested, he stared down at his belt line. A couple of pounds had come off during the last twenty-four hours.

He took a step, feeling that familiar twinge of pain in his right rib cage. Amazing that one Michigan linebacker's zealous tackle could leave him with pain for a lifetime.

He walked off the gray throw rug onto the hardwood floor, cold under his bare feet. Reaching the master bedroom, he cracked the door, immediately repulsed by a rank odor.

"God!" He shut it. Then, feeling obligated to Amy, he held his breath, opened the door, and stepped in, catching a glimpse of her bare feet, her legs, and finally her entire body.

This stiff corpse couldn't be Amy. Not this grotesque prop from a horror film. Cracks of red and black crisscrossed every inch like the flaking of clay on the floor of a desert. Dry skin had scaled away, and crisp ridges of tissue stood out, giving her the unearthly look of a scabby crustacean.

Forcing himself, Devin stepped toward her head. His gut wrenched. Her face, a burned pizza; muddled features were nearly indistinguishable. Dried eyelids peeled back, pale blue eyeballs stared emptily into space, floating in a crusty amber slime.

Devin began to retch and stumbled back toward the door. He managed to get his hands on the knob and forced himself into the cleaner air of the living room.

He shut the door quickly, doubled over, and dry-heaved. Ribs under his right arm ached with the contractions. Between spasms, he panted like a dog, bent over with hands braced on his knees. Amy had dried out. Not like the Skerits, who had been immersed in an alkaline solution. In Amy, he witnessed the result of diseased skin exposed to open air. It well might have been him. He visualized his own face, dried and crusty, and pushed the image from his mind.

Maybe best to leave her and call the coroner. Medical people would have a body bag. God, how she needed that. She would be put in an aid car wrapped up like a seedpod.

Had to get home, curfew or no curfew. The jet? Clemmer was probably fully infected. Maybe Freeman had heard from him. If the jet was unavailable, he could fly in an air-force transport. His press pass was his ticket.

He stood upright, and a surge of heat rose from his stomach, traveling up to his face. Perspiration washed his forehead. He suddenly became terribly weak. Considering the way he felt, travel might be inconceivable. He hadn't eaten in thirty-six hours. He had to have food. Gain strength. *Then* call CNB.

His weakness was reminiscent of the aftereffects of the flu. Food would help.

Regaining his balance, he moved feebly toward the kitchen, searched the cupboards. Cereal. Soup. Crackers. Yes. Start there. His weakened hands found even the wrapper of the crackers difficult to tear.

He managed to wrench the package open, stuffing the crackers in his mouth. Surprisingly tasty. Munching the doughy texture, his tongue danced with small stings of salt. He swallowed gratefully, grabbing another handful. Crackers were good, but dry. He needed something wet. The idea of a screwdriver entered his mind . . . orange juice and a shot of vodka with its obvious medicinal benefits. Hampered the microbe.

The sink was more accessible. Bracing himself on the edge, he put his face under the faucet and pushed the handle with his spare hand. Water, cool and sweet, washed away the bile taste.

He wiped his mouth, straightened up, and enjoyed more crackers.

As he ate he felt his body respond. Strength returned, and he regained determination to return home, filled with thoughts of his apartment, the black-and-white contemporary furniture, the arched lamp over the suede chaise longue, and the view of the bay beyond.

What was happening back home? He spotted a radio.

He turned and walked over to the small dinette, switched it on, and sat down by the yellow curtains, looking out at the birch trees in the courtyard. No one in sight. The condominium complex looked drab under cloudy skies even with spring growth on the trees.

The radio was tuned to the emergency broadcast system, giving instructions regarding the curfew, repeating that no one should leave their homes under the declared martial law. No statistics on the number of dead. Lack of information to avoid further panic. Devin pushed "scan" on the dial. No other stations in Richmond were on the air, only the two emergency frequencies, identical on both AM and FM. The announcer's words blended into a dizzying drone.

He'd open a can of soup. That would clear his head.

While the announcer rambled on, Devin got up and rummaged in the drawers, looking for the can opener. Suddenly he heard Ginelle's voice in the living room.

"Devin, where are you?"

She entered the kitchen wearing a dark green bathrobe. She studied him intently. "What are you doing?" she asked.

"I was hungry," he said. His tongue felt thick. "Making some soup."

"Let me do that."

"I didn't want to wake you." He backed up to the counter.

She pointed to the radio. "Anything new?"

"Just curfew instructions."

"You shouldn't be moving around so soon."

"I feel like it. I've got to get back," he said apologetically.

Her face fell. She switched off the broadcast and walked briskly into the living room. She turned, faced him, and sat down on the arm of the sofa. "Back? To what?"

"My office."

"What's happening there, Devin?" She clenched her hands, dropped them in her lap.

He stood among the tapestries, barefoot on the hardwood floor, feeling like a plaintiff at a trial. "That's just it. I don't know. I just feel unhinged, somehow. I understand the importance of having met you. But, we've done it, you know what I mean? I've got to get out and do my job. I feel like I'm *in* a goddamn story instead of reporting it."

"Oh, I see. All this is too real for you. Is that it?" She rose, walked to the window, looked into the courtyard.

"You don't understand," he said. "I've been on battle-fields, crime scenes, you name it. This is different . . . being here, now . . . I mean, Amy dying." He retreated to the kitchen doorway, put a hand up on the transom, and leaned against the frame.

She stared out the window. Her silence frustrated him.

He turned and paced the kitchen floor, confused. Something about her behavior didn't make sense. He stared down at his bare feet. What was she doing? Was she angry? He stepped back into the doorway, began to speak, and hesitated.

Suddenly she pushed back from the glass and shielded her body with the curtain.

"Devin," she said. "Come here!"

Her frightened tone made him reach her side fast.

She pointed through the window. "Look. Those men."

He focused on the stone walkway that led across the courtyard, connecting the buildings. Three men, dressed in black turtleneck jerseys, looked around, apparently checking house numbers on the condominiums.

"Who are they?"

"They're Asian," she said.

"I can see that."

"Dad told me he had escaped from . . . some Asian men." She clutched his arm. "Devin, I think they've come for me." An overtone of fear in an otherwise matter-of-fact statement. "What will we do?" *We*, she said.

"It'll be all right." He reassured himself. He'd handled panic situations before. Friends, with whom he'd ridden, crashed a car on a country road on New Year's Eve. Hurt himself, he'd carried a bleeding man two miles to a farmhouse and saved his life. Adrenaline served him then, and it surged into him now.

She walked back and forth, bathrobe swinging wildly. "There's no place to hide here," she said. She started for the front door.

Devin glanced out the window. The men. Gone. God, they must already be in the hall. "No! They'll catch you out there." He grabbed her by the elbow. "In here. It's your only chance." He dragged her across to the master bedroom.

Devin heard the latch on the front door, clicking. Someone picking the lock.

With a hand on Ginelle's back, he opened the door, pushed her through it. The foul smell of the decaying body hit him harder the second time.

Devin pushed her past the bed toward the louvered closet doors.

Ginelle looked down at Amy. "God, look at her," she whispered. "I can't breathe."

"Just hold it," he wheezed. He opened the folding door and shoved her in among the clothes, joined her, and shut the door behind.

He stood among the garments, that included several nightgowns. Ginelle. In nightgowns? The image faded as she clutched his arm, hard.

"They'll search every room."

"Maybe not," he whispered. "Now shush."

The bedroom window's light streamed through the louvers, painting soft stripes across her face, highlighting her eyes, suddenly wide with apprehension.

Movement.

He peered through the louvers.

The bedroom door opened.

Two thin muscular men entered, carrying automatic handguns, silencers on each one. The first man exclaimed displeasure in a foreign tongue, holding his nose, pointing to the bed where Amy's body lay. The second waved a hand in front of his contorted face. He appeared to gag.

Devin struggled to see through the door, noticing a U-shaped scar over the first man's left eyebrow. They argued with one another. Then, the lead man forcefully pushed the second man back out with a flurry of staccato Asian phrases, closing the door.

Devin listened, holding his breath. No sound.

"The smell," Ginelle whispered. "They've left."

"Wouldn't you? Now quiet down."

She nodded and put a sleeve of one of the nightgowns up to her nose, indicating Devin should do the same. He grabbed the other sleeve. The cloth felt soft under his nose. Gratefully, he inhaled the scent of gardenia in the fabric.

Together in half darkness, faces partially covered, they studied each other's eyes. Moments passed. Silence. She reminded him of a deer in danger in the forest. Hidden in a thicket. Big eyes. Long legs. Tan. Yet . . . he admired her cool.

"Do you think they've gone?" she asked.

He dropped the sleeve and pushed the door. "I'll bet they can't stay anywhere too long. Wait here." He edged out of the closet, tiptoed to the bedroom door. He listened intently. Unable to abide the stench any longer, Devin put a hand on the knob and rotated it. He opened the door a crack.

The living room was empty. The pastoral tapestries hung peacefully. The front door was closed.

Ginelle stepped out of the closet, edging toward him, but he waved her back, listening one last time.

Then satisfied, he gestured her forward. "It's all right." He stepped into the living room.

With a grateful expression, she followed.

No other sounds in the condo, but Devin felt compelled to check the den, just in case. He walked into the back room, which contained a desk, shelves filled with books, a television, and an unmade Hide-A-Bed. Convinced they were alone, he returned to the living room.

Ginelle seemed angry.

"What's wrong?" he asked.

"I suddenly realized I was only a few feet away from the men who probably took my father and couldn't do anything about it!"

"What did you expect? You saw their guns. You're lucky to be alive." He felt perturbed. She hadn't acknowledged his resourceful idea of using the decaying body as a ploy.

"I've got to do something." She paced restlessly. "If only I could report this."

Her independence reinforced his yearning to get home. "Go ahead. Why didn't you call the authorities in the first place?"

She ran both hands through her hair. "Too risky. I might make the news, and they'd find me again."

He remained confused, torn between empathy for her and the desire to return to San Francisco. There was one way to force the decision. "I'm going to phone in," he said. "You mind if I . . . make a private call?"

She pointed to the rear of the apartment, looking lost. "On the desk in the den." She apparently understood the need he was feeling. "Do what you have to do."

Seated at Ginelle's desk in the low light of the small den, contemplating his next move, Devin had turned on the television set only to find the same local civil-defense official he had heard on the radio repeating instructions. It appeared that national feeds had been completely interrupted. He switched off the TV and the set sat lifeless in the corner. In the curved screen, he saw a fish-eyed, distorted reflection of himself holding the phone.

He dialed and finally reached Frank Freeman on his private line.

After enduring a diatribe from his boss, Devin gave an emotional report of Amy's death.

Freeman was deeply shaken.

Devin followed with an explanation about Hendrix's mysterious disappearance and Ginelle's own close call.

Then Freeman gave Devin an update. He reviewed the progress of the disease, including the unfortunate word that Carl Clemmer had become infected and admitted himself to a hospital in Richmond. Without the vaccine, he would likely die. Devin felt terrible about Clemmer and the cab driver but Freeman reminded him that had Hendrix arrived on time, everything would have been different. Devin bemoaned the circumstances, but Freeman insisted that both men had become involved only because of the need to save Amy and retrieve the vaccine.

With that, he forced the conversation to the subject of the immediate future.

Devin said he wished to return to San Francisco with Amy's body.

To his surprise, Freeman disagreed, arguing that CNB should make those arrangements. "We'll handle things from here, Devin. You've got more important things to do."

"Like come home!"

"No! Don't you realize you're right in the middle of the biggest story of the century? New projections for the next two months show the epidemic could make the bubonic plague look like a head cold. Unchecked, it could eventually wipe out the U.S. . . . maybe other countries."

As he listened Devin watched his own reflection on the blank TV screen. "Are you on the air?"

"Not yet. For twenty-four hours we're preempted by local emergency stuff."

"That's what I've got here. What do you hear over satellite? Or wire. Where does the government lay blame?"

"I hear rumblings from the attorney general's office. Something's not right about that, Devin. Hendrix's name came out of nowhere."

"Nothing comes out of nowhere."

"Exactly. He's become a scapegoat. Government people are screaming for his head. I'd love to break the story about you and Hendrix."

"Then let me come back. I'll do a feature on it."

"Be patient. We don't want every periodical in the country on your ass. We've got the exclusive! You have to stay with this."

Freeman's comments created new burdens. "Frank. I'm beyond exhaustion, for God's sake!"

"I realize that, but this could be the turning point in your career."

"I don't need another one of those."

Freeman audibly bristled at the sarcasm. "Suck up your guts and get fired up. You're right on the mark. I can feel it. If Hendrix is innocent, imagine the story! Hendrix: either satan or savior, likely one of the most important men in American history."

Devin eyed the research books on the shelves and toyed with the laptop computer on the desk. "Okay, Frank. I'm all over this. But I've got to tell you, I feel stranded."

Freeman remained unsympathetic. "You're just not used to the road. Consider this: you and Ginelle may be the only people out there who've had a vaccination.

You're safe. And unique. And mobile. You can move around freely with your press pass."

"Feels like I'm out here flying blind," Devin said.

"Bullshit. I'll feed you information when you need it. Now, the research department has been running cross-references on scientists, to see if there are ties to Hendrix. A few surfaced . . . missing or recently deceased, and not from the disease. This morning's sat-com out of New York mentions a Dr. Ahmar Kahvahl, drowned in a boating accident off Rhode Island two days ago."

"Kahvahl?"

"Found his sailboat near his home at Newport. No one else on board." Devin heard the rustle of Frank's computer sheets in the background. "And more, over the wire yesterday: a Dr. Glant missing in Maui, the day before a Dr. Metzger got pumped full of an unknown toxic substance while getting a tan. Dead. Are you catching on?"

"Holy shit. Ginelle mentioned those guys."

"She did?" Freeman sounded suddenly out of control. "In what context?"

"They were all involved with Hendrix on a research project that started this mess."

"Don't you see! Ginelle's your ticket. If you're with Hendrix's daughter, you're sitting right in the chute. It's your exclusive, buddy. Find her dad."

"Frank, you make it sound easy. She doesn't have a clue. Where the hell would I start?" Devin looked at a gold-framed photograph by the desk pad.

"For openers, you said Hendrix wanted to deliver the formula to the Disease Control Center, the hub of this crisis. I think I can get you in there."

"How?" Devin asked skeptically.

"Through an old army buddy of mine, Burt Williamson, a bird colonel at the Pentagon. I got his ass out of a jam in Vietnam in sixty-seven. He owes me. I'll have him contact Atlanta. You'll clear security."

"What about Ginelle?" The frame on the desk held a picture of Ginelle and a white-haired man Devin felt sure was Hendrix.

"Take her with you."

"She's a fugitive. They're after her." A moment of silence. "Frank?"

"Okay. I've got it. What's she look like?"

"Who—Ginelle?" He studied her in the photograph as he described her. "About five six, long blond hair, green eyes. She's beautiful." The four-color exposure showed Hendrix in a maroon blazer with his arm around his daughter.

"Tough duty. Take her with you as Amy Klein."

"Are you crazy? They don't even look alike."

"Have Ginelle cut her hair and carry Amy's ID."

Devin's eyes rested on Ginelle's long blond hair in the picture. "That'll never work." He studied the photo. Hendrix smiled warmly from the photograph. A kindly face. The face of a father.

"What are you going to do with her, leave her at the bus station?" Freeman asked. "She can't stay in Richmond. She can't move around. The streets are jammed with troops. Amy's press pass is her only way to get out. That way you can keep her on a leash."

Devin looked back at his own image in the blank TV screen. "In Atlanta? That'll be hard to pull off."

Freeman stepped up his pitch. "With Williamson's credentials, they won't question it. I'm telling you."

Devin had heard the hard sell before. "What if Williamson refuses?" he asked.

"In the muck of 'Nam, Williamson and me got down to mud and blood, do you understand? He'll do it, I guarantee it."

"And Amy? What about her identity?"

"From what you've told me, she's unrecognizable, a casualty of this war. Thousands more will fill the morgues. Don't worry. I'll make sure her remains are treated with respect. Now, do what I tell you and go."

Devin reached out, placing the gold frame facedown on the desk. Commitment to his job now meant a commitment to Ginelle and her problems. Freeman seemed to sense his ambivalence and interrupted his thoughts.

"Devin. What the hell's wrong with you? You were all over me to get on the road. What is it?"

Devin tried to regain his perspective. Perhaps the illness had drained him. "Amy, I guess," he said.

"I fully understand, but this is a battlefield situation. We put the dead aside and move on. Listen. Some of us never get a shot like this. Your whole miserable life could be wrapped up in this one story. If you have any balls left, do it. Tell me you'll do it!"

Devin tilted the photo up again, looking at Ginelle's face. Then her father's. He felt isolated and alone. He belonged somewhere, he knew that. But, where? On Ginelle's unlit TV screen, his own reflection sat at the desk suspended in milky nothingness. All he had to do was reach out, turn a knob, and the screen would light up once again.

On-screen, the one place he truly belonged.

Life was just an erratic dot pattern anyway. He was lost in the middle of it. So was Ginelle. Interesting that they shared that. And she had saved his life. Oddly enough, he hadn't even thanked her properly.

"Devin?"

Deep in thought, Devin ignored Freeman's voice. We're all just an assemblage of molecules and atoms . . . so many multicolored, multifaceted dots. He looked back at the photograph of Ginelle and her father. If we're lucky, the dots come together long enough to make a meaningful picture. Pictures only become meaningful with meaningful people in them. Ginelle needed him.

There was still time. Before the pattern flew apart into nothingness . . . before the picture went to black, forever.

"Devin. Devin! Are you there?"

Devin nodded. "I guess I am, Frank. I was just tuning in." He smiled to himself. "I think I'm back on TV."

THE FOURTH DAY
10:16 P.M.
Somewhere on the Road

Dr. Hendrix lay in darkness in his mobile prison with no stimuli save the buzzing of his own brain. Occasional injections he had received over the last days kept him groggy, incoherent.

Prior to the drugs, Hendrix remembered speaking at length to one of the guards, who seemed less vicious than the others. The young man hid a respectful decency behind his harsh exterior. He had even made it a point to get Hendrix's glasses out of the Mercedes's backseat, where they had fallen during his abduction. His name . . . what was it? Wu Sun. Yes. Friendly eyes. But they had taken the young man away, drugs had clouded reality, and the clouds were only now beginning to disappear.

Hendrix struggled with veiled memories of writing to Ginelle. Images of his hands signing a letter to her in black ink. Had he called her? Impossible.

The mind cleared slowly.

As he lay strapped on the cot, his thoughts flitted through the past. Hendrix let the mind pictures play, spin like a kinescope. Many years of research had demonstrated that his subconscious acted independently of his will.

Through mental discipline, a premise or proposition could be extracted from the subconscious. Even complex scientific schematics would appear. He marveled at them. Though complex, they were often quite complete.

Hendrix found this coexistence with his own brain amusing, a pleasant form of schizophrenia, if such was possible. Often detached himself, he could give his mind a problem, it would back-file it, actively addressing more immediate material. Then, miraculously, the problem could be recalled, and answers would rise into the amphitheater of his perception: intricate mathematical calculations projected from his unconscious onto the screen of his intellect.

My mind, he thought, has always been old, even when I was young.

Young. What a concept: that euphoric tender state.

Hendrix smiled as he flashed back to his innocent teen years, a curly-headed scamp, playing soccer at YMCA camps in Switzerland, Austria, and Germany. His father, a philosophy professor, frequently on sabbatical in Europe, brought young Hendrix along. His mother, also an educator, tutored him through his school years.

Then, back in the United States, Yale University, cum laude upon graduation, and a return to Europe, where he met Ginelle's mother, Eva, the gentle Romanian ballerina, with a heart of gold and intellect to match. She performed *Swan Lake* in Salzburg on that snowy evening, and he impetuously proposed marriage over midnight champagne.

Eva's angelic expression. Eva's gone to God. Lisa with her. His daughter Lisa's body had never been found in that Swiss glacier. And now his only surviving daughter was . . . where? Safe?

He cringed. Ginelle's present vulnerability was his responsibility.

"God forgive me," he said aloud, confronting his guilt. He had found God in recent years and spoken with Him often, searching for redemption and forgiveness.

Fear had driven him to the research. Insufficient funds

for his retirement made him join the Black Diamond Project. He had sacrificed peace of mind for $750,000.

The research became an abomination.

At least he had stopped before it was too late. During the last months, in the New Mexico desert, he refused to divulge a connective formula he had discovered, withholding the chemical key that would have made the Black Diamond device a viable weapon.

Thank God we didn't have fraxination back then, he thought. The ability to hypersplice molecular particles would have given his associates the replicator much sooner.

Hendrix had abandoned the project, believing they might never find it. Glant and Metzger had been excellent chemists, of course, second to none, experts in toxic synthetics. And Kahvahl, a microbiologist with a strong background in infectious diseases, had developed the germ. It was clumsy, inefficient. But the U.S. government hadn't merely asked for an infection; they required a weapon. There was an immense difference between isolating an agent in a test tube and launching it into a battlefield. When Hendrix left, the Black Diamond bug had proven to be slow in developing. Still an unrealistic possibility for use as a weapon.

Hendrix's responsibility had been to create the replicator, the triggering device for cloning. He had done his research well. But after seeing the effects of Kahvahl's disease, its destructive capacity had horrified him. He'd had nightmares about the weeks of experimentation, the monkey cages, the black flesh.

One day he had looked in the mirror and wept at the destruction he held in his hands. He resigned, forfeiting two-thirds of the money. Financial security no longer mattered. He simply had to get out.

Feigning a lack of progress with his assigned task, he had signed a nondisclosure agreement and left.

Throughout the last decade he read periodicals and watched the newspapers, hoping what he had discovered would never be found again.

The hissing hydraulic door at the end of the chamber opened, interrupting his thoughts, forcing Hendrix into the present.

One of the Asian men in black fatigues entered, flicked the switch of an overhead light, washing everything in the chamber with a ghostly pale blue.

Hendrix strained to see the man's face and recognized him. This wasn't his original guard. This one was a bit older, with slicked-back black hair and, a notable feature, a horseshoe-shaped scar over his left eye.

The Asian gave him a sidelong glance, took a seat in the corner of the chamber on a metal stool next to Hendrix's Mercedes, expressionless, staring.

"You," Hendrix said to the Asian man. "Can I ask you a question?"

The man didn't move.

"Tell me how many are dying out there."

No response.

"Has my . . . has a cure for the disease been issued to the people?" The stone-faced man looked past him and said nothing. "Keeping me isn't doing anyone any good," Hendrix said. "I want to talk to that Jaktar fellow. Call him." He strained under the straps that held his chest and legs. "These damn things are too tight. I'm losing circulation. Can't you loosen them?"

The man shifted slightly, but continued to stare at the steel wall behind Hendrix.

"You speak English, don't you?" Hendrix continued. "What about my daughter? Any news? Surely, even you people have children. You understand a father's concerns."

The man closed his eyes, as if to sleep.

"Listen, I obviously have nothing to lose here. I'm going to start screaming at the top of my lungs until somebody hears me. Maybe that'll make you more talkative." Hendrix took a deep breath and began to scream. "Help me! Somebody help me! Help! Help!"

The guard opened his eyes. He rose, walked calmly to a switch that closed the overhead vent.

Hendrix kept shouting.

The man turned. He was beside the cot in three energetic paces and struck Hendrix across the face with the back of his hand, knocking the doctor's glasses off.

The shock of the blow forced Hendrix to stop shouting momentarily. He was about to resume his screams when his captor leaned down and grabbed his throat.

With fingers clamped firmly around the doctor's larynx, he spoke in broken English. "You wish die now?" he said, tightening his grip. "No scream, you understand? I rip your neck out!"

Hendrix's eyes bugged out. He needed to cough. He exhaled and chose to utter two words with his remaining breath. "My daughter," he wheezed.

"I have seen her," the man said, clenching his teeth. "She is dead." As if to seek a response from Hendrix, he loosened his grip on his throat just enough to let him gasp in anguish.

"Dead," Hendrix croaked. "Oh God."

The guard tightened his grip once more, and Hendrix began to weep. He heard another hiss in the background.

The man called Jaktar entered through the hydraulic door. "Sing Chu! Let him be!"

Sing Chu looked over his shoulder and reluctantly released his grip.

The blond man approached, pushing Sing Chu out of the way. As the guard left the chamber Jaktar bent down, retrieved the glasses, and pushed them onto Hendrix's face.

"I advise you to restrain yourself, Doctor. You have a chance to live. Why ruin it with a foolish outburst? Can you breathe?"

Hendrix nodded painfully, gasping for air, as tears ran down his face. His mind began to replay an image of his two little girls in the backyard of his New Haven home. Ginelle always wore a red ribbon, Lisa a yellow one. Ginelle had played ballerina, Lisa the athlete. Now they were both gone.

Jaktar placed a hand on his shoulder. "You look upset."

Hendrix sobbed, hardly able to speak. "My daughter."

"Yes. Sing Chu and his associates found her in her apartment. It's a shame you didn't have the opportunity to vaccinate her with your serum."

"What?" Hendrix's heart leaped.

"Apparently the effects of the microbe were quite dramatic." Jaktar seemed to relish the opportunity to shock him.

"What did you say?" Hendrix asked, confused.

Jaktar leaned down. "I said she was a disease victim."

Hendrix's sobs subsided. Something didn't jibe; he tried to unscramble the conversation. He wasn't an actor, but at this opportune moment he became one, feigning grief. Easy to cry when he thought about Ginelle. Easier yet, when he realized, with a rush of relief, that whomever Jaktar referred to, it certainly was not his daughter.

Ginelle had been vaccinated.

Who could the disease victim be? The only possibilities were the two newspeople he had prepared to meet.

Devin Parks. And a woman: Amy Klein. Was there a link between Ginelle and the female reporter?

Hendrix wept, sustaining the charade, then coughed several times, looking up. How unique Jaktar was, with a dark, Middle Eastern–looking complexion, white-blond hair, and a ragged line of a mouth that hung under a narrow, ridged nose, framed by one brown eye and one blue eye.

Jaktar gestured toward the door. "We bring you a cell mate, Doctor." Two guards struggled with their heavy burden, dragging a mass of black cloth across the chamber floor, as Sing Chu hurried past them with another cot.

On the bed, the top sheet of the black bundle was thrown back, revealing an Iranian man in his mid-seventies. His face was ruddy, bruised, and battered.

Hendrix strained against the straps to see. "My God," he said. "Ahmar Kahvahl!"

Jaktar gave the man a gallant wave. "Your esteemed colleague."

Kahvahl hardly breathed. A shock of curly white hair stood out from both sides of his head. His broad nose and high forehead made his head appear too large for his body.

Sing Chu pulled the black cloth out from under the unconscious doctor's body.

Hendrix's tears subsided at the shock of seeing his former colleague. "What have you done to him?"

"Basically what we have done to you." Jaktar stepped back, surveying both doctors with a prideful look. "Taken him out of circulation. He no longer exists."

"Is that my case as well?"

"Precisely." Jaktar appeared to enjoy taunting him. "You have been taken out of the world."

Hendrix contemplated the statement's implications. "Maybe this world is no longer desirable," he said.

"Good. Then you won't mind being a memory . . . and an unpleasant one at that, you old relic." Jaktar pulled a cigarette from his leather jacket, placed it into a pearl cigarette holder, and lit it.

"I don't understand," Hendrix said.

Jaktar stepped closer, bringing his face next to Hendrix, who smelled licorice and cigarette smoke on the blond man's breath. "You opened Pandora's box." He chuckled, clamping the cigarette holder between his teeth. "But the novelty vanished the moment your microorganism was analyzed."

"Don't speak in riddles."

Jaktar seemed angered by Hendrix's confusion. "Is this plain enough? You're finished. An extinct predator."

Hendrix could see that Jaktar was mentally disturbed, and tried not to show his fear. "Who do you work for?" he asked.

"A very powerful group of men," Jaktar said, exhaling smoke.

"They must be insane."

Jaktar squinted at him. "Not at all. They attend to business. Business rules the world."

"Who are these maniacs?"

"Visionaries."

"Name them."

Jaktar smirked, stared at him.

"You're not going to tell me?"

"I will whisper it to you before you die."

Hendrix became angered by the intimidation. "You speak of plagues, yet you're the ones who are sick," he said, words his only remaining weapon. "Your affliction appears to be presumption, incredible arrogance."

Jaktar grabbed Hendrix by the collar with a strong,

sinewy hand. "Who is more arrogant . . . God? Or the one who plays God? You were such a player yourself."

Hendrix found himself uncomfortably deciding which of Jaktar's eyes to look into, the brown one or the blue one.

Jaktar let go and pointed off into space. "The Hendrix name is on every one of those dead bodies out there."

"That's not true," the scientist said.

Jaktar took a deep drag and exhaled, hovered above him in the smoky blue light like a broad-shouldered demon. "It no longer matters what you think, you and Kahvahl." He laughed, waving his long arm through a cloud of smoke. "The survivors of your goddamn plague—if there are any—will remember both of you as the greatest murderers of all time."

THE FIFTH DAY
10:17 A.M.
Disease Control Center
Atlanta

Devin stood on the front steps of the DCC. The building was guarded like a bunker, sandbags stacked on the front steps, leaving only a small opening to the front entrance, which was blocked by an army captain.

His name tag read BURWELL. He was flanked by four soldiers in fatigues holding attack rifles.

Burwell looked at the two press passes and handed them back to Devin from the top step. "No members of the press allowed inside, Mr. Parks. I'm sorry." He maintained a polite, aloof tone. He glanced at his watch. "You and Ms. Klein should have been here for this morning's briefing."

Devin glanced back at Ginelle, who waited near the curb, dressed in her denim skirt and a red sweater, looking markedly different with her now-short blond hair.

"You might try the downtown Hilton," the captain continued. "They've set up a media center in the lobby. Press members are invited back tomorrow at eight A.M., just like today."

"We're not here as reporters."

The young officer's blue eyes squinted skeptically. "Then why give me your press passes?"

"Purely ID." Devin tucked the passes into the pocket of his camel-colored blazer.

Burwell shook his head.

Devin formed his words carefully, as if he'd been mis-
understood. "You should have had word from a Colonel
Williamson in Washington. I have an appointment with
Dr. Gordon."

"No, you don't."

"Why do you say that?"

"No one does, right now. As you might guess, he's
busy as hell."

"Please, check. It's very important."

Burwell smirked. "Isn't everything these days?"

Devin decided to deal with this khaki-clad adolescent
more firmly. "You've heard of Colonel Williamson,
haven't you?"

Burwell countered with a pert smile. "What branch of
the service is he?"

Devin became suddenly embarrassed. In his euphoric
discussion with Freeman, he had forgotten to ask details.
But it was only logical if Freeman was the colonel's
buddy. "Army, I believe." He felt Ginelle's eyes on his
back, and for a second he felt cloddish. "I just know
Williamson's a liaison for the joint chiefs."

"Really? Never heard of him." Burwell pointed down
the pavement. "Now, why don't you and your friend
move along."

"Devin," Ginelle called. She seemed anxious.

"Just a minute," he shouted back in her direction.
"Look, Captain. Dr. Gordon's expecting me. Please
check again."

Burwell rubbed his lower lip with a gloved hand. "Mr.
Parks, I'm sure you're good at your job. So please
respect me for doing mine. My responsibility is to keep
unnecessary personnel off these steps."

Devin felt strange having someone this young push
him around. "Don't you realize how far we've come—"

"Well, have a nice trip back."

With that, Captain Burwell stepped up the staircase and assumed a rigid position. He set his gaze off to the willow trees across the street.

Devin gave him a last look and descended the stone steps to Ginelle, who showed her disappointment by moodily slinging the strap of Amy's purse over her shoulder. She had packed a few clothes and her laptop computer, which she felt might be useful on the road.

"Not too impressed, was he?" she said as he joined her, taking her elbow, leading her back to the VW van. "I didn't even have a chance to fool him with my haircut."

"I think you look cute in short hair."

She pulled her arm away.

"What's the matter?"

"Cute? No one's called me that since I was six."

He couldn't tell if she was truly bothered. She had a spunky expression on her face. "Maybe if I curtsied for the captain, he'd let us in."

Smiling nervously, Devin looked back at Burwell. "Keep your voice down." He hustled her along, reaching the vehicle, then remembered a passing conversation with Ginelle in which he had used the "cute" word to describe Amy. Amy's comment about condescension that night at the restaurant echoed in his mind, and again he wondered if he had too often condescended to Amy with diminutives. "I'm sorry, Ginelle. Does the word *cute* upset you?"

She smiled. "You could use it again and find out."

Devin opened the passenger door and helped her in.

She hiked her skirt up to manage the climb into the high seat. Devin noticed the firmness of her upper leg.

She caught him. "I think I can manage this myself, thank you." She punished him with a glance.

"Not much you can't handle, is there?" he said under his breath. He walked round the front and got into the driver's seat. Putting the key in the ignition, he sat staring out the windshield.

"Well?" She crossed her arms. "Now what?"

"I'm thinking." He searched his mind for possibilities, still feeling weak from the last seventy-two hours.

"*I'm* thinking maybe I should call the FBI. We're running out of options."

"That's inadvisable with all the negative press about your father." Radio newscasts on their drive to Atlanta mentioned an APB for Hendrix, now wanted in fifty states.

"It makes me ill." She did look sickened by it.

"You can't call the FBI."

"What else am I going to do? Every minute puts Dad further out of reach."

He spoke gently, turning toward her. "Look. You and I are in this together."

"I know," she said, nodding emphatically. "And I'm grateful to you for coming along . . . and saving my life back there at my apartment."

"That makes us even," he said, not really believing it. He still owed her.

"Even," she said. "Like fifty-fifty?" She extended a hand.

He took it reluctantly and they shook. He couldn't quite read the glint in her eye.

"Fifty-fifty means I get to make half the decisions," she said.

"What do you mean?"

"You decided we would cut my hair. . . . Now it's my turn."

"Wait a minute."

"So it's my decision to go . . . in . . . there." She pointed back at the large granite control-center building. "There's nowhere else we can go."

Before he could prevent it, she was out the passenger door with the purse thrown over her shoulder, walking the eighty feet toward the army captain.

Devin leaped out of the van, broke into a run, and caught her, spinning her around. "What the hell are you doing?"

She had burning determination in her green eyes. "I'm telling them who I am."

Devin looked over at the guards. They were still out of earshot. He grabbed her and stopped her again. "Don't do that. They'll never let you go." He might never see her again.

"You mean you'll lose track of an exclusive news story." She resumed her march toward the steps.

"Wait! Just give me a minute." He matched her stride for stride. "At least let me do the talking. I'll tell them about the phone call from your dad. All right? But nothing else about you. Please. I don't want them to take you away. You said we were in this together."

She stopped and stared into his eyes, as if measuring his feelings. "Then come along."

"Only if you let me do the talking. Please. For your own safety."

"We'll see how you do."

Before Devin could respond, off she went, walking briskly up the steps toward the captain. Devin brought up the rear. Burwell saw them coming and his gloved hand shot out like a traffic cop repelling an onslaught of vehicles at an intersection.

Before the soldier or Ginelle could say anything, Devin made his pitch. "Captain, tell Gordon I've been in touch with Dr. Thomas Hendrix."

Captain Burwell looked at Ginelle and tilted his head in Devin's direction. His eyes narrowed.

"Go on, give him a call, and tell him what I just said."
Devin threw a cautioning glance toward Ginelle.

"Authorization is based on proper credentials, not on
your knowing some doctor," Burwell said stoically.

As Ginelle stood a few feet behind, Devin crowded the
officer. His voice dropped down to a grating, peevish
growl. He was face-to-face with the young man, almost
whispering. "Don't you realize who I'm talking about
here, Burwell? Weren't you properly briefed? Dr.
Thomas Hendrix is considered the guy who started the
goddamn epidemic. Now, what if your commanding
officer found out you let an opportunity slip by? Hmm?"

The captain slowly relaxed his aggressive stance. He
seemed to think things over.

"Wait here," he said, spun on a polished heel, walked
briskly past the guards, and disappeared through the
heavy glass doors.

"What do you think?" Ginelle whispered. She had
moved up to Devin's right arm.

"I gave it my best shot," Devin said. "I thought I
played the heavy pretty well. He was either impressed or
pissed off. Probably both."

From the landing, the four guards stood at ease, eyeing
them silently.

After a few moments the young captain appeared,
flanked by four more men in battle dress.

"You'll come with me, please," Captain Burwell said
as the new soldiers surrounded Devin and Ginelle, two
in front and two behind. With the captain leading,
they walked as a group across the stone landing toward
the door.

They passed through the black glass into the lobby,
which housed even more troops, lined up against the
far wall.

"You're taking us to Gordon, then?" Devin asked, addressing the captain.

"I've been told to hold you for questioning," Captain Burwell said, in a dry, precise tone. "That's all I know."

The soldiers behind Ginelle closed ranks.

A hint of panic flashed in Ginelle's eyes.

Devin grabbed her by the elbow. "Take it easy," he whispered as they were herded down the hall. "Remember just the phone call for now, no mention of anything else."

He looked back at the glass doors, which suddenly seemed uncomfortably distant.

THE FIFTH DAY
5:27 P.M.
The Ministry of Commerce
Khartoum, Sudan

"Sir. What was the name of the township, again, please?"

"Baghigra," Galbreath said, "just north of Melut, in the old Doapu Province."

Abra, the Nubian clerk, was dressed in white muslin. He stood in a beam of sunlight cast by a small cross-hatched window high on the wall of the alcove. Small dust particles swirled in the beam. Abra's military-style cap, made of white cotton, shone like ivory against his dark complexion. His small brass reading glasses had over time gouged a deep indentation in the fleshy sides of his nose.

Galbreath wondered how long it would take for the skin to reshape itself if the glasses were permanently removed.

Abra fingered the worn beige cards in the teak file. "These new republican folders are mixed in with the old British colonial files, you understand. Unfortunately there is still some confusion. We inherited this filing system from the British, which occurred before my time." He paused and smiled. "I mean before I worked for this department. I was alive, of course."

"I understand." Galbreath smiled in return. The Nubian was polite, articulate. The Englishman appreciated his good manners.

The clerk's black hands flicked the file cards. He reached the end of the row and looked up over his cheaters, as Galbreath would call them.

"I'm so sorry, sir. After all this time it would appear the only records in existence would be in the unmarked stacks at the rear of this building. You see, from what I understand, Colonel Nimeri's regime reorganized everything in 1969. Then it remained untouched until eighty-five, when the Swar al-Dahab government urged us to reorganize. A good deal of our filing is, to our national shame, incomplete and replete with error. This is the unfortunate legacy of repeated revolution. No one has time to organize, because everyone is busy reorganizing." Abra smiled, revealing a silver front tooth.

"I don't mind," Galbreath said, shifting his cane from one hand to the other. "Let me look myself, if you will."

"No, sir. I am ashamed but not helpless. I will accommodate you. You would never find them by yourself."

Abra beckoned with a chubby arm. "If you please, sir." He waddled ahead down the dusty hall.

Galbreath followed with his uneven gait, checking the aisles of the antiquated earthen brick building. They passed a secretarial area that was quiet, save the clicking of old typewriters. Galbreath nodded warmly at several black women who busily worked away.

An ancient portrait of King George hung on the wall, off to the side by a mahogany coatrack. Galbreath eyed it pensively, noting it was likely not displayed out of respect for the past, but rather as a curio of early twentieth-century Africa. To think that all of Egypt and the Sudan were once governed under the Union Jack.

Galbreath was fiercely loyal to his country but critical of lingering colonialist attitudes. He considered himself a transitionalist, helping England influence its former African subjects to think favorably of enlightened British policy: England for the English, Africa for the Africans, with the caveat that Africa needed some occasional guidance in the face of anti-Western influences from the Middle East. His posture remained diplomatic rather than overbearing.

Galbreath's liberal leanings ran against the grain of his family and its aristocratic heritage. He was ten when his mother, Lady Barrington, took him to Westminster Abbey. It was there, in St. Edward's Chapel, that he had seen England's most precious relic: the ancient coronation throne, made to hold the historic Stone of Scone dating back to Edward I in 1300. The chair had been used in every coronation of English monarchs since that time. Young William had pictured kings and queens being crowned, wielding British power that influenced the entire world. The massive abbey possessed him, flooding him with its ornate complexities.

His mother had leaned down, parted her veil, and whispered sweetly, "You see that chair, William?"

"Yes, Mummy."

"What does it consist of?" She had smiled that wonderful taciturn smile with those transparent blue eyes.

"Wood, I suppose."

"No longer. It is now *an idea*. As were the ones who sat upon it, symbols of things decent and enduring in this life. You will remember that, won't you?"

He did remember. And believed it. It was not until he came to Africa and learned the existence of other, simpler truths that he rebelled against his own background.

He had examined his past and found it pompous and ridiculous.

In Africa he discovered a reservoir of life. Britain's influence was superfluous. If left to evolve naturally, the native people and the land blended into a pool of harmony. England had been a cultural blight in some instances.

As a member of the foreign office, Galbreath had come to prevent other outside influences: communism, occasionally capitalism, and now Islamic fanaticism from enslaving people.

He had found Eden and regarded its inhabitants with warmth and respect.

Abra pulled on a warped drawer, sliding it from the ancient cabinet. "Let me try here, sir. It will take me but a moment."

Galbreath mused about fate and how it often hinged on a series of accidents. First, his position in life was due to his father, who died in the Second World War. Second, social status gave him wealth and the education it afforded. Naturally, this led to Oxford, where his life would have been entirely different if he had not met Arthur Kensley.

Arthur had been raised in Africa. Arthur's stories and the affection he obviously felt for the continent ultimately caused Galbreath to visit the wilds firsthand.

Two decades later Arthur was crushed under the weight of a dying bull elephant.

"Yes. I think this may be the one." Abra blew the dust off the manila folder. "Baghigra. Doapu Province. You asked about the economic activity of a very small town. At last count, which was eight years ago, there existed three thousand one hundred and eighty-seven people. There is not much to report." The clerk squinted through the spectacles and poked the paper with a meaty finger. "There, sir, on the last page, several certificates of occupancy are noted. Not for ownership, but simply for lease of agricultural farmland."

"Farmland? What year?"

"It was 1974."

"Wasn't that when the great famine began?"

"Yes, sir. The drought of 1973."

"One would think that foodstuffs would have simply been transported. Surely farming near the town would have been futile? Even today, the area is sparsely inhabited and dry."

"That may be, but here—you see?" Abra palmed the page. "A grant from the parliamentary government of Colonel Nimeri, given to an international company of primarily English ownership named Fertile Crescent Limited."

"English?"

"Yes, sir. And, if you will, notice the permit to construct an agricultural research facility."

"I can't read that. What does it say regarding the purpose of the building?"

Abra turned the page. "It mentions a permit to import chemicals from Europe for the purpose of developing fertilizers."

"Wouldn't the native population use organic materials from livestock?"

"You may not remember, sir, but in the early seventies the drought killed thousands of our cattle. The Sudanese government was anxious for the means of increasing productivity of parched land. Cow manure was scarce, since the people ate the livestock during the famine. It says—let me see—in exchange for the land grant, the Fertile Crescent Company was charged with"—Abra pronounced the words with laborious precision—" 'agricultural growth enhancement through chemical additives to be specifically developed for local soil and climatic conditions.' "

He held up the certificates for Galbreath to see.

Galbreath waved them off. "That's fine. But if all that

did transpire, what were the results? Dry grasses and ruins are all that remain in that area."

"I cannot ascertain those answers from these certificates."

Galbreath took the weight off his cane. "The ruins . . . any clue as to what the structure may have been, or why it was destroyed?"

"I only see the final stamp of tax-exempt registration, marked 1985."

"The year the Nimeri regime ceased to function."

"Well done, sir." Abra smiled broadly. "Yes. That is quite correct."

"Good. Now, could you give me just another few moments?"

"I'm at your service," Abra said.

Galbreath pointed into the stacks with his gold-handled walking stick. "Look into your master files and see if you can locate further information on the Fertile Crescent Company. Could you?"

"Had we only known," Abra said, with the silver-toothed smile, "the international business files are near the front desk from where we came." He extended an arm like a maître d' at a restaurant. "This way, good sir."

After twenty minutes of shuffling paper in files near the reception area, Abra located a two-page memo, which he handed to Galbreath.

"Here you are, sir. A rather limited sheet of information on Fertile Crescent Limited. As you see, the Sudanese division of the company was established in 1969."

"You said that was the year the Nimeri regime came to power."

"Yes."

"And that regime was basically a coalition formed by a

group of military officers who rebelled against a previous government."

"You have a remarkable grasp of our history. But as you may know, the government the Nimeri coalition revolted against was also a military one. Our past is marred by power struggles."

"An odd choice, to do business in such unstable conditions," Galbreath said, wiping his brow with a white-laced handkerchief. "There must have been other options for that company . . . other locations for agricultural endeavor."

Abra seemed to have anticipated this comment and waved more papers in front of Galbreath. "According to this brief, the firm had other African enterprises. A note is made of former business enterprises in Kenya and Tanzania in the late 1960s."

"Really? Does it mention the owners of the firm?"

Abra began to leaf through the paperwork once more, fingering the pages as he went. "I believe that is mandatory on a foreign business license. Let me see . . . yes . . . there it is." He stabbed the parched paper with a stubby finger. Galbreath attempted to see the scribbling on the page, but Abra had already pulled it away and held it to the light of the cross-hatched window above the desk. "International holdings are indicated."

"International? You mean ownership by citizens of various countries?"

"Yes. But due to our former British affiliation, the documents merely required proof of English ownership, which came to pass in 1969. The names are . . ." Abra hoisted the glasses up on the bridge of his nose, straining to make out faded writing. "Two gentlemen: John Blythe-Taggert and Wesley Cunningham. Yes. Those are the names."

"Good God. How odd."

"What is it? Are these men familiar to you?"

Galbreath remembered the occasions he had seen the names in the *London Times*. "Yes, by reputation. Both those men are currently senior members of the House of Lords."

Was English nobility somehow connected to an abhorrent attack on the citizens of a Sudanese village?

Galbreath carefully considered the implications.

THE FIFTH DAY
12:28 P.M.
Atlanta

"Just a few more minutes," Captain Burwell said as he opened the door and peered in.

"It's been two hours," Devin said. He tossed the magazine he was reading on the coffee table and stood up.

Ginelle watched from her seat in the sparsely furnished waiting room.

"They know you're here," Captain Burwell said matter-of-factly.

Devin was angered by what seemed to be the young captain's cynical tone. "Who the hell is 'they'? We just want to see Dr. Gordon."

"As you can imagine, sir, the control center has many priorities at this time. Now, if you'll just sit down."

Just then a Chinese-American woman in her thirties dressed in a white smock appeared behind the captain and tapped him on the shoulder. He stepped out of her way.

"Dr. Chang, excuse me," Burwell said, politely allowing her to enter the room. She was pleasant looking, graceful, exuding a natural charm.

"Mr. Parks, I apologize for the delay. I'm Stella Chang. I'm currently assisting Dr. Gordon."

Ginelle rose, smiling.

Devin extended a hand. "Well, now we're getting somewhere. Where *is* Dr. Gordon?"

172

"In a meeting, I'm afraid, for just a few more moments. We realize you've had a long wait. I'll take you to him by way of the main floor of the facility. It might be interesting for you." She put her hands together in front of her chest, seemingly pleased with her suggestion.

"I'd find that informative." Ginelle smiled, stepped forward, and shook Chang's hand.

Devin interpreted her warmth as an indication that she related kindly to a fellow scientist.

"Nice to meet you," Chang said, "Ms. Klein, is it?"

Ginelle nodded, seemingly reluctant to acknowledge her false identity.

Chang turned back to Devin and smiled. "I must say, it appears both of you are considered rather special. If you didn't have friends in very high places, you wouldn't have had access to us at this rather critical time."

"What friends?" Devin asked.

Chang ignored the question and gestured to the hallway. "Shall we go?" she said.

Devin silently wondered if Freeman's call to Williamson hadn't been effective after all.

Ginelle led the way out the door onto a metal grated platform, leaving Captain Burwell behind at the door, gazing after them.

"Dr. Gordon is meeting with Jonathan Swain, the president's national security adviser," Chang said as she took the lead. "Since we have time, I'll show you the heart of the crisis center. This way, please."

As she walked ahead of them the clanging of her heels on the metal plates drew Devin's eyes down to her legs. They were compact and muscular.

Dr. Chang led them along the steel-railed platform, which ringed a very active work area beneath.

As they reached the top of the grated stairs, Devin took Ginelle's hand to help her down, but she pulled it away.

They descended the stairwell into a large U-shaped pit, about a hundred and twenty feet in diameter, where several dozen technicians in light blue smocks sat in gray, leather-padded cubicles, working on computers.

They reached the first landing and started down to the second flight of stairs as Dr. Chang looked back and spoke over the noise in the room. "The platform below is known to our staff members as the Flashpoint, the hub of the crisis building of the Disease Control Center. It's fortified like a military installation."

"I noticed," Devin said. He looked around and noted the guards from various service branches stationed at the entrances to the large chamber.

"Even though we take our orders from the Pentagon in a chemical-warfare crisis, when it comes to a war with an infectious disease, this is still the tactical command post," Chang explained as they reached the bottom level, their shoes clanking on the metal stairs.

"Why so much glass?" Ginelle asked as they began to walk across the platform.

"In case of computer or electrical failure, the designers felt that visual contact among personnel would be advisable."

Chang led them across the Flashpoint deck to the other side of the large U and one of the computer bays, operated by a pretty, dark-haired woman, also wearing a light blue smock. Her lustrous eyes shone from behind pearl-trimmed glasses.

"This is Alisa Avery, Mr. Parks. She's our head statistician. Alisa, meet Devin Parks and Amy Klein from CNB. They're here on official business."

"Good afternoon," Alisa said from her seat.

"You might as well explain the status of the current crisis," Chang told her, picking up a computer readout.

"We're currently assimilating as much information as

we can to read the progress on the flash fire," Alisa said, crossing her legs.

Devin smiled at Alisa and stepped forward, focusing on the brightly lit computer screen, on which a column of statistics slowly scrolled upward.

Alisa turned back to the computer and pointed. "What you're seeing here are the confirmed number of cases caused by UD number seven. Unknown or unclassified diseases are coded yearly in the order of their appearance."

"There have been seven this year?" Ginelle asked, apparently shocked.

"Oh yes. They're happening more and more frequently all the time. Of course, most aren't deadly. They simply disappear into the population pool in a matter or days or weeks without further damage."

"Do you analyze each one?" Devin asked.

"If we can. We have to isolate them in test vials, develop cultures, and classify them. Unfortunately, some mutate quickly, so classification becomes impossible. If they're viruses, they're particularly problematic. Viruses are frequently quite changeable—as opposed to this killer."

"This one's consistent?" Devin asked.

"Yes. Early analysis shows a holding profile."

"What do those numbers on the screen represent?" Ginelle asked, moving closer.

Devin watched columns forming in codes: 34-6-17-5-01, 34-3-9-2-02. . . .

"We've assigned census codes to keep logs on patient conditions around the country," Alisa said. "The first number represents a state—one through fifty, obviously. The second represents a county within the state. The third represents a case name in the order in which it was reported. The final number indicates a medical facility or hospital where the patient is housed. So, forty-seven-nine-eighteen-seven-oh-one would be—here, let me punch that up—the state of Idaho, Clark County, the eighteenth case reported, in Kellogg General Hospital."

"You're missing a number. What's the last one?" Ginelle asked.

"Oh. That's either one or two. One for a male, two for a female. The zero in front of the number indicates the patient is deceased."

"Punch up the updated frequency grid," Dr. Chang said, looking over.

Alisa's fingers danced on the computer keyboard. She brought up the enlarged screen with a steel blue map of the continental United States. A red dot pattern appeared. "This is the end of day one. Dr. Gordon commented that the early infection pattern looked like a nuclear strike."

"Virtually every state," Devin said, noting the red dots scattered throughout the country.

"Now watch day two, day three, and day four." The dots grouped and blended so that in some areas a solid pattern of red emerged. "Over seventy-seven thousand cases projected by tomorrow," Alisa said, adjusting her glasses.

"Seventy-seven thousand dead?" Devin asked.

"No, potentially infected," Alisa said.

"We never anticipated this type of pattern," Dr. Chang said. "Our sixteen flash-fire teams went to over fifty different concentrations. And from what we can tell, primary victims in each location were children."

"Don't you find that strange?" Ginelle asked.

"Yes," Chang replied. "Propensity for certain diseases isn't unusual for the young, but the oddity here is that adults were also secondarily infected by UD number seven in a matter of days. That's usually not the case. Age barriers normally hold for longer periods during the life cycle of an organism."

"Any idea how these children contracted number seven?" Ginelle asked.

Devin watched her carefully. He found himself admiring her intensity.

"Not yet. That's still a mystery," Chang responded.

"Any pattern of similarity?" Ginelle asked.

"Difficult to establish, since so much information was based on parent testimonials, usually emotionally charged and impressionistic. The consistent aspect is age, of course, between seven and nine years, and the fact that many of them were baseball-team members . . . since it's springtime, I suppose."

"Baseball?" Devin asked, remembering Amy's comment about Gordi's mitt on the porch. "Even girls?"

"You have that kind of detailed information?" Ginelle asked.

"Flash-fire teams ask surviving family members a flood of questions, just in case similarities surface," Chang replied. "And yes, Mr. Parks. Some of our little baseball players were girls. Although we have an eight-to-one ratio of boys. These restrictions disappear in secondary infection groups, only occurring in the initial hundred cases or so."

"I don't get that," Devin said.

"If you did, we'd want a full explanation," Chang said, giving him an oblique glance. "In any case"—she pointed at the map—"the concentration of initial cases indicates artificial contamination. We're convinced it's a conspiracy."

"By whom?" Devin looked back up at the screen.

Chang smiled accommodatingly. "That's the burning question," she said, trading looks with both of them.

Ginelle's attention was now riveted. "Is there confirmed evidence of conspirators?" she asked.

"I'm not aware of concrete proof," Chang said. "But

the restricted target area, namely the continental United States, suggests deliberate implantation."

At that moment a red light flashed on the panel over the computer screen. A man's voice spoke over the intercom.

"Dr. Chang, please report to the briefing room."

"That's us," Chang said, looking from Devin to Ginelle. "I told you it wouldn't be long."

Dr. Chang showed Devin and Ginelle across the Flashpoint to a long ramp, decked in red carpet. They walked past a series of glass-enclosed offices toward the other end of the pavilion, turning left through a set of heavy metal doors that opened into a large conference room. The heavy gray drapes—for soundproofing—along the glass window and recessed overhead lighting gave the room a serene, if weighty, atmosphere.

Three men sat in three of the eight dark blue chairs on the other side of the long oak table.

When Devin and Ginelle entered, Chang excused herself.

The huge black-haired man in the white smock at the middle of the table gestured to two of the chairs on the opposite side.

"Sit there, both of you."

It was a cold greeting, in contrast to Dr. Chang's hospitality, but Devin remained cordial. "Nice to meet you," he said as he and Ginelle took their seats.

"Parks, I'm Samuel Gordon," the big man said. "I'd like to begin by making my views clear. Your presence here is an imposition on our time." He shuffled the files on his desk. His hands were strong and gnarled like the branches of an ancient tree, the hands of a feisty-looking man in his mid-fifties. Gordon looked over at the man in the army uniform. "You've apparently fascinated Colonel Williamson. He flew here in the last two hours to join me in my meeting with Mr. Swain." Gordon nodded to the blond-haired third man, who wore a charcoal suit.

Colonel Williamson, dressed in army uniform, had salt-and-pepper hair and a lean, angular face. He eyed Ginelle with intense interest, which Devin interpreted as something more than the fascination Gordon had alluded to.

Gordon seemed to notice Devin's drifting glances and regained his attention by raising his voice. "You're a disruption to all of us. I warn you. If you two prove to be no more than reporters looking for leads, you will pay for it, I can promise you."

Devin's gaze met the doctor's. "You seem convinced enough to put up with us," he said. "I don't think it'll be a waste of your time." He noticed that the bulk of Gordon's weight appeared to hover around his rib cage.

"We'll see." Gordon coughed several times. "That short tour you got . . . that was my idea. I wanted you to see the havoc caused by this microbe before we had this little chat. Now you realize you're in a war zone. So I'm sure you won't mind if we ask whether the two of you are friend or foe."

"That's a strange thing to say," Devin said, perplexed.

Gordon pushed back from the table in the swivel chair and crossed his arms. "Not from my perspective. What's this nonsense about you knowing the whereabouts of Dr. Hendrix?"

The bags under Gordon's eyes revealed the depth of his fatigue, though he wore his exhaustion well. Devin assumed he had probably not slept since the crisis began.

"I didn't say I knew *where* Dr. Hendrix was," Devin said. He searched Williamson's face for support and found nothing but bullish stubbornness.

The colonel glared at Devin. "So, just exactly what are you saying?"

"Let's say I've made contact."

"Oh, you're clairvoyant," Gordon said sarcastically. "Have you seen him or not?"

"I spoke to him—by phone." Devin crossed his arms, trying not to act defensive.

"In the last two days?" Gordon's eyebrows rose. He sat up straight in the dark blue leather chair.

"Yes," Devin replied, "just before all hell broke loose."

"Why would he call someone like you?" Gordon's impatience was understandable, but his rudeness disturbed Devin nonetheless.

"He told me he had a cure for the disease."

"Really? Don't you think that's odd coming from the scientist who's accused of starting the whole thing?" These were Swain's first words. They were delivered bitterly and in a Southern drawl.

Devin couldn't help looking at Ginelle. Her eyes flared at the remark. She sat forward in her chair, cleared her throat, but Devin jumped in.

"What makes you think he's the one?" he asked quickly. "No one's pressed charges, have they?"

"I told you this was a war zone," Gordon said. "You saw what's going on out there." He made a sweeping motion with a thick hand. "No time for such matters in the face of a national panic."

Swain adjusted the pinkie ring on his left hand and looked directly at Ginelle. "We're led to believe Hendrix is the ringleader of a conspiracy against the sovereignty of this country."

"Who says so?" Ginelle responded angrily.

All three men focused their gazes on her.

Gordon held papers in a muscular fist. "Documents exist, Ms. Klein. Condemning evidence proving that

Hendrix was the instigator of the disease presently killing tens of thousands of people."

"That's a lie," Ginelle snapped. "There were others involved."

Devin felt the heat in the room, some of it under his collar.

Williamson pointed to the files in Gordon's hands. "All of Hendrix's colleagues are dead."

"How do you know Hendrix isn't dead as well?" Ginelle's voice cracked with the remark, and Devin attempted to cover for her.

"Amy is of the strong opinion that Dr. Hendrix was a victim . . . like the other researchers."

"CIA files from the eighties show Hendrix to be a highly paid chemical-warfare researcher, who left a classified project under false pretenses, unlike his associates. We have reason to believe he consorted with the enemy," Swain said, with the acidity of a prosecuting attorney.

Ginelle covered her mouth with her right hand and stared at the floor.

"Which enemy would that be, Mr. Swain? Some congressional special-interest group?" Devin asked.

"Unlikely," Swain answered dryly, "considering the evidence we have in our possession. Hendrix was in touch with a foreign power."

"That's fabricated bullshit."

"It's a matter of record with the CIA. And I object to your tone, Mr. Parks."

Devin glared at him, but didn't reply.

Swain directed his attention to Ginelle. "Ms. Klein, you seem distressed. Are you all right?"

"Perfectly," she said, although she was visibly upset.

"You don't look it." Gordon picked up one of the files and walked around the end of the conference table. "As a matter of fact, you don't look like yourself at all." He pulled a color fax out of the file folder and laid it in front of them. Amy Klein's portfolio photograph.

"Good God," Devin said. "What is this?"

Gordon sat down on the corner of the table, crumpled the fax, and flipped it at Devin, who caught it in midair. "A war zone, Mr. Parks, complete with reconnaissance reports and an intelligence branch. Did you really think we would be unprepared for you?"

Devin pointed at the fax. "Why the charade? How did you know?"

Gordon deferred to Swain.

"As I'm sure you can understand," the security adviser said, "CIA personnel were intensely interested in Ginelle Hendrix, due to her father's involvement in the epidemic. So Langley had a follow-up team in Richmond almost immediately. A cross-check of dental records from an unknown corpse in Ginelle Hendrix's apartment made things more fascinating. Then your boss, Frank Freeman, calls Williamson with this vaccine story, and you, Mr. Parks, show up on our doorstep with a woman whom our computer data shows is deceased. That's when we decided to keep you around. Williamson flew in just minutes ago."

"It's a bit out of my line," Williamson said, "but the joint chiefs are grasping for anything that points to the origin of the attack. They wanted me to follow up on this . . . and make sure your involvement isn't a scam." The three men watched them expectantly from across the table.

Devin remembered the adage that the guy who talks first loses. He kept quiet.

A silent pall hung in the room. "Are you going to arrest me?" Ginelle finally asked softly.

Swain unbuttoned his double-breasted jacket, leaned forward in his chair. He extended a hand. "Not until we've been properly introduced. May I call you Ginelle, Ms. Hendrix?"

Ginelle looked helpless, ignored Swain, and turned to Devin.

Devin felt compelled to speak. "I think Ginelle would prefer an attorney be present." He hooked his thumbs in his belt.

"This is no time for legalistic maneuvering," Gordon said angrily. He paced back and forth behind them. "Thousands of human beings are dying out there. If you people know something, you better spit it out. Ms. Hendrix, your father is about to become the subject of a national lynching. Now let's have it. What's going on?"

"We don't know," Devin said.

"I want to hear it from her!" Gordon trumpeted, hovering over Ginelle.

Devin felt protective of Ginelle. "Don't badger her, damn you. We came here to help!" He leaned over and put his hand on Ginelle's forearm. She didn't pull away.

"Help? Assuming the identity of a dead woman? That's a sham," Gordon said. "We've had enough deceit, don't you think?"

"Under the circumstances, she naturally feels insecure. What's with the judgmental bullshit?" Devin suddenly realized he was shouting. He paused, breathing hard. The awkward silence made him feel like a quarterback who had just fumbled the ball. "Okay," he said, "excuse me. Let's all calm down and talk." He shot Ginelle a supportive smile. "You better tell them what you know."

Gordon lumbered back to his seat and listened intently as Ginelle recapped her story: her father's phone call, Devin and Amy's subsequent involvement, Amy's death, the arrival of intruders at her apartment.

She also went into her more distant past, and it became apparent she knew little more about Black Diamond than

Swain. She could only remember the identity of the principal researchers, the location of their laboratories in New Mexico, and . . . the manufacture of potentially lethal biochemical attack weapons.

When everyone in the room had witnessed her paucity of information, Devin intervened, questioning Swain's similar lack of knowledge regarding a government-funded program. Swain replied that democratic systems weren't perfect. Agencies had rights to withhold facts from one another, and from the executive branch as well.

Concerning her father's alleged guilt, Ginelle tearfully asserted that Hendrix had been killed or kidnapped.

Williamson suggested that the scientist's disappearance could also mean he was in hiding, to avoid being implicated in the biggest sneak attack since Pearl Harbor.

Devin assessed Williamson carefully. Despite being Freeman's old friend, the colonel's attitude seemed only remotely supportive of Devin and Ginelle. Devin attributed his halfheartedness to the weight of his present responsibility.

"Look," Devin said, unable to tolerate Ginelle being grilled further. "She's had enough. Let's address factors that suggest Hendrix's innocence. For example, if he did develop a vaccine, wouldn't that prove that Ginelle's account is accurate? I mean why would the perpetrator of a plague give anyone the cure?"

"All right. Since you brought it up," Gordon said, rising from his chair. "We've had a team check your lab at Commonwealth University. Your colleagues know nothing, and we couldn't make heads or tails of any of your other work."

"I had nothing to do with it," Ginelle asserted.

"I don't believe you," Gordon said. "The vaccine. Where the hell is it?"

Devin pictured himself in a contestant's booth of a

game show. The bonus question had just been asked. "It's running in my veins," he said tentatively. "And hers. That's all we had."

"There must be more," Gordon bellowed.

"There was, but it was in my father's possession when he disappeared."

"You're a biochemist, Ms. Hendrix. Surely he shared the formula with you," Gordon said.

"I'm a viral researcher, not a microbe programmer," she replied. "The exact replicator quotients were too intricate."

"But couldn't you duplicate it with some additional work?" Swain said.

"I don't have sufficient background."

"Then let's find someone who does," Swain concluded. "Pharmaceutical firms are working on a cure as we speak. Perhaps you should help them."

"Please understand me," Ginelle said weakly. "I'm not in any position to reformulate the microbe."

"You mean you refuse," Gordon said, bitterly.

"No, I mean I can't."

"Can't you extract it from the bloodstream for analysis?" Swain asked.

"No," Gordon said. "Correct me, Ms. Hendrix— excuse me, I suppose I should address you as doctor— don't you agree that once settled in the blood, critical elements of antigens are altered when absorbed by white blood corpuscles? Finding it and isolating it at this stage would be impossible."

Ginelle nodded. "Particularly after thirty-six hours."

Both sides of the table fell silent.

The interrogators finally seemed to have no more questions. Devin interpreted this as a mute acceptance of Ginelle's credibility. He felt it was time to end this meeting.

"Don't you see?" He looked from one face to the other. "If you're discussing Ginelle's potential ability to duplicate a vaccine, you've already accepted the fact that it existed. Amy's body proves that she was infected. My being here in one piece proves that the vaccine works, *and* that Dr. Thomas Hendrix produced it. Otherwise I'd be dead." He looked at Dr. Gordon. "Am I right?"

Gordon's eyebrows knitted. "I suppose you have something there."

"Then I'm asking you—please, let us go. We've told you all we know. We're of no further use to you."

"Shouldn't you keep them for observation, Gordon? They're carrying the vaccine," Swain said.

"If they are, there won't be any visible manifestations in the system. Flu-shot recipients show no traces once the body absorbs the antigen. This wouldn't be any different."

Devin saw an opening. "Well, regardless of her father's guilt or innocence, there's no reason to detain Ginelle, is there?" The three men glanced at one another. Devin shrugged. "Then she's free to come with me." He turned to her. "What do you think, Ginelle?"

She gazed at him.

Devin thought he discerned a spark of warmth in her eyes.

"We can't just let you walk the streets, Parks," Williamson said. He appeared suddenly paternal. "What if the assassins return?"

"Keep watch on Ginelle's apartment," Devin suggested.

"I think we'll keep a tail on you as well," Williamson responded. "You're right. Capturing one of her assailants might lead us to the conspirators. Beyond that, I'm sure both of you would appreciate the protection. Swain, don't you agree?"

"I'll have FBI people assigned to you," Swain said.

"We don't need excess baggage," Devin said, distrustful of interference.

"I'm addressing Dr. Hendrix, if you don't mind," Swain said coldly. "Don't interpret our offer of cooperation as acceptance of your story, Dr. Hendrix. Consider it precautionary protection against the conspirators *and* against an angry American public demanding revenge on your father. And don't underestimate mob behavior. I'd be careful if I were you. Even if you *are* immune to the disease, you might die at the hands of the people. Be clear about this. We're offering you protective custody, right here and now, if you wish."

She looked from face to face, then settled on Devin's. "I have no family except for my father. If they're looking for me, I don't want to lead them to my friends. Besides, I can't help my father if I stay here." A tear formed under her left eye. She glanced at all three men. "I'll go with Devin."

"Your choice," Williamson said. "But in the national interest, we may have to maintain surveillance of you as best we can manage it. And for your information, Amy Klein's body has been removed from your apartment and laid to rest in a morgue as a Jane Doe, at least temporarily."

"Can't I at least notify her father?" Devin asked.

"Not yet. Leave that to us," Williamson said, then turned to Ginelle. "And considering the state of affairs, Dr. Hendrix, for the time being, I think it's advisable you maintain your false identity."

THE EIGHTH DAY
6:00 P.M.
CNB studios, San Francisco

Freeman, Devin, and Ginelle were the sole occupants of the green room, an area reserved for special on-air guests. Caricatures of guest celebrities hung neatly along the emerald velvet walls. The atmosphere was tense.

"I think you're going too far, Devin." Freeman pulled up on his suspenders, straightening his shirt. His belly held the garment taut around his middle, but the cloth tended to bunch at the shoulders. He turned and faced Ginelle. "Surely *you* understand."

"I'm not sure at this point." Ginelle put the coffee cup down and ran a slender hand through her blond hair.

Devin threw her a reassuring glance. "They've prepped the studio. The script is finished. Why stop now?"

Freeman shifted his massive weight. "Because I hadn't checked the TelePrompTer copy," he said sternly, taking two steps back, folding his arms as he leaned against the opposite wall. Like the rest of the world, he was in a controlled panic in the face of the continued epidemic. The beaded perspiration on his forehead confirmed the stress.

Freeman's opposition seemed unfair to Devin. "I outlined my plans," he said. He turned to the makeup mirror, checking to make sure the two blue towels shielding his shirt were still properly tucked into his collar.

"Yes. But your material goes beyond editorial jour-

nalism." Freeman pointed a finger. "If Hendrix is innocent, you're baiting unknown felons and conspirators.
And you'll have Washington all over me."

That was a new twist. Devin suddenly became skeptical, turned to Freeman and searched for deceit in his
face. "What does Washington have to do with it?"

"Senator Kemper called me this morning."

"Who's Kemper?" Ginelle sat on the velvet couch.
She looked striking in a beige blouse and a maroon skirt.

"He's a presidential hopeful in the next election, currently chairman of the Armed Services Committee,"
Devin said. "A big gun."

Freeman nodded to her. "He's a bigger gun now. As of
yesterday, he's spearheading a congressional investigation on the disease conspiracy. Dr. Thomas Hendrix is
number one on the docket."

Ginelle's face dropped at the mention of her father's name.

"Why would he call you?" Devin asked suspiciously.

"My guess is, someone leaked the fact that through
you, our network is in the loop on the Hendrix issue."

"A leak? What do you know about that?" Devin asked.

"Me? Nothing. It must be someone you met with in
Atlanta." Freeman seemed oddly conciliatory.

"Like Williamson?"

"Could be. He and Kemper work closely together."

"Oh, great," Devin said.

"Now don't get upset."

"What a good friend you have there." Devin's sarcasm
touched a nerve.

"I'll call Williamson and ask," Freeman snapped.

Devin paced the floor in front of the dressing table.
"What difference does it make? If Williamson knows, the
cabinet knows. I don't care if the president knows. I'm
going on."

"Maybe before you stick your neck out, I should call Kemper and go before the Senate investigating committee," Ginelle interjected, picking up a green coffee cup.

Devin looked at her and shook his head. "We're not ready for that."

"Your editorial will put you in a fishbowl." Freeman stepped forward. "Anyone can take potshots at you."

"That's the idea. You wanted an exclusive. You've got one. And we're going to make the most of it."

"I'm against it," Freeman said.

With Ginelle's eyes on his back, Devin felt his adrenaline flowing. He went nose to nose with Freeman. "I don't understand. First you taunted me. Talked about me being my old self. Here I am, taking an aggressive tack to find Ginelle's father, and you want to snuff it?"

Freeman appeared momentarily set back.

Devin glanced at Ginelle. Her green eyes softened with apparent confusion.

Devin stayed in Freeman's face. "There's no real evidence. Just those old lab photos showing him with the monkeys."

"I've seen them," Freeman said, disgusted.

"And who leaked those?" Devin asked. "Ginelle doesn't know. Somebody's manipulating this whole thing. And I want to flush that *somebody* out into the open. You agree with that?" He punctuated his final question with a finger on his boss's chest.

Freeman relented, stepping aside. Mulling over the options, he straightened a drawing of Billy Crystal on the adjacent wall.

Once again, Devin could feel Ginelle's eyes on him. "Mr. Freeman may be right," she said. "Perhaps we should let Washington do its job."

Hell. Last night on the plane she had agreed to the editorial. Perhaps Freeman's news about Kemper had unnerved her. Ginelle avoided Devin's glare and took a sip of her coffee.

Devin turned to Freeman, deciding to confront one obstacle at a time. "This journalistic propriety of yours. I don't get it. You wanted me focused . . . well, I am. You stop me from going on the air . . . *you'll* be the guy who's lost focus."

Freeman's eyes narrowed; the determination in Devin's voice had apparently affected him. "What about Washington?" He nodded toward Ginelle. She seemed reluctant to answer.

"They know less than we do," Devin said. "Their focus is on capturing conspirators. That's their priority. Our focus is on finding Hendrix. That's our story."

Freeman shook his head. "I just didn't envision you getting reckless, Devin. We report the news. We don't create it."

"Well, goddammit. Make this an exception." Devin walked over behind the couch and grasped Ginelle's shoulder. "Don't tell me CNN or any other network wouldn't be itching to use Ginelle as an angle."

He hadn't intended to imply that he would take the story elsewhere, but once he said it, he felt good. Blood pulsed up the side of his neck. He kept the momentum going. "You said this might be the hottest story of the century. Well, they're ready for me on the set, and I want to do the broadcast."

Freeman's belly heaved with a pensive sigh. He bit his lower lip and hooked his thumbs in his suspenders, looking back and forth from Devin to Ginelle. Then his gaze settled on Devin.

Slowly, a smile rippled across his black face, and he nodded. "I'll be a son-of-a-bitch," he said. "I haven't seen that fire in your eyes since you came to work here. You *are* back."

Devin was amazed at his change of tone. "Frank—"

"You're on." Freeman pointed a thick finger, turned, put a hand on the brass doorknob. "I'll be in the booth." With that, he left.

Now able to concentrate on his upcoming editorial, Devin gave Ginelle a cautious smile as he walked back to the makeup table. Checking himself over, he noticed that his face was thinner; he had lost a few pounds.

He picked up a tortoiseshell brush and smoothed his hair, looking at Ginelle in the mirror. "Do I have your support?" he asked.

"Yes. I suppose you do."

He spun around and faced her. "No supposing," he said, shaking his head. "The injection you gave me the other day . . . you said you needed *my* complete consent. This is a different kind of shot, a shot in the dark. And I need *your* complete consent."

"That was a medical issue." She crossed her legs.

It was the first time he had seen her in heels. He noted the smooth tightness of the black nylon over a tan knee cap.

"The situation is analogous," he said, turning back to the mirror. "We're going on this ride together. I want you on board all the way." He ran the brush through his hair again, waiting for her response. She gave none. Ignoring the silence, he straightened his tie, careful not to loosen the blue paper makeup towels sticking out of his white collar.

"I *am* on board," she said softly. "I just want to be cautious."

He blew face powder from the lapel of his charcoal-gray suit and walked over to her. "My editorial may not shake anything out of the branches, Ginelle. But the rest of the news is slandering your father. We've got to try and change that."

"But we're legally powerless. I still feel I should go to the investigating committee, convince them Dad is innocent."

Devin considered the brutal photographs of Hendrix in the papers. "Who's going to believe you with those pictures on the street?"

Her green eyes hardened. "They believed me in Atlanta."

"Gordon did. We can't be sure about Williamson, now that he's hobnobbing with Kemper and other senators. Swain? Who knows. They're on a witch-hunt." He put a finger to his chest. "I'm the one who wants to save your dad."

"And I suppose if you succeed, it certainly won't hurt in attaining your ultimate goal."

"My what?"

"Well, you obviously have Freeman's attention."

"Is that it? You think I'm just using you to get a lead story?"

"The hottest story of the century, in your words."

"All right. I admit it. It's my opportunity." He sat down beside her. "But that's not what's driving me."

"Something is." She edged away.

He couldn't believe the strength of the feelings he had for this woman, whom he'd known for only a few days. He searched his thoughts for the right words. "The way we met . . ." He leaned closer to her. "If this were a different time, other things would seem more important. . . ."

She quickly rose and left him leaning on the arm of the couch. "There's only one thing that's important to me."

I've driven her back into her fortress, he thought, standing up. "Ginelle, please don't misunderstand. . . ."

She walked away. "There's no misunderstanding. My first objective is to find my father."

"And that's what we'll do."

She reached the makeup table, fussed with the brush, looked back at him. "I appreciate your help, but I'm not completely helpless, you know."

"Forgive me, I'm pushing you." Things were moving too fast. "I guess part of it . . . I want to express my gratitude to you . . . for saving my life."

"Then I'll accept your help on that basis." Her green eyes cooled. "No other expectations."

The awkward silence was broken by a knock at the green-room door. Devin went over, shielding Ginelle from sight and looked out. Tony Cavello, his frizzy-haired on-line producer, stood chewing gum in the hallway.

"Excuse me," Tony said. "They're ready."

"Give me a couple of minutes, Tony," Devin said, perplexed.

Tony tapped his wristwatch. "I would, but you've got just three minutes."

"I thought I'd have a ten-minute call."

Tony shrugged. "The feed from L.A. ran short."

"All right." Holding the door shut, Devin stepped back in and gave Ginelle an apologetic look.

"That's all right, Devin," she said. "Let's get on with it."

"I just wanted to tell you—"

"Let it be. I think I know." Did she? How could she really? "I'll wait here," she said. She had to. Freeman insisted that her presence at the studio be discreet. She had been signed in under a false name at the back gate.

Devin leaned over the dresser and flicked on the green-room TV monitor. On screen, Brook Hanford, the acting on-air anchor in L.A., was wrapping up. Devin turned to her and tried to wipe the slate clean. "Watch my smoke."

She smiled, seemed to understand his resolve.

He launched himself into the hallway toward Studio A.

"Why is Hanford's feed finishing early?" Devin asked, hustling along behind Tony, aware of the death symbols on the producer's Grateful Dead sweatshirt. In light of the current state of affairs, they had taken on a whole new, and rather unseemly, meaning.

"Control says he's feeling sick," Tony said, chewing gum.

From working with Tony, Devin had acquired an appreciation of his honesty. "Who? Hanford? You don't think—"

"Hey, man, nowadays, who knows?"

With a national case count of over ninety-six thousand, the grim truth had come home to CNB. The network had twenty-three dying employees.

The corridor opened into the expanse of Studio A. Three silver cameras with operators clad in headphones sat under the lights, ready for the shoot.

Jack Tade, a slender floor director dressed in a bright orange shirt and jeans, shifted sheets of paper on his clipboard, motioned to Devin frantically. "Two minutes, Devin, hustle!"

Doris, the heavyset makeup woman, waited for Devin under the lights, powder puff in hand, anticipating a final dusting of his face.

"Jack will count you down," Tony shouted as he peeled off toward the stairs leading to the control booth overlooking the floor.

Devin scurried toward the red-carpeted risers on center stage, where Doris and a single tan leather armchair waited for him in a halo of light.

Suddenly Dan Canon, the science editor, stepped out

from behind one of the baffles and hurried after Devin. As usual, he looked pasty-faced, with a white shirt and narrow black tie; a narrow tie to match a narrow mind, Devin thought.

"I need to talk to you," Canon said.

"Dan. I'm on in one minute." Devin brushed him aside, knowing full well Canon would feel slighted about the Bellingham story.

"What's the source of your information?" Dan asked.

"What?"

"Where are you getting your facts?"

Devin felt no particular compulsion to share anything with the science editor. Dan had shown disdain for Devin on many occasions. "Just watch my editorial, Dan."

Canon would not be put off. "What happened to Amy?"

"Later." Devin couldn't tell him without compromising everything.

"Who's the woman with you?"

"Did you see her?"

"Not yet. But they say she's beautiful."

"I'm sure she'd be delighted to hear that," Devin said. "Now please . . ."

Devin approached the platform. A sound technician crowded in, snapping a LAV microphone on Devin's lapel.

Canon was pushed aside in the confusion.

"How ya doin', Doris?" Devin asked casually. The makeup woman moved in front of him as he sat down in the tan leather chair.

Canon was back, peeking over her shoulder.

"Hold still." Doris grabbed Devin by the chin. He smelled the cinnamon mint on her breath as she dabbed fresh powder on his forehead.

Canon weaseled his way past Doris's elbow. "Who is she, Devin?"

"Just a minute." Devin ignored him and pushed Doris's hand aside. "Sound test. One, two, can you hear me up there, Tony?"

"Loud and clear." Tony's voice rang out from speakers mounted above the overhead lighting grid.

Doris went back to work on him with Canon edging in.

"I have a suggestion," Canon said. The studio lighting glared off his horn-rim glasses. He crouched on one knee, next to Devin's arm.

Devin felt suffocated by the bodies on the set. "Frank? Frank! Tony, is Freeman up there with you?"

Freeman's unmistakable voice boomed from the booth. "Here, Devin."

"You're dry. You look fine." Doris gave a last dab to his nose.

Devin brushed her hand away. "Frank, get Canon out of here, will you?"

Doris finished under his chin, removed the blue paper towels, and waddled off beyond the cameras.

"Step off the set, Dan." Freeman's voice had a familiar impatient ring to it.

Canon looked up into the lights, gave a sheepish wave, and moved off into the darkness.

Jack Tade stepped out next to Camera One. "Five seconds. On my mark."

Devin looked off the set into the monitor, where freckle-faced Brook Hanford stood on an outdoor location, capping his report.

". . . and so, the search for a cure continues. Recent signs of hope come this morning from several pharmaceutical companies around the country, all of which are working twenty-four hours a day. Among these, Alcor Petrochemical in Houston, EDI Industries of Harrisburg,

Pennsylvania, and Maxillar Chemical Corporation in Cleveland claim to have made some progress in formulating a vaccine. Meanwhile speculation continues as to the origins of the plague."

Devin took note of the mention of the vaccine, wondering how close any of these companies could possibly be to Hendrix's formula.

Hanford was closing. "In a special editorial, here is Devin Parks, from CNB studios in San Francisco, with thoughts about the future and observations about the . . ."

As he finished his introduction Devin looked up under the lights.

The floor director had yelled for quiet and gave him the countdown. In the darkness next to the camera, Devin saw Tade's right hand forming a five, a four, three, two, and then an index finger pointing right at Devin's face.

The red light on top of Camera One lit up, and Devin was on . . . live, to the nation and the world.

The words A CNB EDITORIAL flashed on the lower portion of the on-air screen.

Devin looked straight to camera and spoke.

"Those of you watching me have all shared in the tragedy of the last week. Like others, I believe this is a war . . . a war as devastating as any other, and even more disastrous because it is taking place on our sovereign soil."

Devin was fully aware that up in the editing booth, Tony was manipulating the switchboard, pushing keys on the computer.

As Devin continued, scenes of UD#7 victims flashed on a screen superimposed next to his face. Battered bodies of infected children around the country, like the Collins girl in Macon, appeared.

In each shot, a "before" picture from school files was

followed by an "after" version of each child's face, blackened by infection.

"This is the face of America today." Devin referred to the photographs. "It's an ugly face. A terrible face. A face scarred by plague. And I'm not referring just to the unknown disease. In our nation, there's an even more despicable malady behind the epidemic . . . the sickness of the people who caused it." A picture of Dr. Hendrix appeared next to Devin. "It's commonly believed that this man, Dr. Thomas Hendrix, whose whereabouts are unknown, was the responsible party. You may have heard of his research on a project called Black Diamond in New Mexico some years ago. And you've undoubtedly seen the newspaper photographs and heard broadcasts stating that he's being sought for this crime."

Pictures of the three doctors flipped into position.

"These were his three known associates: Victor Glant, Leo Metzger, and Ahmar Kahvahl. Today, Metzer is dead. Glant is presumed drowned, and the third man, Dr. Kahvahl, is missing."

Jack Tade cued him. Devin shifted his weight and looked sharply into Camera Two.

"In covering this story, I've had personal experience with disease victims." He knew he had better not mention his recovery from the disease; it would cause a riot at CNB. People would come by the thousands seeking the vaccine.

He continued. "And in following up leads on the story, I've had indirect contact with Dr. Hendrix and his work. This contact convinced me that news stories condemning Hendrix are in error."

He turned toward Camera One, catching the close-up out of the corner of his eye. "Whether he's dead or has been abducted, I'm sure Dr. Hendrix's disappearance is part of a massive cover-up. If we are to assume a conspiracy against our country, I believe Dr. Hendrix is a victim of the perpetrators, as we all are. He is innocent and decidedly not the cause of the epidemic.

"Still, while it's unclear exactly how the epidemic began, I believe the conspirators themselves are vulnerable. They fear facts Dr. Hendrix might divulge. As a reporter, I have privileged information that suggests who the guilty parties may be. Yet evidence is incomplete. Nevertheless, on the strength of that evidence, I am, from this point on, dedicating myself to determining exactly how the disease began. I welcome you to join me in that search.

"If you have any information regarding Dr. Hendrix, Black Diamond, or other knowledge about the disease and its origins, I ask you to call me through our CNB operators at 1-800-555-1300 immediately. A special task force here at the network will process your calls." Devin saw the 800 number stay on the screen as he wrapped up. "I have CNB's mandate to clear Dr. Hendrix's name and to assist federal authorities in their investigations. And with CNB's continued cooperation, I will be reporting to you whenever new information surfaces. I'm Devin Parks."

Devin remained frozen, staring into Camera Two.

"We're clear!" Jack Tade yelled, stepping out in front of the camera. He glanced in Devin's direction. "Looked good, Dev. Right on the money." He gave Devin a thumbs-up and hustled toward the playback room.

Devin unhooked the microphone and stepped off the risers, squinting under the hot lights, looking around. Dan Canon was nowhere in sight.

Freeman came downstairs from the control booth, nodding. "Well, Devin, you were credible as hell. I hope things turn out the way they should." He adjusted his suspenders with both hands.

"Thanks. It felt good."

Freeman corralled him with a huge arm and led him off toward the back of the studio. "Give me a moment," he said. As they reached a darkened corner near a prop table, Freeman lowered his voice. "Devin. Let's be clear about this. I'll give you my support. But with this committee in Washington convening and calls from Kemper . . . I want to be assured there are no warrants out for Ginelle."

"Warrants? Come on, Frank."

"All right. Don't get excited. I just want to make sure no crimes were committed. We can't harbor a fugitive, you know that."

"It's just as I told you."

"Good. Good. Now, here, take these." Freeman held out a set of keys, looking like a father about to consign the family car to a teenage son.

"What's this?"

"Keys to my beach cabin in Monterey. I think you and the young woman could use a safe haven until things sort themselves out. What do you say?"

"I thought an out-of-the-way motel—"

"Nonsense. This is private and serene. You know Max Davis?"

"Head of security?"

"Yes. He's been with CNB over thirty years. I've assigned him to keep an eye on you two."

Surprised at his kindness, Devin wondered if Freeman merely wanted to protect an exclusive news story. "I'm grateful, but I'm not sure I want to be responsible—"

"He won't get in the way. He's got a Chevy van that he'll use for surveillance. You won't even know he's there. All right?"

"Well . . . okay. Thanks." Devin pocketed the keys

and, for the first time, noticed Dan Canon standing in the shadows.

"How long have you been there, Dan?" he asked.

"Just got here," Canon replied, with a strained look on his face. He ignored Devin and stepped up next to Freeman. "Frank. You know who the woman Devin has in the green room really is?"

Freeman turned, like a feeding Brahma bull interrupted by a pesky insect. "What are you saying, Dan?"

Canon appeared to hyperventilate; he began to ramble. "It wasn't that tough, you know. Dr. Hendrix's files are public record. I cross-referenced academic records out of the state of Virginia. The *Richmond Chronicle* had a picture of his daughter on file from the Lee Center ceremonies—"

Freeman had a hand up, looking around nervously. "Keep your voice down. You actually went to the green room, Dan?"

"Well, just to be sure. I peeked in."

The Brahma bull seemed to want to protect its offspring . . . a hot news story in its infancy.

"You're out of line," Freeman breathed.

Canon continued his machine-gun prattle. "She had Amy's purse. I recognized it. It's quite obvious we need a full explanation about Klein's death. And what about Parks and this—"

"Shut up, goddammit." Freeman hunched his shoulders. "I made the green room off-limits to all personnel."

Canon suddenly seemed taken aback. "Understandably." He stepped aside.

Freeman reverted to his military vocabulary. "You countermanded a direct order."

Devin was pleased to watch the impromptu court-martial unfold.

Canon scrambled to cover his ass. "I wasn't sure you knew—"

"Oh. You're taking care of *my* business now? Wait in my office!" Freeman's stubby finger pointed upstairs.

Canon leaned in that direction but seemed unable to let go. "Why give this to Parks? It's a science story, after all. I've just done some comprehensive viral research—"

Canon had no chance to finish. Freeman signaled for Devin to leave, closed a large black hand around Canon's elbow, and led him toward the elevators.

"I normally admire your inquisitive nature, Dan," Freeman said as they moved away. "But I have some news for you. . . ."

Devin couldn't hear the rest of the sharp-edged reprimand, because he was on his way toward the hallway at a brisk walk. He made it to the green-room door in a matter of moments, pushing it open. Ginelle was watching the national feed on the monitor. She looked up, startled.

"Did he bother you?" Devin asked breathlessly.

"Who?" She seemed nonchalant. "Oh. The thin one. No. Not at all."

"He knows who you are."

"Not from anything I told him."

"He did a computer check and found your picture."

"Isn't he one of CNB's people?"

"I don't trust him. Let's get out of here. Freeman gave us a place to hide." Devin reached over and grabbed Amy's handbag and Ginelle's new coat.

Someone knocked at the door.

Devin put a finger to his lips and opened the door a crack, relieved to find Tony.

"You've got a call, Devin," Tony said pleasantly. "A response to your editorial."

"Already?"

"Yeah, man. Interesting. I told them to route it here."

"Okay," Devin said. "And they're calling from—"

"Africa." Tony smiled.

"What?"

"Yeah. The power of television." Tony turned to leave.

"All right. Thanks." Devin slowly closed the door and gave Ginelle a confused glance.

"What do you think?" she asked.

He thought back to the recent phone call from Hendrix that had thrust him into chaos. "One way to find out." He picked up the green telephone on the dresser and said, "This is Devin Parks," sitting down on the velvet couch.

"Mr. Parks, William Galbreath here. I'm calling you from Cairo." The voice was British and upper class. "I saw your broadcast just moments ago here at the hotel."

"You've got satellite reception?"

"Oh yes. An excellent station out of Dubai in the United Emirates. They carry CNB broadcasts in Arabic and English."

Devin looked at Ginelle and shrugged. "What can I do for you?" he asked.

"I think it's a matter of what we can do for each other, Mr. Parks. I think we may be at similar crossroads. I, too, have reason to believe that things are not at all as they seem in this matter. This leads me to believe it might be helpful for us to get together."

Devin frowned. "I don't understand."

"I can't express my feelings adequately over the telephone. Suffice it to say I've been most disturbed by certain findings I've made here. Seeing those pictures you had on the screen . . ."

"Yes."

"They look unfortunately similar to photographs I recently discovered of natives here in the bush country of this continent."

"What are you trying to say?" Devin was listening very carefully now.

"Disease symptoms, sir. Like those in America."

"I wasn't aware that the infection had reached that part of the world."

"It hasn't . . . not in recent history, at least."

Devin was thinking hard.

"Hello, are you there?" Galbreath asked.

Devin's mind had drifted to an imaginary Africa, where diseased phantoms roamed a parched plain. "You're saying *your* photographs relate to *our* current epidemic?" he asked.

"Precisely, sir. It occurred to me that all this may impact on your efforts to clear the name of your Dr. Hendrix. The disease saga is apparently international, if you get my meaning."

"I believe you're right, Mr. Galbreath."

"Excellent. I can arrive in approximately twenty-four hours."

"Now? How can you travel here under the circumstances?"

"Diplomatic privilege." The voice was confident. "I'm an official of Her Majesty's government. I've arranged a Canberra Bomber. I'll be on it in four hours. I connect in London and should be able to make San Francisco by tomorrow evening, your time. Can you suggest a place to meet?"

Devin thought quickly. "Public places are closed, Mr. Galbreath, but military facilities aren't. My superior, Mr. Freeman, is a retired military officer. I think he may be able to arrange a liaison. Route your flight to Nellis Air Force Base in Nevada. That's an hour-and-a-half flight for me. I'll meet you there in the officers' club. When you hit London, call this number back to confirm."

"Will do. And incidentally, Mr. Parks, I considered

your broadcast an inspiration. Due to circumstances I will explain when we meet, I had few options—until I saw you, that is. I commend you for what you're doing. You are a beacon of hope in the darkness."

Devin couldn't help smiling at his words. He looked over at Ginelle. "If that's true, sir, it's because I recently had my fires lit."

THE EIGHTH DAY
11:55 P.M.
Alexandria, Virginia

Thick fog covered the country near the Potomac. A temperature inversion had moved over the greater Chesapeake Bay coastline. Mild onshore flow brought the oceanic mist inland.

Street lamps around Capital Park resembled luminous dandelions, dotting the darkness, strung in a symmetrical arc around the perimeter of the grass.

Disguised in a black hairpiece and wearing a wide-brimmed hat and raincoat, Jaktar waited to the rear of the truck. He lit a cigarette in his pearl-handled holder and exhaled, watching the gray smoke float above his head.

He leaned against the back doors of the semi truck his driver had parked in the alley behind the Pepper Pot Restaurant, deserted due to renovations. The abandoned eating establishment was a safe place for the transport to remain undisturbed at this hour of the night.

This particular tractor-trailer was the first of five mobile units, identical to the one that held Dr. Hendrix captive. Two others waited in the Midwest. On his drive east, Jaktar was told a fifth vehicle had been allocated to the West Coast under Sing Chu's command, due to a disturbance in California, where the meddling of some television newsman demanded immediate attention.

All five mobile computerized command centers were capable of housing personnel, as they had during the initial disease infestation. Operatives could comfortably sustain themselves inside for days.

On this particular trip, which lasted only thirty-two hours, Jaktar had headed east to make a delivery.

His driver, Kim, and another man, Wu Sun, who was Sing Chu's cousin, sat in the forward cab. Jaktar had insisted Wu Sun be present on this trip so he could keep an eye on him. As Hendrix's original guard, Wu Sun had become too friendly with the doctor. Jaktar considered his behavior insubordinate. He wanted to kill Wu Sun, and only Sing Chu's pleas had prevented it.

Jaktar stared into the night, waiting for the tiny blinks of light that he anticipated near the old stone bridge. He expected three successive bursts from a flashlight, signaling him to approach. He pushed his black leather glove down to see the face of his Swiss watch. The digital LED read 11:57 P.M.

As he dropped his hand Jaktar's gaze drifted to the silver metal briefcase that sat on the pavement at his feet.

Jaktar knew very well what the case contained, even though he had not looked inside: over two hundred prepared syringes to be delivered to Bethesda Naval Hospital, each one filled with a 10-cc dose of vaccine. These were specially made, not from the regular production line.

Although an amoral mercenary, Jaktar occasionally wondered about his future. He felt the flow of destiny's tides, and had been cheered by the fact that things were going well, with over one hundred thousand suspected cases of the disease reported.

Jaktar knew that the waiting was nearly over, and that his employer, an international organization of great influence and power, would soon be able to act with impunity.

A moving vehicle on a distant street caused him to

hold his breath, gauging the size and proximity. Traffic noise was rare, because of the curfew. The hum passed from east to west on a causeway beyond the park, likely a police patrol, not a military truck, not National Guard. Their troops made their rounds on foot.

Jaktar reached inside his raincoat and patted the Beretta, his close-range weapon of choice. Shifting his hips, he felt tightness under his belt, assuring himself that the nine-millimeter he carried was also secure at the small of his back. The rough texture of the handle gently scraped his skin.

His preferred weapons also included a combat knife, which he carried in his right boot, strapped to his ankle. The fierce-looking, two-edged, stainless-steel blade had a metal handle tethered in cowhide, ideal for throwing.

To amuse himself, he flexed his foot and heard the soft creaking of boot leather against the knife sheath.

Then he hesitated. From the corner of his eye, Jaktar saw something in the darkness. At first, he thought he was experiencing retinal fatigue. But another quick glance validated his suspicions. There they were . . . two more flashes out near the bridge.

Jaktar tapped the side of the truck with his gloved hand twice to let Kim know he was leaving.

He picked up the briefcase, looked in both directions, and ventured out of the alley into the street.

Fog made excellent cover, and he felt strong moving within it. Poor visibility favored the natural killer, who struck without hesitation when confronted.

Jaktar visualized himself as a stalking panther, walking lithely in the darkness. Years of martial-arts training had honed his innate athletic abilities and he reveled in the sense of his own physical well-being.

Crossing wet grass, he approached the stone bridge.

A dim streetlight sparkled off the moist granite pieces

on the bridge wall, the sharp rough angles of the rock refracting the light.

He reached into his trench coat, found the small pen-light, and began flashing it as he walked.

Responding flashes answered from under the bridge.

The contact recognized his approach. Good. It would be a shame to be killed by a killer. Not that he feared death; he merely understood that his own would be a ter-rible waste.

As he drew near he saw the silhouette of a man dressed in heavy layers of rain gear. A large hood covered his liaison's face. Even in daylight, it would have been diffi-cult to recognize anyone in those clothes.

Not that Jaktar would know this man. He had only heard of him.

Jaktar was allowed to have inklings of knowledge about his organization's big picture, but he was given very little detail. He had simply been told that his contact was a longtime operative who held the confidence of a key man in Washington. The Washington man's identity, on the other hand, was top-secret. He was referred to only by a code name.

Jaktar switched the briefcase and penlight to his left hand. Clamped in his fingers above, the beam shone steadily down onto the case. He wanted the contact to see that he had the delivery as promised.

Still shielded by the gloom, he reached across his chest inside his coat, took the Beretta out of the holster, and put it in his raincoat pocket, leaving his right hand free.

Jaktar stepped under the stone arch of the bridge within a few feet of the man.

"I've heard much about you," the contact said in a deep voice.

Jaktar didn't welcome chitchat. He came right to the point. "I need the name."

"The name of lore?" the man asked, the pat greeting, as instructed.

"The lore lives." Jaktar gave the planned response.

"The code name is Karryot."

"So it is."

Jaktar extended the briefcase to the man in the inky blackness. It was difficult to determine the contact's build in the mass of clothing. Jaktar estimated that, like himself, he was well over six feet tall.

A hand emerged from the cloak and took the case.

"These are for the hospital," Jaktar said coolly. "A shipment of three thousand will follow through military channels after the announcement."

"Are they specially treated?"

"Naturally," Jaktar said. "Why would I come, if they weren't?"

"No need to be abrupt. I was just checking."

Jaktar enjoyed being abrasive. The meeting stimulated him. The contact remained reticent.

"They said you would have word by now," Jaktar said.

"There *is* word."

"Then say it."

The dark mass of clothing had enshrouded the briefcase and stepped farther away.

Inside his pocket, Jaktar's grip on the Beretta tightened. The contact's response should have been immediate. If the contact moved away another step with the case, he would kill him. Jaktar began to pull the weapon.

"The shepherd sleeps in four days," the contact said.

Jaktar's hand relaxed. He dropped the gun back down in the pocket. "Is there more?" he asked, disappointed he had not been able to fire, yet realizing the kill would have been impractical.

"That's all the prophet said." The contact shuffled off under the arch, then apparently turned for a final exchange. "After the shepherd sleeps. How will I know you?"

Jaktar barely heard the question that echoed emptily under the stone bridge.

Concealing himself in the cover of night, he had darted away onto the grass, satisfied the contact would marvel at his sudden absence.

THE NINTH DAY
8:10 P.M.
Officers' Club, Nellis Air Force Base
Near Las Vegas, Nevada

Devin attempted to adjust his vision in the darkness. It was difficult to see in the low light of the officers' club lounge.

A few men and women stood near the bar with its neon beer signs. The rest of the room felt like a cave, with an eerie blue glow cast by candles inside glass landing lights on each small table.

Air-force personnel had apparently decorated their lounge like a plane cockpit with dials and knobs spread along the walls among shelves of bottles. Old flight helmets, pre–WW II leather headgear, and jet-age plastic bonnets hung among the black-and-white photos of test pilots and planes.

Under the watchful eye of Max Davis, the middle-aged CNB security officer, Ginelle had settled into Freeman's cabin in Monterey. To keep herself occupied in Devin's absence, she planned to monitor the Internet for world news on her laptop, hoping to stay abreast of any developments of the epidemic. Max had parked his van a few yards up the hill in a grove of trees, assuring Devin he would keep a watchful eye on his charge. With the assurance that Ginelle was safe, Devin had flown to the Nevada airfield to meet the mysterious Englishman who had telephoned him the previous evening.

Detained briefly at the gate by a guard clad in

biohazard gear, Devin had shown his press pass and checked in at a medical station, where masked on-duty physicians gave him a quick examination.

Diagnosis of the disease in its incubation stage was, as yet, impossible, but military bases throughout the country checked transient personnel in the hope of eliminating the risk of exposure to advanced cases. Anyone with flu-like symptoms was immediately isolated. The nation-wide curfew allowed interstate shipping but restricted personnel travel to the military, medical staff, and the press.

A cocktail waitress in her forties, scantily dressed in black satin shorts and fishnet stockings, noticed Devin's restlessness and asked if she could be of service.

"I'm looking for an Englishman," he said.

The waitress's heavy eyeliner gave her a raccoonlike appearance in the low light.

"Englishman? How could you miss him?" she answered, then cracked her chewing gum. She nodded to the back corner of the room. "All that khaki and not a rhino in sight."

Brushing past the waitress, Devin squinted in the indicated direction.

At a secluded table, a man dressed in light tan safari clothing sat sipping a glass of water. A white cane with a brass lion's head leaned against the back of the metal chair. A beige Akubra hat lay on the table at his elbow.

The tall Englishman rose as Devin approached.

"Mr. Parks, I'm William Galbreath," the Englishman said.

Devin shook his hand, moved around the table, and settled in the other chair. "It occurred to me after your call . . . I hadn't asked you what you look like."

"Different from the others in this environment."

Galbreath smiled. "Of course, I knew you from the broadcast."

Devin studied the Englishman, who looked serene and sincere, with his striking brown eyes, dark skin, silvery eyebrows, and white hair.

Galbreath glanced around, keenly aware of his surroundings. Not much noise in the bar. Military personnel appeared glum due to the crisis, speaking in subdued tones.

"Mr. Parks," he said. "I've been struggling with the ethics of this meeting ever since I called you. Since I'm here on my own accord, and not as a British official, I need your assurance that this conversation will be held in the strictest confidence. And if your responses are unsatisfactory, I may terminate this conversation at any point."

"You're a man who needs reassurance . . . but I'm in a similar position."

The cocktail waitress approached the table. Her legs looked soft and white. Her mouth was plastered with red lipstick, and her cheerful demeanor contrasted oddly with the sober atmosphere in the lounge. "What can I get for you, gentlemen?"

"What'll it be?" Devin asked, nodding to Galbreath.

"I have an abiding affection for Scotch," the Englishman replied, pushing his water glass aside.

"I'll have a Scotch and soda . . . make it Cutty Sark," Devin said.

"Johnny Walker, Black Label," Galbreath added. "No soda."

The waitress gave Galbreath a coy smile and put two cardboard coasters on the table, revealing her ample cleavage.

Galbreath recoiled at the scent of her musk perfume. The waitress gave him a look and oozed her way back to the bar.

"I'm sorry," Devin said. "This may not be an appropriate place to meet."

"Nothing is appropriate just now, old boy. We must all do our best. I advocate any kind of resistance in the face of chaos."

"And what are we resisting?"

"Criminal acts perpetrated behind an obvious veil of deceit," Galbreath said pointedly. "I believe you and I may have something in common—persistence. I, about details of heinous events in continental Africa. You, about your knowledge of Dr. Hendrix." He folded his hands carefully and continued. "Mr. Parks, I came because I do not accept media accounts regarding the epidemic you are facing here in the United States. They cannot be correct."

He was forced to pause as the waitress returned with a full tray.

"Your drinks, gentlemen." She bent over the table and placed Devin's drink in front of him. "And here's the Black Label." She put a glass in front of Galbreath. "Oh, look at that," she said, holding another glass in the air. "Looks like the bartender made an extra Black Label. What'll I do?" she asked, with coy perplexity.

"Just leave it," Devin said impatiently.

"For you, or for you?" She smiled, moving the glass back and forth in the air between the two men. She appeared to be enjoying the little game.

Galbreath furrowed his brow. "Dear lady," he said in a patronizing tone, "if that orphaned cocktail needs a home, let it join my glass of Black Label. Why on earth would Mr. Parks mix his Scotches?"

Confused, she set the glass down in front of Galbreath and left without further comment.

Galbreath followed her with his eyes and then smiled

at Devin. "Astounding the capacity for triviality even in the face of disaster."

"Triviality, I suppose, is what we're fighting *for*." Devin grinned.

The Englishman hoisted his drink. "May I call you Devin?"

"Of course, but I refuse to call you Bill."

Galbreath smiled. "A bit of hands-across-the-sea, then?"

They clinked glasses and enjoyed their first sip.

Then both men sat forward in their chairs.

"What have you found?" Devin asked.

"I will share that with you in a moment. But with your forbearance, some background first." Galbreath scratched his chin. "As a member of the British Foreign Office, I was assigned to visit Baghigra, in the Sudan, to secretly investigate illegal activities by an Islamic terrorist group called Nahda, operating out of Tunisia. During my posting two native boys led me to some ruins where photographs were buried."

"The ones you mentioned on the phone?"

"Precisely. Buried in a metal container, each showing native children scourged and battered."

"Like ours on television?" Devin took another sip of his drink.

"Too similar for me to discern a difference. Burned. Skin torn from their bodies in places. Of course, I had not seen any of the American victims by then. I went to Khartoum to enquire about the ruins. And several days later, when I saw your pictures, the experience shattered me." Galbreath spoke with considerable feeling. "I felt I was peering down a time tunnel at some horrific monster."

"What do you mean?"

"My dear fellow, further investigation revealed the

ruins were at least fifteen years old, like the photographs." Galbreath reached into the jacket of his khaki
suit and placed an envelope on the table. "I verified their
age with a friend of mine in Cairo—a lab technician for
the British Secret Service—all hush-hush, of course. The
degradation showed them to be at least that old. The idea
of twentieth-century technology being used to ravage an
African people . . ." His face twisted in disgust.

Confounded, Devin picked up the envelope. "May I?"
He opened the flap and examined the pictures, nodding
grimly as Galbreath silently sipped his Scotch. Devin's
mind filled with visions of atrocities. "What do you make
of this?"

"I may have a clue. You'll see how the whole thing
falls together." Galbreath put both hands up to his face,
rubbing his nose, and then clasped them together, staring
at the table lamp. "I discovered that the ruins in Baghigra
were once owned by Fertile Crescent Limited, a division
of Persian Pride Enterprises, a company licensed in Iran
under the shah, later seized by agents of the Ayatollah
Khomeini. The company dealt in exotic foodstuffs."

"Have you shared this information with your
government?"

Galbreath sighed deeply. "No. I chose not to."

"Why not?"

"Two of the major stockholders in what was then
known as Persian Pride are currently members of the
House of Lords, Wesley Cunningham and John Blythe-
Taggert. Frankly, I'm somewhat intimidated by these
two. They're part of what we refer to as the Eton old-boy
network. Terribly influential."

Devin clutched the table edge. "Are you suggesting
that the ruins in . . ."

"Baghigra, yes. That two British statesmen had connections with Fertile Crescent . . . which was conducting

experiments with the microbe causing this disease fifteen years prior to the current epidemic."

Devin tried to fathom the implications. "An American epidemic with African—and international—roots."

"Let me get into that further, after I finish with Baghigra."

"Please, go ahead."

Galbreath reflected a moment and then continued. "Sudanese locals remember the ruins as stone buildings used to store grain and agricultural equipment. Over the years many dozens of white men came and went. The townspeople thought the European company would develop farms in the area, farms to make crop production during a drought possible. Scientists experimented with soil and used laboratory facilities. That part seemed legitimate. But through some old official business documents, I found requisitions which indicate the project director for Fertile Crescent was a man born in Iran. He received his doctorate in the United States. A man named Ahmar Kahvahl."

Devin pushed his glass aside. "Kahvahl did research in Africa?"

"So it seems."

"Could the other Black Diamond researchers have gone to the Sudan with him at one point?"

Galbreath shook his head. "I don't know. But Kahvahl was quite busy in Africa. Baghigra was the site of his third project, after Kenya and Tanzania."

Devin felt the hair on his neck bristle as he digested Galbreath's comments. He looked apprehensively over his shoulder at military personnel seated several feet away, and lowered his voice. "If British government officials owned a part of an Iranian company, how would that relate to an epidemic here?"

"Now we begin with the speculation," Galbreath said.

"The ministry of commerce in London lists Persian Pride as an oil company with affiliations in the United States. Have you heard of the Maxillar Chemical Corporation of America?"

"Who hasn't? They're a multibillion-dollar corporation."

"Maxillar was founded by a man named Arthur Quail. He was part owner of both firms."

"Quail's an industrialist. Makes the news occasionally. Owns various conglomerates. Shipping companies, pharmaceuticals, chemical laboratories. He's got clothing companies, I believe, manufactures lots of things, cleaning solutions, agricultural chemicals . . ."

"Agricultural chemicals?"

"Yes."

"Like those that might be used by a company like Fertile Crescent, perhaps?" Galbreath said softly.

Devin stared at the Englishman. The dancing light of the table lamp created ghostly shadows on the wall behind him. "So you are assuming Quail was involved in sponsoring the initial research?"

"A place to begin. Baghigra, or perhaps other villages, may have been chosen as test sites for fledgling experiments."

"God forbid there were others," Devin said, visualizing the victims.

Sipping his Scotch, Galbreath went on to explain that Fertile Crescent had operated in Africa for two decades, likely producing food in nations besieged by famine, easily acquiring operating permits. Galbreath was visibly disturbed that these inhumane activities had ostensibly been directed from afar by two English noblemen and an American industrialist, but Devin could see there was more . . . and he had to coax it out of him. "What else is bothering you?"

"Have you ever heard of the mythical Trilateral Commission?" Galbreath asked grimly.

Devin recalled hearing the name. "Some legend about an international group of wealthy politicians, business-people who've attempted to change the course of history."

"Yes. Arisen from the Knights Templar, centuries old."

"Centuries old? You're telling me that's what this— this conspiracy is?" Devin asked.

"I haven't had time to speculate, but we may be faced with something like that—a conspiracy among influential individuals in various nations, Quail included. According to my research through the secret service, the link to Fertile Crescent, a.k.a. Persian Pride, extends into conglomerates in several nations, Japan, North Korea, Iran, and Britain as we mentioned, Colombia, Germany . . . and of course, the United States." Galbreath leaned forward, as if to add emphasis to what he was about to say. "I would speculate that multiple corporations in various countries and their directors are involved in a conspiracy, and that terrorism became a tool of these conglomerates."

Galbreath's statement hit Devin like a punch in the stomach. Challenging villainy on such a scale seemed suddenly beyond him.

He leaned back in his chair, staring incredulously at the Englishman. "God," he said. "If it's really that big, where the hell do we begin?"

THE NINTH DAY
8:26 P.M.
Atlanta

"Dr. Gordon," the operator's voice said over the speakerphone, "the White House is calling. Just a moment please."

Dr. Gordon stopped pacing the floor. He'd been expecting the call.

The president had finished delivering his latest address, the third of what were becoming daily broadcasts to the people of the United States, whom, it was judged, needed constant reassurances. Though presidential messages had been simulcast on all television stations as well, Gordon had chosen to listen rather than watch.

Looking out through the glass to the floor of the control center, he had sipped his coffee, able to picture the president as he spoke, preferring not to see the growing signs of stress on the president's face. It was obvious that the most powerful man in the world had been hobbled by an unknown enemy.

Retribution was impossible under such conditions.

Naturally, military bases all over the world were ordered to go to DEFCON 1, security tightened, and missiles were armed, though as yet without a specific target. Speculation about the source of the biochemical terrorism was rampant and wide-ranging. Certainly, Dr. Hendrix was considered the prime mover, but who had abetted the researcher in an effort so ambitious? Perhaps most confounding for the Pentagon was the fact that those nations that would automatically be most suspect— Libya, Iran, Iraq, and China among them—were themselves frantically voicing concerns about eventual contamination, and closed their borders to Western air travel. Of course, that could have been no more than a smoke screen.

There were no answers, not yet . . . and that's why Gordon knew the phone would ring . . . as it had every morning and every evening for the last three days. And as had become his habit, rather than be interrupted on the floor of the DCC, he patiently waited in his office for the eight-thirty call.

Coffee in hand, he stepped back to his desk and sat down on one of its corners, staring at the clock radio on the credenza. Seconds after the LED flashed 8:31, the phone on his desk buzzed. Gordon touched the red button.

"Yes, sir."

"Did you hear me tonight, Sam?" The president had taken to using Gordon's first name.

"I did, sir."

"How long do you think I can keep the dam from bursting?" The president sounded exhausted.

"Sorry?"

"We're just barely in control of our inner cities. Frankly, I think we may have lost Detroit. A large group of people have broken out through the eastern perimeter. They're storming the border at Windsor, trying to get into Ontario. How do you think the Canadians feel about that?"

It was a rhetorical question and Gordon had no way to answer it.

"They're scared to death, that's how they feel," the president continued. "Seventeen people have been shot by Canadian police. You know how hard it is to contain our borders?" Another rhetorical question. Gordon had become a sounding board for a president under siege.

"I'm sure we're doing our best," Gordon said quietly.

"Yes, we are, but we can't patrol every inch of land between San Diego and Brownsville, Texas, either. Did you hear about the renegade boat traffic out of Florida and Seattle . . . we've got an Armada sailing off to the Caribbean and the strait of Juan de Fuca. The Coast Guard can't board them all . . . things are out of control."

Gordon interpreted this report as a plea for help.

"I'm trying to avoid panic, but it's damn near impossible. How long do you think I can keep lying to these people?" the president demanded.

"Lying, sir?"

"Yes. I keep telling them we're on the verge of finding a cure."

"I'm in touch with Pendergast at USAMRIID almost hourly, Mr. President. This afternoon they achieved nucleic separation of the microbe's elements."

"Congratulations . . . what the hell does that do for us?"

"Pendergast says that separation will allow integral analysis of the protein residues . . . a key to understanding the antidote. But these things take time . . . it's a trial-and-error process."

"There's no room for error, does he understand that? What's the latest from the pharmaceuticals?"

"The companies appear to be at roughly the same stage as USAMRIID, perhaps slightly advanced. Frankly, with their greater resources—"

"Listen, I'm not asking for a turnaround. What's the latest projection—a quarter of a million by next Saturday? A million in a month?"

Gordon envisioned the incredible task of disposing of the mass of bodies, dumping the dead in fire pits on the outskirts of town, reminiscent of scenes he had seen in paintings of the black plague in Europe.

"Isn't there even something to slow it down, Sam," the president asked, a most unstatesmanlike desperation in his voice, "to give us some time? Why couldn't you people have foreseen something like this?"

Gordon wanted to mention the lack of government support for biochemical-warfare-prevention research, but realized its futility. "I'm on it every minute."

"Well, of course you are." Fearful of alienating an important ally in the medical community, the president controlled his frustration. He had few friends in this crisis. "Get involved personally if you have to. Maybe you should visit these pharmaceutical companies. . . ."

Gordon couldn't see leaving the DCC in this crisis. "I'm needed here—" he began, but the president interrupted.

"Well, then Pendergast, or one of your other people—"

"I could put Dr. Chang—"

"Fine, but get a handle on it. Make it a top priority. Will you do that for me?"

"Immediately. And I'll keep you apprised."

"Good. And Sam, let's understand each other. The first thing that comes along that helps . . . gives us some hope, we'll put all our guns behind it, if it does any good at all. . . . Panacea, wonder drug, nicotine patch—whatever—if it buys us some time, I want to hear about it."

THE NINTH DAY
8:31 P.M.
Officers' Club
Nellis Air-Force Base

William Galbreath stared into the candle flame, momentarily stumped by Devin's question. "Where to begin? Reminds me of an old Hindu tale about the seven blind men who were to identify what kind of animal an elephant was simply by feeling it. Do you know it?"

"Vaguely." Devin reluctantly went along with the diversion.

"You know . . . the blind man who touched the trunk said it was a snake, the one with the tail in his hand said it was a large rat . . . and so on."

"I'm sorry. I've lost you."

"The elephant's body is like the international organization behind the epidemic. It must be right here in the United States, where the disease struck. We don't have time or the means to conduct overseas investigations, so I suggest, given our limited resources, we focus our thoughts on the corporation nearest at hand. Maxillar Chemical."

The name rang in Devin's mind. He'd recently heard it on the news. Studio A. Brook Hanford's lead-in to his editorial. "Prior to my broadcast, one of my colleagues mentioned that Arthur Quail's company, Maxillar Chemical, has made some progress on formulating a vaccine."

"Are you certain?"

"Yes, I'm certain. Why shouldn't I be?" Devin looked momentarily confused.

Galbreath seemed troubled. "Maxillar working on a vaccine disproves our theory."

"I'm sorry?"

"It contradicts our belief in a conspiracy. If Quail and his affiliated companies are behind the disease . . . why should they want to develop its cure?"

Devin had used the same argument with regard to Thomas Hendrix. He rubbed his temple, weighing the alternatives.

"Because they stand to make millions of dollars if they succeed."

"Yes, that may be it. Of course, Quail is already obscenely wealthy," Galbreath said.

"Then, as a cover." Devin pointed a finger in the air. "Other pharmaceutical firms are working on vaccines. To avoid negative speculation, Maxillar would have to announce its own efforts." He looked into his empty glass.

"On the other hand, suppose the epidemic were the result of some kind of accident. Quail might be covering for an embarrassing error in a lab somewhere," Galbreath suggested.

Devin shook his head vehemently, remembering the map he had seen in Atlanta. Red dots scattered on the U.S. map. "It was no accident according to the Disease Control Center, given the initial pattern of infection. But a conspiracy brings up another central question. Who did the dirty work? I mean, even if Quail, your British Lords, or other foreign corporations were involved somehow, who traveled around the country infecting kids? It would have taken a complex, coordinated effort."

Galbreath clicked his tongue against his teeth like a man concentrating on a chess move. "A world without borders," he muttered.

"I beg your pardon?"

Galbreath explained that his investigation had convinced him that modern terrorism relied on economic and religious bonds that transcended geographical boundaries. He was convinced that Kahvahl had acted through terrorist operatives in the United States. Since Kahvahl was Iranian and Persian Pride was founded in Iran, he believed those terrorists to belong to some Islamic rebel faction.

Devin objected. "Islamic? Isn't that just a bad rap? Lately, when the FBI can't solve a crime, out comes the same old scapegoat."

Galbreath frowned, shook his head. "Intelligence suggests that Islamic fundamentalists form the most openly aggressive anti-American international organizations in existence. With Quail involved, somewhere between Baghigra and Black Diamond, I think big business bought big terror."

"Business interests using religious radicalism? I guess it's possible," Devin conceded.

Galbreath raised his eyebrows. "Fanaticism as a business tool, yes, why not? Then add Kahvahl, a fanatic with scientific expertise."

Devin shook his head. "Somehow that bothers me. If, as you say, Kahvahl had a killer bug in Baghigra fifteen years ago and the capacity to cause major mayhem, why would he risk exposure by working for the United States?"

Galbreath frowned. "Why indeed?" Then he looked down at the table and tapped his fingers as if he were playing a piano. "He would only have to do that if—"

"He needed help," Devin interrupted excitedly.

"Yes. Go on."

"For whatever reason, Kahvahl had a germ he couldn't perfect. He didn't have it exactly right, somehow."

"So he engaged in a research project with other experts

to help perfect the bug," Galbreath speculated, furrowing his brow. "But Hendrix—"

"There's something I haven't told you," Devin said cautiously. "I have inside information about the formula and Dr. Hendrix."

Galbreath looked startled. "What are you saying?"

"I'm in direct contact with his daughter, Dr. Ginelle Hendrix, who knows more than anyone else about the disease."

"You've actually seen her?" Galbreath seemed astounded.

"She saved my life with a vaccine that Hendrix himself formulated just before he disappeared."

Galbreath's expression changed to disbelief. "A vaccine? You were infected?"

"And cured."

The Englishman's jaw dropped. "You r-recovered?" he stuttered, looking more closely at Devin's face. "There is no sign of infection at all!"

"I was inoculated in time," Devin said, thinking sadly of Amy.

The Englishman leaned forward excitedly. "Why can't we simply take the vaccine straight to the authorities?"

Devin shook his head. "It was the last remaining dose. There isn't any more—that I know of. And I met with the authorities. In Atlanta." He recounted his meeting with Williamson, Swain, and Gordon, then suggested that he take Galbreath's photographs to them.

Galbreath, however, was reluctant. "Do you trust these men?" he asked.

"How could I? I hardly know them," Devin replied.

"We could be undermined. I fear unknown enemies even more than those we've identified. I prefer we keep evidence to ourselves rather than revealing it to someone simply because they are in positions of authority." Galbreath fingered the lion's head on his cane.

Moments passed. Then Devin leaned forward on the metal table and stared into the landing light. "Our advantage, Mr. Galbreath, is that no one except the two of us knows the *extent* of our knowledge."

Devin saw Galbreath's eyes shine with new resolve. "Devin, you have a point. Our knowledge is a powerful weapon. We can intimidate them and shake their confidence. We have resources to fight."

"Yes. But fight how?"

"With the element of surprise." Galbreath's eyes gleamed. "We possess facts that no one would suspect, plus the advantage of your acquaintance with Hendrix's daughter. Let's return to the notion of focusing on Maxillar. At least we know its founder is *not* in the government. Imagine how dangerous our knowledge could be for Mr. Quail."

"Are you suggesting we confront him?"

"Why not? You went on television to get the pot, so to speak, boiling. I have arrived to season it with spices. Now, we can feed our soup to Mr. Quail."

Devin smiled at the metaphor. "I'm a reporter. I could request an interview to learn about the progress on the vaccine, in light of Quail's statements to the press."

Galbreath smacked the table with the tip of his cane. "Yes!" A few officers on the other side of the bar looked over. The Englishman glanced in their direction and lowered his voice. "And if Quail is as guilty as we suspect, he's no doubt heard about your editorial. He knows who Devin Parks is by now. Let's see if his curiosity overrides his confidence."

Devin realized the ramifications of this suggestion. "You realize, of course, that he could also kill me on the spot."

"Oh. Yes. I suppose he very well might." Galbreath rubbed his chin. "Particularly if you mention Baghigra."

Devin visualized the moment. Facing Quail, he would name the African town, and a bullet would slam into his forehead. Still, succumbing to fear would leave them nowhere. "I'll do it. I'll photocopy your photographs and send them to my boss, Frank Freeman, with an explanation. If I'm threatened by Quail, that's my ace in the hole. Freeman's a retired officer. Maybe he can notify the military in Cleveland and give me some kind of support, even if it's only symbolic. At least I'd appear to have some backup strength."

"Can you arrange that?"

"I'll try."

"Excellent. I want to be there to see it."

"You'll go along? Why?"

"Let me show you something," Galbreath said, putting his cane on the table. He looked around the room to see if anyone was watching. "I'm afraid I'm somewhat influenced by my past—Her Majesty's Secret Service." He grasped the handle of the walking stick. With one sharp turn, the lion's head separated from the shaft, revealing a nine-inch stiletto blade.

"Son-of-a-bitch," Devin said. "That's wicked."

"Yes." Galbreath smiled. "Watch closely." He twisted a small button at the base of the blade. The blade unfastened from the lion's head. Galbreath tucked it in the breast pocket of his jacket and held the handle to the light. "This instrument has several uses," he said. He tapped the handle of the cane and a small black cartridge slipped out.

Devin saw a blinking red LED at one end. "What the hell is that?"

"Observe." Galbreath turned a section of the cartridge. "Son-of-a-bitch, that's wicked," said a tiny voice.

"Tape?" Devin asked.

"A DAD. Digital Audio Diskette. Hours of recording on a miniature disk."

"You're going to record Quail."

"Precisely. We'll shock him into some kind of incriminating reaction and record it." Galbreath bristled with confidence.

"Can that be reproduced?" Devin asked.

"Only in an advanced sound lab."

"But it plays back! I'd feel good taking that kind of evidence to court. Or back to Dr. Gordon at the Disease Control Center."

"What do you think, old man? It appears to be the two of us against the world." Galbreath extended a hand with grave determination.

Devin gripped it strongly. "Into the pit?"

"Yes. Armed with the truth, we'll pull the devil's tail," Galbreath said. "Let's see if he retaliates."

THE TENTH DAY
3:29 P.M.
Maxillar Chemical Corporation
Cleveland, Ohio

"Thank you, Corporal," Galbreath said, as the surgical-masked soldier handed him an identification card. The interview had been granted immediately, as the Englishman had predicted, though no cameras were allowed.

Devin showed his press pass, pinned to the lapel of his camel-hair blazer.

The six soldiers stationed outside the building were part of a standard contingent assigned to guard priority-one companies, in this case, Maxillar Chemical Corporation.

As they stepped up to the huge brass-framed glass doors, Devin asked the corporal, "Were you contacted by your base regarding our arrival?"

"Yes, sir. My CO mentioned assisting you. Requested by a Captain Freeman, retired. What exactly are we expected to do, sir?"

"Well, for one thing, make sure we come back this way." Devin smiled. The soldier looked confused but nodded. "And, Corporal, could you and three of the others remain inside during our interview?" There was little other protection they could hope for.

"Yes, sir," the corporal said blankly.

"Good. If I wave, come join me, won't you? Keep your eyes open."

The corporal herded three of his men inside the

entrance as Devin and Galbreath walked in, armed with the tiny recording device, a briefcase, and a newspaper that Devin had folded under his arm. The photographs remained in the rental-car glove box. As a precaution, copies had been sent to Freeman, who was excited by Devin's contact with Galbreath and the potential of the story.

Ginelle, on the other hand, rebelled at having to wait in California and said that Galbreath's pictures should be immediately revealed to the congressional committee. Devin convinced her otherwise, arguing that the national news media and even the Internet were already brimming with reports of her father's guilt, and this was a chance to clear his name.

Devin carried her concerns with him as he and Galbreath walked through the huge lobby.

Behind them, the sunlit street was empty.

Like all other cities, downtown Cleveland was deserted, except for military traffic and foot patrols wearing masks. With a strict curfew in effect, only certain businesses—utilities, communication and transportation firms, and pharmaceutical companies—were allowed to remain open. All were guarded by National Guard troops.

"I hope our soldiers look convincing," Devin said as they walked.

"I hope *we* look convincing," Galbreath said softly, brushing the sleeve of the tweed suit he had worn for the meeting. "Thank God, Quail is a curious man."

Devin stared around their ostentatious surroundings. "Either that or a publicity hound." He pointed at a fifteen-foot-tall statue of Arthur Quail, sculpted out of granite, holding a freighter in one hand and an oil derrick in the other. Quail looked out toward a far-off horizon, a look of visionary fervor in his eyes.

Galbreath and Devin walked across the spacious marble floor. There were no employees, guests, or soldiers in the immense anteroom.

Devin's heels clicked on the stone surface, whereas Galbreath's soft safari shoes were silent. Occasionally he tapped his cane.

"Look at that." Galbreath pointed. The miniature freighter in Quail's hand sported a flag with three horizontal stripes, all the same bronze color. "Several European countries have striped flags, to say nothing of Russia, Yemen, Syria, Iraq, and Iran, among others. See the insignia on the oil derrick?" He thrust with his cane at an eagle with the initials *AQ* emblazoned upon it.

Devin looked down, noticing the inscription on the rock, and read it aloud. "The world awaits."

"Really," Galbreath said sarcastically. "You'd think he was the second coming." He nudged Devin with his cane.

"Is that baby turned on?" Devin asked, motioning to the lion's head.

"Indeed," Galbreath said.

The two men continued down the long empty corridor to a glass-enclosed office. As they approached the reception area a woman seated at a makeshift desk in a small, apparently airtight glass enclosure acknowledged them. Beyond her, two large leather-padded doors led to what Devin assumed was Arthur Quail's office.

"Good morning, gentlemen," the woman said, through the intercom speaker. She was young, blond, in her early thirties. "Forgive the isolation booth. With the infection, we've been forced to take precautions."

"Understandably," Devin replied. "We have an appointment with Arthur Quail."

"And you are. . . ?"

"From CNB. I'm Devin Parks." He showed his press card.

"Oh, yes, of course. Mr. Quail will be just a few minutes. He asked that you go in."

"He's not here?" Devin asked.

"No," she said, smiling. "But he's expecting you."

Galbreath chimed in. "In a glass cage as well, no doubt?"

"Oh no." She smiled. "Once past me, you're cleared." She pushed a black button on the counter. They heard a loud click at the lock. "Please go in."

Devin noted how heavy the glass door was, yet how easily it swung open, perfectly balanced on its brass hinges.

He took a last look at the two soldiers at the front door.

Beyond the glass reception area, they entered an immense chamber. No one was present in the huge marble-floored office.

"I feel like we're in purgatory," Devin said as the leather-padded doors closed behind them.

The circular room was huge, over seventy feet in diameter, and topped by an enormous dome. Soft indirect light glowed from behind the columns that ringed its base.

"More like the bowels of hell." Galbreath looked up, awed by the spectacle in spite of himself.

The entire ceiling had been painted dark blue and spotted with metallic silver flecks, giving the dome the appearance of the evening sky, with a million stars shining in a darkened firmament.

Devin checked the walls. Twenty-one backlit photographs measuring several feet across hung around the circular chamber. They portrayed industrial scenes from around the world, including oil-drilling desert shots of the Middle East, an oil tanker off the coast of Japan, and a myriad of refineries and manufacturing facilities. Quail appeared in several of the shots, sun-drenched, wearing a hard hat.

"Egomania at its best," Galbreath said.

Devin walked toward the center of the room. "Galbreath, look at this."

The Englishman joined him at a partially sunken circular aquarium, measuring some fifteen feet in diameter. Tropical fish swam in the thick glass enclosure.

The two men studied the lavish display.

The three-foot-high fishtank was lit from below, with polished black onyx around its edge. A pedestal stood in the center of the tank, emblazoned with a replica of the world; Africa was given the central position, the other continents spreading out around it.

Galbreath pointed his cane. "Look there."

Devin noted a bronze pyramid sitting where Egypt would be. A solitary eye looked out from all four sides of the pyramid.

"The symbol on American currency," he said. "Complete with the inscription."

"You've a good eye, Mr. Parks," a voice said. Startled, Devin whirled around to see a man in a black suit, who had apparently entered the room through a hidden door. "I've never been hesitant to make the entire world my place of business," the tall man said, stepping forward from the shadows. The darkness set off his graying mustache and brilliant pale blue eyes under heavy brows. Devin's first reaction was unease, as if he were in the presence of someone unpredictable. "Welcome, gentlemen." The man ambled toward them, as if his legs were hinged metal. "I'm Arthur Quail."

Devin took Quail's outstretched hand and found himself almost wincing in its strong grip.

"William Galbreath," the Englishman said, in turn taking Quail's hand.

"Really, with the British press?"

"Yes," Galbreath said dryly. "Collaborating with Mr. Parks, here."

"Well, that's fine. I have many friends in England."

"So we understand," Galbreath said.

Quail dismissed the ironic comment and walked toward the giant world map. "I see you've been examining my aquarium."

"We have, with amazement," Devin said. "We've never seen anything quite like it."

"Good. It was meant to be one of a kind." Quail pointed to the far end of the chamber. "Why don't we sit over there. We'll be more comfortable."

He led them to a furniture arrangement comprising a couch, two black leather chairs, and a highly polished, creamy-blue coffee table hewn from a single piece of granite.

"Spectacular," Devin said, indicating the enormous table as he took a seat in one of the leather chairs. Galbreath took the other, leaning his cane against the arm.

Quail sat down on the couch across from him.

Devin put the leather valise and the newspaper on the granite table. The newspaper, a copy of the *Cleveland Plain Dealer*, flopped open.

The headline read CONGRESSIONAL HEARING TO CONVENE—EVIDENCE AGAINST HENDRIX PRESENTED over a large picture of Dr. Hendrix in a lab next to a disfigured chimpanzee. The caption read: *Hendrix with Experiment Victim in New Mexico.*

Arthur Quail refused to glance at the paper. "I'm pleased you like my office," he said. "I use it for inspiration. I had it built for that purpose."

"What does it inspire you to do?" Devin asked, giving Galbreath a sidelong glance.

"Excel." Quail smiled. "Lack of new challenges leaves

me stagnant. With the advent of computer technology, previously unknown challenges arose and have been overcome. It's mind and machine, isn't it, gentlemen? The mind and the computer can do it all."

Although he smiled ingratiatingly, a sardonic glint danced in his eyes. Devin studied his face. Quail's skin stretched tautly over his facial bones, as if a plastic surgeon had fashioned it. It appeared oddly artificial . . . like his hospitality.

Quail scratched his nose with his right hand.

Devin noted a huge diamond ring and obviously manicured nails, covered with clear polish.

"Well?" Quail's smile faded. "An interview, I believe?"

Quail's arrogance angered Devin. "That was the purpose of the meeting," he said, shifting his weight and pointing to the coffee table. "Nice handiwork."

"It's Peruvian," Quail said, "a rare blue granite found only in the Andes."

"I'm referring to the newspaper, not the coffee table," Devin answered coldly.

Quail glanced at the paper. "Oh, yes, the disease business." His tone was oddly neutral. "We're proud of the progress we're making on a vaccine."

"I'm not talking about that," Devin said.

Galbreath intervened. "I believe Mr. Parks is referring to the false accusations about Dr. Hendrix."

"False? I'm afraid I don't understand." Quail crossed his legs. His Italian leather shoes gleamed even in the low light. "The evidence indicates that the man is guilty."

"We have evidence that states otherwise," Devin told him.

"So you indicated during your recent editorial. I would find that interesting if I didn't believe it weren't simply some ploy to improve ratings. I've found that people with evidence don't just talk about it, they submit it.

Frankly, Mr. Parks, I considered your statements nothing more than irresponsible journalism."

Devin felt heat on the back of his neck. "Then why did you agree to see me?"

"Why not? I had no idea your statements about Hendrix related to an interview with me."

Devin glanced at Galbreath, trying to gauge his timing of the conversation and sense the moment when he could force Quail into voicing an incriminating statement.

Galbreath merely nodded.

Devin viewed the next few minutes as a verbal chess game. "Mr. Quail, I'm not here to defend my editorial. But I can tell you that my beliefs aren't groundless. In fact, Mr. Galbreath and I are convinced you *and* your grand plan are in trouble."

Quail studied Devin. "The only grand plan I have is to supply millions of people with a lifesaving vaccine. I think you know that. Why don't you come to the point? My time is worth about fifty thousand dollars an hour."

Galbreath took his cane and held it across his knees. "Your time may be limited, sir," he said. "Opposition will bring your schemes to an end."

"What?" Quail's face reddened slightly. He sat forward in his chair. "Is one of you wearing a wire? Or do you have a tape recorder in that briefcase?"

Devin and Galbreath remained silent.

Quail looked from face to face and gave Devin a whimsical smile. "Now, I don't want to seem rude, gentlemen"—he brought his two hands together as if he were praying—"but the tone of this interview has taken a rather ridiculous turn. If you want to discuss our corporation in the context of helping America survive this crisis, I'll be happy to continue. Any other misguided contentions on your part will bring our tête-à-tête to an end."

"Hendrix is innocent, and you know it," Devin said.

With this, Arthur Quail rose abruptly.

In response, Devin noticed Galbreath grip the lion's head of the cane. It appeared as if he planned to strike the billionaire.

Quail appeared oblivious and picked up the newspaper. "For the record, and the benefit of anyone else listening, what I know of Dr. Hendrix, I've read in the press. This story on page one? It validates what everyone has suspected."

"Hendrix is innocent," Devin repeated.

"Then why doesn't he come forward and defend himself?" Quail threw the newspaper in Devin's lap.

"Because you killed or kidnapped him . . . you or one of your coconspirators," Devin said, rising.

Quail reached down and handed Devin the valise. "This interview is over. I suggest you both leave." He turned, walking back to the hidden doorway from which he had entered. "Please show yourselves out."

Devin and Galbreath exchanged looks. "How much do you know about Baghigra?" Devin said suddenly.

The word stopped Quail dead in his tracks. He stood with his back to them, staring at the wall. "What did you say?" he asked, not turning.

"Baghigra," Devin repeated.

Quail swung around. As Devin watched he walked calmly to the aquarium and pushed a small black button set into the black onyx rim.

Almost immediately three men stepped from the hidden doorway. All were large and well muscled, wearing black turtlenecks and blazers.

Devin nudged Galbreath's arm.

The Englishman nodded and grasped his cane as if he were about to brandish it like a sword.

Quail joined the men as they approached, whispering

something. Then he turned toward Devin and Galbreath and pointed at the men. "My assistants have decided to join us."

"What a pleasure to meet you all," Devin said sarcastically.

The three bruisers in brush haircuts walked over and surrounded Devin and Galbreath. "Pat them down," Quail said.

Galbreath protested. "This is outrageous."

Quail stood back with arms folded. "Unbutton your collars and raise your hands, gentlemen."

Galbreath and Devin complied as two of the men checked their clothing. The youngest of the three looked at Quail and shook his head.

"Empty the briefcase," Quail ordered.

Devin became incensed. "This is totally uncalled for—"

"Give it to them," Quail said forcefully. His raised voice echoed in the stone chamber.

Devin handed the briefcase to one thug, who flipped the case open and spilled the contents on the floor, while a second sifted through the scattered paraphernalia and the third eyed them aggressively.

"Anything?" Quail asked. He kept his eyes locked on Devin's.

"Not a thing, sir."

"Take the case in the other room and examine it thoroughly," Quail said sharply.

Galbreath leaned on his cane. The two remaining thugs held their positions next to Devin and Galbreath while the other left the room with the case.

"You've become a rather fascinating enigma to me, Mr. Parks," Quail said, ignoring Galbreath. "A TV reporter requests an interview and then starts spouting strange foreign names that by all logic, he shouldn't know."

"Does the word *Baghigra* bother you?" Devin asked.

"Not at all. I'm fascinated with foreign words."

"It's African," Galbreath said. "Sudanese, to be precise."

Quail deliberately shifted his glance to Galbreath. He stepped over in front of the Englishman until he was virtually nose to nose with him. "And you, sir," he said icily. "How did you become acquainted with the term?"

"He's fascinated with foreign words, too," Devin said, trying to draw the attention back in his direction.

Quail retreated a step and looked Galbreath over from head to toe. "He must be more than fascinated." His eyes narrowed. "That's an equatorial tan you have there, Mr. Galbreath. I've spent some time in the Middle East."

Quail began to pace in front of the Englishman, like a big cat in a tiny cage, as the thug with the briefcase returned. He simply shook his head at Quail, who continued: "I'm familiar with a particular coloration the skin takes on from long bouts with the mid-African sun. You should be very careful." Galbreath remained mute. Quail stopped pacing, clenched his teeth, and flashed a wicked, menacing smile. "I understand overexposure can lead to stroke or even death."

Devin watched him carefully. "The soldiers out front said you might be too busy to see us for very long, Mr. Quail." He eyed the other men as he spoke.

"Soldiers?" Quail asked. "You mean the National Guard? What do they have to do with you?" He gestured to one of his henchmen, who moved to the door, opened it a crack, and looked down the hallway.

"We put them on alert in case we were detained," Devin said, relieved to see the man at the door look back at Quail and nod. "I think it's time we moved on."

Quail's glance shifted to him, and Devin felt the chill as their gazes met. "Give him the case," Quail said quietly. The young muscleman handed the valise to Devin. "Yes, you may leave now," Quail said. "And leave knowing that we're about ready to enter a new level of conflict."

"Conflict?" Devin smirked. "Really?"

Galbreath and Devin began their retreat toward the large leather doors.

Quail clenched his teeth. "I'd love to have you stay."

"You've been quite hospitable, but no. We've struck home, haven't we, Mr. Quail? Baghigra represents trouble, doesn't it?" Devin asked.

Quail and his henchmen accompanied them to the doors. Devin knew they were dying to get their hands on him.

Quail smiled. "You wouldn't be so brave if the National Guard weren't out in the hall."

"You'd kidnap us like you did Hendrix, wouldn't you?" Devin said.

Smiling still, Quail reached out and gave Devin a slight shove. "I'm warning you, Parks."

Devin turned to face Quail, and the youngest henchman moved to intervene. Quail restrained his man.

"You'll be seeing us again," Devin said.

"I guarantee it," Quail replied. Then, strangely, his body relaxed, seemingly resigned. "Let them go," he said to his men. They stepped aside.

Devin moved to the leather doors, letting Galbreath trail behind, hopeful the recording device would continue to pick up Quail's voice.

"Since you seem fond of rare diseases," Devin said, stopping at the door, looking back, "it's a shame we can't share some snapshots of infected children that we picked up in Africa . . . in Baghigra to be precise."

"What are you talking about?" Quail sounded genuinely shocked.

"You didn't expect that, did you?" Galbreath asked. "Dr. Kahvahl must have been careless."

"Kahvahl," Quail said, clearly off balance. "Maybe there *is* something to discuss."

Devin gripped the door handle. "And what would that be?"

"More power and money than you've ever dreamed of."

"A payoff. If we give you the photographs?" Devin asked.

"Something like that." Quail was scrambling. "Come back and sit down."

"No thanks," Devin said, opening the large leather door.

"Walk out of here now, and you're both dead men," Quail said quietly, through clenched teeth.

"Nice to have met you, too," Devin muttered as he and Galbreath crossed the reception area, past the woman in the glass booth.

Devin glanced back at Quail's ashen face, then opened the large glass doors and pushed Galbreath ahead. He hurried down the marble hallway toward the corporal, with Galbreath struggling to keep pace.

"Well, you wanted his reaction. I think you have enough of it, don't you agree?" Galbreath whispered, referring to the diskette in his cane. "Shall I go on to Atlanta, as planned?"

"Yes," Devin said softly so only Galbreath could hear. "Use Freeman's name when you check in at Dobbins Air Base. I'll pick up Ginelle in Monterey and meet you tomorrow afternoon."

As they passed Quail's statue and approached the soldiers, Devin felt the adrenaline surge through his body. He smiled at Galbreath, appreciating him, enjoying the taste of conquest.

As they continued out toward the sunlit street together, the clicking of his heels on the polished stone floor rang in Devin's ears like gunshots.

THE TENTH DAY
7:46 P.M.
Near the Monterey Peninsula

It was a clear California night as Devin speeded toward the cabin, eager to return to Ginelle. The smell of the sea had moved in on the coast road and he had the top down on the Chrysler convertible he had rented.

He had called Ginelle from the chartered Learjet after a special national network broadcast announced that Maxillar Chemical had just discovered a cure, a vaccine now being called "Quaillium" by the national press, which the White House had embraced. Devin wondered if his visit to Quail had prompted this sudden news, and Ginelle had sounded extremely upset, since official acceptance of Quaillium robbed her father of his discovery of the vaccine and of his chance to clear his name.

He got off the main highway and drove to the beach. Rounding the bend into the gravel driveway, he caught sight of the weathered wood cabin with its cedar-shake roof. As his headlights hit the front porch he was surprised to see Max Davis, the CNB security guard, coming down the front steps.

"Max, what's going on?" he asked after leaping out of the car.

"Mr. Parks," Max said sheepishly. "She got me."

"What do you mean? Where's Ginelle?" The lights in the cabin were on, lighting up the trees near the house.

"She just called. She's probably right behind you."

"Called?"

"From the van. She's been at CNB."

"San Francisco? I thought you were supposed to—"

"I was." Max's gun belt creaked as he leaned on the holster.

"What the hell happened?"

"Well . . ." Obviously embarrassed, Max gestured to the porch and sat down on the top step. He looked out at the crashing surf. "Late this afternoon, I was in the front seat listening to the radio, letting the day go by in the shade, when she showed up."

"At the van?"

"Up there on the knoll." Max glanced up, his blue eyes showing his chagrin. "She said she'd been restless and asked if I wouldn't mind joining her for some coffee . . . a bit of conversation to pass the time. She's a very pleasant person when she flashes that smile, you know."

"What time was that?"

"Three o'clock or so. We were in the living room. Three cups later I asked to use the head. When I came back out she was gone. So was my jacket and hat."

Devin put a hand to his forehead. "And your keys . . ."

"Yep," Max said, frowning. "In the jacket. She took the van."

"Holy shit." Devin shook his head.

"I'm really sorry."

Seeing the older man's eyes, Devin tried to contain his displeasure, and sat down on the porch with Max to wait. After about fifteen minutes of stilted conversation, the Chevy van's headlights washed the cabin, pulling in behind the Chrysler. Ginelle hopped out of the front seat, wearing Max's jacket and holding his hat and some papers.

Both men stood as she approached.

"Look at this," she said, holding up the computer

printouts. "A complete rundown on the Maxillar corporation. And I picked up your list of calls that have come in since your broadcast, Devin. Over two hundred of them. What's the matter? You look upset."

Devin nodded to Max. "Would you mind leaving us?"

Max nodded and stepped forward, his hand extended.

"I'm sorry, Max." Ginelle smiled and handed him the hat and jacket. "But those worked great. With that special security sticker on your license plates, I drove right through National Guard checkpoints and they never stopped me."

Looking at Devin, Max shrugged, took the clothes. He started his van and backed it up the hill under the trees.

"You know it's dangerous for you out there?" Devin glared as Ginelle joined him on the stairs.

"I don't care. Do you realize I've become completely dependent on you, your opinions and your judgment?" She walked toward the screen door and he followed. "Without consulting me, you agreed to withhold Galbreath's photographs from Senator Kemper's congressional investigating committee." Her green eyes flashed as she opened it. "You casually tell me on the phone that you agreed not to show them because Galbreath is *nervous* about it?"

"He came to me of his own free will, can you respect that?"

"And my father may be dead by now. Do you respect that?" She slammed the door behind her. Frustration from her long ordeal had finally surfaced.

Devin was right behind her in the hall.

"Then this Maxillar fiasco." She waved the printouts in the air. "I'm going to study this stuff tonight and I'm off to Washington in the morning."

"The hell you are. Galbreath's in Atlanta."

"And Kemper's in D.C."

"Kemper's in bed with the pharmaceutical lobby. Swain's just an adviser. How do we know we can trust either of them?"

"Freeman's friend Williamson, then. Someone at the Capitol." Her eyes moistened with anger. "Where are the photographs, anyway?"

"In the car. Freeman has copies."

"May I have them, please?"

Without saying a word, Devin walked out the door. Finding the envelope in his camel-hair coat on the front seat, he turned and paused. Ground fog had begun to waft through the reeds outside the house. Up the knoll, the grove of madrona trees had blended into a hulking mass, with the silhouette of the van barely visible underneath. Beyond, on the hills above the coast road, distant head-lights of a vehicle sparkled. Military, he thought.

He looked out at the ocean.

The famous seventeen-mile drive was only minutes to the south. He wished he could take Ginelle on that ride in the morning instead of a plane ride back east.

Returning to the porch, he opened the screen door and handed her the pictures. She took them, examined them, her face occasionally twisted with disgust.

"These poor innocents," she said. "I can see why Gal-breath was moved to call you."

"Wait until you meet him." Devin leaned against the wall next to the oak umbrella rack. "He's an incredible man." He envisioned the Englishman in his Akubra hat and cane, smiling as they said good-bye in Cleveland. "Look, Ginelle. He's expecting to carry out the plan we devised. Let's rendezvous with him in Atlanta. Then, if we all agree, we can fly on to Washington."

She shook her head. "If we meet at all, it'll be in Washington. Call and arrange to have him come."

"I can't get through to him on the base at this hour."

"In the morning, then. I'll call Kemper. If he's not in, I'll call Swain." She looked at him apologetically, sensing his distress. "I'm sorry, I feel I should take a stronger hand in these matters now. It's my father, after all." She walked to the banister. "Now, if you don't mind, I'm going to go to bed. I've got an early morning."

He watched as she climbed the stairs, remembering past demonstrations of her willpower: her inner strength when she saved his life; her determination at the Disease Control Center. He also understood her pain. Too much time had passed since her father's disappearance. She had crossed the line.

He walked into the living room and stared at the pictures of seals and seagulls over the living-room couch and felt restless, not knowing what to do with himself. Bothered by the incompleteness of their conversation, he needed some sort of closure to the evening.

Reaching the top of the stairs, he paused at her bedroom door and knocked. "May I come in?"

"I'm asleep."

He opened the door and looked in. She was curled up in bed. "I'll do whatever you wish," he said quietly.

She looked up, reading his face, then sighed, pushing the blanket back. "I know you're doing the best you can, Devin. I appreciate that. I want you to understand. When my mother died and my sister Lisa was killed in Switzerland, Dad naturally clung to me. But I hurt him. I was so upset with his work. It was abhorrent to me. And for good reason. For the last two years I had actually shunned him." She choked on the last words. "Now he's the only thing I want back in my life."

He took a step toward the bed, but she extended a flattened hand.

"Please," she said. "I think I just need to be alone."

He felt suddenly empty, wanting to share her grief.

Perhaps he'd overwhelmed her, bullied her into com-
plying with his decisions.

"Whatever you want to do," he said.

"I want a good night's sleep."

Devin watched her settle down. Even in these
moments of desperation, dressed in Freeman's wife's
blue pajamas, she looked every bit a woman. He couldn't
help notice her soft outlines as she turned from one side
to the other, and suddenly felt a little ashamed of himself.
"I need rest, too." He grasped the door handle, wondering when he would ever find another woman in
his life.

She pulled up the blanket, turned her head, and closed
her eyes. He began to leave.

"Thanks for trying so hard, Devin," she said, her voice
muffled by the pillow.

"I'll wake you at six." He leaned back through the
doorway. "We'll leave for the airport at seven."

No reply. Wisps of her short blond hair curled along
the edges of the maroon blanket.

He watched her for another brief moment, then closed
the door.

Alone once again and filled with ambivalence about
Ginelle's demands, Devin decided to take a walk.
Clearing his mind would help him sleep.

After changing into beach shoes, jeans, and a black
shirt, he quietly passed her bedroom door and went
downstairs.

Feeling self-indulgent, he stopped in the kitchen and
checked the cupboard. A nightcap would help calm him.
He poured himself a shot of bourbon, adding some water
from the sink. Drink in hand, he wandered out through
the front door onto the wooden porch facing the ocean.
He looked up the knoll. Max was likely asleep in the
back of the van.

The tide came in under a half-moon as he walked in the sand.

Good to be out by the roar of the surf. He stood by the long grasses on the edge of the beach, sipping the Jack Daniel's, inhaling the salt air. The alcohol warmed his gut.

As ocean breezes swept his face Devin watched sandpipers looking for food. The luminescence of the bubbling surf gave the scene an eerie, surreal appearance. The sandpipers' underbellies shone as they scurried about upon the flattened waves, black mirrors dissecting themselves in long planes of continuous motion.

His thoughts kept returning to the woman asleep upstairs in Freeman's quaint cabin. He felt isolated from her. Even unappreciated. Why? he wondered. Because she would not agree to "his" plan? Would her demands cause him to betray the Englishman?

Her assertiveness made him feel oddly removed. Yet he was attracted to her. Perhaps he wanted what he couldn't have, or desired something different than he'd ever experienced. She was certainly different from other women . . . at least, from those whom he had taken the time to get to know.

She was no Susan. Susan had been attentive and possessive in a wifely sort of way, until he ignored her.

But Susan never challenged him. She had seemed submissive to his career ambitions—that is, until she finally tired of it and walked out without warning. The minute she was gone, he'd felt the enormity of his loss. He had been in love with her but had, temporarily, fallen in greater love with his own broadcast career, leaving Susan to fend for herself, which she did poorly. He realized too late how blind he had become to her needs. Susan had endured the passing months with bitter tolerance, dismay, and finally rebellion. Submission had turned to resentment.

No submission in Ginelle. He could read the signs in her green eyes. In these untoward circumstances she might need his help. But, otherwise . . .

Ginelle. He had only known her in this time of crisis. Was she truly that fiercely self-reliant? Or simply uninterested in him? Or was there someone else? Perhaps both. Strong women often had high expectations. Perhaps he wasn't intellectual enough. The world of academia was certainly very different from that of the media.

His brow furrowed as he looked out beyond the birds at the cold ocean.

Dr. Ginelle Hendrix and her intellectual sophistication.

He took another sip and stared at the bourbon in the glass.

This would be over soon. They would go their separate ways. In the morning he'd call Dobbins Air Base in Atlanta, tell Galbreath of Ginelle's decision, and be done with it.

The wind had come up. He took the last sip of his drink and looked up at the clouds moving across the slate-colored sky. Occasionally, they obscured the moon. The luminescence on the waves came and went as the clouds' dark shadows moved over the beach.

Minutes later, in his room, he sat on the quilted bedspread and removed his shoes and socks. Grains of sand fell on the hardwood floor. He took his shirt off and lay back on the pillow, intending to get up in a few moments to go to the bathroom. He fell off the edge of awareness into a sound sleep.

Dread: his next conscious thought. Was it a nightmare? No, something else had disturbed him. Distant surf . . . the only sound in his room.

But downstairs. A small noise. He lay still.

Perhaps it was Ginelle getting something to eat.

He took a moment to clear his head, staring up into the darkened room. His gaze traveled along the cedar ceiling, coming to rest on the knots in the wood. Some appeared to be staring back at him, hollow eyes from a fallen tree.

Then he heard it again. A branch on a window. No, too metallic for that.

He decided to investigate. Bare-chested, barefoot, dressed in jeans, he moved to the landing. He pushed Ginelle's door open a crack. Ginelle lay motionless under the covers. Clearly, she wasn't the source of the disturbance.

Devin closed the door and crept toward the top of the stairs, cursing to himself as the floor creaked. He shivered, feeling the cold wood floor under his bare feet.

As he ventured out onto the top stair he could see the front door below. No lights in the house, just the front porch. The glow from the outside bulb illuminated the living room with a dim blue aura.

Another stair. He moved slowly, stepping down sideways, feeling along the banister with his hands. Then he heard another sound, toward the back of the house, perhaps from the spare bedroom next to the kitchen. Would Max have returned to the house? Certainly not without announcing himself. Devin would have to check.

He reached the bottom of the stairs and stood on the dark brown throw rug in the entry next to the front door.

Silence buzzed in his ears.

Wait. There. Yes. He heard it again. Definitely toward the right side of the house, behind the living room.

He tiptoed across the living room, making as little noise as possible. Blinds were partially closed. The shadow of the window frames fell on the hardwood floor.

Reaching the door to the spare bedroom, he groped in

the darkness for the handle. The door didn't budge, wouldn't open, locked from the other side. Strange. He didn't remember locking it. Perhaps Ginelle. Or even Max, while she was gone.

He would approach from the kitchen.

As he turned right at the hallway his bare left foot caught the phone cord, yanking the antique phone across the top of the stand. It emitted a hollow ringing sound.

"Son-of-a-bitch," Devin whispered, glancing up at the second-floor landing, hoping he hadn't wakened Ginelle.

He peered into the kitchen at the yellow counter and the large cutting board. Nothing.

The back door was secure. But yes, again, a tiny tapping sound in the next room. Could a bird have gotten in? The door to the spare bedroom was closed, but there was no lock. He tiptoed across the linoleum. Should he call Max? Probably nothing anyway, mice in the walls. He'd feel ridiculous. But just in case, he picked up a large carving knife that stuck out of the wire dish drainer next to the sink.

He slowly pushed the door open.

Darkness. The spare bedroom had no overhead light. He tried to remember the location of the furniture. A single lamp rested on the end table next to the plaid Hide-A-Bed on the far wall, beneath a curtained window, and a small wooden coffee table sat in front with old issues of *Reader's Digest* stacked next to a seashell ashtray.

He would check the window.

Clutching the knife in his hand, he stepped across the throw rug toward the bed. Nothing odd here.

He knelt on the bed on one knee, pushed the curtain aside, and heard tapping; the roller shade was halfway down, hitting against the window frame. A gentle breeze caressed his face.

Strange. The window wasn't open.

In the dim light from the backyard, he could see the latch on the window in the lock position. Why the fresh air? He reached out to the window's lower panel.

His hand touched . . . nothing. The pane was missing. The metallic sound. The pane. Glass cutter.

Fingers of fright danced down his back. As he slowly turned his head toward the kitchen door, his eyes adjusted to the darkness. He saw a dark shape moving toward him. It wasn't Max.

From his diaphragm, Devin emitted a sound he had never made before in his life, something between a shriek and a wail, forming one word . . . a name.

"Ginelle!" Devin screamed, as loud as he could. The man was on him, wearing a black sweater and ski mask.

Devin stood and thrust the knife downward, striking at the man's chest.

His adversary squatted slightly, crossing his hands over his head. Too late Devin recognized the defensive karate move. Devin's wrists came down hard at the man's crossed wrists. And in a split second his assailant seized his right hand in a viselike grip. With a sidestep, the man twisted Devin's arm, and Devin found himself in the air, spinning head over heels.

He landed on the coffee table, the wood splintering under his weight, magazines scattering.

His attacker still had his right wrist clamped and quickly fit a foot under Devin's armpit. The other foot was already in a back swing.

Devin felt the crushing blow to the right side of his stomach. The body kick thrust air out of him, and he was unable to breathe. A searing pain shot up from his hip to his arm. He wanted to grab his side, but his left arm was pinned beneath him.

In the fury of the moment he became aware of Ginelle yelling his name from upstairs.

Devin now heard the kitchen door splinter. Four men stepped through into the kitchen and then ran up the stairs. The second floor creaked above. Ginelle screamed again, this time a panicked painful shriek. Devin struggled to get up, but his assailant had him firmly pinned.

The man brought a gun down to his cheek. "You! Up!" he ordered, shifting the muzzle under his chin.

Devin was forced up with the lift of the gun.

His assailant gripped him on the side of the neck, fingers digging deep into his flesh. The gunman yanked Devin toward the kitchen door.

Other men rambled down the stairs. Devin watched dark figures moving down the hallway toward the kitchen. Where the hell was Max?

The man holding Devin barked a sharp command to the others as they passed, carrying Ginelle, whose pajama top had been torn, revealing her pale skin.

Seeing her partial nakedness angered Devin. He threw the bulk of his weight back toward his captor, hitting him with an elbow strike across the face.

The blow stunned the man just enough to allow Devin's superior size and weight to slam him into the refrigerator. Straining to look outside, Devin saw Ginelle disappearing.

Two men were headed back toward him.

Then everything went into slow motion. A blow to the neck forced him to his knees. Then he heard tires on gravel. A vehicle had come to a halt.

"Max!" Devin shouted.

The gun butt came down just over the temple. Everything exploded into blinding white light. He hung in a limbo of pain and crashed to the floor.

He felt himself being dragged, held by the wrists, a sack of bones, bumping out the kitchen door, down the two steps, onto the grass. Several sets of hands gripped him, lofted him into the air above their shoulders. Then they started to run. Their bobbing, trotting motion caused blood on his forehead to stream downward into one eye, along his nose, and over his top lip. He tasted the salty sweetness.

He fought to regain his vision, trying to get a free hand to his face, and then saw why Max had not shown up. Up on the knoll, the Chevy van was aflame under the trees. Then whose car . . .

Sudden exclamations in an Asian tongue from his attackers.

A back door slammed.

"Stop! FBI!" someone shouted.

Devin strained to look back with his good eye and saw dark shadows of two men in full chase.

He heard whooshes. Several of them. The silencer on a pistol.

Then the sound of a bullet striking flesh very close. One set of hands holding him fell away. Then the other.

Cold grass on his face. They had dropped him to the ground.

He squinted up with his good eye in the darkness and saw one of his masked captors unsling an AK-47.

The man yelled something in a foreign language. "Sing Chu! Sing Chu!" he barked, and pulled the trigger.

The rapid-fire weapon spit shells down onto Devin as he lay on the ground.

His other captor knelt on one knee, facing the house, firing a semiautomatic handgun. A third lay bleeding only a few feet away.

From ground level, Devin watched as one of the FBI men took a hit and dropped to his knees. The other fired rapidly in his direction. He heard the sound of another bullet striking the man kneeling to his right.

The man cried out as his shoulder squirted red onto the

black turtleneck and he vaulted backward, hitting the
ground on his back.

Magnum, Devin thought. Powerful.

Realizing the remaining FBI man might be his only
hope, Devin kicked at the assailant who stood above him,
trying to dislodge the weapon from his grasp, or at least
spoil his aim.

But the man sidestepped and fired another rapid volley
of rounds. Flashes spit from the barrel of the rifle, and
Devin heard the FBI man's shout of pain as he, too, was hit.

Then silence.

The hooded man with the automatic rifle breathed
hard, then looked down at Devin. His body language
spoke anger; he took the rifle off the sling.

Devin barely saw the butt of the weapon descend. The
blow struck him in the forehead and the world went
black.

THE THIRTEENTH DAY
7:32 P.M.
An abandoned Maxillar
Chemical Truck Depot
Topeka, Kansas

For forty-eight hours Devin traveled through various stages of delirium like a blind swimmer in a cauldron of cognition. As he regained consciousness sounds from some tortured hell surrounded him: pitiful whimpering from an animal caught in a trap, senseless cries, mumbling of a creature possessed.

Then another sound. Someone saying his name. "Devin . . . please, Devin. Shhhhh."

Cold compress on his forehead. Gentle hands stroking his hair.

He tossed his head back and forth. The whimpering drew closer. Louder. Interrupted by gasps of air. He lifted one eyelid. The other wouldn't open. Shocked, he understood that the anguished sounds came from his own throat. Thrashing. Wanting to get up. Being held down. The coolness of the rag. Moisture on his cheek.

There, next to him, Ginelle, with a look of extreme concern on her face. "Dad, he's coming to."

What did she say? Dad?

More whimpering. Words. Forming on his lips. He could speak.

"Ginelle. What happened?" Stabbing pain in his rib cage.

"Quiet, Devin. Lie still. You'll be all right." She stroked his head. Why so considerate? Did she care for him? Another hushed voice. On his right. A man. Holding his wrist.

"His pulse is slowing. The seizure is abating."

"Thank God," she said.

Dim light. Or was he hallucinating? "I couldn't talk," Devin said, embarrassed over the sounds he apparently had made.

She put a hand to his mouth. "I know. But please, speak softly."

"Why?" He struggled to sit up. She clutched his wrist. Looking down, he noticed he wore a black shirt, blood spattered down the chest.

She looked over her shoulder nervously. "We're in trouble." In light blue pajama bottoms and a black turtle-neck top, she lay next to him on a blanket covering a grated metal floor.

Devin reached up and touched his face. "Where are we?" Left eye swollen, forehead bruised and cut. The bridge of his nose felt heavily scabbed. He must look like a beat-up fighter.

"We're inside a truck. You're seriously hurt," Ginelle said. "But you'll be all right."

He remembered the capture. Her nakedness. "Your clothes! Did they hurt you?"

"No. Just made lewd remarks," she said bitterly, "but finally they gave me something to wear."

"I feel weird."

The voice on his blind side spoke. "They injected you with a sedative."

Devin strained and recognized a haggard, gray-haired man with glasses taking his pulse, also lying on a gray blanket next to him. Devin tried to sit up. "You're—"

"Dr. Hendrix, Mr. Parks. Thank you for helping my daughter."

"I did a bang-up job, didn't I?" Devin winced. "God,

my head feels like it's going to come off. Maybe it already has."

"Kahvahl experimented with mind-altering depressants based on an extract of curare," Hendrix said. "They gave you that injection. Recovery is extremely painful."

Devin could relate to that. A knifelike pain traveled from his left eyebrow over the top of his head and down his spine.

"Kahvahl?" he asked incredulously. "He's here?"

Hendrix pointed. "He is still heavily sedated under the same drug they gave you. Over there."

Several feet away an emaciated dark-skinned man with a matted gray Afro slept. He lay flat on his back in the corner of the stainless-steel grating, dressed in a set of gray overalls.

"That's Kahvahl?" Devin asked in a hushed voice. "Is he always like that?"

Ginelle shook her head, showing a glimmer of a smile. "Good. You've retained your sense of humor," she said.

Dr. Hendrix moved closer. "They literally gave him a bit of his own medicine, a generous injection. He's been like that for days."

"I guess he deserves it." Devin studied him. Kahvahl's broad forehead and flat nose made him look as if he'd been beaten. "Is his face swollen?"

"No. Those are his features. Though he's looked better in the past. They starved him, prepared to let him die, fed him intravenously until today."

Devin tried to fathom their dilemma. Friends in peril. He remembered the Englishman.

"Ginelle! What about Galbreath?"

"They captured him in Cleveland just after you left. He was here when we arrived. He looked terrible. They tortured him. He had knife cuts all over his face. And now . . ." She motioned to the door. Two guards resembling his assailants in Monterey sat silently on either side on metal stools.

"He's out there?"

"Somewhere."

"Did you talk to him?"

"Briefly. He asked about you. Then they dragged him off."

Devin now fully understood their plight. Galbreath might have been their last hope. "You realize what this means, don't you? No one knows we're here."

"Max does," Ginelle said.

"I suspect Max is dead," Devin said sadly.

"But Ginelle said there was other resistance."

Devin tried to focus on Hendrix. "Resistance? Two dead FBI men. Some resistance."

"But it means they followed you," Hendrix said. "Jaktar's men tailed you as well. They planted a tracking device in your briefcase."

Quail's office, Devin thought. That's why they had taken the valise to the other room.

"The agents might have radioed in," Ginelle said hopefully.

"We wouldn't be here if they had." Devin got up on one elbow, looked down the length of the truck, noticing the rancid smell of human sweat. He marveled at Hendrix. "Doctor, you've been in here this whole time?"

Hendrix nodded. "I'm the senior prisoner."

"Any hope of escape?"

"That door." Hendrix nodded toward the metal-plated opening. "That wall opens hydraulically. And of course there's the vent." He motioned to a small fan ten feet above.

Devin assessed their situation. They were encased in steel, huddled together at one end of the trailer. Thirty feet away, guards sat with semiautomatic weapons slung on their shoulders. The men appeared uninterested in their conversation. Devin wondered if either of them had been involved in the assault on the cabin.

Hendrix read his thoughts. "There are more of them. I've seen as many as five or six, commanded by a strange-looking blond man named Jaktar. He's large and very unpleasant."

"He's a maniac," Ginelle said. "He nicked Galbreath's cheek with a large knife he carries in his boot."

Devin was starting to organize his thoughts. "How many of these damn rigs do they have?"

Hendrix adjusted his glasses. "Wu Sun says there are five."

"Who's Wu Sun?"

"A guard. He's more friendly. It took time, but I convinced him to speak with me, several times. He seemed somewhat sympathetic, different from the others. He's a broad-faced fellow, like a bear. A student at Columbia for two years, pulled into all this because his cousin Sing Chu is one of their leaders."

"Sing Chu? I heard that name in Monterey." The backyard. Firing. Someone yelled the name. "So, they travel in these trucks?"

"Command centers," Hendrix said. "Behind that door they have a bank of communications equipment. I've caught glimpses when it opens. Impressive, isn't it? That entire wall actually moves sideways so they can load men and gear. The rest of the chamber remains a solid piece, heavily reinforced. My car was in here the first week. The only good thing is that at least we're together."

Devin's head finally cleared. "Yes, why do that? Put us all together in one vehicle."

"They're using all the other trucks," Hendrix said. "Quail's orders, I assume."

"You know about Quail!"

Hendrix quieted him with a finger to his lips. "Yes. Ginelle told me. I've made some assumptions from what I've learned. An incredible story, Mr. Parks."

Devin looked back at the guards, who remained immobile. "Well, tell me what you know. If we all know the facts, no matter which of us survives, we have a chance to retaliate. Do you agree?"

"Of course." Hendrix nodded thoughtfully. "Even if one of us escapes, he or she better have details."

The idea sent a chill down Devin's back. Here they were, huddled somewhere in a fortified mobile fortress, possibly the only hope of thwarting a plot against the country.

Devin decided to get the ball rolling. "I've got a million questions, of course, but please begin."

"I'll reconstruct parts of the story. Some of it will be based on inferences I've made, and some from what the guard, Wu Sun, told me." He squeezed his daughter's hand. She sat on her haunches next to Devin. Hendrix made himself more comfortable. He sat cross-legged next to his daughter.

"Ginelle tells me you know about Africa."

"Yes. Galbreath told me. The Sudan and all that."

"By 'all that' I assume you mean Kenya and Tanzania." Hendrix removed his glasses and cleaned them with his ragged shirt. "Kahvahl worked with molecular experimentation for decades." He placed his glasses low on his nose. "But the molecular machine didn't become viable until after Black Diamond's replicator technology helped make it an efficient attack weapon."

"Through Glant and Metzger and yourself."

"Not exactly. They must have taken it to the next phase. The replication code was incomplete when I left them."

"Is that the reason nothing came of the Baghigra experiments?"

"Baghigra was brutal, inhumane, and primitive. Yet Kahvahl's work in that hovel of a laboratory generated a new core. The core microbe would be classified as a virus, since that term covers a myriad of foreign particles. Kahvahl developed something quite deadly, but from a strategic perspective the killer microbe was ineffective."

Devin listened as Hendrix went on to explain how after Hendrix resigned from Black Diamond, Kahvahl, Glant, and Metzger had persevered and succeeded in hypersplicing molecular particles, using Kahvahl's virus and molecular trigger parts, formulating an attack microbe while the government was told the experiment was incomplete.

Apparently, Arthur Quail had paid off Glant and Metzger, but once he was in control of the microbe, he ordered them both killed. Hendrix suspected that he himself was only alive because of some undisclosed plan Quail had in mind.

Devin was struck by the look of tranquility on Hendrix's face. He had confronted the imminence of death and made peace with himself.

"Understand. Kahvahl's motives," Hendrix continued, "were purely ideological."

Devin found himself at odds with that idea. "What ideals justify mass murder?"

"In this case, religious fervor. History teaches that fanaticism always accompanies dogma, often condemning dissenters to death. I believe Kahvahl was a zealot who, when offered the opportunity, joined his countrymen in an act of war against the United States."

"His countrymen?"

"The men who spread the infection."

"They were Iranian?" Devin asked, looking over at Kahvahl.

"Yes, according to Wu Sun, though they were joined by some Iraqis and Lebanese. Mostly immigrants planted here since 1979, a few American converts—young men tied by an oath of death. For one reason or another, they felt abused by our system and chose to retaliate."

Devin remembered Galbreath's assessment of Islamic radicalism. "Did this guy Wu Sun say how they did it?"

Hendrix frowned. "An odd scheme, really. Ironically, many Middle Eastern immigrants, particularly those without much English, are relegated to doing menial tasks. A number of these terrorists found jobs as janitors in schools. This allowed them to infect children with the microbe. Thereafter, trucks like the one we're sitting in retrieved the terrorists. Wu Sun was on one of those missions. On his route, he dropped twenty-three men between Minnesota and Wisconsin. They walked across the Canadian border to prearranged pickup points. Cars were left for them in the forest."

"They're in Canada?"

"No. Not any longer. A ship picked them up in a remote area near Port Alberni on Vancouver Island. They sailed for North Korea twelve days ago."

"An Islamic–North Korean connection," Devin said pensively, remembering Galbreath's comments at the bar. "Obviously, the North Koreans and Islamic terrorists were convinced to work together in this instance." He remembered the map at the DCC in Atlanta. Infection pattern like a nuclear strike, Dr. Chang had said. "Did Wu Sun say how the terrorists spread the epidemic?"

"Wu Sun described it as best he could in laymen's terms. I've put the rest of the pieces together myself." Hendrix coughed.

Ginelle moved to his side and gave him a pat on the back. "Dad. You should rest."

"I've explained it to Ginelle," Hendrix said, red-faced. "Let her tell you." He turned, convulsing with another spasm of coughing.

Ginelle continued to rub his back and turned to Devin. As Hendrix's discomfort subsided she folded her hands in her lap. Even in these bleak surroundings, she looked beautiful.

"Long story short, Devin." She sounded like a teacher starting a lecture. "From Wu Sun's comments and Dad's extrapolations, we believe Quail recently added a clothing firm called First String to his long list of companies."

"I'm familiar with that."

"Well, First String manufactured baseball jerseys that were shipped to various schools. Each jersey was contaminated, soaked with poison in the crook of the right arm."

"Wait a minute. Schools. And terrorist janitors. Did First String ship haphazardly, or just where their janitors were employed?"

"You misunderstand. First String has been around for years. Their list of clients was extensive. Far too many schools to cover. We assume a limited number of terrorists sought jobs at specific schools already on the order list."

"All right. Contamination in the cloth. The microbe?"

"Only partially. Remember at my apartment I told you that for safety and transportation, the replicator was handled in two parts: alpha and beta. Both harmless until mixed together." She changed position, crossing her tan legs, and continued. "We assume the shirts were soaked in an alpha solution; thick enough to stay in the fabric and yet water-soluble, to respond to body heat and perspiration during exercise, slightly toxic but not deadly."

"Okay, I'm with you. The kids received their shirts." Devin visualized hundreds of children like Gordi, proud in their new uniforms.

"Right. Then our 'janitor' randomly chose a victim—or several, for that matter. During recess or lunch, whatever the opportunity, the conspirator inserted the beta portion of the replicator into the fingers of the kid's baseball mitts, likely in the form of a salve, or even leather balm."

"The kids now had the alpha portion in the crook of the right arm and the beta portion in the mitt."

"Exactly. And since the alpha portion of the replicator in the jerseys was toxic, it caused the skin to itch. After running around, our baseball player had a right arm inflamed with a rash inside the elbow. The rash spread to other parts of the arm. The child, wearing the contaminated glove at practice, used a beta-contaminated left hand—or so we must assume—to scratch an alpha-contaminated right inner arm, and the two mixed. You've seen how kids brutalize insect bites. Through sufficient abrasion, skin in the crook of the arm breaks and the replicator enters the bloodstream."

"Seemed like a lot of trouble to go to. I suppose an eyedropper into some soup wouldn't have been sufficient," Devin said.

"Not without risking unpredictable contamination. Remember how easily this bug spreads. They found a safe way for the microbe to become activated while on the victim's skin."

"All right, but what about Amy? If she picked up Gordi's glove—"

"She must have come into contact with mixed formula residue, possibly some blood. Gordi must have worn that glove again after scratching his arm several times. Traces of the mixed replicator would have been harbored in the leather."

Devin visualized Amy innocently putting on the child's mitt, dooming herself. The hiss of the hydraulic doors interrupted his thoughts.

The guards on the metal stools rose to their feet as two others dressed in black dragged a limp body into the room.

Shocked, Devin recognized the body's tweed clothing, the silver-blond hair; Galbreath, or what was left of him. His tan face resembled a pincushion; blood dotted his cheeks.

Devin got to one knee as Galbreath was hauled in and unceremoniously dumped on the floor by two men, one tall and one stocky.

Hendrix whispered in Devin's ear. "The short one is Wu Sun."

As the guards stepped back a large blond man in a black leather jacket entered, an empty cigarette holder clamped in his teeth. He carried Galbreath's cane.

"That's Jaktar," Hendrix whispered apprehensively.

As he approached, Jaktar threw the cane on the floor. It clattered across the metal grating and came to rest at Devin's feet.

Jaktar stared down at Galbreath's limp body. He raised his eyes; Devin noticed that one was blue and one brown. He looked up and their gazes met. Devin felt the chill of the blond man's icy glare.

"The English gentlemen spoke of you often," Jaktar said pointedly. "He told us everything."

"Did he?" Devin said coldly, trying not to glance down at the cane, wondering if they had discovered the DAD inside the handle.

"He's a fascinating man." Jaktar leaned over, grabbed Galbreath by the collar, and dumped him to one side.

Devin noticed a gun in Jaktar's shoulder holster under his left arm.

He checked Galbreath's tweed jacket, the breast pocket of which had been torn away. The material over the chest expanded and contracted ever so slightly. He was breathing.

Jaktar left Galbreath's body and approached Kahvahl. "Has he moved?" he asked loudly of anyone in the room. No one responded. Jaktar kicked Kahvahl's thigh and glared at Hendrix. "Answer me, old man."

"No," said Hendrix, "not at all."

Jaktar spun on the heel of his black boot. "Sing Chu," he yelled.

A fifth man stepped through the hydraulic doorway. Devin recognized him by the U-shaped mark on his brow.

"I want Kahvahl awake," Jaktar said. "Get an injection of amphetamine and B-twelve. How can he sign the documents if he isn't awake?"

The horseshoe-scarred Sing Chu nodded silently and left.

"What documents?" Devin asked, squinting at Sing Chu.

Jaktar sprung at Devin like a striking cobra, covering six feet in an instant, and landed a blow to his puffy right eye. Devin went down grunting. Excruciating pain blossomed over his eyebrow as he fell to the floor. As he brought a hand up to his forehead, he felt the fresh gush of warm blood run through his fingers.

Jaktar leaned over. "I didn't ask you to talk."

Devin felt the gloved hand on the back of his collar jerking him up off the floor.

"Please don't," Ginelle said. The gloved hand let go.

Devin rolled over and saw Jaktar face her.

"Ginelle," Jaktar said, taunting her. "I forgot. We pulled the two of you from your little love nest. You were bare-chested, from what they tell me. What an exit. The men say your breasts are quite shapely. I regret I wasn't there. Perhaps you will avail me of a private showing when all this is over."

Ginelle's face reddened.

Devin tried rising, but Jaktar stepped on his back, driving him down onto the grated floor. He heard leather creak and felt the tip of something very sharp behind his right ear, a searing sensation and a sharp tug as the tip nicked his earlobe.

Ginelle gasped.

Warm wetness covered the side of Devin's neck. He realized his earlobe had been split open.

Jaktar removed his boot from Devin's back.

In pain, Devin watched Sing Chu walk over to Kah-vahl, who had remained motionless by the back wall.

Jaktar joined him. "Give him the injection," he said.

Sing Chu and Jaktar bent over the Iranian. As the Asian inserted the needle Jaktar watched, dropping his hand by his side, dangling the knife, blood dripping off the blade. Devin's.

Ginelle slid over to Devin on her knees, touching his arm. She pushed the compress into his hand, motioning to his ear.

With his good eye trained on Jaktar's back, Devin nodded grimly, took the rag, and placed it up under the damaged earlobe.

Looking for openings, Devin became acutely aware of his adversary, the albino hair, oddly stark against his dark skin, the broad shoulders and narrow waist, the lanky muscularity. He also noticed the glint of metal just under the seam of the leather jacket at the small of Jaktar's back, another gun tucked into his belt. Judging from the shape, he guessed it was a nine-millimeter.

Jaktar barked something to Wu Sun and the other man

who had entered with Galbreath. They bowed and exited briskly. Two other guards took their positions by the door. Jaktar examined Galbreath, shaking him by the shoulder, then, apparently satisfied that there was no fight left in the man, he turned to Devin.

"You." Jaktar stared him down. "Why are you involved? You don't look like a man who seeks trouble. A television puppet, mouthing empty words. Why? For her?" He pointed a gloved hand at Ginelle.

She knelt, flushed, glaring back at Jaktar.

Dr. Hendrix froze.

Jaktar rocked back and forth on his boots as he spoke. "Is she that desirable? Maybe I should find out. You could watch." He stepped toward her, obviously enjoying the game.

The thought of Jaktar even touching Ginelle was too much for Devin. "Don't touch her, you fucking freak."

Jaktar pulled the gun from under his arm, cocked the weapon, and pointed it at him.

Devin felt the perspiration on his forehead.

Jaktar stepped closer, brought the gun forward until the tip of the barrel pressed on the red bruise below Devin's hairline. "Words? From the puppet?" He leaned down. "I'll sever your strings."

Devin knew the gun could go off any second. Jaktar's face was inches away. Devin smelled licorice on his breath. No one in the room made a sound. Seconds ticked by.

"If you were going to kill me, you would have done it by now," Devin said.

The gun's muzzle lifted off his head, then tapped him hard between the eyes, splitting the scabbed flesh on the bridge of Devin's nose.

"With me, you never know," Jaktar said, standing upright. "But I assure you, Mr. Parks, before this is over,

I will provide you with an invigorating moment of death." He stepped back, surveyed the group: Kahvahl and Galbreath unconscious, Hendrix kneeling by Ginelle, frozen in fear at Devin's side.

Apparently satisfied with the spectacle, Jaktar spun on his heel, then strode through the hydraulic door with Sing Chu in his wake.

THE THIRTEENTH DAY
8:00 P.M.
Ritz Carlton Hotel
Washington, D.C.

"I appreciate your coming, Sam. I know how busy you've been," Senator Kemper said, shuffling papers on the coffee table. His broad, meaty face showed his weakness for Southern cooking.

"I admit it. I haven't had a sound sleep in nearly two weeks." Dr. Samuel Gordon sat across from him, his huge body occupying nearly all of a love seat.

"God. Is that all it's been?" Kemper looked up through his bifocals. His gray suit jacket hung on the back of his chair.

"Thirteen days since the first sign of it."

With the curfew still enforced, the hotel was empty. Only essential personnel were permitted within so they could deal with visiting government officials and military visitors. The vast majority of the population was being vaccinated. Lingering paranoia prevented the president from lifting the curfew until he was completely assured the danger was past.

"You've given your deposition?" A lock of Kemper's gray hair kept falling in his face.

"I have. I'm driving to Maryland tomorrow and flying back to Georgia."

"So you're not going to be at the hearing?"

Gordon had to get back to Atlanta. Cleanup work yet to be done. Lab reports. Damage analysis.

"No, but Blake Pendergast, the virology specialist from USAMRIID, will be in attendance in case there are any technical questions about the epidemic. He and I will meet at his lab before I leave. Pendergast is sharp. When Quail testifies, he'll act as our own specialist to corroborate findings."

"Good." Kemper sat back in the chair, assuming a casual pose. "But even with Pendergast there, I need your take on things now. For my report. And so, you understand, our conversation is completely off the record. The president expects me to submit your views prior to the hearing. Purely committee business. Of course, it may eventually be passed on to the Justice Department."

Gordon disapproved of Kemper's blatant political ambition. His voluntary fact-finding mission for the Disease Investigating Committee had put him firmly in the national spotlight.

"Off the record or otherwise, ask what you like."

"I think the president's interest revolves around the state of the union, if you will," Kemper said. "He's scheduled several press conferences in the next few days. I want him to have answers." Kemper's severe underbite gave him the appearance of a bulldog. It also caused spit to spew when he sounded his *S*'s. "I need answers from *you*."

"Fire away."

"All right. Are you fully confident we've licked this thing?"

"Yes. The Maxillar vaccine appears effective." For political and professional reasons, Gordon wanted to sound sure. In reality, he wasn't sure at all, not with an untested vaccine and a sudden unexplained cure. He hoped Pendergast would set his mind at ease.

"How'd they develop it so fast?" the senator asked.

"I haven't seen Maxillar's lab specs. They're confidential. Only Pendergast at USAMRIID saw them, along with a few people at the FDA. And that's understandable. They don't want Merck or other pharmaceutical firms to do a knockoff. As you know, it had to be pushed through for quick approval. Concern for long-term effects were secondary . . . since there may not be a long term. Generally, it's not unlike polio in the 1950s, when everyone flocked to get vaccinated. But to get back to your question, Senator, if the microbe is synthetic, you can conclude that the antidote is also. Nanotechnology allows what they call replication once molecular particles are correctly analyzed."

"Do you understand all that?"

"Unfortunately, no. Pendergast got me most of the early information. Thank God for him and his associates. I've had too many fires to put out. Pendergast is in the process of writing up a full report on the epidemic. It's my understanding he'll have it available at the hearing. But for your purposes, or the president's . . . the key word is *replicator*. The microbe and the antidote both *replicate* or *duplicate* themselves under specific conditions. They're essentially machines, the size of a molecule, unprecedented in the annals of medicine. A synthetic cures another synthetic; the vaccine works because the antidote version deprograms the plague version."

"I never thought of it that way. I've got little machines floating around in my blood." Kemper created a fine mist of saliva when he pronounced the word *machines*.

"After vaccination, we all do, antigen replicators and hundreds of thousands of their clones. Don't let the word *machine* throw you. Think of it this way: Human organisms are large protoplasm machines. It's a matter of complexity and scale. Replicators are miniature machines. Normally, natural antigens recede after the job is done, but these puppies stick around. For good reason. They'll be there to prevent reinfection."

"How do you feel about Quail's offer to do the entire operation at cost?" Gordon felt Kemper was fishing.

Gordon had doubts about Quail's apparent generosity, and he threw the bait back. "A fine gesture, if it *is* free."

Kemper appeared to bristle at the remark. "What do you mean?"

"You should know, Senator, since you deal with lobbyists every day. Quail bought himself some worldwide notoriety. His name will appear on half a billion vaccine bottles, for Christ's sake. I understand he's being treated like an honored guest at the hearing."

"Yes. Of course, he asked to be there." Kemper smiled and seemed to backpedal. "But let's not misrepresent his philanthropy. The vaccine isn't exactly free. Maxillar wanted four dollars a vial. That's their base cost to manufacture."

"Who's picking up the tab?"

"The Department of the Interior . . . under a National Disaster Relief Fund. And, of course, Maxillar's getting paid for the international market."

"European shipments?" Gordon had had to field calls from Paris, questions from French scientists.

"That, and Japan. Canada and Mexico, quite obviously. Russia's requested the vaccine. You realize the damned Europeans are making this a scandal. The British press call it the Yankee Plague."

"I heard," Gordon said.

"France is trying to bring a lawsuit against us in the World Court, and I think they'll get it."

"Justified by what?"

"A couple of thousand cases at this point . . . exposure in Paris, other cities. If they charge negligence, they've probably got a case. Black Diamond was government-subsidized, after all. Here . . ." He handed Gordon the brief. "Take a look at these exhibit documents in the Hendrix case. A contract with Hendrix for research in New Mexico in 1978. You'll notice the signature of General Robert Drury, the head of intelligence for the United States Air Force in the seventies."

"An air-force project?" Gordon asked, taking the papers.

"Not officially. Never officially. As far as Congress was concerned, the Pentagon did business with the Black Diamond Corporation, a research company, a project initiated by Dr. Victor Glant. Metzger, Kahvahl, and Hendrix joined him. Look on page fifteen. Biographical information. Glant and Metzger were well known in their field."

Gordon leafed through the pages. "Impressive. Metzger wrote a thesis entitled *Computer Analysis of Neurophysical Functions*. And"—he turned the page—"here . . . 'Machine and Mental Linkage: Neurotherapy Through Chemical Encoding.' And I see Kahvahl was a biochemist."

"Yes. But Hendrix and Kahvahl appear to be the guys with the ultimate key." Kemper leaned forward. "Check page seventeen."

Gordon leafed forward. "Kahvahl pioneered viral research. He was born in Iran, which doesn't help him. A notable rebel. A hermit in Africa for some years. Hendrix, on the other hand, looks good on paper. He was a neurologist specializing in computer-applied messages." He read out loud: " 'Hendrix researched electromagnetic fields and their effect on cellular exchanges in the body.' "

"Mean anything to you?" the senator asked.

"Not much. Exchange of proteins, I suspect. I'm a doctor not a scientist. It's a damn shame Hendrix used his knowledge that way."

Kemper pointed. "Look at the pictures."

Gordon turned to the glossy eight-by-tens of Hendrix in the lab with dissected chimpanzees. Close-ups showed the animals' fur shaved away, evidence of blackened skin deterioration.

"Talk about animal rights," he said quietly.

"The FBI confiscated material from Hendrix's home in Williamsburg, proving conclusively that he had the knowledge and the means to head the disease conspiracy, including a journal with daily notes on experimentation with animals. And one final condemning item," Kemper said. "The last page." Gordon flipped to it as Kemper continued. "Special Agent Curtis, who conducted the search of Hendrix's home, submitted that," he said. "You'll notice it's addressed to Hendrix at his home address. Dated March seventeenth. Roughly a month and a half before the outbreak of the disease. Notice the postmark? Cairo, Egypt."

Gordon looked the letter over carefully. "It thanks the doctor and wishes him good luck in his 'quest.' "

"You see the signature?"

"Mahmoud Kahedeen," Gordon read.

"Few people would know him. CIA has him on file as a suspect in the murder of Anwar Sadat. He's a Muslim terrorist and leader of the Red Hand, an Islamic revolutionary force operating a worldwide ring of terrorist organizations throughout the Middle East, in Europe, and here in this country."

Gordon paged through the brief. "So that's where we're headed with this thing, prosecuting scientists who sold out to terrorists?"

"Apparently, Doctor. The president is determined to have answers. In the face of national panic, we have to find the goat. With the two other researchers dead and Kahvahl suspiciously missing, there's enough evidence to put Hendrix away. That's where we go. That letter seals it."

"The letter's a bit convenient, don't you think?"

"Maybe. Except we also have a Swiss bank account we traced to Hendrix from a receipt we found in his home. It was opened over a year ago. We got some international cooperation through Interpol and another account surfaced for Kahvahl. One million dollars deposited in each by a Lebanese businessman named Travak."

"Red Hand?" Gordon asked, studying the photographs once more.

"Yes."

"So Hendrix and Kahvahl might be in North Africa."

"We're serving extradition papers to every Middle Eastern country that will listen." Kemper took the file from Gordon. "At this point their whereabouts are less important than a public denunciation and conviction." He checked the last page. "Oh, one last loose end . . ."

"Hmmm," Gordon said, lost in thought.

"Ginelle Hendrix . . . daughter of the scientist, surfaced a few days ago in Atlanta. Now she's disappeared."

"I don't blame her, considering . . ."

"It wouldn't be much of an issue except that it's somewhat coincidental."

"What do you mean?"

"She told officials at the DCC that she was headed for San Francisco. Two FBI men are missing in that general vicinity since the day before yesterday. Naturally, they're investigating . . . oh, and she's a scientist, too," Kemper added as he closed the folder and set it down on the table. "The hearing may yield further information."

The hearing. Like the president's demand for answers, government response to public opinion was the driving force on the Hill.

Gordon shook his head, looking past the purple drapes toward the Capitol dome on the horizon. "They're really not a new phenomenon, are they?" he asked.

"Excuse me?"

"Scientists accused of crimes against society," Gordon said bitterly. "Nazi Germany had plenty of them. Communist Russia. Now the United States. Hendrix, his daughter, and Kahvahl. Dead or alive. I wonder where the hell they are."

THE FOURTEENTH DAY
9:01 P.M.
Union 76 Truck Stop
East of Kansas City on I-70

It was deadly quiet in the truck.

Jaktar sat in the front seat of the Ford Bronco in the dark.

The lit end of the cigarette cast a reflection in the windshield as he pursed his lips and pulled on the pearl-handled holder, exhaled, and watched the smoke float toward the driver's-side window, open just a crack.

He had parked away from the overhead lamps that lit the parking lot. Off to his right some fifty yards away, a farmhand filled his pickup at the pumps. The small diner was still active with a late dinner crowd.

As his thoughts wandered Jaktar watched a waitress move along the aisle, laden with plates for a party of four men seated in a booth by the window.

The black-haired woman in the pale blue outfit set the plates down. One of the men patted her on the butt as she turned to leave. She whirled and scolded the man, although from this distance, Jaktar couldn't tell if her anger was genuine. The waitress moved seductively. Perhaps she invited flirtation. Perhaps she enjoyed it. Perhaps not.

Jaktar's relationships with women had been largely nonexistent.

His impotence stemmed from his repulsion for white women in general. Images of his mother haunted him whenever he attempted sex. Whenever he was aroused, he fully intended to dominate and penetrate, but with white women he was repeatedly unable to manage even an erection.

Frustrated by whiteness, he had tried black women, yellow ones, mulattoes. Repeated failure led to violence and several unidentified corpses. Yet Jaktar discovered that killing women he had failed to have sex with gave him the orgasmic sensation he had missed. Quail appeared to understand Jaktar's aberration.

Jaktar watched as the waitress returned to the table with a tray of beer. She leaned against the vinyl booth, engaged in a conversation with the same man who had patted her.

Games of sex, much like games of conquest.

We are here to conquer or submit, Jaktar thought, reassessing his position as a conqueror in the scheme of things.

Quail understood because Quail *was* the ultimate conqueror. Few realized the depth of ambition within the man, ambition driven by his own brand of hatred. Yet Jaktar had never met anyone who suppressed his emotions so well.

He had worked for Quail seven years. During that time he had gleaned bits of information about his employer's background.

Quail's mother had died at his birth.

Quail had grown up in oil . . . Oklahoma black gold. He had also been fried in oil by his father. It wasn't common knowledge, by any means, but rumor had it that Quail had been physically abused to the point that he had to have his face surgically reconstructed—not once, but several times as he grew up. That explained the oddly taut skin on his face. It also explained Quail's amorality. Feelings for other people had been cut out of him.

In his twenties, Quail inherited the family fortune, and his ambition took on worldwide proportions. With the strength of his oil business as a foundation, he began to shape the world to his fashion. Quail sought out other business magnates whose characters demanded unrelenting conquest.

Choked by taxes and despising governments who levied them, these men from England, Japan, Colombia, and other countries sought the ultimate triumph: not to be subservient to any power, any government. Jaktar was not a political scientist, but Quail had explained to him that the late-twentieth century, with its increasing fragmentation of large nations into smaller ones, allowed the rise of an entrepreneurial body . . . to intercede, to finally unite the world through its unique force.

That's where Kahvahl came in. Kahvahl's two valuable assets: knowledge and religious fervor.

Quail had used both, acquiring a killer microbe and a group of radicals whom Kahvahl had recruited to spread it.

Quail's cartel convinced Kahvahl's people and a new rebel group from North Korea that they had few other alternatives to achieve their goals. With Quail's worldwide connections and huge financial resources, the cooperation of the North Korean Communist party and the Islamic Liberation Front, and a killer bug in his possession, the overthrow of the Western democracies *was* feasible.

The communists and Islamic radicals recognized that after the American victory in the cold war, the future of communism was bleak, and life in the Middle East would remain grim and impoverished. American culture was constantly intruding, and peace signaled the decay of Islamic ideals, which needed conflict and the hatred it engendered in order to thrive.

Quail promised them a new order.

Jaktar's musing was interrupted by the arrival of the long black limousine that pulled into the truck stop. It slowed by the pumps as the driver surveyed the grounds. Then slowly it moved next to the Ford Bronco and stopped.

Quail had arrived.

It was to be their last meeting before the takeover. At this moment in the conspiracy, Quail had opted to distance himself from Hendrix's imprisonment, refusing to come to the truck facility, and to forgo any phone contact with Topeka. He was confident, yet cautious.

The rear door of the long Lincoln opened. A hand beckoned.

Jaktar tossed his cigarette onto the pavement and stepped down. He walked over to the limo.

"Well? Get in," Quail said from the dark brown leather seat.

Jaktar stooped and slid in. The limo was spacious, equipped with a bar, TV, telephones.

"Any surprises?" Quail asked as Jaktar closed the door.

"The Englishman, Galbreath, is with the foreign service," Jaktar said, settling himself.

"I thought as much," Quail said. "What did he say about Baghigra?"

"The photographs were no bluff. They exist."

"And how, do you suppose?"

"Kahvahl buried them. As an insurance policy. To use against you in case things didn't work out. At least that's what he said before he passed out."

"The treacherous idiot."

Even in the dark, Jaktar saw Quail's pale gray eyes glisten.

"Where are they now?"

"The photographs? We have the originals. CNB apparently has copies."

Quail shook his head. "Well, that's inconsequential. I've conferred with Washington. Everything's fine. We're set to knock them on their butts."

"When?"

"Three days. I'm leaving for D.C. this morning. Do you have the signed confessions?"

"No. Kahvahl hasn't recovered to sign them." Jaktar was to have brought them to their meeting.

"Dammit. I need them."

"Why not just forge the signatures?"

Quail looked angry. "They have to be authentic in case something goes wrong. What if I wind up in an inquiry? The Europeans will be more convinced. Besides, I don't pay you to think, Jaktar. You're a soldier. Soldiers execute directives."

"I will. I apologize. Sing Chu was overzealous with the drug."

"All right. Back these guys off. Shoot up Kahvahl with stimulants and let's get a signature. And send the papers to me by tomorrow night; my appearance at the hearing is set. I expect your compliance with my wishes. You know where I'm staying?"

Jaktar nodded. "I do. You'll have them." With the takeover so near, he dared not fail to carry out Quail's orders. Quail reached for the door handle to let Jaktar out, but Jaktar stopped him. "There is one last thing."

"Yes, what?" Quail gripped the handle impatiently.

"The others. Parks, the woman, Hendrix . . ."

Quail smiled. With a cavalier gesture he pushed the limo door so that it swung wide. "Your pleasure, Jaktar. I don't care how you amuse yourself. Do as we planned and kill them."

THE FOURTEENTH DAY
10:41 P.M.
Topeka, Kansas

The soft hum of the ceiling fan was the only sound in the chamber. The Asian guards were gone. The room seemed hushed in the wake of Jaktar's threat. The prospect of his twenty-four-hour deadline hung in the air.

Devin lay on his back, eyes closed, unable to sleep, contemplating means of escape, while Ginelle and Dr. Hendrix dozed on their blankets.

After trying to open the lion handle on Galbreath's cane without success, Devin placed it next to the Englishman's limp body. The handle was trickier than he remembered. Better to leave it alone than chance destroying the diskette, which he hoped was still in there.

Kahvahl, the man with the answers, remained comatose.

Devin found himself replaying the scene with Jaktar in his mind. During the Iraqi war, whenever things seemed to happen too quickly, he'd mentally rewind and study an event, attempting to sort out and logically understand it.

He did this now, and was somewhat surprised at his own reaction as he faced the prospect of death. Without a weapon, he had nonetheless defied Jaktar, and now he was intrigued by his motive at the time. Certainly not a death wish. Protecting Ginelle? He might not have confronted Jaktar at all, if she hadn't been present.

If Amy had been there, would he have reacted similarly? Protective, certainly. Willing to die? No.

Since his injured eye was swollen shut, he rolled over and looked at Ginelle with his good eye. She lay in a fetal position with one arm tucked under her head, her short, baby-fine blond hair matted from the humidity.

Devin followed the line of her back down her hips to her long legs. Rare to find spirit as well as intellect in a body like that. Ginelle was an anomaly . . . a confident, good-looking woman who didn't obsess about her beauty. Her ease with herself stood in marked contrast to his own inner battles.

He was distracted from his thoughts as Ginelle stirred, rubbing her forehead. He watched her affectionately, aware of the deep respect he felt for her.

He lay back and closed his good eye again.

Strange, it had come to this. The truck's chamber was a sort of microcosm of a life—with friends, enemies, and a woman to whom he felt deeply attached.

A hand touched his shoulder. He started.

"Please excuse me, Devin." It was Dr. Hendrix. "Were you asleep? I didn't want to wake the others. I thought we should talk." He had addressed Devin by his first name for the first time.

"If you like."

"Forgive me. I wondered if you had any inspiration that might help us."

Devin was amused. For days, he'd been swept along by Dr. Hendrix's actions. Now this man was asking him what to do. "I'm pondering a way out."

Hendrix moved closer. "Good. We can't just sit here and let them kill us."

"On the surface, it would seem like we don't have a prayer."

"Odd you would say that," Hendrix said softly. "That's all I do, lately."

"Pray?"

"Penance for the sins I committed in the name of technology." Hendrix's face became stern. "I'm a fine candidate for eternity in hell."

"There's an old axiom about a gun and people who use it. Don't you think that applies to you?"

"I prefer not making assumptions, but rather ask forgiveness." Hendrix looked him straight in the eye. "Do you mind if I ask yours?"

"Forgiveness?" Devin felt humbled. "I'm not sure I'm the guy to whom you should ask anything."

"You underestimate yourself. I think what you've done for Ginelle is incredible."

"I acted as a professional."

"Really? And when Jaktar pointed his gun at your head, in what capacity did you respond?"

Devin couldn't think of an answer.

"I'll tell you," Hendrix continued solemnly. "As the Jews would say: you acted like a 'mensch,' a human being." He sat down. Devin could see that the man was seeking camaraderie, no doubt a result of his long isolation. "I hope you don't mind my asking, since we may all die at any moment—tell me, Devin . . . do you believe in God?"

Devin found Hendrix's question touching. "I went to church as a kid."

"You evaded the question. Let me make it easier by telling you first, that I do believe in Him, with all my heart."

"They say every dying man does."

"You make light of my avowal," Hendrix said.

"Sorry, perhaps I wasn't prepared to discuss it."

"If not now, when? If we are to live, faith will aid us. Without faith, we invite death."

"Doctor, it's your turn to forgive me. I tend to be skeptical, particularly about religious assertions. You see, this

little group of ours is a reflection of a greater reality."
Devin pointed at Kahvahl. "Look over there. A religious
zealot who acted out of his beliefs. That's what you said
about him, right? He's Islamic and you're . . ."

"A Christian."

"Fine. So in this microcosm of ours . . . is God at odds
with Himself? Or have Muhammad and Jesus agreed on
the behavior in this room?"

"You will find that Kahvahl's jihad is founded on
faith, no matter how heinous a crime he committed."

Devin was revolted. "Please, Doctor, I don't see—"

"Wait. It's important to me that you understand. Islam
believes that what they call evil, the corrupt values of
Western society, must be obliterated for a higher spiritual
good. That's what they consider the greater jihad."

"Rather inconvenient for those of us who stand in their
way . . . living our lives in accordance with those same
corrupt values."

"I only mentioned it because the first step to getting
along with our enemies is to understand them."

Devin was disappointed. Hendrix was taxing his
patience with complexities. "I don't want to understand
any justifications for the atrocities he committed. I want
none of that."

"But we have to abide by some principles; love for our
neighbors and empathy for our enemies . . . enemies like
Kahvahl over there. Because in a way . . . I allowed his
acts to take place. I made them possible."

Devin felt suddenly overwhelmed by Hendrix's struggle
with his guilt. "I think you're blaming yourself for something others did."

"But I should have prevented it. Long ago. That's why
we must stop them now."

Given their situation, the idea was absurd. Devin
motioned to the hydraulic door. "I'm afraid that that

necessitates being *un*neighborly to that blond weirdo out there."

Hendrix's eyes hardened. "Don't misunderstand my empathy for my fellow man. Kahvahl is a sinful man. Jaktar is less than human, more like the devil himself."

As if on cue, Kahvahl suddenly uttered a high-pitched whine. Then he whimpered, as Devin had done in his recovery phase.

Hendrix crawled to him and took his pulse.

Casting a glance at the unconscious Galbreath, Devin crawled after Hendrix to the other side of the trailer, where Kahvahl lay wheezing.

The commotion disturbed Ginelle. She joined them, sat at Kahvahl's feet.

Hendrix lifted Kahvahl's head. Devin was amazed to see Hendrix raise a hand high in the air. He brought it down hard, smacking Kahvahl's cheek.

The sharp report of the blow startled Ginelle. "Dad," she said, "what are you doing?"

"He's close to coming out of it," Hendrix said breathlessly.

"Well, then why not let him?"

"We must speak to him before they come back."

Hendrix struck the Iranian again. Kahvahl shuddered. The whimpering ceased. He began to cough. Hendrix took him by the shoulders and shook him violently. "Come on Ahmar. Wake up."

Kahvahl's eyes opened. They were glazed. He looked around, bewildered, then recognized his old colleague. "Thomas," he said, speaking with an accent. "I feel like I'm dying. Am I dying?"

"I don't believe so, Ahmar."

"They've taken everything," Kahvahl said. "Who is that woman?" His gaze moved slowly around the room.

"My daughter."

"Here in the laboratory?" He was still incoherent.

"No laboratory. You're a prisoner, Ahmar," Hendrix said. "Why did you allow this?"

Kahvahl stared at the others blankly. "A prisoner in my own house," he said.

Hendrix clutched his shoulder. "Why did you work with Quail?"

"I was Allah's servant," Kahvahl said simply.

"But Quail. Why him, of all people?"

Kahvahl moaned, twisting about on the floor. "A promise. Victory. For Islam to escape the yoke of the West. We trusted an infidel and were betrayed."

"Us? Who is us . . . Iran?"

"Not Tehran. All governments spawn corruption." Kahvahl closed his eyes, murmuring, "True believers. From all countries. Like streams into a river. The flood of Allah."

"Why were you betrayed?"

"The man is a beast." Kahvahl's eyes burst open, stared at the ceiling. "Used us. He has hidden power . . . in other nations."

Devin couldn't help himself. "England? What about England?"

Kahvahl focused on him. "Who is this foolish man? Not just England. Many others. Many epidemics after this one. First the United States will fall, then Europe."

"What? How?" Hendrix's voice shook with urgency.

"Biochemical blackmail. The microbe is merely a device to frighten. Children first . . . to make panic. Watch for the cure. The cure is ultimately lethal. Vaccine for the president, the cabinet, and Congress, the entire population. The vaccine contains . . ." Kahvahl paused, trying to gather his breath.

"What? Contains what?" Hendrix asked furiously.

"A molecular code, encrypted with a trigger." Kahvahl sighed.

"Is that possible?" Devin asked.

Hendrix shushed him. "Ahmar. The trigger you put in the vaccine . . ."

"A blackmail device, a cipher," Kahvahl continued, again delirious.

"How did you develop this blackmail cipher?"

"Based on your equations." Kahvahl struggled to become coherent. "Replicator expansion. You were right. Mycoplasmic cofactoring works. Allows the microbe to utilize an independent source of proteins. An osmotic reaction."

"What does he mean?" Ginelle asked.

Kahvahl responded to the question, speaking to no one in particular. "Once . . . in the blood . . ." He paused, moaning. "Quail is the only one with a blocking mechanism."

Hendrix panicked, turning to his daughter. "Dear God! I think I understand. The vaccine Quail distributed has a blackmail cipher, a coded molecular time mechanism that puts the body in constant danger of infection. It confuses the immune system with a rotating kernel code that changes the microbe's character every few months in a prescribed fashion. The microbe remains impervious to a permanent cure due to its adaptability. Since Kahvahl built the code, a cure with precise antidotal codes to match would have to be administered every few months . . . to prevent recurring epidemics. Quail can hold the country hostage, since he is the only one with the rotating code."

"For what purpose?" Devin asked.

"The government will be overthrown," Kahvahl said. "The president, his cabinet, and congressional members took an accelerated version of the vaccine. They will die."

Hendrix's face became red, as his anger began to surface.

Devin's thoughts hurtled through the various scenarios he and Galbreath had discussed. "Quail didn't plan this alone. Ask him who else is involved. Someone set this up."

Hendrix leaned down to Kahvahl. "Is there someone else? In Washington?"

"I never knew. Quail knew. The code name is Karryot."

"Karryot?" Devin frowned.

"The president is the shepherd. The cabinet, the disciples. The code name is Karryot," Kahvahl repeated.

Devin slapped his own forehead, then winced, having forgotten about his injuries.

Ginelle put a hand on his shoulder. "What is it?"

"He's not saying 'the code *is* Karryot.' He's saying 'the code: Iscariot!' Judas! Someone planted inside the government. It must have been planned for years."

"It was," Kahvahl said weakly. He appeared to recover his senses, speaking more clearly. "I have known Quail since his early years in Africa. As a young man in the oil business, he was interested in me. He had heard about my experiments in eastern Kenya. You remember, Thomas, my work in Africa gave us the basis for the replicator. My finest killing machine."

Hendrix's voice shook with rage. "Yes, but you've corrupted the cure . . . made it into a doomsday device." He bent over Kahvahl. His glasses slipped down his face, rested on his chin. "How could you?"

"I'm a professional, Thomas."

"You made a mockery of science and of me!" Hendrix

grabbed Kahvahl by the collar. "I defended you to this man," he said, referring to Devin.

Ginelle came to her father's side, tried to restrain him.

Devin heard the hiss of the hydraulic doors as Hendrix scolded Kahvahl. "You've become a monster, Ahmar. No better than . . ." He looked back. Jaktar had entered with Sing Chu at his side. "These maniacs," he shouted in Kahvahl's face.

Sing Chu sprang forward and gave Hendrix a round kick under the left arm.

Hendrix's glasses fell to the ground as he slumped across Kahvahl's body.

The blow to the old man enraged Devin. Recalling his martial-arts instruction, he was up, throwing a straight punch that landed on Sing Chu's neck under his right ear. Caught off balance, Sing Chu fell, landing on the unconscious Galbreath.

A blow to Devin's head from the rear told him Jaktar had entered the fight. Devin went down, seeing white behind both eyes. Immediately Jaktar lifted him back into the air. The blond assassin was strong, holding Devin's nearly two hundred pounds with his left hand. He jammed a Beretta pistol under Devin's nose with his right.

"It's your time, asshole," Jaktar said.

Even in a fog, Devin thought the expletive sounded comical when spoken in an accent. However, he had little time to enjoy the humorous effect. Jaktar pistol-whipped him across the temple, dropping him to his knees.

Devin slouched from the blow. Jaktar jerked Devin's head upright. Devin's face was a sea of pain, and he had the business end of the Beretta stuck in his right nostril.

With a gloved hand locked on Devin's collar, Jaktar shouted at the others in the room. "All of you, back away! Or I will shoot this man now."

THE FOURTEENTH DAY
Almost midnight
United States Army Medical Research
Institute of Infectious Diseases
(USAMRIID)
Fort Detrick, Maryland

Frowning, Dr. Gordon sat on the brown metal chair in the low light of the lab. As Pendergast had told him, even in the middle of the night, the virologist required as little illumination as possible. His eyes were extremely sensitive, as the large lightly shaded glasses he wore testified.

Dressed in a white lab coat, Blake Pendergast turned from the computer screen, facing Dr. Gordon. "Well, what do you think?"

"What do I think? You're asking me?" Gordon said, disconcerted.

"Yes. I am. The use of this vaccine falls into your province."

"The hell it does. It falls under a presidential order as dictated by FEMA. Don't try to lay that off on me."

Pendergast's eyes, magnified within the silver frames, fluttered several times in dismay. He was disturbed by Gordon's remark. "Yes, but I'm the one who'll be sitting at the hearing, not you."

Weary, Gordon responded, trying to hold back his irritation. "You realize what a madhouse my office is right now? The disease cleanup is overwhelming. I don't understand what you expect at this juncture."

"All right, Doctor." Pendergast raised both hands in the air, as if he were being arrested. "At least I've mentioned it. That's all I can do."

"What are you trying to accomplish? With thousands dying in the streets you want R and D protocol?"

"I'm going on record. . . ." Pendergast pointed at the screen. "The computer shows a slight anomaly between the infective model and the antidote."

"Does that surprise you? They're from different sources, after all . . . Hendrix and Maxillar."

"Right. But they're both synthetics. Theoretically, the microbionic signatures should align."

"And they don't?"

Gesturing, Pendergast moved to the computer monitor. "These columns of numbers at the top of the screen are a digital interpretation of the microbe's biochemical and electromagnetic makeup. The lower half of the screen is an identical reading of a molecular particle . . . the antigen." He used a pencil to point to a specific grouping of numbers. "There's a binary aberration on the antigen grid."

"So?"

"The binaries should align as a mirror image of the microbe."

"Suppose it's because of the retention factor . . . it's my understanding that the molecules are made to stay in the bloodstream to prevent long-term infection."

"But I need extensive diagnostic work to tell you that," Pendergast said, somewhat defiantly.

"Well, fine. You'll have that opportunity."

"Perhaps. But I'm going on record now."

"What are you asking me to do?" Gordon suspected the answer was one he didn't want to hear.

Pendergast removed his large silver glasses, cleaned the lenses with the fringe of his lab coat, apparently mulling over his words. Without the lenses, his eyes shrank to half their previous size, pale blue and squinting beneath his gray eyebrows. Gordon waited patiently as the virologist replaced his glasses, now

ready to resume. "I don't know if it's possible," Pendergast said hesitantly, "but I think it prudent to hold off on
the rest of the vaccinations until we can test these elements thoroughly."

The suggestion pushed Gordon over the line. "You
think this is the FDA? I've got a beleaguered president
on my ass—who's had his shot, by the way—and with
thousands still dying, you want ingredient statements on
each syringe?"

"I'm just saying we're on uncharted ground. We've
just begun to deal with biosynthetics from a diagnostic
perspective."

"Meaning?"

"We can analyze but not create."

"Ain't that a familiar tale. We're *re*active not *pro*-
active because we're underfunded. The private sector
has us beat. Sure. How do you think Hendrix and Maxillar were able to produce miracles of nanotechnology,
while you and I sit around holding our dicks waiting
for developments? USAMRIID and the DCC are
the clearinghouse for every new accident that comes
around."

Pendergast appeared confused.

Gordon checked his watch. He would have to leave
now or miss the twelve-thirty red-eye to Atlanta. He
lifted his ponderous weight out of the chair, stepped over,
and put a thick hand on Pendergast's shoulder. "Here's
my advice. Attend the hearing. Let the testimony against
Hendrix run its course. Let Quail's people have the
chance to present their findings. Then I suggest you and I
appeal to the investigative committee to have Maxillar
interpret these numbers. It's probably a manufacturing
variance of some kind . . . who knows? What we *do*
know, thank God, is that the vaccine works. We're
saving lives, yours and mine included. Compared to

death, I welcome a slight aberration flowing in my veins. . . . Hell, I've probably had worse from a bad bottle of rye."

THE FOURTEENTH DAY
Midnight
Topeka, Kansas

Needles of pain danced on Devin's face. The grip on his collar had him wheezing, trying to recover his breath. Down on all fours, with a gun stuck in his face, he heard Jaktar yell at the others.

"You do as I tell you . . . or I will blow this man's head off!"

"Daddy. Please. Do what he says."

Devin strained to look back. Ginelle had joined her father, who sat holding his side, still suffering from Sing Chu's kick. Both of them knelt next to Kahvahl on the floor, with Galbreath on the other side. He had not stirred since Devin knocked Sing Chu onto him during the scuffle.

"So, Ginelle," Jaktar said. "Your boyfriend's life does make a difference, doesn't it?"

Devin felt a new stream of blood moving down over the dried mass that covered his right eye and cheek.

"Sing Chu," Jaktar said, "give them the papers."

Sing Chu removed a roll of paper and two pens from his belt and threw them on the ground in front of the kneeling men.

"Cover them," Jaktar said. Sing Chu stepped back, leveling a nine-millimeter handgun at the others. "Sign your confessions, both of you," Jaktar said to Hendrix and Kahvahl.

Hendrix looked up at Jaktar. "If your forces control the government, who cares if we sign this?"

"We may need to convince the Europeans of your guilt. It documents your involvement."

Kahvahl stared at Jaktar and picked up the pen. "I'll sign it," Kahvahl said. "Just don't kill me." He pushed a scrawl across the sheet.

Hendrix pushed the papers away. "I refuse."

"Do you?" Jaktar snarled. "Bring the woman here."

Sing Chu dragged Ginelle over next to Devin. They were on their knees, side by side, with Jaktar's Beretta in their faces.

"Suppose I destroy your daughter with this gun, one piece at a time, until you sign the documents," Jaktar said, moving the pistol from Devin's nose to Ginelle's right ear, far enough that Devin could now see across the room. "I might begin with her ear." He pushed the barrel to her lobe.

Devin sensed they were going to die. All of them: himself, Ginelle, Dr. Hendrix, Kahvahl, and Galbreath.

During that realization, Devin noticed movement on the metal grating behind Sing Chu. A gray head stirred. A blood-spattered face raised. Under silvery eyebrows, a pair of brown eyes looked straight at his. Galbreath had apparently been roused by Sing Chu's collision with him on the floor.

"Dad. He means it," Ginelle cried. "Please sign it. Kahvahl's right. What difference does it make now?"

"I *do* mean it." Jaktar brought the Beretta down, brushing Ginelle's forehead with it. "Are you prepared to watch me splatter your daughter's features?"

Devin observed how, without Sing Chu noticing, Galbreath had managed to grab the cane that had been lying at his side. The North Korean stood astride the Englishman's legs, looking toward the other captives. Now Galbreath held the ivory walking stick with both hands in that peculiar fashion Devin had remembered before, his right hand curled up over the lion's head.

"Wait," Hendrix shouted.

Devin watched as Galbreath disengaged the handle.

"You've angered me, Doctor," Jaktar said nonchalantly.

"Here." Hendrix put pen to paper, leaning over on his knees. "I'm signing it. Look!"

Galbreath silently unsheathed the blade.

"Little matters to me anymore," Jaktar said. "This whole thing is a bore."

Galbreath had his wrist curled downward, parallel to the floor, his arm in a back swing, under Sing Chu.

Devin looked nervously at Ginelle, who closed her eyes. She was trembling.

"We'll liven things up with some bullet surgery." Jaktar cocked the Beretta just as Galbreath struck upward forcefully.

Galbreath's blade thrust into Sing Chu's groin midway between his genitals and his buttocks all the way to the handle.

The world went into slow motion.

Sing Chu lifted his face toward the ceiling, bursting forth with an animalistic scream as Galbreath twisted the blade. Then the Englishman grabbed Sing Chu's gun with his free hand. The weapon went off repeatedly into the floor, throwing sparks off the steel.

Devin watched one of the bullets splash a red hole in Galbreath's thigh.

Jaktar turned his head, startled by the commotion.

In that instant, calling on his karate training, Devin knocked Jaktar's right arm upward and vaulted toward him, driving his left shoulder into Jaktar's waist. The Beretta went off next to his left ear, deafening him.

Ginelle fell to the deck at the sound of the explosion.

Devin prayed she wasn't injured and spun his body hard to his right, groping for Jaktar's gun.

At the same time, Galbreath clung to Sing Chu's nine-millimeter pistol with his left hand, driving the blade into the North Korean's abdomen with his right. Galbreath yelled Devin's name repeatedly, which Devin could barely hear, due to the ringing in his head from the Beretta's recent close-range report.

To Devin's right, Galbreath hung on as Sing Chu undulated in pain and fell to his knees, continuing to fire the nine-millimeter, spraying the wall behind Hendrix and Kahvahl.

Devin heard Kahvahl cry out and fall to the deck.

Devin's tackle drove Jaktar toward Galbreath. Both of them fell to the grating only feet from the English-man. Weak from his ordeal, Devin summoned all his remaining energy and grasped Jaktar's gun hand around the wrist.

Jaktar displayed immense power as he grunted, got to his feet, and lifted Devin with him, clamping a gloved hand around his throat. Devin's feet hardly touched the ground as he smelled licorice on the big man's breath. Jaktar's brown eye stared blankly; the blue eye shone with a gleam of hate as he throttled Devin, back and forth. Clinging to Jaktar's wrist, Devin glanced down and saw Galbreath drive the knife repeatedly into Sing Chu's abdomen.

The screaming North Korean lay on the grate.

"Damn them to hell, Devin," the Englishman shouted as he struck.

Jaktar stumbled closer to Sing Chu's body, apparently wanting to get to his henchman.

Devin's strength waned. With his airway clamped shut by Jaktar's gloved hand, he felt building pressure in his head. As Jaktar's fingers and thumb began to meet under his jaw, stars danced behind the tears welling in Devin's eyes. He felt power leaving his hands. His grip on Jaktar slackened. Jaktar's gun hand would be free in a moment. Devin would lose consciousness and die. His last memory would be Jaktar's cruel, squinting mask thrust in his face.

Then Jaktar's glowering expression changed to one of wide-eyed shock. Miraculously, the hand loosened on Devin's throat.

Devin looked down.

Galbreath had rolled, grasped Jaktar's leg, and driven his blade through Jaktar's boot, deep into his foot.

Jaktar roared, rearing like a stallion away from his attacker. As he fell to the floor in agony Devin went with him. The impact of their fall forced Devin to lose his grip on Jaktar's gun hand. Sloughed off behind Jaktar, still in contact with Jaktar's upper body, Devin was horrified to see the blond giant sit up on one hip and fire two rounds toward Galbreath, striking him in the chest and shoulder.

Galbreath fell back, emitting a sickening moan.

The sight stirred the last of Devin's resolve. He threw his legs around Jaktar's waist, desperately clinging to his broad back.

Remembering the spare weapon at the small of Jaktar's back, he dug hard and grabbed the nine-millimeter from the blond man's belt. Yanking Jaktar's hair with his other hand and holding on with his remaining strength, he pushed the semiautomatic weapon to the base of Jaktar's skull.

"So," Devin said breathlessly, leaning forward to his ear, "is this the invigorating moment of death you wanted?"

Jaktar squirmed, trying to dislodge him.

"Drop the gun, you son-of-a-bitch," Devin growled through clenched teeth, but Jaktar twisted, rolled hard to his right, bringing the Beretta across his own body around his left hip. It was pointed straight at Devin's gut.

Devin squirmed to his own right to avoid the muzzle of Jaktar's weapon, keeping his own gun pressed to the base of Jaktar's skull. Then both men fired simultaneously.

Devin felt the burn at the top of his left hip as the back of Jaktar's head sprayed red tissue onto his face. The blond man's body went stiff for a moment, then slumped back heavily onto Devin.

Under Jaktar's weight, Devin reviewed the damage. If he had taken a belly shot, he might die. In shock, he couldn't tell exactly where he'd been hit.

After what seemed like an eternity, someone pulled on Jaktar's body, rolling it to the floor. Devin tried to check himself out.

Ginelle and Dr. Hendrix bent over him. Hendrix removed Jaktar's Beretta and held it in his hand.

Suddenly the young guard named Wu Sun ran headlong into the room, a gun at his side.

Hendrix looked up, startled, then rose, stepping forward. Hendrix pointed the Beretta at the young Korean. "Put it down, Wu Sun." The scientist's hands were shaking.

Wu Sun looked around the room.

From his vantage point on the floor, Devin saw Wu Sun's cousin, Sing Chu, lying in a pool of blood near Galbreath on the far side of the trailer.

Was Galbreath alive?

"I don't want to shoot you, Doctor," Wu Sun rasped. "Please disarm yourself, or I will be forced to kill you!"

"Don't," Ginelle said, kneeling next to Devin. "My father never meant you any harm."

Hendrix's voice quavered. "No more killing, Wu Sun. Your family has suffered enough. Your cousin is dead."

Eyes wide with emotion, Wu Sun's gaze drifted to

Sing Chu and then to Jaktar, who lay on his belly on the floor, the back of his blond head blown away. "Drop the gun and step back," he shouted, his voice full of fear.

"You are not like these men, Wu Sun," Hendrix said kindly. "You and I talked, remember?"

"I should have never listened to you." The young man's moist eyes darted nervously around the room.

"This is ended," Hendrix said. "Go back to your studies. You still have a life. Put the gun away."

Wu Sun blinked several times, staring at Hendrix. "My life?"

"Yes, think of yourself." Hendrix had his full attention.

Wu Sun inhaled deeply, looking down at the floor. His shoulders relaxed. He dropped the pistol, which clanked noisily on the grating.

"Good." Hendrix sighed. "Now, where are the others?"

Devin suddenly realized the gunfire should have drawn immediate response. Why weren't other guards arriving?

"They took the trucks to Cleveland." Wu Sun spoke in an oddly boyish voice. "To prepare for the takeover." Hendrix was right. The kid had been here under duress. At the moment he resembled nothing so much as a grinning bear cub.

"Come with us," Hendrix said. "You'll be treated well."

The young man was obviously torn. A tear trickled down his cheek. He looked around the room, his expression hurt and bitter. "You cannot win. They have already won," Wu Sun said desperately. Then, panicked, he bolted through the door.

"Wu Sun, wait!" Hendrix shouted, then dropped his head to his chest, apparently exhausted from the confrontation.

Outside, a vehicle started and drove away.

Devin remembered Galbreath and felt compelled to get to him. "Ginelle, help me."

"Devin, please don't move."

"I've gotta see him." Devin dragged himself across the floor. She helped him along, tears streaming down her cheeks.

"Dad." She brought her hand up from Devin's waist. It was covered with his blood.

God, I'm dying, Devin thought as he crawled. If I am truly dying, let it be for her. To get her out of this hellhole. For one clearly definable instant he valued someone else's life more than his own, not symbolically, mumbling a wedding vow, not poetically, whispering love promises. No lights. No makeup. The cameras weren't rolling. This was real.

"Dad!" she repeated.

Hendrix knelt over Kahvahl. What was he doing? Hendrix looked up.

Devin traveled what seemed a hundred yards, though it was only a matter of fifteen feet. Hendrix joined him by the time he reached the Englishman.

Devin hoisted himself onto his elbow to look into Galbreath's face, ravaged by knife cuts.

A glimmer of recognition showed in Galbreath's eyes. He was barely alive. Even in this battered state, his chivalrous manner remained. "Devin," he said. "We did it."

"Yes. We beat them."

His chest a mass of red, Galbreath breathed laboriously. "Well done. Well done, indeed," he said weakly. "Now you must get Quail."

"He's next. I promise."

"Parks, old boy," Galbreath whispered. A look of fear replaced the bravado.

"What is it?"

"Africa," Galbreath said. "Scatter my ashes on the plains of Tanzania, near the mountain where Arthur Kensley is buried."

"Who?"

"A man I cared for." A tear trickled from the corner of Galbreath's eye, making its way down ridges of rent flesh.

"Good-bye, Mr. Galbreath," Devin said, his throat thick with sorrow. Once again, he had lost someone special.

"Devin." Hendrix pulled on his shoulder. "Come. He's gone. Let me look at you." He forced Devin to lie on his back next to the Englishman.

Devin noticed the doctor's cracked lenses, crushed in the firefight.

Hendrix reached down.

Devin felt the tug of the shirt as it came away from the wound.

"Let me see, Devin. Remove your hands." Hendrix leaned farther down. A sharp knifelike pain shot through Devin's left side. He flinched. "Sorry, my friend," Hendrix said. He squinted through his spectacles and sighed. "Good. The bullet came out just over the hip. A deep flesh wound. Muscle damage. No organs."

Ginelle squeezed Devin's hand.

"We've got to get out of here," Devin said painfully.

"Yes." Hendrix got to his feet. "Ginelle, we need a bandage."

"Here." Ginelle tore her pajama bottoms, shredded the cloth on her legs into strips.

"Good." Hendrix crept toward the hydraulic door as she bunched some of the cloth into pads, applying them gently to Devin's side and, with his help, wrapping others around his waist.

Hendrix was back in a moment. "I tried to use the

phone in the control room. It's encoded somehow. We're in a deserted trucking yard. I don't see anyone."

"Help me up." Devin winced, using Hendrix's arm for leverage.

"What now?" Ginelle asked.

"Find a phone booth. Call Freeman. And . . . I need that." Devin pointed at Galbreath's cane. "The handle and the shaft." She leaned over and handed him the pieces. "He'll have his own sweet revenge." He took the cane in both hands.

They hobbled to the door, leaving Sing Chu, Jaktar, Kahvahl, and Galbreath behind.

"When we call the police, we'll make sure his body is handled properly," Devin said.

They stepped through the red glow of the control room.

Hendrix and Ginelle supported Devin as they descended the grated stairs onto the Kansas dirt. Open air. Stars in a clear spring sky.

Hendrix looked up into the heavens. "Thank You, Lord, for Your gifts of mercy," he said. "And dear God, give me the power to find answers quickly."

"Dad. What answers are you talking about?" Ginelle asked.

Hendrix looked anxiously at his daughter in the moonlight. "Kahvahl whispered something disturbing to me before he died. He could barely speak and did not finish."

"What was it?" Devin punctuated the question with a groan.

"Pi . . . plate," Hendrix said.

"Pie plate, like apple pie?"

"No. I'm sure he meant *pi*, the Greek letter. The rotating code Kahvahl concocted appears to be based on a random seed, *pi*."

"Knowing that, you can break the code." Devin smiled, wincing.

"I doubt it. I am not sure what 'plate' means . . . some private jargon they used after I left, perhaps. But pi is an irrational number. That means the rotating codes go to infinity."

"And?"

"The code would become unbreakable," Hendrix said, looking out toward the horizon. "If so, Quail is in full control."

THE FIFTEENTH DAY
4:29 A.M.
A Dirt Road

The gravel shoulder of the road felt rough under Devin's right buttock. The wound over his left hip throbbed, the pain seeming to penetrate through his gut. He grunted with each wave of discomfort, his skin sticky with dried blood under the cloth pajama strips. Occasionally, a sting shot up under his left rib cage. Fine, now he'd have aches on both sides.

They had walked for hours, and now were resting.

A cursory search of the abandoned truck depot revealed that Wu Sun had taken the last remaining vehicle, a pickup or a large four-wheel-drive truck, judging from its tire marks. Jaktar, Sing Chu, and Wu Sun had apparently planned to take off in it after murdering everyone else.

Devin stretched painfully and got up on one elbow. Galbreath's cane lay on the ground next to his leg.

Off to the east, miles of open plain. A dim glow on the horizon forecast the coming of dawn. In the dark, a stiff breeze blew over deserted farmland.

Stop Quail . . . the idea turned over in his mind. Galbreath's dying wish. But how, with no transportation? And no means of communication. Perhaps Ginelle was the only solution. She stood above him, looking off to the east.

"I don't want you to go . . . but you may have to," he said to her.

She looked at her father. "I can't leave him."

Hendrix sat on the ground in his shredded clothes, shoulders slumped, knees up to his chest. His hands lay palms up on the dirt by his sides. He appeared asleep, exhausted from the ordeal.

"We've come a mile, maybe two," Devin said. "We're just not moving fast enough. At this rate we'll be out here for hours. It's ridiculous." Hendrix remained motionless. "I wouldn't be surprised if Maxillar owns some of this land. No farms around here. We can't even get to a phone."

Ginelle appeared reluctant to speak. She stared at the ground.

"It comes down to you, Ginelle."

She turned toward him, wiped her hands on the front of the turtleneck, and looked away, her eyes on the horizon. "I'm not leaving him."

"Look, I hate to put it this way. But I can't walk. Your dad is too weak to travel. There may be no options here."

Again she turned, pointing to the strips of cloth, soaked dark red around his waist. "You've lost a lot of blood. Quiet down and save your strength."

"Talking's about all I *can* do. Now, I know how you feel about your dad—"

"No, you don't."

"If you want to keep him," he said gently, "you may have to leave him for a time."

A look of determination settled in her green eyes. "Let's stick together," she said. "If someone picks you up while I'm gone, we may never see each other again."

Devin understood. The prospect of losing her was unbearable. "No one's picking us up. No cars. Not with the curfew," he said.

She was silent, digesting his words.

He remembered a sign he'd seen a while back indicating the Potowatomi Indian Reservation twenty-five miles east and a town called Wamego six miles ahead. "Now, from the direction of the sunrise, this road appears to lead south and east. You can walk the six miles to Wamego. Otherwise, none of us will make it anywhere."

He watched as she looked from her father to Devin and back again, trying to decide. "But what if someone does comes by?" she asked.

Devin tried to exude confidence. "We'll hitch a ride to the first town. Let's agree to meet at the first public building on the right-hand side of the road. Whether motel or store—whatever, we'll meet there." He knew she would never forgive him if his plan led to permanent separation from her dad. He also sensed that if she trusted him now, it might bring them closer.

She walked around the two men, radiating nervous energy.

"Ginelle," Devin said. "Maybe it's asking too much."

"When I get to a phone, what do you want me to do?" She tucked the black turtleneck sweater into what was left of her pajama bottoms. She had made her decision.

"Come here," he said.

She squatted by him. He reached out. She accepted his hand. He squeezed hers, gave her a smile, and she couldn't help but smile back.

"You should see your face," she said sympathetically.

"I look funny to you?"

"Only when you smile."

"Sure, if it didn't hurt so much." Then he noticed her bare feet, cut up from their walk across the rough terrain. "You're bleeding," he said. "I didn't realize—"

"I had bigger blisters in ballet class. Just tell me what you want me to do."

"Call Freeman," Devin said, wincing. "The hearing in Washington must be under way by now. Have him bring the copies of the African photos." The originals had been left in Monterey, probably taken by the raiders that night.

"We're simply going to walk into the hearing?"

"I don't know. I haven't thought it through yet. We have to stop Quail, somehow."

"All right. I'll call your office."

Devin looked over at Hendrix, who still hadn't moved. "We need a plane. Your father can't travel publicly. He'll be assaulted."

"All right. A charter. Landing where?"

"Your father said we were in eastern Kansas. Land in Kansas City, I guess. Or Topeka. They must have a large enough airport."

"Ginelle." Dr. Hendrix spoke with his head between his knees.

"Dad." She bent down next to him. "Don't try to stop me. I have to go."

"I've been listening. I understand. Tell Freeman I must get to my lab in Richmond. If we're to have any chance, I must have my computer and my old fraxination stats."

"I'm sure he'll call Williamson, Doctor," Devin said quietly. "We'll see you have what you need."

Ginelle walked over and knelt by Devin. "Promise you'll take good care of him."

"This isn't good-bye, Ginelle."

"I know. But in case something happens, see it through to the end, Devin. Just as you wanted."

He looked up, pleased at the admiration written on her face. A wave of affection swept through him. She was the last person he wanted to part with. "It feels like we've been together for years, not a couple of weeks."

She extended a hand and touched his, then saying good-bye, went to her father's side, kissing him on the brow. "Rest. I'll be back," she said.

Hendrix looked up at his daughter. "If I don't get there, find the fraxinations—"

"Shush, Dad, I wouldn't know where to begin. You'll simply have to make it." She put a hand on his head, stroking his hair. She rose, and without a look back, began to walk.

Devin strained to watch her leave. He followed her silhouette against the dim glow of the morning.

She walked strong, determined. But several hundred paces away she stopped.

Devin squinted to see why.

She stood motionless, staring out at the horizon. Then she turned and began running back toward them. "Devin!" she shouted. "Lights!"

He looked past her toward the horizon. A gleam. Ahead of a rising cloud of dust, headlights were coming in their direction.

She reached his side, out of breath, and looked back. "God. Do you think it's Jaktar's men?"

Devin was torn between a desire to hide at the roadside and to remain visible so they could be picked up. "Take your dad behind those bushes!" he said. "Hurry!"

"Why?"

"If it's a ride, I'll flag them down. If it's the North Koreans, they'll only take me. You could still get your father back to his research."

"No," she said angrily.

"Ginelle," Hendrix interjected. "He's absolutely correct. Please help me." He struggled to his knees. With Ginelle's help, he half crawled, half rolled to a thicket of brush near the road.

Devin watched apprehensively as the lights drew closer. He grasped Galbreath's cane, twisted the lion's head, and unsheathed the blade, placing it tight to his body. Unsure how he could fight in his weakened state, he focused on the horizon in an attempt to identify the vehicle. It was dark in color, possibly black or blue, only some fifty yards away, kicking up dust and rock.

As the headlights hit him Devin waved from his prone position.

A black Ford Bronco pulled to a stop twenty feet away. Dust swirled forward past the grille, making it difficult to see.

He was blinded by the light.

The driver's-side door opened and slammed shut. Silhouetted against the headlights, the figure of a man strode toward him. The dirt crunched under his boots. He was short, stocky. The man stopped.

"I need your help," Devin said, squinting up at him, shielding his eyes with one hand. He gripped the knife handle with the other.

"That's why I came back," the man said.

Devin suddenly recognized him, but unsure of his motives, looked frantically to see if he was holding a gun. It was Wu Sun.

"Where is the doctor?" Wu Sun said. His hands were empty.

"I'm here," Hendrix croaked from the bushes.

Ginelle got to her feet in the glow of the headlights.

"Come, Doctor," Wu Sun said. "There is a town close by." He bent over Devin, who struggled to sit up and take him by the arm.

"Are you really trying to help, or do you have something else in mind?" Devin asked skeptically.

"No questions, and no talk, Mr. Parks. I came because of the old man. I will get you to safety and then you will not see me again."

Devin allowed Wu Sun to help him to his feet.

THE SEVENTEENTH DAY
2:45 P.M.
Washington, D.C.

Flanked by two MPs on a street a mile from Capitol Hill, Devin shielded Ginelle from the breeze that blew up Pennsylvania Avenue. She wore a tan leather jacket, a new denim skirt, a Yankees baseball cap, and sunglasses to avoid being recognized.

Without divulging their identities, Freeman and Colonel Williamson had arranged a military escort. The soldiers stood behind them next to a telephone pole, which, like others along the avenue, bore a Red Cross sign. Large red letters on white cardboard read: VACCINATION NOW! VIOLATORS WILL BE PROSECUTED. Smaller type below read: *Report to Your Local Dispensary or CALL 1-800-555-SHOT.*

Martial law dictated that everyone receive a dose of Quaillium.

Devin, dressed in chinos and a blazer, used Galbreath's cane as a crutch. He favored his left side, heavily bandaged under his clothes.

A few hundred feet away pickets paced back and forth in front of the complex known as the Federal Triangle. Placards demanded Dr. Hendrix's death, and the marchers chanted angrily that Hendrix must be captured and killed.

"Where the hell is he?" Devin said, turning to her. "Quail is likely having a field day. I'm getting jumpy as hell." He turned to the MP in charge. "Couldn't we just go, Lieutenant?"

"No, sir." The lieutenant, young, lean, and perfectly groomed, gestured to the Buick parked at the curb. "When Mr. Freeman arrives you are to get in the back of the car. We'll take you in."

"Couldn't we use your radio to check on him?" Ginelle asked, straightening her cap.

"Sorry, ma'am. No radio contact. Colonel Williamson's orders."

Ginelle turned nervously to Devin. "I feel like I'm about to die."

He smiled reassuringly. "You've been through that already." He held up Galbreath's cane. "No one's going to hurt you again."

"Do you think they'll listen? Everything seems so stacked against us." She straightened the collar of her jacket, looking fashionable, a far cry from the ripped pajama bottoms and bare feet of two days ago.

The roar of a Jeep caught their attention. It raced up to the curb with Freeman in the passenger seat. Two more MPs in back. As the vehicle squealed to a stop behind the Buick, Freeman leaped out and ran over. The big man hustled like a Jell-O mold in motion. He huddled with Devin and Ginelle a few steps from the MPs.

"Well?" Devin said. "Where's Hendrix?"

Freeman did a double take as he saw the damage to Devin's face at close range. They had spoken only on the phone since the Kansas incident. "Devin, you're a mess."

"Never mind that, goddammit, tell me!"

Freeman lowered his voice. "A U.S. marshal showed up on base at the last minute with an extradition order from the attorney general. Williamson is delaying Hendrix's release until he can get him over here."

After the Learjet picked them up in Topeka, Hendrix

had been under military escort for forty-eight hours, most of which were spent at the lab in Richmond. He had arrived in Washington that morning.

"How can Williamson hold him?" Ginelle asked.

"Claim he's a prisoner, taken during a state of war." Freeman, whom Devin had normally seen in shirtsleeves, looked oddly formal in a gray pin-striped suit. "If that doesn't work, he'll have to turn him over to the feds."

"We'd have to wait months for a trial," Devin said angrily.

"Believe me, Devin. Williamson's doing all he can." Freeman turned to Ginelle so the MPs couldn't hear. "Williamson's with your father at the army barracks at Andrews Air Base. Your dad's signed confession didn't help matters, by the way. I wish you hadn't left that piece of paper where the police could find it."

Devin leaned in. "We were kind of preoccupied . . . with survival."

"Won't Galbreath's recording help?" Ginelle asked, the breeze causing her skirt to billow around her legs.

"Don't count on it," the big man said. "The confession states that your father and Kahvahl engineered the epidemic crisis. It takes Quail out of the picture."

"But the use of Quail's equipment . . ."

Freeman looked around nervously, then shook his head and whispered patiently, "Quail could claim Kahvahl commandeered the trucks for his own purposes. Somehow you have to link Quail to the Kansas captivity and the conspiracy. Right now that connection doesn't exist. You need someone to corroborate those events."

"We don't have time," Devin said. "With Quaillium running in everybody's veins and a European epidemic already under way, we have to convince Senator Kemper and the committee of Quail's guilt." He felt the window of opportunity closing. He gestured to the Buick sedan. "I'm sorry, Ginelle, we should go."

She tugged his sleeve. "Can't we just wait a few more minutes?"

Devin looked at his watch. "They've been at it all morning. The hearing could adjourn early." He remembered how she'd fought him in Monterey. Now she seemed suspended between fear of the unknown and a newfound faith in his judgment. Something had changed in her since that night on the dirt road in Kansas. Their eyes met. A surge of energy passed between them. He felt her trust.

With a calm dignity she touched his arm. "All right, Devin." She nodded toward the car.

"Lieutenant," Devin said, looking at the officer. "Let's go."

The two MPs ushered them into the car. Three others prepared to follow in the Jeep. Freeman settled into the backseat with Devin and Ginelle.

"I had Brook Hanford cover the hearing since this morning," Freeman said.

"I'm surprised you didn't let Canon cover it," Devin quipped. The Buick began to move.

"Why Canon?" Ginelle asked. Her expression revealed her dislike of the pushy science editor.

"He's kidding, Ginelle," Freeman said. "I fired him yesterday. Canon leaked your location in Monterey to someone who claimed to be with the FBI. When the *real* FBI men were killed at my cabin, Canon panicked and told me about it."

"I thought the FBI were assigned because of Williamson," Ginelle cut in.

"They were, of course, but Canon wouldn't have known that."

She fumed. "He nearly got us killed."

The Buick turned and drove up the hill to the Capitol.

"Frank, I'm sorry about Max," Devin said.

"I am, too. He did his best. We've suffered a few casualties."

"And I want you to know how much I appreciate your taking care of Galbreath's remains," Devin said.

"No problem. His ashes will be at Andrews tomorrow in your name." They rode silently for a few moments. Frank stared at him. "Speaking of casualties, you look great, Parks. The photographers are going to love it . . . like you went twelve rounds with an elephant, man." He examined Devin's swollen face and the large bandage he still wore on his ear. "Come to think of it, you look like the elephant man."

"You should have seen him two days ago," Ginelle said.

The Buick pulled up at the federal building.

Freeman patted Devin on the knee and handed him an envelope. "The Baghigra pictures," he said. Devin nodded and took the photos. "You've had a long haul, Devin. We're with you the rest of the way."

As the car door opened the MPs jumped out and formed a wedge to keep them away from reporters and pickets. Though curious, most of them seemed ignorant of the newcomers' identities. Freeman had been tremendously helpful, making sure that Williamson's people kept them cloistered. Their story had been kept out of the press. Fortunately, most reporters were inside the building, covering the hearing. The handful outside fired questions in their direction. The MPs kept them distant.

Devin began to take the steps one at a time, using Galbreath's cane. Ginelle supported his elbow. Freeman followed slowly. They worked their way up to the great entrance to the rotunda. Devin gave Ginelle a smile of encouragement. Although she was apprehensive, she returned the smile. He watched her, appreciating her warmth. They had been through a great deal in a very short time, but they were here, together, ready to do whatever it took. Devin felt a rightness to it all, and his past faded away. He felt focused, ready to direct his energy, as if the recent confrontation with death in Kansas had pushed all the emotional debris out of his mind.

As they reached the top step and approached the entrance, Devin knew the importance of crossing this threshold. It somehow seemed appropriate that this momentous confrontation take place within the grandeur of this building. They would emerge from these halls as free people in a free world, or as hostages of Arthur Quail, who at this very moment was likely in control of the hearing inside.

He turned to Ginelle, feeling somewhat humbled by his responsibility. "I don't know if we *can* do this alone," he said, pulling a copy of Galbreath's recording out of his pocket, "or if Galbreath's diskette will mean anything. But at this point there seems to be no choice."

They approached the large door, still flanked by the MPs.

Screeching tires at the base of the Capitol steps made Devin pause. He looked back and saw a platoon of soldiers jump from an open army truck. Colonel Williamson and Dr. Hendrix stepped from a Jeep just behind.

The reporters and pickets reacted immediately to the sight of Hendrix.

Williamson intervened, shouting orders.

Soldiers formed a line of resistance, pushing the violent crowd back.

Armed MPs carried Hendrix up the steps. As he approached, Devin saw the strain on the doctor's face. He appeared not to have slept in the last two days. He was barely able to stand.

Horrified, Ginelle grabbed his arm.

Hendrix pulled an envelope from his breast pocket and pressed it into Devin's hand.

"Devin," he said weakly. "Take this in there. Read it and . . ." Hendrix collapsed and was laid down on the pavement by the troops.

Having removed her cap and sunglasses, Ginelle knelt next to her father as the rest of the soldiers formed a circle around him.

Colonel Williamson barked an order to the lieutenant. "Get him inside. Barricade the door and get a doctor." He stepped to Devin's side. "You can see what he's put himself through."

Devin opened the envelope and read Hendrix's note, a computer printout with a hand-scrawled message at the bottom, then leaned down to Ginelle. "He's done it."

She looked up and smiled weakly.

Williamson placed a hand on Devin's shoulder. "Are you ready?" Devin nodded in response. Williamson turned to the four remaining MPs. "You men come with us."

The lieutenant had immediately ordered the soldiers to carry Hendrix indoors, away from the crowd.

As Devin walked in he looked back at Ginelle, who remained at her father's side. He felt lost without her as he walked toward the north wing and its conference rooms. A few people milled about the hallway.

Brook Hanford met them as they approached the door, where two more MPs stood guard.

He recognized Devin through the bruises and bandages and gave him a broad freckle-faced smile. "Stuck more than your nose into this story, huh, Dev?" He shook Devin's hand.

"Hello, Brook."

"What's up?" Freeman asked impatiently.

"Just finishing with recess. Brutal condemnation of Hendrix this morning. Huge blowups of the chimps in New Mexico. They read Kahvahl's signed statement aloud. Senate Majority Leader Harmon mentioned an extradition order, enforced by the attorney general's office. The U.S. special counsel representing the government quoted charges against Hendrix. He's being blamed for all the deaths."

Devin assessed the weight of the negative evidence, anticipating the conflict ahead. "Colonel, before we go into that room and raise almighty hell," he said, "can we leave the troops here—so we get a feeling for what's going on?"

The colonel nodded affirmative. "Sure. I asked federal security officials to turn the metal detectors off. We can bring in our weapons at any time."

"All right. But before you do . . ." Devin turned to his colleague. "Brook, come in and show me who's who."

"You got it."

Brook took off, pushed past the MPs. Devin was impressed and encouraged by the young man's energy.

Together, they entered the rear of the large wood-paneled room.

Devin surveyed the scene. In a chamber some seventy-five feet square, he looked over heads and shoulders of some one hundred people standing in the gallery that sloped down to the committee-room floor. They blended in with the crowd.

Over the microphone, Majority Leader Harmon, seated with others behind a long elevated table, droned on, reviewing the evidence against Hendrix that would soon be turned over to the Justice Department.

Large blown-up photos were displayed on easels: Hendrix with disfigured chimps, a black-and-white picture of the Black Diamond research facility, and images of Hendrix, Kahvahl, Glant, and Metzger in a lab.

Colonel Williamson and Freeman moved in behind Devin.

"Okay, fill me in," Devin whispered to Brook.

"The federal special counsel is seated to your right," Brook said, pointing to an individual table. "His name is David Tooms. He specializes in prosecuting terrorist cases. At the head table, we've got government officials." Devin studied the lineup on the dais as Brook continued. "The majority leader of the Senate, Harmon, is presiding, along with Senator Kemper, chairman of the investigating committee, and his five committee members. Seated to your right at the other table are Dixon, the secretary of defense, several cabinet members, and Jonathan Swain, the national security adviser to the president."

"Yes. I know him." Devin looked off the left to another riser, where Arthur Quail was seated with eleven men. He noticed the three with brush cuts . . . the henchmen from Quail's office. "I know those tough guys, but who are the rest of the men in Quail's group?" he asked softly.

"His lawyers and biochemists. Maxillar Chemical lab people are material witnesses to the epidemic for any future trial . . . since they formulated the vaccine."

"Kahvahl did that," Devin said, "not them. Is there a spokesperson from the Disease Control Center?"

"See that guy in the thick silver-rimmed glasses and gray hair . . . just off to the side next to the congressmen?"

Devin located the man at a separate table, busy examining paperwork. "Got him."

"That's Blake Pendergast; he just testified this morning. He's the main man. The army's virology expert. He works with USAMRIID. Worked with the FDA on the vaccine clearance."

"Okay," Devin said, trying to formulate a plan.

"What do you want to do?" Freeman asked quietly.

"Nothing yet. Let's see where we stand."

Majority Leader Harmon continued speaking.

He reminded Devin of a kindly penguin with slicked-back white hair, long narrow nose, and kindly, wrinkled face.

Harmon addressed the court reporter, peering over his bifocals. "Further, you may record that the findings of this hearing against Dr. Hendrix are sanctioned by the Congress of the United States to be submitted to the Department of Justice for further deliberation." He shifted his glance to the special counsel. "Mr. Tooms, are you prepared to proceed with the secondary charges against Dr. Ahmar Kahvahl?"

Tooms stood. "I was, Mr. Chairman, as they relate to the charges against Dr. Hendrix." He looked like a book-keeper, not a lawyer. "But after consulting with Mr. Quail during recess, it appears there may be a more urgent matter to deal with. Mr. Quail wishes to make a statement."

"With all due respect to Mr. Quail and his contributions to all, a statement at this time seems irregular. We'd planned to hear from him in due course with reference to the"—he studied some papers on the table—"administration of the vaccine."

"It seems something's arisen that pertains to national security," Tooms said.

"As does this entire proceeding." Harmon smiled at Tooms. "Is this diversion absolutely necessary?"

Tooms looked over at Quail, then back at Harmon. "So it appears."

"Well, all right then, Mr. Quail, please step to the microphone."

Devin watched as Quail rose, his eyes shining, and walked toward the small table that faced the dais. When he reached his destination, he looked around the room. He projected an air of indefatigable confidence.

Harmon seemed uncomfortable with the delay. "Would you like to be seated, Mr. Quail?"

"I prefer to stand, if you don't mind." The sound of his voice sent a chill down Devin's spine, a reminder of their last meeting. Silently, he renewed his pledge to Galbreath.

Arthur Quail cast a glance at each of the members of Congress. Then he paced back and forth, preparing himself, and turned to the reporters in the room. "I came here today—"

"Mr. Quail," Harmon interrupted.

"What is it?"

"Are you addressing the gallery or the committee members?" Harmon waved at the officials on the dais.

"Well . . . all concerned," Quail said contemptuously. "And believe me, you will be concerned." He walked off to the side of the floor, from which vantage point he could address the entire chamber. "There, is this better?"

"Thank you," Harmon said. "Please continue."

Quail rubbed his hands together. "I have something to tell this fine gathering which will change"—he chuckled—"well . . . just about everything." He glanced at Harmon. "In fact, there won't be any further need for a trial when I get finished."

"That's a judgment for this committee to make," Harmon countered.

Arthur Quail ignored him, casting a cold eye at the congressmen, then swept the room with a haughty gaze. "What I'm about to say to you refined ladies and gentlemen will shock you. I suggest you remain calm and listen carefully, since I will likely not address you again."

Devin grabbed Williamson by the shoulder. "This is it. Have the MPs come in quietly with their sidearms. When I give you the word, tell them to rush the floor and cover Quail and his group." As the colonel excused himself Devin worked his way forward in the gallery.

Quail continued. "You should understand that the epidemic in this country was a direct attack on the government of the United States," he said, with his back to the dais. "And the assault isn't over. In fact, it begins again today."

Some of the congressmen traded looks of confusion, speaking to each other in hushed voices. Senator Kemper and Jonathan Swain remained focused on Quail as he walked the floor.

"I want you to be clear about my background," Quail continued. "I'm a patriot. For thirty years I was also a member of an international cartel of businessmen sometimes naively described as the Trilateral Commission. In the opinion of our cartel, the economic future of the United States is no longer viable. Failure to reduce deficit spending and balance the national budget as well as the forces of uncontrolled deflation at work around the world present us with a forecast of immediate decline at best. We believe that balanced budget amendments and such nonsense are illusory panaceas that disguise the depth of our economic woes. They're Band-Aids and not solutions. Lobbyists and their hidden agendas are the most powerful force here on the Hill. And have been for generations. It doesn't matter which party controls Congress or the White House, entitlement waste and hidden spending continues.

"Beyond that, the cost of keeping current in the information age and the vicissitudes of the global economy are draining American wealth at a frightening pace. It's not providing us access to their resources. Rather it's giving underdeveloped countries access to *our* economic base. Billions of our dollars go overseas every year. Oh, I know it doesn't look that way to you, listening to stock-market reports, but whether you realize it or not, you're witnessing the beginning of the end for Western democracies along with the demise of the welfare state, and the termination of nation states." Quail continued pacing angrily in front of the government officials. "With revolutions occurring in every corner of the world, and the military supremacy of the United States in a state of decay, we're inviting global chaos, followed by decades of anarchy around the planet.

"My associates and I, the businessmen I mentioned, refuse to sit by while Third World countries like China and India and others unite against us to capture future markets, future growth, and ultimately attempt worldwide control."

"Mr. Quail," Harmon said, interrupting, "I'm sure your economic speculations are very interesting, but—"

"Do I have the floor, here?" Quail asked, scowling. The senator gave him a polite nod. "Then let me finish. I think you'll find what I have to say fascinating."

"As you wish, but please try to be succinct." Harmon settled back in his chair.

Quail gave a quick forced smile, appearing to recover his train of thought. "I'll come to the point. The international group to which I belong holds power throughout the Western democracies. We are affiliated with government and business leaders everywhere. With my guidance, our group has devised a way to halt this one-way trip into mediocrity." He looked directly at the congressmen. "We decided to make moves the United States government couldn't make due to bureaucratic red tape, congressional gridlock, and foreign-policy claptrap." His voice rose. "Do you realize how many little skirmishes like Iraq, Panama, and Bosnia we are forced to settle around this planet? Is that what you look forward to . . . foreign aid, American soldiers policing foreign countries, and higher taxes? Wouldn't you rather have a single means of controlling all other peoples that guarantees that if they do not comply, they simply do not exist?" He glared at Harmon.

"Controlling? What exactly do you mean?" Harmon said. The congressmen looked at each other, bewildered.

Quail crossed his arms, assuming an arrogant pose. "Our cartel successfully introduced, cured, and now controls the code key to what people call the replicator," he said.

The congressmen gasped.

The gallery exploded in an uproar, which gave Devin the opportunity to move through the crowd to the front of the chamber. A look behind him told him Williamson and the MPs had entered in the rear.

Harmon pounded his gavel. "Please quiet down. Order," he yelled, standing up. The uproar calmed. "Let him speak. I want to get this for the record."

"Yes, please, do that." Quail smiled. "It'll be in the first chapter of your history books." He turned back to the congressmen. "Our organization, with the help of several Middle East terrorist groups and a North Korean commando unit, engineered the epidemic. We also gave you the cure. We've given it to Europe and Japan, where the epidemic is just beginning.

"Why the cure? you may ask." He turned and glanced at his contingent. "Three of my top chemists seated here can corroborate this information. The deceased Dr. Kahvahl cleverly devised a molecular cipher which guarantees—listen to me—guarantees that *without* continued doses of vaccine, every single individual who received a Quaillium vaccination will be dead in a matter of weeks."

Pandemonium erupted in the room.

Devin watched as members of the Senate stood up, shouting at Quail.

Several security guards in dark blue uniforms moved onto the floor as if to seize Quail, but he stood his ground, immobile in the middle of the room. He raised his hands, palms out, asking for quiet. The guards looked up at Harmon, confused about what to do.

Harmon held a hand up, temporarily restraining them.

With everyone standing, Devin noticed Jonathan Swain, dressed in a pale gray suit, ambling out from behind the dais toward the floor as the chaos subsided.

"Are you saying you infected us?" Senator Kemper asked, spraying spit.

"Exactly." Quail ignored the guards. "As you all know, an antidote usually contains a bit of the poison. Our poison is temporarily impotent. But it will gain its full power shortly. Now, AIDS, for example, has a period of dormancy. The replicator does, too. But not two-to-ten years. Weeks. Then it takes another run. Cure it, and it runs again in three months. It comes back, regenerated every three months, until you die."

"Hogwash," Harmon said. "We ought to arrest you right now. What's the point of all this?"

"The point? Your lives!" Quail said. "You'll be forced to turn over the power of the United States and the other Western democracies to us. You can put me away. But some morning just weeks from now, the nation's population will wake up with a hell of a fever, and you know the rest. Mass deaths everywhere."

"You're admitting to having already murdered tens of

thousands of people just to get your way?" Senator
Kemper said bitterly.

"Oh, you question my integrity, here in the city where
it was decided to kill many more people in Hiroshima
and Nagasaki? The hypocrisy never ends."

A hush fell on the room.

The guards retreated, watching Quail as he strutted
about. He turned his attention to the congressmen.

"What makes you think other countries will support
you?" Senator Kemper yelled.

"What makes you think they won't?" Quail laughed.
"They've had a bellyful of your methods."

Swain, looking calm, had moved out onto the floor
next to Quail.

"Mr. Swain, here, will work closely with the president
during the transfer of authority, and ultimately assume all
power," Quail said. "And by the way, the president,
cabinet members, and most of Congress received vaccines at Bethesda Naval Hospital that will kill them in
three days . . . unless they comply with my demands and
then receive another injection."

The congressmen turned to each other, yelling questions. A cabinet member at the side table dropped to his
knees. Harmon banged the gavel repeatedly, trying to
maintain order.

Kemper shouted at Quail, unheard through the
mayhem.

"Silence!" Harmon screamed.

As the confusion settled, Kemper's voice rose over the
din. "We'll arrest you right now," he snarled, turning to
the guards.

"Go ahead," Quail said. "I have sufficient vaccine to
reverse your deaths. But it's under guard, safely stowed
away. If my colleagues and I are not released from this
building this afternoon, unharmed and free, my associ-

ates holding the antidote have instructions to destroy the liquid that could save all of you, including the president."

Kemper fell silent, as did the others.

As Quail continued to list his demands Devin felt a nudge at his right shoulder. Turning, he was astounded to see Wu Sun, their former captor and unexpected ally, who, true to his word, had left them in Wamego, Kansas, less than sixty hours ago. Wu Sun looked every bit the student, wearing a Columbia University sweatshirt.

"I see you made it," Wu Sun said.

"What the hell are you—"

"Where is Hendrix?" he asked stoically.

"He's outside."

"His life. My life. All lives are together now."

Devin noticed an expression of apology on the young man's face. "You're right! You want to help Hendrix?"

Wu Sun nodded.

"Then come here." He guided Wu Sun to the front row of the gallery.

They were in plain sight, only feet from Quail, who ranted on about his demands.

Devin took his weight off Galbreath's cane and tossed it. It landed with a clatter, echoing through the chamber, coming to rest several feet from Quail, who stopped in mid-sentence, looking down.

Quail searched the crowd with his eyes. Devin and Wu Sun stepped out of the gathering onto the floor.

Devin noticed with satisfaction the expression of fury on Quail's face.

"Wu Sun and Parks," he said, obviously off balance. Swain took a step backward as Devin limped toward them.

"Mr. Quail and Judas Iscariot," Devin said. "After all the shocks both of you gave us," he said, leaning down to pick up the cane, "it's gratifying to see there are still things that surprise you as well."

"You've got no authority here," Quail said fiercely.

Devin signaled to Colonel Williamson. Williamson and Freeman worked themselves down through the gallery, accompanied by the MPs, their guns drawn.

Suddenly Devin hurled himself at the startled Quail, brandishing the cane. He lifted it high in the air and struck Quail twice, across the face and on the top of the head. Quail fell to one knee. Blood oozed from a cut on his forehead. Quail's thugs leaped from their seats, but the MPs blocked their paths with weapons held high.

"That's for Galbreath and the thousands you brutalized," Devin said, standing over him.

Wu Sun seized Swain's arm in a control hold.

Devin turned to Williamson. "Colonel, you can arrest this man for his crimes against the United States. And he's wrong about his formula."

Confusion erupted again. Several soldiers and security guards surrounded Quail. Three others grabbed Swain. The rest of the Maxillar staff were also held at gunpoint.

Everyone hurled questions at Devin.

Harmon, the congressmen, and cabinet members, unable to contain themselves, rushed down to the floor.

More of the colonel's troops entered the gallery from the back, along with Ginelle, who pushed her way through the confusion to Devin's side.

"Wu Sun, you were one of us," Quail said incredulously.

"I was one with my family. Now my cousin is dead," Wu Sun said bitterly.

"Parks. I'll see to it you're the first to die," Quail shouted.

"I didn't have one of your injections." With obvious effort, Devin heaved himself up on a chair and faced the crowd. "My vaccination came from Dr. Hendrix, the man who did the research to prove that Quail's formula won't work as he says it will." He held the computer printout high over his head, showing the rest of the people in the room. "Hendrix's research demonstrates how Quail put a cipher in your vaccine. . . ." The panic started again. "But it's reversible! Dr. Hendrix has the formula for a permanent cure right here on this paper. You have nothing to fear. You can be cured for good." Devin felt the elation in the room rising, but was interrupted by Quail, who screamed at him.

"The man's a liar," Quail shouted. "You're all dead without me. The code is unbreakable! We made sure of that!"

Using the cane as a pointer, Devin glanced down at him from the chair. "Hendrix analyzed your vaccine, Mr. Quail. You're right." He read from Hendrix's page. " 'The rotating code is unbreakable based on the irregular number of pi. But the RNA trigger in the cipher has a positive charge.' " He smiled down at Ginelle. "The filter or 'plate' of plutonium mesh you used to purify the plasma was never negatively ionized. Kahvahl realized that error just before he died. By nature, the replicator will change polarity when it assumes a new cytoplasmic shell. A negative microbe with negatively charged regulatory proteins cannot morph. It will ultimately repel itself! The first time it goes through the run cycle, the microbe becomes impotent. It's all right here."

Devin looked up, addressing the crowd. "That means once you're vaccinated with Hendrix's new vaccine, you're *permanently* cured! Furthermore, Dr. Hendrix has advised me that he has enough vaccine in the lab to treat those government officials in immediate danger!"

Majority Leader Harmon was red in the face with impatience. He turned to Pendergast and shouted, "Is that true? Can you tell if that makes sense?"

Stepping down, Devin handed the paper to Pendergast. The virologist moved forward and examined it eagerly.

Pendergast pushed his silver glasses high on the bridge of his nose. The room fell to a hush as he studied the printout in his hands. Then, with an expression of both awe and relief, he began to nod and kept nodding as the crowd's hum in the chamber grew into a roar.

Quail's face was twisted with frustration. He looked over at his biochemical staff, who were still under guard. "What does this negative charge mean?" he screamed at them. "Is he right? Could he be right?"

Two MPs fought their way through the gathering. Devin was delighted to see Dr. Hendrix supported between them. People parted in his path, as the doctor was escorted down the center of the room.

Wu Sun took Hendrix's hand for a moment. The young man smiled warmly, said a few words of thanks, and disappeared into the crowd.

As the MPs pinioned him tighter Quail finally lost all remnants of his composure. He started to squirm, kick out with his legs.

Devin felt the irony of it all: the power-hungry tyrant now stripped of power; the ultimate absurdity of the printout Pendergast still held in his hand—as had happened before throughout history, one sheet of paper had dictated the future of the world.

Tears formed in his eyes, and he realized with relief that he was at last mourning the dead.

Dr. Hendrix and Ginelle approached, and they joined in a three-way embrace.

Behind them, Quail was taken from the room and his staff was escorted away at gunpoint. Jonathan Swain gave Devin a contemptuous glare as the MPs cuffed him.

Senators and cabinet members came by in turn and shook Devin's hand and patted Dr. Hendrix on the back.

Ginelle had hold of Devin's right arm.

"Devin," she said jubilantly. "We've done it."

Freeman and Colonel Williamson came down the walkway from the gallery and approached Devin. Freeman seemed to have a newfound spring in every step.

"Devin," Colonel Williamson said, smiling, "I've just been on the phone with the president. He wants to congratulate you and Dr. Hendrix personally."

"Me? It was Hendrix."

"Yes, but you took it upon yourself to find him. That saved us."

"Tell the president I appreciate it." Devin had an arm around Ginelle's waist.

"I don't think you understand," Williamson continued. "Frank worked it out for you. You're to be congratulated on national television at the White House. And"—the colonel paused for emphasis—"the president wants to announce your special appointment to his staff, as director of public information acting as liaison to America and the world during the cooldown phase of the epidemic. We have to mend some important fences with the U.S. allies."

Devin wiped the moisture from his face and flinched as he inadvertently brushed his bruises. "You think I'd look good on TV right now?" He smiled at Freeman. "Me? The elephant man? Thanks, Frank, but there's only one job I still want."

"Devin, the anchor position can be yours anytime. But think what a presidential appointment could mean to your career." Frank was selling hard. "You'd be the most visible man in the country for months."

"I want to head the six o'clock news, Frank."

The frustration on Frank's face turned into an understanding grin. "I'd be proud to have you start tomorrow night if you like," he said.

Devin smiled. "How about some time off to let this face heal up?"

"Of course, whenever you're ready."

As Freeman and Williamson moved off, Devin turned to Ginelle, exploring her eyes. They were still green, but he glimpsed some blue sky somewhere deep within them. "Hello," he said. "I feel like introducing myself. I don't know what it would be like . . . just being with you without chaos crashing all around us."

A curious smile played at the corners of her mouth. "Oh, I think we were getting to know each other fairly well."

He moved closer. "You think we could make that a habit?"

"Devin, I . . ." She was unable to finish.

He gripped Galbreath's cane in his right hand. "After I turn over this recording device to a judge, I'm off to Africa to see that Galbreath's ashes find a resting place near Kilimanjaro . . ."

She studied him for a moment, then warmth flooded her eyes. "Yes," she said. "I'd like to go."

"And after that?"

She smiled and touched his face. "Let's take our time."

He leaned down to kiss her and was overwhelmed as she put her arms around his neck and kissed him back.

"Time?" He held her gently by the shoulder, gazed into her eyes. "We'll enjoy every minute."

Her face softened into a knowing, contented smile. "Every nanosecond."